MOONLIGHT IN VERMONT
a novel

By John Hilferty

Moonlight in Vermont
a novel

ISBN: 145054875X
EAN: 13-9781450548755

Part I
Prologue

Duplicitous and crafty, another Machiavellian cloud sneaked over the lake, leaving no trace. The morning sky had begun with a deep blue, backing up a brilliant sun's light and balancing the sharp Arctic air. The light and the crispness met in a way so wintry fair that one would have to be gallows-bound not to rejoice in their presence.

But the light fled by the time Ed Phoebe had slowly slalomed down the trail called Sidewinder. The clouds that appeared were neither white nor fluffy, but suddenly were gray and stringy. Unwashed and dirty, they raced to the east and New Hampshire.

As he seated himself on the lift chair for another run and swung away to the summit, the bright glow had returned, lighting up the snow with dazzling reflection. Ed Phoebe, at eighty years old, preferred skiing with the sun. Dark days flattened the ski trails, hiding the ice and lumps that his not-so-strong eyes could see.

New England skies are fickle friends. As Mark Twain was alleged to have said about the consistency of its weather, "Wait a minute."

Hopping off the lift once more, Ed took in the horizons of the Adirondacks to the west, rising above the gray line of Lake Champlain, and New Hampshire and the Presidential Range and Mt. Washington to the east, the region's highest peak, and where winter lions roared. Quebec lay up north, and Camel's Hump, a thorn-shaped Vermont mountain, dominated the view. Spruce and hemlocks, dwarfed by many winds to the equal of Ed Phoebe's slight height, were reshaped the night before into frozen, white puddings.

Atop Mt. Washington, as the winter wind hurled, as usual, in eighty-mile blasts outside the isolated weather station, Bob Guion held a steaming cup of coffee as he read the communiqué that had just arrived from Burlington:

```
THE NATIONAL WEATHER SERVICE WILL CONTINUE
ITS WINTER STORM WARNINGS THROUGH TODAY
FOR NORTHERN NEW YORK AND NORTHERN
VERMONT.

AS LOW PRESSURE MOVES NORTH OF NORTHERN
NEW YORK AND VERMONT THIS AFTERNOON AND
EVENING, ARCTIC AIR WILL BEGIN TO
INFILTRATE. TEMPERATURES TONIGHT WILL FALL
TO BELOW MINUS 20° F.

DOPPLER PICKING UP MASSIVE CLOUD FRONT
TORONTO. PRESSURE 30.10 FALLING SLOWLY.
INCREASING FULL GALE WINDS EXPECTED.

HENDERSON.
```

"Bastard's gonna wallop New England!" Guion whispered.

Snow fell nearly every winter night in these mountains of New England, but forecasts were often misguided. The pattern on this January day called for cold air from the north to meet and join with moist air arising from the ocean waters of the southeast. Without a doubt, an alliance of these two would form a single, unfaltering army that was hell-bent to rush, determined to leave a wind-whipped pillage on the mountains and villages below.

Cirrus clouds were now thickening, looking like boiled wool.

Only moments before, the bright light of the sun had glanced off the silvery stubble of Ed's chin. He removed his old-fashioned goggles, merely sunglasses with pieces of leather attached on each side to thwart the breezes. He tugged at the collar of the dirty, yellow, quilted vest that was all puffed out, resembling a life jacket. It was the one he had bought the year Jack Kennedy was shot.

When Ed skied, he always moved slowly with deliberate but perfect turns. Unscrubbed and unwed, he was the happiest of bachelors as he looked forward to skiing at the age of 100. He quit defining his emotions or intellect long ago. He never thought too deeply about any subject, instead letting either a smile or frown reveal what he felt and thought inside. He now frowned as a breeze drove the sun behind another swiftly moving cloud. Even though there was a blizzard in the forecast and Ed and every other hard-bitten regular at the Maple Glen Ski Resort welcomed the prediction because it meant a dump of good powder, he did not wish to be caught in the indiscriminately grip of a bad storm on the way home.

By late afternoon, the storm-to-be had begun its prelude with a gentle drop of flakes. At first, it was scant. Then trillions of them lay down so very silently upon the hills and valley. In the many pastures, cows left their feed bins and began walking single file to their barns with their swollen bags swaying and skunk stripes of white forming upon their backs.

In the purple cast of twilight, there was still peace in the valley. Dots of glowing window lights in isolated cabins and homes appeared on the mountainsides as well as on the farms and the village of Lowgate Springs. However, by nightfall, the flakes of snow ceased wandering. Taken up by an intensifying wind, they began hurling in angry straight lines from west to east and down upon the ground.

Hours passed. The wind found a voice as it howled and struck a banshee's tune atop the mountains. Very little traffic moved. The heavy snowplow trucks were defiant as the chains clinked, and the wipers clicked while the drivers squinted into an ocean's flood of white flakes hurtling against the windshields. An occasional single light, a snowmobile racing home from the tavern, sped across a stunted cornfield. No human would survive what would come later this night when temperatures would drop to twenty degrees below zero. The wind chill was far more serious than that.

From the west, blasting over the darkened lake, came the storm with an arctic rage at its tail. The pines at higher elevations, some of them already encased in six feet of a previous snow, held fast. Farther down the mountain, the birches and beeches waved skeletal arms. Moose, deer, and bobcats had already headed toward protected stands away from the ridges. Black bears had no opinion, as they lay snug in trancelike torpor in their winter caves.

Around midnight, the cyclone winds lessened, but snow continued falling. At the summit's 4,000-foot level, silence descended except for a slight click when a brief burst of wind tickled a tree limb against its neighbor. White piled upon more white, obliterating the traces of human activity of the previous day.

Before the morning sunlight edged over the eastern hills, a few cars and pickup trucks bearing the first shift of workers—lift maintenance mechanics, lift operators, ski patrollers, and cafeteria workers—slowly approached the base lodge of Maple Glen Resort. All were under orders from the day before to not be late. The first wave of powder hounds would be right behind them, waiting for the lifts to open at 8:00 AM, an hour earlier than usual.

For a skier, first tracks in powder down a steep mountainside constituted a high to be equated with sex, opium, or a vision of God Almighty. Nothing could duplicate the rhythmic push of deep powder against the bottom of the skis as it extended through the feet, up to the knees and thighs, and as far as the deep-breathing lungs and heart while the skis and body plowed white feathers.

It was still dark when Pete Finley mounted his snowmobile and sped uphill, the single headlight poking between the narrow band of trees marking the Spruce Lodge lift line. A lift mechanic, he was headed toward the summit to see if the storm had done anything that would forestall the opening of the Summit chair. The afternoon before, the top operator had reported to dispatch that the sheave approaching the uphill side of the bull wheel was making a rather cranky sound, an indication of bearing failure.

As he dismounted, the first sign of grayness, like a veil, spread over the snowcapped trees that had grown lumpy with little igloos upon the branches and boughs. Even though the temperature had warmed to zero at the base lodge, it was minus twelve degrees on the lift shack thermometer at the summit. Heavily encased in two suits of expedition-weight underwear, a turtleneck shirt, and a thick, wool sweater beneath his quilted, dirty brown coveralls, Finley was comfortable enough. He wore a greasy ski mask beneath a battered hard hat that had been originally painted red.

As the darkness tiptoed away, silhouettes began appearing. Finley spoke into his radio that was strapped with Velcro to his coveralls.

"Hey, Al, I'm here at the top of the Summit chair. Let me know when you're ready to spin it," he said, knowing his partner, Alvin

Green, would soon be arriving at the bottom of the lift to conduct maintenance checks.

Green's voice crackled from below, "Hey, turd face, I'm already here! Give me a couple of minutes."

Green initially had trouble pushing open the heavy sliding steel and glass door to the bottom lift shack because of the snowdrifts. Nevertheless, he soon shouldered it aside, allowing the wind to chase candy wrappers and dirty paper cups across the shack floor.

He turned the power on and radioed to the top, "Here we go!"

He gave two short rings of the "ready" signal. Up top, Finley repeated the rings by pushing the "ready" button twice with a gloved finger. The huge bull wheel, easily ten feet in diameter, began turning.

As the lift and chairs moved slowly, Finley kept his eyes and ears attentive to the sheave above his head. There were four steel wheels over which the heavy cable ran. He turned his left ear to the sheaves, listening for the telltale grind and whine of a cranky bearing. He heard a rhythmic click as each chair's steel hanger rode over the suspect sheaves, the sound of smoothness.

"No trouble here."

His eyes peered down the line of chairs approaching slowly from the bottom of the lift. One by one, the chairs danced slightly in the soft wind. He wiped his gloved hand across his runny nose. Dawn was taking over now.

Far down the steep pitch, Finley looked for swaying chairs. Wind holds, an imposed shutdown of the lifts, were common this time of year, irritating skiers and frustrating management.

"Looks okay," Finley whispered into the radio.

Each chair cascaded into dots far down the mountain. As the faraway chairs rode the towers, they gave a slight lurch skyward and then immediately sagged, one after the other, as the steel rope held taut. Finley knew haste was important this morning.

As Finley's eyes cast its fixed stare down the line, he noticed something odd. Something was teasing his vision. It was probably the early morning lightness bouncing from the shiny steel. A lump?

"No...no lump."

He blinked. The cold brought tears to his eyes as they focused on the line. He looked to the sky and blinked to clear his vision.

His lips moved, "A lump. What the hell is it?"

As the chair clicked upward, the shape grew. A bag of something left on the lift? A roll of soft fencing? Blankets wrapped in a tarp left by the ski patrol?

"That's what it is. It's gotta be! Careless pricks!"

Finley held his breath, as if staying still would help his vision. He focused hard on the approaching chair. Something was definitely there.

"Hey, Al!" he said carefully and slowly as he held the radio close to his lips. "There's somethin' on one of the chairs. There's somethin' there. I can't see what it is, but there's somethin' there!"

Seconds later, he shouted to the radio. His fingers shook as he held it.

"Jesus Christ, Al, it's got legs. It's a skier! Did you let the operator get on?" he yelled angrily.

It was a strict rule that, before the lifts could be opened to the public, no one could ride the lift until maintenance had given the all clear to dispatch. It was the signal the mechanisms were functioning the way the manufacturer assured they would. That is, they were safe enough to ferry another 1,500 skiers to the high peaks for another day. Then—and only then—could the top operator or the ski patrol get on the chairs.

"There's nobody on that fuckin' lift!" Green yelled defensively from the shack below. "I just started spinnin' the sucker!"

Finley started to reply, "There's…someone…"

As the sound of his voice evaporated in the winter wind and cold, he stared at the double chair. He watched it ride slowly toward the ramp opposite the lift shack where he sat, like a small ferry toward its dock. His hand trembled on the stop button. With the chair about twenty feet from the ramp, he slowed the lift to half-speed and then to its slowest gait, which was barely as fast as a person could walk. Creeping along, the double chair approached and reached opposite to where Finley stood transfixed in the lift shack. He pushed the stop button.

For thirty seconds, Finley stared at the frozen, human clump. It was as still as one of the evergreens covered with a blanket of white. The head of a skier barely protruded above the snow-filled collar of a whitened, stiff ski jacket. Goggles blinded in white gazed toward the ground. The shoulders of the victim, mummified in a wintry shroud, were hunched in a final, futile protection from the previous night's blizzard. The two legs, barely swaying, were immobile with the skis attached.

Finley began crying when his eyes took on what they did not wish to see. His voice shook and then screamed, "Send the patrol quick! It's a body...a body...it's a body!"

Chapter 1
To Conquer Europe

Dances with Wolves was the in-flight movie, which Calvert had enjoyed until the last half hour when the United States Cavalry went on a butchering and maiming rampage against the Native Americans.

"Why do the white guys have to be the bad guys all of the time?" Calvert muttered to himself as the flight attendant came past with an armload of pillows and blankets.

Passengers, sated with supper, were settling in for their mid-Atlantic naps. Some were desperately—and therefore futilely—trying to sleep. They knew, in a little while, it would be 8:30 AM and they would be facing the day in Zurich, Switzerland, instead of Waycross, Georgia, robbed of a night's comfort.

Calvert rarely slept on overseas flights. Engine drone was one cause for insomnia, and even his short legs sometimes suffered cramps in the tiny space between the seats.

"Should have bought business. Never fly coach again. Best goddamned sales record in all of the United States and Europe. They tell me we gotta cut back."

He stretched his stubby legs beneath the seat in front of him and scratched his light, incessantly curly hair He snapped his eyes shut and, reflecting on the movie, imagined himself going to bed with a Sioux squaw. But the eyes opened quickly as the back of the seat in front of him came bounding his way, like the unleashed spring on a rat trap.

"Goddamn!" Calvert muttered again.

Just as instantly as the seat swiveled back, a shock of dark hair poked over the top of it. Calvert could see a pair of wide, youthful, blue eyes.

"Does that bother you? The seat being back that far?" the eyes asked. "If it does, I'll move it up."

"No, no, that's all right," Calvert lied as he settled deeper into the little pillow, trying unsuccessfully to fluff it around his stout neck.

He sighed in resignation before getting up and stretching his arms to the ceiling of the swiftly moving 747. He walked the few steps toward the midsection bathroom and waited in line.

Except for occasional stabs of faint light where a non-sleeper read a book or magazine, the plane's interior had settled into semidarkness. From the reflected light of the galley where the flight attendants were busy depositing the mess from supper, Calvert could see the young man who sprung his chair at him. In repose with his eyes closed, he had the relaxed but vapid face of someone who would do well in this world one day but was obviously untested. With its high cheekbones, the features seemed strong and molded. However, there was a softness to the flesh, particularly around the mouth. His lips, now slightly parted in pre-sleep, spoke of decency, perhaps humility, or "a fairly good upbringing," thought Calvert.

Three minutes later, as he washed his face in the tepid trickle of water in the lavatory, Calvert reflected that the young man at least apologized for invading his space. He had been surprisingly polite. Calvert was at that period in middle age when anybody younger than thirty was a potential pain in the ass.

He then remembered the voice of the pilot a few minutes before the plane had taxied out to the runway. "At this time, I'd like to welcome aboard some of the members of the U.S. Ski Team on their way to another World Cup season in Europe. We wish you well."

There had been a few "yips" and some scattered applause. Calvert then forgot all about it because someone's carry-on bag struck him in the head when it fell from the overhead storage he had just unsnapped above his seat.

As he returned to his seat from the lavatory, Calvert said warmly, "I beg your pardon…Are you one of the ski team boys?"

"Yes," the young man said after his eyes popped open. The seat beside him in the midsection was empty. This was often the case on evening flights from JFK to Europe.

"Do you mind if I sit here a minute?"

"Not at all," the young man said as he lifted a copy of *USA Today* from the seat beside him.

"Name's Calvert Thomas," he smiled broadly as he extended a hand.

"That's not Calvert, comma, Thomas, like a lot of people think," he chuckled. "Calvert's the first name. Thomas is the last, good ol' Welsh name! I'm from Georgia. Well, I guess you could tell that."

The young man grinned, though weakly.

"We don't have snow down there, and I don't know shit from shinola when it comes to ski racing. But, my daughter, she's nineteen and in college, she skis. Well, she's been about three times now and swears it's the most fun of any sport that is, but I suspect it's the boys that ski that make it fun. I really wouldn't know, but she'd just about kill me if she knew I took this trip and told her the U.S. Ski Team was aboard the plane and I never got to know any."

"How do you do," said the young man. He was smiling more openly now, but he was fervently wishing he had traded seats with Klecko before the flight. He glanced to his right, toward an aisle seat along the starboard side. Arnold Klecko's bristling blond hair barely poked above the pillow. Klecko always slept soundly. Always!

For his part, Calvert was now in sales mode. He functioned as he best knew how, even though he did not have any intention at all of selling a Caterpillar earthmover to the U.S. Ski Team. Nevertheless, he could pump the young man for knowledge about World Cup skiing and then store the newly obtained information in the resource part of his brain, like a ready-made pamphlet from which he could extract the knowledge—offhandedly of course—to soften European clients, most of whom were men. Calvert lost a big sale, he had once convinced himself, when he could not bullshit comfortably with a German contractor about the slalom race that was on the television in a bar in Hamburg. It was the same with Formula I auto racing. He lost another sale because he revealed—no, blurted—he had never heard of Alain Prost, the former world champion from France.

"And the son of a bitch I was trying to sell was French! It's like sayin' you never heard of Hank Aaron or Mickey Mantle."

Calvert was ready to take control of the conversation. "What kinda racin' you do?" Calvert asked.

"I'm a downhiller."

"Yeah, well, it's all downhill, isn't it?" Calvert chuckled

"Yes, but some skiers ski slalom and giant slalom. That's called technical skiing when they go in and out of gates, past flags." The young man wiggled his right hand snake-like before Calvert's eyes. "You've probably seen them on TV. That's slalom. Then there's giant slalom, or GS. That's where the gates—those flags—are farther apart. Other racers, like myself, race downhill and super G. It's called speed skiing. You start way uphill and ski down against the clock."

"Your kinda skiing sounds harder to me," said Calvert. "And your name is?"

"Atwood. Ethan Paul Atwood. Most people call me Ethan."

"Forgive me if I admit I've never heard of you. How long you been on the team?"

"Oh, about three years now," said Ethan. "I'm still working my way up. I haven't won a race yet. I haven't even finished in the top fifteen, but I'm getting closer. I figure, if I keep at it, I'll be mediocre someday."

"You're probably too modest," said Calvert. "Sounds kinda like sales. I myself sell earthmoving equipment, heavy machinery, for Caterpillar." He slipped a business card out of his front shirt pocket and handed one to Ethan. "What I sell ain't a trinket, not at six tons, or even like sellin' used cars, which is how I got started in sales. Damn things are expensive. Spent thirteen years up and down the East Coast. South mostly. Did real good! Good enough, they shoved me over here to Europe. But it's a whole different ball game dealing with the Europeans. If I can win just one out of ten tries, I'm in hog heaven."

Calvert said he was on his way to Eastern Europe. It was new territory—new horizons—now that the jackboots and tanks of communism were finally out of there.

"If they wanta' go anywhere, like join the European community, those guys gotta have somethin' to move the dirt around first. I'm headed for Prague, that's in that new Czech Republic; used to be Czechoslovakia. Then I'm onto Budapest, Hungary."

His pretense out of the way, Calvert asked, "Who are some of the good skiers? Oh, I mean, excuse me. I'm not saying I don't know who you are and all that. I apologize. But, you know, is there anybody with name recognition? That's what I'm tryin' to say."

"Otto Gerbisch of Germany and Franz Kluckner of Austria," Ethan named. "They're usually one and two. The Europeans tend to dominate, and our best skier on the U.S. team is Arnold Klecko…"

"Klecko? By Jesus, I've heard of him. He the fella does the commercial for some kinda' cereal?"

"Krispy Korn Kisses!" Ethan answered.

"Krispy. That's right. Of course, I've seen him. Slurps 'em right up. Like he really enjoys 'em."

"He does enjoy them!" answered Ethan. "Eats five or six bowls a day!"

Calvert brightened.

"He's sitting right up front. Over there on the right." Ethan pointed toward the back of the nearly perfectly square crew cut head that was lying comfortably back against the little, white pillow. Klecko was deep in slumber.

"Oh my gosh, I just hafta' meet him!" gushed the salesman as he fast-forwarded down the road to a successful closing of a contract, which was achieved in great part to the casual worldliness of the salesman. *"Arnold Klecko. I know him personally."*

"Do you think you can…could you introduce me?" he asked.

"I'll be happy to," smiled Ethan, who was, in fact, elated at the opportunity to hand off Calvert Thomas to Arnold Klecko.

Two years before, during his rookie year, Atwood's servile compliance toward the elder Klecko would have prevented that kind of ploy. Klecko had invented the game they played, passing along well-meaning, but tiresome, fans from one racer to the other.

"You've just got to meet this guy. He'll be the next Jean Claude Killee!"

Now approaching thirty, the twilight racing years, Klecko had enjoyed a better than mediocre career. The winner of six World Cup races over a span of a decade, he was the only American male downhiller to burst the rank of the top fifteen skiers in the late 1980s. In Austria, Switzerland and France perhaps, his results would win him a respectable middle-of-the-pack recognition. To the struggling American team in the early 1990s, he was the star as he earned a comfortable amount of endorsement money that was sufficient to build a massive log cabin just off the lower reaches of Independence Pass in Colorado. There and in hotel rooms and in his Subaru wagon, he had pulled down the panties of some remarkably pretty women. Only occasionally did thoughts of life after skiing come as a concern.

"Acknowledged veteran" is what the other, younger ski team members called Klecko.

The plane landed and on the moving ramp in the Zurich International Airport, Ethan felt pleased with himself by the deft manner in which he transferred Calvert Thomas to the "acknowledged veteran."

"Arnold, here's a gentleman from Georgia who's been dying to meet you!"

As they later climbed into the bus that would take them to St. Moritz, Klecko acknowledged, "Well done, Atwood! Well done! And thanks! Calvert's quite a man. He wants me to meet his daughter!"

Chapter 2
Hoping and Dreaming

Riding in the bus that would take the U.S. Ski Team to the first European race of the season, Klecko sank back in his seat and smiled at the recollection of Ethan's ploy.

"The man wants to sell you a bulldozer. Jee-zuz!" It was a far cry from the shy but affable young rookie named Ethan Atwood from Vermont of a few years ago. Atwood was so green that he tripped and fell backward at the top of a moving airport escalator at Orly Field in Paris. He was so green he would mumble when introduced. He was incapable of looking any person directly in the eye and would actually stutter if a girl attempted to make his acquaintance.

"Ethan, you're a big boy now! You don't have to read a book under the covers with a flashlight anymore! Go in the goddamn bathroom!"

Klecko had first met Ethan at Portillo, Chile, during summer training in the Andes Mountains. An awkward boob with tangled, dark hair, Ethan was carrying a huge, plastic bag of tortillas, which, during the bus ride from Santiago into the tall mountains, had puffed out to the size of a large balloon as the altitude increased. Atwood marveled at how the bag of chips resembled a basketball. He refused to open it. Instead, he wanted to take it home, just as it was, to show his girlfriend. He had the grin of a simpleton.

"For Christ sake's, don't they have *any* mountains in Vermont?"

Klecko was so initially unimpressed with the kid that he found ways to dislike him. It was perhaps a jealousy that segued to respect the first time Ethan Atwood snapped boots to bindings, and, in a sinister tailwind, took the mountain called Roca Jack by the throat, beating the best times of the day by a full two seconds.

They soon became big brother/little brother and protector/protectee. With unreserved glee, Klecko took on the task of molding his protégé into a formidable social. He succeeded halfway. Ethan would never play the fool. He would become the quiet one with a half-smile.

"Arnold, I'm here to save you from yourself."

The beginning season was difficult.

"Seventy-fifth place ain't too bad for your first World Cup race," Klecko had said that day at the finish line at Wengen. Once more, he hugged the boy, whose sad, beagle eyes reflected nothing less than loss of life.

Without the support of the veteran, Ethan's first year—eighty-seventh in the standings at Groden, forty-fifth at Vail, and thirty-ninth at Crans Montana—would have been as crippling as it was enlightening. Conversely, like many good but quiet athletes, his social depression, the awkward pain-filled self-absorption, the shyness, were all unleashed in a bundle of fury out of the start gate.

The safety he sought in social settings, like being in the middle of the pack, would do no good on the race course, where there is nowhere to hide.

Now, after leaving the level smoothness of the Autobahn to the exit at Chur, the bus ground gears as it went up the switchback highway toward the first race of the year at St. Moritz. It would soon be there. The skiers began reflecting that all of the Austrian, Swiss, German, Italians and French skiers were probably already there—already there with their head starts. They had attitude to match ability. They were always ballsy, snarling bastards who were pissed off half the time, but they were shaving quarter-seconds off their runs. They were followed by frantic partisan crowds, clanging bells, and blowing whistles that chilled your blood with their crazy yodels. A World Cup race in the Alps was Monday Night Football in Green Bay, Wisconsin.

True to his adverse nature, Ethan slept even as the bus awkwardly lurched around sharp corners of the mountainous road. Stabs of sunlight entered the dirty window, which, as the bus changed direction, was followed by shadow. Ethan's head bounced off the window glass. The back of his neck settled deeper into the cushion at the top of the seat.

Still, he slept as he saw Mary Ann Queensbury in the translucence of memory. On a hot, summery day from long ago, her long, muscular legs were carrying her uphill. With ease, she leaped from rock to rock up the side of Britches Gore Mountain. For the first time, he noticed that his longtime, platonic female friend looked like a woman. He felt a slight, sweet queasiness in his groin. Mary Ann's face was beaded with sweat, but Ethan observed strangely that it was suddenly preserved in cream.

It was the sweat, though, that teased his urges as he watched it glisten on the backs of her knees as she bounded upward on the rocks. Those smooth, tanned, muscle-hard haunches. Up to that day, she had been Donny Naples' girl. Donny was witty and bright and thought he was good-looking. He was too conceited to admit, even to himself, that Ethan Atwood was skilled enough or aggressive enough to steal his girl. Later, when he had mastered the wonderment and rage, he would say, "Ah, I could see it comin' with you two. I saw the looks." Moreover, when the new love deepened between Mary Ann and Ethan, he promised to be best man.

Donny never really learned what happened the day Ethan got to his girl, a day that was—by now—deeply cemented in Ethan's brain as the best day of his life. Heaven answered! He relived it repeatedly, savoring the moments leading to what happened. On the bus, he once more recalled the logging road, where the hardwood trees had given way to pines with their black-green branches fanning in what little breeze there was that hot afternoon. A hawk circled overhead in silence. They were perspiring heavily by the time they reached the deep woods and hiked down into a low-lying creek valley. There was some old, rusting machinery that had been abandoned when the sawmill that was located there had moved to another place down in the valley fifty or sixty years before. An old, Ford truck was half-mired in muck. Dull, blackened paint flaked off its rusting Tin Lizzie hide. Ethan kicked at a fender, and it rattled almost to the ground. It dangled only by a strand of thin, green creeper vine.

"I can't understand why they just left this stuff here," said Ethan, grabbing a handful of blueberries.

As they climbed higher into the woods, the trail all but disappeared where it ran parallel to an old, out-of-place stone fence running without purpose through the forest. The moss-covered wall marked the boundary of a long-abandoned farm field that was now overgrown with aspens, birches, and heavy sugar maples. Many had trunks a foot-and-a-half thick, which measured the years since the family that lived there had abandoned their fields and, like the sawmill, moved on.

In the late 1800s, Vermont was nearly stripped of trees due to over-logging of the forests, which fed the Gilded Age's lust for lumber to build an America that was advancing westward. Farmers had moved uphill onto the cleared land and built their own homes as they raised sheep and families. Someone then discovered they could make more money milking cows, and the farming moved closer to the roads again, back down into the valleys. So, a century later, where upland farmers had once plowed their fields, beeches, birches, oaks, and maples now stood, leaning into darkened, deteriorating farmhouses scattered on the hillsides. Their windows were gone as the dirty, empty rooms echoed with memories.

Ethan led the way through a berry patch, stopping every now and then to pick and nibble. He stumbled over a stone that was buried in tall clover and white trillium, but he caught himself. A small tombstone was lying on its back. Mary Ann stared, twisting her head as her golden brown hair dropped to one side of her face. She stooped, dug her fingers into the dirt, and set the grave marker upright. The stone was about a foot high. She focused to read the chiseled letters that were weathered by decades of snow, wind, and rain. She and Ethan searched the undergrowth around them, but they did not see any other grave markers. Mary Ann squinted against the sunlight as she gently touched the carving, letting her fingers help her read.

"It says 'Hathaway Child, October 14, 1885.'

"What?" he asked, kneeling quickly beside her to get a closer look. His cheek brushed her hair, and she felt his breath upon her neck.

"Here," she said, probing the cut. "Hathaway Child."

"Oh, Ethan, she was only about two-and-a-half years old when she died."

Mary Ann felt a catch in her throat as she touched and read a second inscription carved across the curving top of the small piece of gray, speckled granite. It read, "Our Mae."

"They called her 'Our Mae.' Who could it have been? Who were the Hathaways? How long did they live here? Little Mae, how sad! She'd be over 100 now." She stood, hovering over the stone and staring down at it.

"About one hundred and three, I'd say," said Ethan, trying hard not to chuckle. But, when he saw that Mary Ann was indeed deeply touched by the moment, he began tearing away the weeds from the long-abandoned marker. He made a clearing, letting the gravesite breathe some of the mountain air.

"Leave some of the ferns," said Mary Ann. "They're pretty." She gathered goldenrod and leaned the slender stems against the stone.

Ethan woke with a jolt as the climbing, rocking bus met another bump in the road. They were now leaving the Engadine Valley and going past lime-washed houses toward the incredibly prickly alpine cliffs above. Snow was falling.

He looked at his watch. It was 1:00 PM.

"Christ, I'm hungry!"

What would Mary Ann be doing now? Six hours from 1:00 PM would be 7:00 AM in Montpelier. She would be just getting up to go to classes at UVM, the University of Vermont, where she studied resort management.

Around him, the whine of the straining gears drowned the snores of sleeping skiers. Only Klecko was awake. He was sitting in the very rear seat and fingering his Nintendo. Morgan Rutledge and Mack Schultz, two other downhillers, had each sprawled over two seats with their heads encased in their jackets, mouths open.

Ethan let his mind drift back to that hot day on the mountain when he stole Donny Naples' girl, wondering about his own naiveté.

"I did nothing. She did it all," he thought.

The day had begun as just another hike up the mountain, a training run before he was to leave for South America. Leaving the little gravestone, they had stopped to rest and admire the view as they sat on a grassy hump hiding a tree root.

"What time do you leave?" she asked.

"I catch a 10:55 flight from Burlington to Kennedy in New York. Then we have to wait around until after supper before going to Santiago. I'll be up all night."

"You can sleep on the plane."

"Not me. I'll be too excited."

"You never get excited," she smiled, touching his arm and tilting her head back upon his shoulder.

To his stunned surprise, she kept it there. He tried not to stiffen. He slowly forced his cheek to rest upon her head. A hot, damp drop suddenly fell on his arm. She looked up at his face, her own awash in tears, chin dimpled and trembling.

"Oh, Ethan, I don't want you to go!"

He had never before experienced a start out of a gate like this, as he found himself kissing Donny Naples' girlfriend on her sweaty neck and panting lips. It was a frenzied, young love that exploded in a tangle of torsos on the ground as arms and legs struggled for advantage and heaving bodies crushed milkweed and columbine. They finally lay there on their backs, staring but not seeing the canopy of pines above. A crow scolded from afar.

She spoke huskily, "That little girl, Our Mae. Do you know she never saw first grade?"

Chapter 3
Bells and Yodels

The night before the opening race of the European venue of the World Cup season was a giddy time to be alive, especially for the fans, who danced and drank on the cobblestones in the old town square beneath a round and happy moon. They made rowdy, strident noise long into the night. The team had settled two to a room in the plain, stuccoed six-story Hotel Monopol on Via Maistria. Ethan shared a room with Morgan Rutledge, a still-young skier from New Hampshire whom Ethan had raced against many times in their academy years. Like himself, he was one of the "up-and-comings."

Klecko, with whom Ethan often bunked, shared a room during this trip with Emil Girard, an assistant coach. Head Coach Bill Quinn was arriving on a later plane the next day, and Girard asked Klecko for help in setting up practice schedules, a gesture of respect to Klecko's senior status on the team. More than likely, the "acknowledged veteran" would coach one day.

In addition to learning how to race against stronger competition, the younger skiers mostly endured a painful learning experience during their first couple of years on the professional tour. In the beginning, Ethan had suffered most of all. Starting with his grandmother's cooking, he missed the warm, steaming odors from the stove; he missed the comfort of the kitchen and its collection of cow curios, present even in the wallpaper. As if there were not enough cows on every hillside and along every road in Vermont, Grandmom Rose's favorites were ink-blotted Holsteins. Their likenesses were on coffee cups and glasses as well as tea towels. There was an attractive tea cozy that Rose had tailored especially after she sent the artist a sampling of her wallpaper.

Ethan and his grandfather both shared the same given name, but, through most of the younger one's life, the elder one was referred to as Big Ethan. Big Ethan seemed to spend a large amount of time resting his large body in a parlor recliner, his vast stomach working like a bellows as it rhythmically rose and fell. He exhorted snorts, whistles, and occasional farts. Awake, he was affable and lighthearted, with the major complaint in his life being Rose's curio farm. The vast collections of ceramic flotsam spilled over and beyond on both flat and vertical surfaces everywhere in the house.

In their many years of marriage, Rose and Big Ethan were spiritually one, as some traditions called for. Physically, the oneness was oddly crippled. Big Ethan was tall. Although once thin, he was now husky in the shoulders and protruding at the belt line. Once and always waif-like, Rose had a tiny, thin body supported by thin bowlegs. Her gray hair, now going white, was a global frizzle as it stood in many frightened-looking directions. It was as if she had grasped a live wire. A stranger would expect a shrill or squeak from a voice in a physical presence like that, but one would be surprised to hear a mellow baritone, one with a devilish and rapid chuckle. Most everything in life amused Rose. As he lay in bed, young Ethan now reflected how her good humor shaped his concept of himself and life in general. Using absurd exaggeration, Rose turned frowns to smiles and pouts to giggles. "Hold still, we'll have to amputate!" she would say to a whimpering child with a slight cut on his finger. As a toddler, when he would strike his head on a corner of the dining room table, she would kick the table.

"Bad table! Bad, bad, bad!"

The ache of loneliness abroad—the homesickness—was made more intense when Ethan observed the competition. Being American was not fair because he was so young and so far removed from home. The European skiers had the best existence because they had opportunities to go home on occasion. When they could not return home, their friends and relatives stood downhill, cheering them on as they rung their silly bells and twirled ugly sounding klaxons. The Swiss, Norse, Austrians, French, Germans, and Italians attracted the attention of an adoring media, who rarely —it seemed—pursued an American skier unless he stood upon the podium, which, of late, was not often. Except for the Olympics, an American reporter rarely showed up to write stories. Of course, when stories were written, they were about how poorly the U.S. Ski Team would do.

Atwood and Rutledge were immature and painfully homesick during their rookie years. When Ethan could not sleep those first years, he would go into the hallway to quietly stretch his tired muscles, alone. He also called Mary Ann, and they would whisper long into the night. During the first weeks of the first year, he hesitated calling her, lest the others tease him. After one long pause of several days, when he finally reached her in Montpelier, her voice was thin and sounded frightened. This was abnormal for a self-assured, happy girl who was content with her position on earth and her relationship with others.

"What's wrong? You sound different," he finally asked as he held his breath.

At the other end, there was silence. She finally said, "I missed you, that is all. I went to bed Sunday night late, waiting. Maybe he'll call! Maybe he won't! Where is he? Running around? Drinking beer? Met a...met a..." She spoke slowly and with a hesitancy that gave away some uncertainty, an emotion Ethan had not seen in her before. She could not say, "Another girl!"

Ethan gasped in a bright mix of joy and guilt. The urgency of her small entreaty touched him to the spine. This was a girl he had not yet felt totally entitled to. He would have been content to grovel his life away at her feet.

He surprised himself when he shouted into the old wall phone in the empty hallway, "Jesus Christ, I adore you! I adore you!"

He then anxiously looked in both directions to see if anyone heard. He whispered forcibly, "I adore you! Mary Ann, Mary Ann, Mary Ann! I can't tell you how much I think of you. I can never look at another girl! I've just been afraid to call...I didn't want to embarrass you."

"And I have to admit that I was reluctant to call because of what the others might think." The confession made Mary Ann melt. "Same old Ethan!" she said to herself. She was touched.

It became one of those blessed lovers' conversations that occupy the very pinnacle of endearment, making up after a spat, quarrel, or misunderstanding. Always the best moment. They said good-bye with a mutual flood of happy tears.

Ethan slept soundly and marched into the next day with a reaffirmed purpose for life.

This year would be different. He could bear down on his race training. Braced with more experience on the European tour and a dedicated program of summer training behind him, he was able to return to Europe with a picture of a girl—his girl—in his wallet, feeling strong and wise. Ethan would keep the focus narrow and simple. His body also had a full library of muscle memories now, ones that would feel the swift course underfoot. All he had to do was stay relaxed, get some good times, and earn a few more points each race. As the season and his confidence progressed, he would get bolder, get mad, and take charge. Win!

Ethan turned his thoughts back to the present. In the start shack, the jagged downhill course appeared to drop in a near-perfect vertical, forcing racers to dive nearly head first. To a pro racer, it was a maneuver that was not a real bother. However, to the casual weekend skier, it was terrifying.

Konrad Lanzenir stuck his poles over the start wand and breathed deeply. The starter announced, "Racer, ready!" Konrad tightened the muscles of his arms for the push off. Ranked mediocre by the Austrian team he skied for, he would have been an all-star if he were an American.

While waiting his turn, Ethan squatted into a tuck for his mental run. He shut his eyes and visualized each turn and degree of angulation. He stood, inhaled, stretched his arms and waved them in circles, loosening the shoulders and getting the blood to flow. He let his eyes take in the jagged peaks that stood like giant thorns on all sides. He jumped up and down, flattening his feet to the inner soles of the boots. They were buckled as tightly as possible to transfer each ounce of bodily energy perfectly onto the skis. His boots were size nine; his street shoes were size twelve.

One other ritual, the relaxing reverie, was left. He's seven years old and standing atop a wind-driven cold day at the top of Goat, one of the fabulous Front Four black diamond trails at Stowe. Big Ethan, who was ski patrol captain at the resort, was on one knee. On most of his days off, he led his little namesake higher uphill to newer, bolder challenges upon the resort's skinny, icy trails. Ethan had had many coaches in his career. Each had different eccentricities, but none were more beautifully inventive than the gray-haired wizard who made skiing as thrilling and crazy as a nighttime fairy tale.

"Now," the older Ethan asked, "Do you see that big fluffy cloud up there?" He stood at the eye level with the lad with one knee in the snow and a big, gloved hand on his grandson's little shoulder.

When Ethan nodded, the grandfather continued, "I want your big toes…both of 'em…pointing up at that cloud. I want your feet flat on the snow, but I want your toes pointed up. Touch that cloud with your toes! You got it? You know what I'm talkin' about?"

"Uh huh," said Ethan, tilting his head far back in order to see from underneath the thick wool hat that forever slipped over his goggled eyes.

"Well then, tell me what I'm talkin' about!" said Big Ethan.

Ethan drew in a breath, sniffed fiercely to retard his runny nose, and closed his eyes to remember the lesson. He then shouted impatiently against the cold wind, "If I ski with my toes up, it keeps me forward, over my skis, to keep my weight downhill."

"Why that's very good for such a young fellow!" said Big Ethan, patting his head and adjusting the hat as he pulled it roughly over the boy's ears and turned up the front into a brim.

It had always been the same. Whatever the pitch of the slope, Ethan felt his upper torso take command. He loved the thrill of hurtling his body down a cliff toward sudden death, only to have the skis glide beneath him at the very last second and spring his body aloft just high enough to skim the snow. After that day at Stowe, the turns became much easier, and he became much more sure of himself. He went downhill much faster—fearlessly faster.

When the weekend closed, Ethan had finished fifteenth in that first race at St. Moritz. For the first time, he broke the barrier between the also-rans and the elite. He had even beaten Klecko, who had skied off after missing a gate high up near the start. Morgan Rutledge came in directly behind Ethan, a promising beginning for the U.S. Ski Team, tempered nonetheless with the realization that six of the top ten finishers were Austrians.

Still, Ethan's eyes popped wide open when Otto Garmisch, who came in first more than two full seconds ahead of Ethan, extended his hand and said, "I will have to fear you this year!"

"Sure, Otto!" Ethan grinned. "Bullshit, Otto!"

"No bullshit! No bullshit!"

The season pressed on, and the ski team gained some solid—though not spectacular—results. Ethan had advanced in world ranking to No. 20. He was finally ahead of Klecko but he still had a long way to go to reach the golden climes of the Austrians and Swiss.

His eagerness to compete was at a high level. During his rookie year, he dreaded the approach of each race day, feeling his confidence slide right out the soles of his boots. Things felt differently now.

The moments of the week that preceded the next race at Wengen ticked away slowly. The team arrived there on a Sunday night. They took the narrow gauge railroad up from Lauterbrunnen and checked into a small, quiet hotel away from town, which was actually closer to the next resort mountain of Grindelwald than Wengen.

The coaching staff agreed to get the ski team into accommodations that were sparse, colorless, and lacking elements of distraction, such as females, booze, and rock music, particularly early in the season.

Coach Quinn was savvy to every and all possible derailments of concentration, for example, like what happened the year before in a small hotel shared by the Swiss women's team. It was one of those old Alpine hostels where the room keys were made of brass. So heavy and so large, they were impossible to lose, let alone carry around. Most guests, in keeping with the casual security of the hotel, left their keys in the outside lock when the room was occupied.

Alas, as the American team hurriedly dressed to go to practice one morning, a couple of Swiss girls—ski-racers themselves—turned the key to Klecko and Ethan's room while walking down the hallway. They giggled and sped away, eventually showing up in the courtyard below and laughing hysterically as Klecko cursed from his window above.

"I'll get you for this! You'll rue the day! Swiss bitch! I'll kick your ass! Slut!"

The girls blew kisses up at him.

"Your mother's a cow!" Klecko yelled back.

Only when the races neared the end of the season, and if the team was doing poorly, would the coaches hold out the carrot and consider lodgings in the "recreational" parts of ski towns to let the youths break away from their mentally unchallenging rounds of video games to socialize, womanize, and drink beer. They allowed anything to relieve the funk of losing.

However, this was early in the season. At the little Bernerhof Hotel, the team awoke refreshed with extremely high moods to match the sting of cold, fresh air whistling down the Jungfrau.

It was in this mindset that Ethan, overzealous, went down after hitting an icy rut on his very first practice run. He slid skis first into the safety fence, a minor mishap that was repeated a half-dozen times each practice day by the racers of many nations. Yet, he went down softly enough that other competitors laughed.

"Yo, Ethan, the race is Saturday!" yelled one.

Ethan smiled and jumped up quickly. He then bent down to pick up his ski pole lying on the snow beneath the orange, plastic fence. As he reached, the thumb of his right hand failed to move. He removed the heavy glove to examine the numbness and saw a thumb dangling straight down from the rest of his fingers, like the end of a broken candle when snapped in half. Obviously, the ligament was ripped through.

Sitting in the outpatient surgery waiting room of the hospital in Bern, Ethan tried staring at the far wall, but he nevertheless caught glimpses of the sick and injured around him, a man who was old, pale, and sickly with a few days of beard on a sallow, drawn face. Next to him, a slightly built girl, perhaps still a teenager, probably his daughter, gently scolded the old man in German. The old man stared straight at nothing and blinked away a tear until the girl softened. Smiling and crying, she caressed his heavily knuckled hand.

Ethan tried not to look at them because the scene made him guilty about his own selfish distress. Big hanging thumb! So what! Big kid skiing! Too bad! He sighed, mostly from boredom and slightly from apprehension. All he could lose from this accident was momentum during recovery. Just when his confidence was peaking and his muscle power seemed perfectly in tune with his will and his readiness to win, that was when it happened. He would have to fight to maintain the mental acumen. Athletes dread injury because of the interruption in pace. The worst word in the English language is "rehabilitation." He would have to do something.

So, when a nurse announced, "Meister Att...vuld," he jumped to his feet and resolutely walked into the small, white room. While waiting for the doctor, he rehearsed what he would say.

The doctor, a slight, balding man with large glasses and huge smile, was initially taken aback by Ethan's insistence that he fashion the cast out of fiberglass and create a hook to allow Ethan to grip his ski pole. Two hours later, when Ethan was led away after the surgery, the doctor smiled, satisfied with his handiwork.

He vigorously shook Ethan's left hand and said, "I will be watching. I will watch for you. You win!"

He laughed. Ethan smiled.

Lauberhorn was the longest downhill course on the World Cup circuit. On this day, it was frightfully cold. A dark gray obliterated any sunlight, and a sharp wind exacerbated the need to keep lively. The racers danced and bounced atop the peak near the start gate, widely flailing their arms and moving them in windmills.

Swiss Army soldiers, of whom it can be said had never fought a war they did not like, had been employed to stamp down the newly fallen powder, which was hosed with water to bring it to the proper and most dangerous icy slickness

There was a false illusion that the pain in the thumb—which had been excruciating—had subsided with news of the judgment of the Race Committee. The Committee concluded that racing with a hand cast resembling the beak of a parrot or, at worst, a toucan, was not in violation of the rules. Fearful of another medical disqualification, Ethan had stopped taking painkillers days before the race. Now, preparing for the start gate, he could feel the thumb

throb as blood coursed through it, but it was not with the terrible knifelike intensity of the past few days. Klecko came over to him, helped him to put on his one glove, and began rubbing his shoulders.

"Wipe your nose!" he said.

The day after the race, pictures appeared in the European papers of the three winners on the podium, Franz Kluckner, the popular German superstar was at the top. Ethan Atwood was a step down, and Arnold Klecko was in third. It marked the first time in years that two Americans had held such exalted positions in the downhill event. The news stories and TV coverage glossed over, but it nevertheless brought attention to the fact that Ethan skied while injured. The hook was more captivating. One commentator likened it to a lobster's claw. World Cup fans throughout Europe took notice of the "Aragosta. Ethanee Aragosta!"

In a little back alley café in Prague, a bulldozer salesman from Atlanta leaned to the man next to him and showed him the photo in the paper.

"I know these two ski racers here. Met 'em on the airplane!"

The man returned his look quizzically, wondering to himself why Americans so much enjoyed sharing witless information.

Looking back at the paper, Calvert T. Thomas muttered to himself in astonishment, "I'll be goddamned!"

Chapter 4

Kitzbuehel

The skiers were pleasantly relaxed and eager when they reassembled at Kitzbuehel after the Christmas holidays. The mood quickly changed with the weather that visited the old, walled town. It went from a crisp cold to a non-wintry warm and ugly atmosphere. Rain fell in the valley and even up top. Snow rotted and turned from white to brown, running downhill in dirty rivulets.

Melancholy failed to dissipate even when the sun appeared for a day. A chill then followed. Then a snowfall came, a gentle overnight dumping that should have reshaped attitudes as well. They were staying in a small hotel, the Auberge, just a short distance from the Hahnenkamm cable car in the center of town.

The weather was fickle. It was sour, then bright, then warm, windy, and rainy. Finally gentle amounts of snow began falling. The initial frustrations led now to anxieties, worsening at night with the lights out.

Then it happened. At 2:00 AM, Klecko, in a sweat, rose from bed, stumbled to his gear bag, which lay in a pile in a corner along with dirty socks, underwear, and sweatshirts. He fingered the small, plastic thermometer keychain attached to the cloth handle.

Aiming his penlight, he whispered gruffly, "It's eighty-six fucking degrees in here!"

He could hear the steam as it banged on interiors of the pipes deep in the rooms and hallways of the building below. Ethan, getting out of bed, risked a hernia attempting to open the windows, first one and then another. They had been painted shut many times over. The two sleepless athletes banged back on the radiators with their heavy ski boots. They went into the hallway. They met Rutledge in a rage, trudging downstairs to the front desk.

A small man behind the wooden front counter made promises. "Yes, I'll take care of it," he said, blinking sad, bulging eyes and nervously scratching his Hitleresque mustache.

The skiers returned to bed, angrily dropping to the mattresses. They waited. Within minutes, as the wind barked outside, the temperature began descending...and dropping and dropping. At 5:00 AM, Ethan felt for the blanket at the bottom of his bed and discovered he had already pulled it tight.

"Now it's fifty-two degrees in here," whispered Klecko, on his haunches near the gear bag.

Unable to sleep, the skiers roused and went downstairs for an early breakfast, except they had to wait an hour for the kitchen to open.

Practice went poorly that day. Worse, more fire was added to the myth of the Alps, where inhabitants firmly believed in the dragons and demons that were thought, centuries ago, to dwell in the cracks, caves, and crannies of those sky-high peaks. Were they the ghosts of Hannibal, Caesar Augustus, or Attila the Hun, all the conquerors who had trespassed these imperious crowns, seeking trespass to profit and power? Intruders now are mountaineers and skiers, likewise puny beings to be hurled to their deaths for daring to climb forbidden spaces.

Bad signs were everywhere in Kitzbuehel. First, rain mixed the snow to brown. Faulty plumbing then weighed down on frail psyches. It was not depression, but it was a far worse cancer, the one that erodes confidence.

Coach Quinn was quick to notice the fallen tempo at practice. His racers began pacing themselves, being careful not to fall on the steep pitches of the downhill section called "The Streif." Kitzbuehel's Hahnenkamm was fearsome enough to begin with, and it was not just because of the attention-getting prominence of the race. It was the difficulty of the course, which easily intimidated the most fearless of downhillers.

"Funny," said Quinn to Emil Girard, his assistant coach. "You can count a hundred racers at every World Cup event in the year, except Hahnenkamm. Only about half of them show up here."

"They're afraid of this mountain," said Emil.

"You know why?" continued Emil, glaring uphill. "This course has never changed since the first day they skied on it. Remained the same since the beginning—same vertical, same turns, and same drops. It was tough then, but it's tougher now because the skiers are faster now. Better equipment, faster skis, all that stuff. They're goin' twice as fast as they did in 1950."

A couple of nights before the race, Quinn called a team meeting in a small downstairs recreation room of the hotel. Immediately assessing the serious look on his face, the racers stopped short their usual banter, laid down the ping-pong paddles, turned off the video, and clustered on a couch or the floor as they waited for the scowl to soften.

The promise the coach had made to himself to approach the problem with resolute calmness was broken only seconds into his speech.

Quickly turning to an uncontrollable tirade, Quinn shouted, "You have to stay composed, goddamn it!

"I don't like what I'm seeing...and hearing. 'Oh, it's too hot in here! It's too cold in here! The food stinks! The hotel staff stinks! People aren't friendly! They hate Yanks! The snow stinks! The weather stinks!

"'And you know what? We stink, too! We're skiing like a bunch of old ladies.' This mountain will eat you alive if you don't begin attacking it. You hang back here, and you're down."

"Can I interrupt?" Klecko finally asked, raising his hand like a child asking permission to visit the bathroom.

"You just did. No, it's okay," said Quinn, half-smiling now that his steam had been blasted off. "What is it, Arnold?"

"About the heat in the rooms. I don't wanna complain, but I think we're being sabotaged. I think that's the reason for everything."

"Sabotaged?"

"Yeah, sure. It gets hot and then it gets cold in our rooms. It's been goin' on all week. Hot, then cold. We bitch about the heat. Then it gets cold. From one extreme to the other."

Nodding in agreement, some of the others said, "Yeah, that's right."

"I think what's happenin' is the Austrians, in particular. They seen some good things comin' outta' our team recently, like what Ethan did and so forth. They see us comin' on strong, and...well, I wouldn't put it past 'em. I think they put the word in with the concierge here or somethin.' You know." His finger tapped the air. "Fiddle with the thermostat? Things like that?" Even as he spoke, a drop of sweat slid down his brow.

Quinn laughed aloud. "You know, Arnold, maybe they did! You know, I could—maybe I should—tell the hotel people we're not staying here again. They probably couldn't care less. But, what if it's true? What if it is sabotage? What can we do about it now?

"You know the answer as well as I do. Nothing! At least nothing directly. I'll tell you what we can do, though, and this is my whole point."

Arnold's interruption did nothing but make Quinn even angrier.

"Quit, for Christ sake, quit focusing on the negatives! Quit bitchin' about what you can't control. You can't do a damn thing about the Austrians—in the hotel or out of it. You can't do a thing about the weather, the snow, or the sunshine. You can't do a thing about whether some asshole says hello to you or not or whether your eggs are cooked right.

"The only thing you guys can control is how you ski. You should know this all along. You're supposed to be professionals and here you are, letting the distractions distract you. That's exactly what the Austrians want you to do as well as the Swiss, the French, and the Italians. They want you distracted. They want you to ski badly.

"You got to get refocused," he concluded. "I can control my skiing and my equipment. If it's broken, I can fix that. I can make corrections when there is something wrong with what I'm in control of. What I can't control, what I can't do anything about, what is in somebody else's hands, I can refuse to let it get me down." He pounded a fist in his hand, striking with each word. "I refuse to let it bother me. I refuse to whine. Whining is for babies."

Quinn's discordant voice was strident now. And loud!

"Tough guys don't whine. Tough people don't bitch and whine and complain all the time! Who the hell is tougher on this trip? Us or the Austrians?

"Us!" yelled some skiers.

"Us is!" roared Klecko. "Us are!" He blinked and looked to Ethan, who quietly corrected him. "We...we are!"

"We fuckin' are!" yelled Klecko.

That night at 2:00 AM, "clunkety, clunk...clank...clunk clunk." The steam made alternate banging and wheezing noises as the demon of the furnace added more fuel. Ethan imagined a screaming American downhiller, stuck through on a spit with an iron rod poking into his bunghole and out his bleeding mouth. It was turned on the spit, and the skier rolled repeatedly as his flesh peeled from his bones, dropping in wet globs onto the fiery coals below. Slowly, the temperature vaulted.

Clad in shorts, Ethan, resisting the urge to scream, laid flat. Staring at the darkened ceiling, his palms pressed downward on the hot sheets beneath him. He forced his body to tense, tightening the muscles in his feet. He then let them relax, to go limp. He did the same in order with his calves, knees, thighs, hips, trunk, fingers, forearms, shoulders, neck, jaw, eyes, and ears. He closed his eyes and put himself at the apex of the Streif.

Below you squats the entire valley of Kitzbuehel. You breathe deeply, patiently awaiting your turn before sliding your skis forward carefully beneath the wand. Just as carefully, you lift the poles over the wand, planting them, waiting.

"Racer ready!"

"Go!"

The course drops from sight, a couple hundred feet of forty-five degrees, free falling in the lap of gravity. Skis caress the ice beneath. More speed. First flat. Sharp, short turn to left. Mausefalle. The Mouse Trap jump. Take it in the center. One hundred fifty feet of air. Skis down quickly. Set up quickly. Left turn and a right. Now at Steilhang, ugly rock face. Blue ice. Take the highest line. Glide! Skis flat! Speed increases. A curve to the right. Short ledge. Go left, then right. Go into a long, fast, straight incline. Relax. Breathe. Glide. Tuck!

Terrain drops. Quads feel good! Now an S-bend. Need perfect line for the Hausberg jump. The killer jump. Just before the ramp, the hill flattens. Now the ramp itself. Need eighty-five speed here. Pre-jump. Get the skis down quickly. Here come the G-forces.

Thighs on fire. Stay aerodynamic. Tight line. Back into the tuck. Press forward. Cross the finish line.

He fell asleep, muttering "Nothin' to it." There were no banging pipes, no searing heat, and no demon of the Alps.

The next day's practice was the best ever as the flock of American racers put aside, at Quinn's command, their insignificant bitches.

The up-tempo mood rose higher that night in the town square, just around the corner from the hotel. There, on a wooden stage set up in the middle of the street, as celebratory horns blared and drunken people shouted, race officials drew seeds from among the top fifteen skiers. Choosing an elite group put the also-rans at a disadvantage long before the race even started. However, by focusing on the fifteen, the competition became intensified. Those fifteen would take one run and then a second in a reverse order of the finish of the first run. Thus, the fastest skier in the first heat had the advantage of skiing last in the second. Based on the successes of their most recent performances, two Americans, Arnold Klecko and Ethan Atwood, were in the fifteen. Klecko, wearing a green Tyrolean hat with huge, white feather, had been there many times more than Ethan had. He grinned broadly when he dipped into an old leather bucket and chose No. 7.

"Right in the middle of the pack, just where I wanna be," he shouted to the crowd, which roared back, even though they did not understand much of what he said.

Ethan chose 13. He was satisfied. He would know before he started whom he had to beat. He kissed the paper and held it high to the cheering crowd. Then he raised it, with seeming reverence, to the statue of Ludwig the Severe, looking down at him from his high perch near the city fountain.

When he dropped down to the cobblestone street from the stage, he felt a hand on his elbow.

"Ethan!" shouted a boy who appeared to be about fifteen years old with dark, wavy hair nearly covering his eyes.

"We are your fan club—the Ethan Atwood Fan Club," he shouted, spreading his arms to introduce a pack of young Italians. A couple of them were holding half-empty wine bottles. They all pressed forward to shake Ethan's hand. There were about a half-dozen of them, and they huddled around the mostly confused, but smiling Vermonter.

A few clutched felt pens, which they passed from one to the other while Ethan scribbled his autograph. One was on the very back in a wide space of a ski jacket. There had been times in his past when he had difficulty signing his name. He sometimes took the force of concentration to make the signature legible. He thought legibility was important. Now, his signature poured onto the photos of himself and on pads and autograph books with broad, confident sweeps. Nonetheless, it was surprisingly legible.

"You will win!" said one of the fans, another teen with protruding teeth flashing brightly. "You will win Kitzbuehel. Then you will dine with us! Say 'yes.'"

"Dine with you? You mean dinner? Yeah, why not! I'll be happy to…"

In the hotel, Klecko teased as they mounted the stairs, "Ethan Atwood's got a fan club! They're all Eye-tralians! An Eye-tralian Fan Club! Fame and fortune for the Big Ethanaroo! Go, Ethan Babe!"

Saturday morning dawned cold, dropping even colder to about zero degrees, as the skiers departed the lift and stood atop the mountain. They jumped to keep warm. Spectators lining the Streif huddled in small masses, like herds of seals on a rocky, ocean beach, protecting one another from the Alpine blasts. The racers fought to not mind the cold, despite the openness of the mountaintop where the wind whistled and roared. Ethan regarded fifteen degrees below zero in Vermont as "sometimes chilly." January days like that were frequent, and no one stopped skiing just because it was below zero. Ethan, enforcing an old habit, went to each team member and stared at his face. He was checking for the white, chalky patches that were signs of frostbite. He frequently held his gloved hands to his cheekbones and then asked one of the trainers for some clear salve, which he applied to his exposed flesh to protect the skin.

The sky went suddenly ablaze with golden sunlight, glancing off the mountains to the north and west. Ordinarily, Ethan, who had never felt so relaxed just before a race, would not see what surrounded him. For a moment though, his eyes swept over the knifelike peaks that were padded in white only on certain sides or in nooks and the narrow crevices between the giant rock thorns. The frantic, nervous noise of cowbells and alphorns rose to the peaks. He watched the gray shadow cast by a cloud make progress across the face of a nearby massif.

After an hour of what seemed like an eternity of course inspection and bureaucratic decision-making by race officials, the event got underway. Conditions were perfect. There was no fog nor falling snow. The tracks were good and fast. The speed with which the racers left the start house was immediately noticeable. An appreciative crowd accelerated each racer with air horn blasts, shouts, and bells.

One by one, the racers left, but not all reached the bottom.

"Reikel's down," said Girard from his post at the Steilhang, referring to a German skier who slid off course when he slipped an edge.

A Canadian racer went next, swiftly disappearing from the start area, but Girard echoed, "Fluharty's down."

The Steilhang, an icy wall of defiance, was winning. It seemed one skier after another was dropping, their fortunes shattered. Out of the first ten skiers, only half reached the bottom, and those were at incredible speeds. Otto Gerbisch and Franz Kluckner were two who made it. Standing first and second respectively, they were the ones to beat.

Klecko's run was aborted at the final jump when his knees collapsed, bouncing his butt beneath him and hurtling him at autobahn speed toward the orange safety fence. Klecko's out-of-control body tore clear through the fence and piled into some spectators beyond. Four or five went down in a heap. Klecko's brightly striped, blue and red skintight suit flailed to regain balance, frantically flapping in the spider's web.

He disengaged, stood up, and raised his arms. "Okay," he said and then stooped to help the victims of his mishap. All would survive without serious harm, and they would tell the story for years to come about the time the American downhiller nearly killed them at Kitzbuehel.

As the race progressed, the climate of various moods stiffened. Pulses moved rapidly. Both Gerbisch and Kluckner hovered near the finish area, watching the clock and watching skiers fall. They would glance uphill as if to see the next racer leave the starting gate, but that was two miles and two minutes away. Each harbored feelings of increasing rivalry from Atwood, especially Gerbisch, who saw in the American the same disinclination toward losing that he possessed himself. He knew Atwood genuinely feared losing, perhaps the greatest of all motivators. His performance at Wengen was no fluke, especially with that lobster claw impediment. He was a potentially great racer who was just beginning to hit his prime, and the others knew it.

By the time Ethan took one final, deep breath and, with a whoosh, exhaled and shoved off, the course had been narrowed and tuned to an icy groove by the racers who went before him. Adherence to the groove was all that was needed.

He passed the Mousetrap with incredible ease. The bells were ringing, and spectators were roaring. He did not hear anything except the whish of the skis beneath him.

The Steilhang, which felled so many before him, loomed ahead. Denying caution, he pushed forward, setting the steel edges all along the base of his boots. The skis responded by cutting and carving a perfect arc without any skidding or loss of speed.

By the time the final jump approached, like that of an oncoming locomotive, his speed was plus eighty-five miles per hour. His thighs aching, he crouched forward to ease the pain. As the ramp approached, he relaxed his knees, softly compressing them. He skimmed the top of the ramp with only a minimum of launch, quickly brought the skis to earth, and sailed home to first place by a quarter-second.

One more run and Ethan would be a World Cup winner, at Kitzbuehel nonetheless. He knew it. He felt it. His confidence level was brimming. The only control he needed now was to keep feeding that gorgeous mental and physical high.

"What did you feel when you hit that last jump? It was perfect!" yelled a television race commentator, thrusting a mike upward.

Still gasping in the rarified air, Ethan tried bringing his breathing back to normal. The question took him by surprise because the voice belonged to an American television commentator. He noticed NBC on the insignia on the camera.

"I honestly didn't feel anything, except my legs burning," Ethan replied. "I never felt so good in a race. I don't know why. I just felt good."

"Your confidence level is high?"

"Right now, sky high! I feel beautiful!" he said.

An hour would pass before the thirty other racers took their runs. The icy, vertical course tripped up many more, including the No. 15 runner, Carlo d'Ampezzio of the Italian Ski Team. A helicopter carried him away from the Steilhang. His left leg was shattered. His season was finished. The fog then set in, canceling the remainder of the heat for that day. The stage was set for the final heat on Sunday.

Chapter 5
Steilhang

"Go back to the hotel," said Quinn. "Call your girl. Take a nap."

Because of the press interviews, it took Ethan another two hours to get away by himself.

When Mary Ann picked up the phone at home in Montpelier, she knew instinctively it was him, mostly because of the continent-away pause before she heard the voice.

She did not want to ask, "How did you do?" All she needed for him to say was, "I'm in first place. One more heat and I'll have a victory" or something simple like that.

Mary Ann's stomach dropped in a sudden disbelief, but she felt a wave of warmth flow from the pit to her face.

"He's in first place! I want to go outside and shout, shout, shout!"

Ethan grinned at the other end, hearing her voice bounce off the walls of her living room. Oh, the grateful feeling! She would always do for him what he could not do for himself. She could fill in the hollows of his self-imposed diffidence and make him forget who he really was, an ordinary slowpoke who sometimes skied fast. For the first time that day, he felt the thrill of a tingling spine.

Their conversation was brief, but nothing was left unsaid. He understood Mary Ann's sudden silence. He could feel the tears falling from her eyes. If there were any soft spots in Mary Ann's strong psyche, it was sentimentality for underdogs that made her shed, oftentimes, buckets. It was like the first day on the mountain, the memorable hike and the discovery of the little tombstone of the Hathaway child. Both said a lumpy good-bye before murmuring "I love you" and hanging up. He felt so pleasantly fatigued and went to bed. He fell suddenly asleep with Mary Ann Queensbury's face on his mind.

Because the race rules established that ranking first in Saturday's first heat meant Ethan would race last in the final heat, the target Ethan had to shoot for would be an absolute time on the clock. With the others all going ahead of him, there would be no guessing about whom he had to beat or the time to beat.

Sunday church bells clanged in the village and up the mountain. He arrived at the course early, mainly because of more scheduled interviews with NBC, *Ski Racing* magazine, and the European press. Ethan was surprised about how less threatening it was talking to the press now. At the apex of triumph, every question is easy to answer, including what is unknown.

"I'll just do my best."

At the top near the start shack, Gerbisch approached Ethan and extended a hand: "Do your best, Atvud!" He grinned. "Today, I'm going to beat you."

"Thanks a lot, Otto, just what I need to hear."

Otto's gesture, his psych move, was easy to figure. It was meant to entangle the young Vermonter into self-doubt.

A trainer approached and began pounding and slapping Ethan's thighs, rubbing away any unwanted tightness. It was looking like a short race day, especially with a shrunken field. Many good skiers had been eliminated. Not only had the strongest survived, it was the most fearless. Among elite racers, the only fear worth possessing was the fear of failure.

A young Austrian, Peter Miller, who had not been seeded before, skied first, thanks to the attrition that attacked the elite group on Saturday. He set the time at 2:06:38, not too swift and nothing for the other racers to worry about. Miller was elated to be where he was, despite having little chance of winning.

As the racers came and went, some fell to the blue wall. Some fell to the jumps, and others fell to the orange nets. The course became ragged and chewed. Fog was quickly laying down its gauzy mist atop the summit, but, so far, it affected only the start shack.

"Please, dear God, don't fog it in!" Ethan prayed, uncertain whether his once-peak confidence and his ability would hold up. A voice inside him suddenly said, "You're backing off, dumb bastard. Keep positive. Focus!"

He decided to concentrate on breathing. Closing his eyes, he dropped to a stationary tuck and mentally let the Streif come alive to his mind's eye. He remembered the course during inspection, which seemed like several hours ago.

Kluckner, racing thirteenth, missed a gate and skied out. This caused Girard to exclaim into his radio to Quinn, "That's one down. One to go." The latter was a reference to Gerbisch.

The fastest time so far was 2:05.24. It was registered by Canadian Bill Reilly, one of Ethan's good friends who came from a resort not widely known in British Columbia named Red Mountain. It was, however, a mountain that over the years had produced about one-third of the Canadian Ski Team.

Only two racers were left, Otto and Ethan. Just before Gerbisch entered the start gate, Bill Quinn, standing with Ethan, stole glances at Gerbisch's face. Normally, the German was the epitome of bravado and concentration. Quinn stared hard to see if Otto's trademark sneer was present. Was Quinn seeing doubt and concern? It then dawned on him that it did not matter.

He quickly looked at his own racer." How do you feel?" he asked while massaging Ethan's shoulders and arms.

Ethan shook his head affirmatively. His lips were a tight line. "Ready! I'm ready!"

Gerbisch took off. His line was tight, but the burst out of the start gate was not so strong as it might have been. He handled the Mauseffale and the two quick turns that followed with ease. Racing toward the Steilhang, Gerbisch took a lesser line than Ethan did on his first approach. He was racing conservatively, carefully. Gerbisch respected Hahnenkamm. His goal today was to finish with a time worthy of the course and the conditions. Even if Atwood skied as well as he did the first time down, Gerbisch felt he could beat his combined time with a typical gliding race.

"He's not killin' it," yelled Emil Girard as he watched the big racer speed past him. "Maybe eighty, that's all."

It was now clear to the American coaches that the German team did not consider Ethan that serious of a threat. The young American had never won a World Cup race, let alone one where he would have to come from behind or on the fiercest downhill course in the world. If Gerbisch could keep his pace and stay out of trouble, he would win the Hahnenkamm with ease.

Indeed, the midcourse clock had Gerbisch at two-tenths of a second behind Reilly.

As he glided toward the last big S-turn before the Hausberg jump, Gerbisch's speed picked up. His gliding ability was coming through for him. He had saved his energy for the end. He hit the jump in a fluid, but compact, squat. His elbows were slightly turned out, and his skis were parallel. Taking a minimum of air, he put the skis down quickly and sailed across the finish line 1.4 seconds ahead of Reilly. He was way out in front, a certain victory.

"He used that big body and his gliding skill to pick up speed at the end of the course, where it counted, and he came in first with ease," said the race commentator, Joel Griffith. "Atwood probably will have to run a perfect race to beat him."

Just before Ethan moved into the start shack, Quinn took a gamble. Ordinarily, he did not like messing with a skier's head, but, knowing this skier, he decided to risk it.

"Gerbisch ran a perfect race," Quinn yelled to Ethan after hearing Girard's assessment. "You're going to have to bust ass, Ethan. Let it go! Let it all go! Can you do it?"

Ethan looked at his coach for a couple of seconds as if he was a statue that had suddenly found a voice.

"I'll kill the prick!" said Ethan in uncharacteristic machismo. He got into the start, breathed deeply four times, and listened to the commands.

"Ready…Attention…Go!"

Ethan steeled his legs to propel his upper body with all of his strength. The start was magnificent with incredible free fall speed. The first left turn was technically perfect, as was the second. The Mousetrap approached. Here, the racer needed the most intense concentration. Any slight bump, rut, or fogged lens could cause a mistake. He hit the jump squarely in the middle. But, in the air, he drifted slightly to the left. His left edge slightly caught the rim side of one of the deep ruts created by the other skiers. The gate was coming up, a sharp turn. Ethan planted his edge with incredible force. His balance shifted, but the sharp, steel band failed to hold on to the ice. With a sudden shock, he went down on his right side. An incredible force.

"He's down! Atwood hit the ice!" yelled Griffith.

The crowd roared in disbelief. Stabbing with his right pole, Ethan grabbed air. His elbow struck the snow and his right hip, but, just as quickly, the force of the blow propelled him upright. He barely made the gate.

He was back on course, but he was, predictably, out of the race.

"There is no way Atwood can make up the time from that terrible fall! What a disappointment for this hard-pressed American team. Just when they started to show some promise."

"But don't give up on this kid yet," interrupted the color commentator, a retired downhiller, Ed Pernitz. "I've seen Atwood ski before. I know he's going to let it all out. And that's what he's doing. He's attacking the course."

In the back of his mind, Ethan knew his fall would mean a poor time. He also knew that only a hell-bent attack would save him face, with disaster looming over the large and threatening mountain. He suddenly decided not to let failure have an easy time of it. Many a skier delayed by a mishap above could make up the speed on the Hausberg.

Nevertheless, he would need a high, risky line across the Steilhang. That was the fastest route. Another tiny mistake would probably send him hurtling past the fence and into the forest of pines. It would take all the strength and concentration he had. As the ice mass loomed up under his feet, he pushed his upper body ever more down the fall line, letting the flats of the skis kiss the snow beneath them. He missed the orange fence by a millimeter. Sensing disaster, the crowd on the opposite side of the course roared while those on the side closest to the hurtling downhiller coming at them dived for cover. In a flash, Ethan was past them, taking a line that was out of the ruts of the other skiers. How he held his edges to the ice was perhaps a miracle. He allowed his skis to drift wider apart to take the pressure off his aching, burning quads, which would be tested severely on the final jump.

Everything Ethan had learned about gliding over the years leaped to his skis. Minimize resistance. Stay true to the fall line. Stay relaxed. Knees over toes. Keep the tuck.

"He's picking up speed," yelled Griffith. "But he's still got eight-tenths to make up. He'll never do it!'

The easiest part of the hill approached. It was straight, long, and fast with a curve to the right. It was a small jump and then a turn to the left, which Ethan took in a perfect arc.

"He lost no speed there! He's flying! He's gotta hit the jump just perfect."

The approach to the Steilhang contained enough of a dip to normally bring a racer's upper body down to the ground in such a g-force that there would be one bounce and then an eternity of sailing into the sky, like a shot from a cannon.

Ethan felt newfound strength in his legs as he kept his tuck as the jump approached. He relaxed the knees, letting them absorb the lip of the head wall. As it happened, he leapt forward, pressing his fists outward to the ground beneath him. He kept the tuck with his elbows pressed nearly tight to his body. He let the skis touch down…flat, smooth, oily, and straight in the fall line.

"Perfect! He hit it perfectly! Listen to this crowd!"

"He nailed it!" yelled Girard to Quinn.

Ethan heard nothing, even though a cacophony of cowbells, horns, whistles, and screams thrust him forward. He sailed across the finish and skidded to a stop, letting his exhausted body slide across the snow. He glided on the left side of his ass and bounced into the orange net, which thrust him upward. He took two wobbly steps backward and collapsed to the ground, finally hearing the freight train roar of the thousands around him.

Klecko leaped upon him, punching him with his open gloved hands. "You won! You won, you bastard! Ethan, you won! You did it!"

By two one-hundredths of a second, Ethan Atwood won his first World Cup downhill race on the toughest ski slope in Europe.

The meteoric rush of a championship feeling engulfed the entire U.S. Ski Team, which, except for occasional bursts of glory, was fixed year by year among the also-rans. Back in Park City, Utah, the team's national headquarters, drinks were poured, and high fives were slapped with exuberance.

"I can't wait 'til next year," shouted Al Bernstock, the team's communications director. "Atwood's the nucleus now. With the Olympics coming up, we're going to market the shit out of that guy."

In Vermont, the Delahantys and the Atwoods yelled and hugged as they watched the delayed satellite rerun of the magnificent race. Mary Ann sat on the couch, staring and smiling at the television. Once again, she felt the hot tears fall. Hours later, Ethan let his limbs fall heavily into the mattress. His gently aching legs and arms were held now in soft warmth.

Chapter 6
The Breakfast

Phone calls that break up sleep in the early morning seem to have the immediacy of a firing squad.

"Breakfast? Breakfast?" he asked without any idea about who was the intruder. "Did you say breakfast?"

"Si, yes."

"Uh!"

"This is Carlo...Biancovello. Your fan club. You remember?"

"Ah, of course! How are you?"

"I am fine. You are better. You are the champion, the champion of Hahnenkhamm!"

Ethan fingered his hair and rubbed his eyes. Out the narrow window, snow—multitudes of heavy flakes—drifted silently down upon the steeply pitched carved gables and overhanging roofs of the Tyrolean buildings across the street.

"You remember your promise?" said Carlo. "You promise, if you win the race, you will dine with us, your fan club. I am the president of the Ethan Atwood Fan Club, and I invite you to enjoy breakfast with us. Today? Tomorrow? Whenever it is convenient for you."

"I...I...I didn't get your name," said Ethan.

"Carlo."

Ethan exhaled loudly and let his head drop in resignation upon the pillow. "Sure, sure, I'll be happy to," he said, emphasizing his diction so as not to let down the young man's expectations.

"But wait!" he suddenly said. "I forgot...We're leaving today. We'll be in Cortina!"

"I know," said Carlo. "So will we. Cortina is a small town. We can meet you at Cinque Torri. That's a ristorante, not the ski slope. Right in the town center. Next to the big clock tower. How about...we'll let you sleep late...ten o'clock?"

He agreed, hung up the phone, and began the downhill mental process of wondering whether the social encounter would present any difficulties for him. Blunders, gaffes, or embarrassment?

He wished to be like Arnold Klecko, who oiled his way through the most difficult passages of life, on top of it all, at ease and in command. There was the occasion when a freckled redhead wishing for an autograph approached Klecko in a hotel lobby near Val d'Isere.

"Sure thing. Gotta pen? What do you want me to sign?"

The girl, grinning broadly and surrounded by a gaggle of giggling friends, handed the skier a felt tip pen. She then turned and pulled down her britches to expose two beautifully shaped ass cheeks.

As though it happened every day, Klecko dropped to one knee and placed his left hand on the girl's lower back. With the pen in his other hand, he wrote "Arnold" on one cheek and "Klecko" on the other.

Klecko leaned back and twisted his head sideways, as if he was admiring a Botticelli. "Perfect!" he continued in a respectful, but imploring, voice, "You know, my grandfather shortened his name from Kleckiszewski. I mean, I could continue right on around."

Riding in the Volkswagen bus down the steeply pitched mountain passes between the Salzkammergut Alps and the Italian Dolomites, Ethan was able to push aside his social worries and concentrate for the first time in a long while on the beauty of the little towns as well as the harmony and splendor of the mountain peaks.

The skiers lamented they had no time to stop and enjoy the mineral springs and mud baths of the numerous spas in the region.

"I love the names," said Rutledge. "Bad Ischl. Bad Aussee. Bad Reichenhall. I wonder if they got any of that warm mud for Bad Skiing."

Later, on the Dolomite Road, as the sun peaked for an instant through the pinnacles, the skiers slept. The monotonous little roar of the Volkswagen engine made them lazy as it strained to climb the twisting road past now-dormant vineyards and orchards.

In Ethan's dream, Rose Delahanty looked down on the curly-haired boy who, deep in his pre-adolescent funk, aimlessly stirred the creamed dried beef on his plate.

With a few well-timed questions, she listened while her grandson with his downcast eyes exclaimed in disjointed sentences, "They don't like me...the kids at the academy...say I'm conceited...call me Ethan Hot Dog."

"What's a hot dog?"

"The way I ski...They say all I know how to do is race and show off..."

"This is the kid who will flatten against the wall of a crowded room," she thought.

"You don't talk because you're shy. Isn't that right?" she asked.

Rose had taught third and fourth grade for thirty-odd years. She had learned all the available tricks for overpowering her own dyslexia, a handicap she saw many times over in children. Was she a better teacher because of the affliction? Some would have been discarded as learning disabled if it had not been for her awareness of the problem and her ability to help the youths overcome it. Determining north from south and east from west were entirely other problems, and it was often of such a magnitude that her husband, Big Ethan, fretted terribly when she left the house. He thought she might never return. He had a whole drawer full of hand-drawn road maps for Rose to use.

"Do you say hello to the other kids?" she asked.

"They don't like me. Why should I?"

"If you want my help, you'll do as I say!"

"Say what?" he answered bitterly.

"Say hello, goddamn it!" Instantly sorry for the momentary loss of patience, she added quickly, "Say hi. I want you to say hi to the first person you meet at school tomorrow."

"I can't. I don't know how."

"Okay, no dessert for a week."

The noisy grind of the Volkswagen engine broke the slumber. Ethan awoke to Rutledge's bemused stare.

"How was it?"

"How was what?"

"Your dream…nightmare?"

"What did I say?" Ethan said, now bug-eyed.

"You said 'hi, hi, hi!' Over and over!" Rutledge guffawed and threw a rolled-up candy wrapper at Ethan. "You're a piece of work, you know that?"

A bell gonged loudly as the bus turned the corner into the center of Cortina d'Ampezzo. It was late in the afternoon as shadows began cloaking the small scrubbed houses and fancy shops. Cortina was a little town with a big appetite for the après-ski life. Klecko panted dramatically at the smartly dressed slick people on the sidewalks. Some were wearing furs and gold jewelry. A woman wore suede boots that extended nearly up to her shoulders.

"Didja ever feel like you're a hick?" asked Rutledge. "Look at these people!"

"I'm a hick. I know I'm a hick," answered Klecko. "Ethan's a hick, too. Right, Ethan? You a hick?"

"Yeah, I'm a hick. Hey, I wonder where the restaurant I'm supposed to be tomorrow is at."

"Hey, yeah, hick meets chic!" said Klecko, smugly pleased with himself. "You know what you oughtta do, Ethan Hick, you should impress your Italian fan club by speaking Italian. They'll love it."

"I can't speak Italian, but I should understand some of it by now," said Ethan. "When my girl gets pissed at me back home, she curses at me in Italian. She learned it from her mother."

"All girls learn that shit from their mothers," said Rutledge.

"Ethan, seriously, you should at least order your breakfast tomorrow in Italian," suggested Klecko, grabbing and shaking his duffel bag that he had been using as a pillow. "It's good public relations. PR. Quinn says we should practice PR wherever we go. I'm gonna help you. I'll write down your menu in Italian. What do you want for breakfast?"

"Oh, God help me!" said Ethan, rolling his eyes.

"Hey, there it is! There's your restaurant, Cinque Torri! Right there on the corner!" said Rutledge.

"And there's our hotel," said Tim Whitney. "Practically next door."

The morning dawned with some hesitancy. Fog, lurking in lower pockets, fled upwards to be seen no more. From the window, the racers could see cheerfully colored cable cars inching up the white-covered cliffs, already carrying skiers to their respective pleasures. They had all slept late, nursing and cursing contusions and sore bones that would never entirely heal until May or June, when racing was shelved for the season.

Ethan combed his hair while staring at the mirror in the small bathroom. Turning to Rutledge, he asked, "Do you want to go get some breakfast?"

"No thanks, pal. I wouldn't dream of it. This is your party. It's your fan club."

As he entered the restaurant, Ethan warily examined the surroundings, stuck his thumb in his belt, and covertly probed the top of his pants fly to ensure it was zipped. It was. There were rows of tiny tables with white cloths and fresh flowers on them. Soda parlor chairs with wire backs flanked the tables. A cream-colored motif, inviting and warm, spread throughout the walls. Immediately, a young man walked to Ethan and extended his hand. Short and slim, he had an aquiline nose and bright, brown eyes and shiny, brown hair.

"I'm Carlo," he said, "and this is Angela, Tonio, Alfredo, Maria…" He carefully introduced the young people, one by one. There were nearly a dozen of them, all grinning and happy to meet the skier from Vermont. All wore expensive, but not elegant, ski clothes.

He soon discovered they were serious fans. Carlo had collected a huge pile of glossy posters, showing Ethan speeding downhill and flying off a jump in a perfect tuck. It was one produced hastily by the ski team headquarters back in Utah soon after his notable race at Wengen. Once seated, their questions were polite, but hurried. It was typical of teens who were impatient with just plain conversation. They wanted to know all about Vermont, the ski academy. The races. The life. The growing up. The team. The mountains.

Carlo thrust a handful of variously colored felt pens at him. He began signing. He was glad he had something to do with his hands.

He felt more at ease as the morning progressed as his fans chatted happily with him. Each spoke to him in a mix of English and Italian.

They then all sat in a specially prepared back room at one long table for brunch.

One of the girls glanced through the door to the street. There, a face beneath a cupped hand was pressed against the glass. Someone was peering against the glare to see inside.

"It's your cousin Angelina, Carlo. Is she looking for you?"

"Ah, si!" Carlo pushed back his chair. He said, "Scuzzi, scuzzi, scuzzi!" as he pressed to squeeze past the others. He came back with a girl, a few years older than the others. She wore a beige turtleneck sweater with very tight-fitting après-ski pants. Her hair was dark and wavy. She was less than tall with broad, strong shoulders. Ethan noticed she had a chest to match. Overall, her body was curvaceous, nowhere near runway thin. However, it was her eyes that commanded attention. She had full lips as well, but the eyes—large and dark but smiling and luminous—were liquid and radiant.

Carlo introduced the girl to Ethan as Lina and insisted she take the seat next to Ethan that Carlo had vacated. The restaurant owner, a baldish Italian with a brief, black mustache, brought an extra chair. Ethan quickly moved his tongue across his teeth, a helpless move to eliminate—at least his fear of—bad breath.

After pleasant introductions, the waiter came and took their breakfast orders. Ethan ordered last, boldly pronouncing the Italian words that Klecko had taught him. He had said them repeatedly for the past hour.

The waiter stiffened. His thin frame was taut, a slight smile appearing as he penciled on his order pad. There was silence at the table. It was almost a concentrated breathless pause. In fact, the Italians, like the waiter, began smiling. Someone cleared his throat loudly. Finally, Antonio, one of the youngest, burst out laughing. The others snickered.

Lina, her hand suddenly to her mouth, smiled and grabbed Ethan's forearm as the waiter, imperious with a knowing smile across his face, bowed to Ethan, clicked his heels, and wheeled toward the kitchen.

"Did I say something wrong?"

Lina, still laughing, stopped and took a breath.

"Dear one," she said, "do you know what you just ordered?"

"Two eggs, I hope!" said Ethan, desperately fighting the inner swell of panic. "Oh no, what did I say?"

"You ordered...two men!" said Lina, erupting again. Those beautiful eyes were helplessly squinted as her grin broadened.

"Two men!" Ethan yelled, lifting from his seat.

"Two men. Due uomini, you said."

Tonio, who was sitting across from Lina, held up two fingers.

"I ordered two men for breakfast?" Ethan shouted.

"Si! Yes!" said Lina, laughing. She then took his shoulder affectionately. "Turned over. You ordered them turned over. Girati! Girati!"

From beyond the swinging door of the kitchen, the waiter and cook staff guffawed.

"I'll kill Klecko! I'll kill the bastard!"

"You dear boy!" said Lina. She was laughing so hard she began coughing. She then wrapped an arm over Ethan's broad shoulders and squeezed.

Eventually, the guest of honor admitted a good time to himself. The party then swung into several hours with lunch and wine. Ethan permitted—no, insisted—Lina order for him. The restaurant owner approached the table with a green bottle, bowed to Ethan, and said, "For you, some grappa. For you, good sport, drink up. For you, breakfast ees on the house!"

Almost mid-afternoon, the party shifted from the Cinque Tori to the cobblestone street outside. Arm in arm, with Ethan in the center, they marched in the middle of the thoroughfare. The Italians sang "Moonalighta Eena Ver Monta!" lustily.

Klecko's day had been full of sinister glee. On one hand, he entertained himself by imagining how disastrous Ethan's Italian gaffe must have been. On the other, he planned the best possible escape route when Ethan would put his hands around his neck. He began the day with window-shopping on the Via Tofana, gazing at necklaces of pearls and gold draped casually around the black velvet, headless throats.

It did not take long for a leggy blonde woman wrapped in sable to approach the rugged-looking athlete. A conversation ensued. Lunch followed, and there was a most sublime roll in her puffy bed in the Hotel Miramonti.

Klecko and his new friend, between episodes of lovemaking, laughed and laughed as he related the Italian lesson. Ethan was standing before the mirror in the tiny bathroom, shaving. Klecko was on the toilet seat, thumbing a book called *The Italian Menu Master*. Ethan was fidgeting and half-listening as he nervously scraped his face with the razor.

Klecko repeated, "Now, when it comes your turn, say 'uomini' carefully. Hold up two fingers. 'Due. Doo-Eh! Doo-Eh Uomini!' Got it!"

"Yeah, yeah. I got it, Klecko, I got it. Doo-aae-oo-ah-mee-nee! I got it! There!"

Getting home around midnight and tiptoeing up the stairs, being especially careful sneaking past the coaches' rooms, Klecko experienced how satisfying a day it had been. It had been a warm and tipsy day, thanks to the schnapps that Hilda Something had shared with him.

Ethan, meanwhile, had finally fallen into a deep sleep, but he was awakened by the sound of thrashing, bed springs rattling, and soft cursing. Klecko was kicking unsuccessfully to slide his feet to the bottom of the bed. The feet were stopped halfway because the bottom sheet had been folded, that is, short-sheeted, with both sides tucked firmly beneath the mattress.

"Arnold, will you stay still?" complained Rutledge from the next bed, unaware of the trap.

"I can't...I can't get my fuckin' feet into...Oh, now I know! Now I got it!"

He smiled, rose from the tortuous blanket and sheets, ripped them from the bed, and remade it. Exhausted, he finally flopped down.

After a moment of silence, he said slowly and sarcastically, "By the way, Ethan, how was breakfast?"

Chapter 7
Conversations

Ethan finished second in the race at Cortina. Gerbisch was first. He had transposed the surprise and anger he had experienced when losing to the American at Kitzbuehel into triumph at Cortina. It is why he won consistently and why he was so very much more professional than the pack behind him. Eschewing thoughts of defeat, Gerbisch, he of the strong psyche, flipped to positive, vowing never again to be beaten by Ethan Atwood or any other American.

Ethan's impression of the race was less exalted. "I'll take it," he said. Fully aware he could not win them all, he accepted with satisfaction his accumulation of FIS (Federation Internationale de Ski) points. He was moving up on Kluckner, who finished a disappointing eighth, for him and the indomitable Austrian Ski Team. It was just ahead of Klecko.

Before the season, Klecko had all but decided this would be his final appearance on the World Cup circuit. The telling signs were there. After each race and each strenuous practice session, several days would pass before his tired muscles rebounded. Concentration was achieved only after a tiresome effort. During practice, after a mental lapse had sent one ski on the wrong side of a gate, he recalled the line a major league ballplayer spoke after throwing to the wrong base, which allowed the winning run to score, "I thought the legs went first."

Quitting now would put a nice cap on a successful ski-racing career. He could enter some Europa Cup events if he liked or the national championships. He could try qualifying for the occasional made-for-TV races. He was, at least, the best American on a team lacking good racers. That is, he was until Ethan Atwood arrived.

"You know, Atwood. Just because of you, I'm thinkin' I gotta race again next year, just to make sure you stay in the right groove. Somebody's gotta push you along."

However, Klecko seriously told others he saw great things coming, and it would be wonderful to be a part of it. He had had more fun this season than ever, especially with his young friend from Vermont.

"With your mastery of foreign languages, Atwood, you'll someday probably get the French Legion of Honor and an Italian Gold Leaf or something. Whatever, I wanna be there!"

The following week, the team drove across the border into Switzerland to Flims-Laxx. Ethan fell to sixth place, chiefly because of a sore left knee that had been bothering him since the win at Kitzbuehel. He had given so much in that race that his physical machinery took a major beating. He tried avoiding recollection of the dreadful pain the g-forces thrust through his thighs as he attempted to maintain his tuck and his speed on that final jump. He was beginning to think there were no wins without losses.

"I guess I have to be happy I finished in the top ten with a bad knee," Ethan said to Mary Ann in one of his transatlantic conversations happening nearly every night. Curled on the sofa with her ankles tucked beneath her, she could tell by his voice that he was tired. She also wanted this long season ended, regardless of its success. Wedding plans were underway. There was a chapel halfway up Mount Mansfield that was tucked in the woods.

"No, I don't think so," she said in harmony with Ethan's minor groans. "Too hokey. Maybe we should get married in my church in Montpelier and have a drunken reception with paper plates in the Elks Hall."

At the end of the conversation, they tentatively settled on the wedding to be held at Mary Ann's Aunt Ellen's farm in the Mad River Valley. It was a place to rival Eden. A lovely lawn flanked the river and backed up to the soft woods that grew steeply uphill. It would be outdoors in the flower garden.

"Sounds good to me," said Ethan.

Mary Ann signed off with a gentle warning to check with her before saying one more word in Italian. He had told her all about the breakfast and how gracious the fan club members were to him, as well as the wait staff and the clientele, during his embarrassment.

"Be grateful for the Italians. If that had happened in France or Germany, they'd have laughed you right out the door," said Mary Ann.

Lina Biancavello and a couple of members of her group had followed the ski team to Flims-Laxx. They first flew to Zurich and then took the Autobahn to Chur in a rented Mercedes.

"If my father ever finds out I rented a Mercedes, he will have my head," she told Ethan at lunch the afternoon before the race. Her father had worked for Fiat in the design division in Milan. Benito Biancavello, now semi-retired and deservedly wealthy, owned a penthouse apartment in a fashionable district of Milan as well as a villa at Lago di Garda at the base of the Dolomites between Brescia and Verona.

Her father was a widower, and Lina had been motherless since the age of 10.

"She died of cancer," Lina said. "At that age, I was both sad and angry. I thought she had deserted me. I was devastated."

"Did your father help?"

"Yes, he helps me by indulging me," she confessed. "He gives me anything I want. He feels guilty for spoiling me." She laughed. "But he says he's just waiting for me to grow up."

She tapped at her wine glass with a manicured finger as she lowered her eyes to the table. She had gotten her hair cut so that it conformed to her oval face. It somehow made her brown eyes even more luminescent.

"And when will you finish growing up?" asked Ethan.

"I don't know," she said, shaking her head and smiling. "When do ski bums in America grow up?"

"Sometimes never," answered Ethan. "Look at me for example!"

"Yes, but you race. You make money. You are successful." She leaned back in her chair to allow the waiter, a portly, baldish man with protruding teeth, to set down the quiche she had ordered. "Tell me this? What would you be doing now if you were not a racer?"

"I don't know. I never gave it much thought. My father's an architect, but I don't think I could do that. I'd have to work outdoors. Probably teach skiing." He shrugged. "I don't know. Probably work for a mountain somewhere. Bruce White—he's the guy who owns Maple Glen where I grew up skiing—asked me if I would consider working for him in some capacity. Probably as a skiing ambassador. You know, local ski celebrity, that sort of thing. Greet the guests. I know I'd have to work on a mountain somewhere. I couldn't leave Vermont, just couldn't do that. Roots are there and all that. Besides," he laughed, "I like the weather."

"It is cold?" asked Lina.

"Yeah, it is. But there's more to it. It can be sunny one second. The next, it can be totally clouded over. Then blue sky." He waved a hand haphazardly to the window, where outside could be seen the Alpine heights of La Sialla, a Swiss mountain just over 9,000 feet high.

"I like the villages, I guess, in Vermont," Ethan continued in a rare, talkative mood. "You know, there's a village about every six or seven miles. It's all historic...well, historic and old for America. Our antiquity is only a couple hundred years old. Yours in Italy is centuries. But, every town in Vermont was located near a mill where the farmers and foresters would come. There's always a general store, and the post office is where people meet and talk. They take care of each other. And there's always a white-spired church and..."

"I know!" said Lina. "I see the calendars, the photos. I love those scenes."

After a minute, Lina confessed, "I would love to come to Vermont to be a ski bum. I have relations outside Boston. That is near there, isn't it? They live in Barr-ee. You've heard of it?"

"There's a Barr-ee, Vermont," Ethan said. "B-A-R-R-E. I don't know of any Barre, Massachusetts. Are you sure they live near Boston?"

How far...how far this Barr-ee from Boston?" she asked. "They left Italy to work in stone. The men, they were carvers."

"It has to be Barre, Vermont," Ethan said. "The place is loaded with stone workers. Granite quarries. You ever hear of Rock of Ages?"

Lina ignored him and said, "Then, after I ski your places in New England, I go to Colorado and Utah. Utah, my God, I see pictures of Alta, is it? And Snowbird! What are those people there, those Mor-Mons something?"

Ethan laughed. "What a life you lead!"

"But I love my Dolomites, especially Madonna di Campiglio. That's my local resort. It's only twenty-five kilometers from my home, and you race there next week. You must come meet my father." Her eyes opened wide as if this was a sudden and a natural idea to pursue.

Ethan, however, was not sure just how far he should take this venture with the Atwood Fan Club. "What are its limitations," he thought, "its expectations, too?" The club was growing in numbers, partly through the effort of its original members and partly because the Italian Ski Team falling on hard times as none of its skiers had any chance for prominence. There were even stories in *Conversations*, the Italian press about Ethan being engaged to Mary Ann. They particularly pointed out she was part Italian. Ethan was astonished when Lina read that to him.

"How did they find that out?" he asked.

Lina smiled.

He liked Lina, but he did know her well enough to get a fix on her motives. There were fans, and there were groupies. He had been around long enough to know that. Girls made themselves available to ski team members in just about every town, but, with Lina, he could not determine if that fine line ran through her or around her or on which side. She was genuinely a fan, that was for certain. On the other hand, she was affectionate, but it was in the sense that many European women seemed to be. He noticed the Italians were not afraid to touch, caress, or coo. These gestures simply came natural to them. They were harmless or nonthreatening on the surface.

He met Lina several times more for lunch, once or twice for dinner with Klecko and Rutledge, or with various fans and hangers-on. During the occasions when they dined as a pair, each became more comfortable than the last for Ethan.

She prodded him about Mary Ann, how they had met, and what their plans were for the future.

"Children?"

"Oh yeah, we'll have kids!"

He did not have to exaggerate his goals in life. Simple and straightforward, they consisted of Mary Ann, kids, and an undemanding job with a mountain. That was it, forever and ever and ever. All was to unfold after his career in ski-racing.

"Your parents? They approve of Mary Ann?"

"Absolutely!" He became mute for a moment, considered, stopped, and continued. "Everyone loves Mary Ann. She's so very sure of herself, bright, energetic, and loving…to others. She picks people up, you know what I mean?"

Responding to the quizzical look on Lina's face, Ethan added, "People look up to her. They come to her and ask her advice. She's very smart and very considerate."

He continued talking, growing more at ease, and once they were long into the night with conversation, he began telling her about his life.

"It's simple," he said. "I don't know why anyone would be interested in my life. It's very simple. I live with my grandparents. I have since I first started at the ski academy."

Lina sat up. "Why do you live with grandparents? Why not parents?"

In telling how it came about, his mind subconsciously vaulted over the reasons for the arrangement. "My mom and dad, they live in Albany. That's a city, the capital of New York state."

"New York City is the capital!" insisted Lina. "Of New York State? Is that not true?"

"No, it's Albany. It's upstate, up the Hudson River from New York City. Anyway, that's where I was born and it's where my dad has his business. They live there."

He continued telling Lina how his mother had desires for him to attend Spring Mountain Academy in Vermont, where the teaching of ski-racing is a serious business along with a strong and tough pre-college curricula.

"My mom grew up near there. Little village of Lowgate Springs. That's where I live, with Grandmom and Grandpop. My parents always come up from Albany on weekends. It's like a three-hour drive."

Ethan's story was all true—every word. However, he did not mention the unspoken cause of why he was put in his grandparents' control. In fact, it was never mentioned, particularly because his knowledge of his father's problems was veiled over. It was only a cloud in the past. It was something his mother and father dealt with, but not Ethan. He was a kid, an innocent kid when it all began.

The problem started soon after Paul Atwood, Sr. had graduated from Rensselaer Polytechnic Institute in Troy, across the Hudson River from Albany. He got drunk at parties, imbibing on weekends. Martinis were had before dinner. Wine was sipped with the meal. Beer then followed before bedtime.

Paul Atwood was a kind, loving, handsome man. He was tall, thin, athletic, brilliant, and quiet. Marge Delahanty's infatuation with Paul's good looks and reserved behavior deepened quickly into love soon after they had met while skiing at Maple Glen so many years ago. She was still not ready to ditch a marriage and sacrifice the future of a son because of booze. However, the good husband and good father grew more internal with each passing month. Introverted is too kind a word for the often sullen moods of a drunk.

Discussing the problem with her closest friends, she answered honestly when the question came to "What kinds of abuse are you talking about?"

"Never physical, no violence," Marge said. "Mental abuse is sometimes worse. The withdrawal. I talk to the wall sometimes. Always, practically always. He is always within himself. It's like he crouches down inside his soul. I get the shivers."

On one occasion, she told her best female friend, "I can't take much more!"

It is why, on a hot, midsummer evening when the crickets and tree toads were going crazy with heat just off the back porch, she suddenly announced. In fact, she blurted it out. She had determined and rehearsed what she would say many times over. There would be no shouting or chance for reprisal. Her words dropped like cold stones, emotionless. She stared straight out the window, not at Paul.

"Ethan's going to live with my parents in Lowgate Springs. I'm enrolling him in SMA. We'll see him on weekends."

The steel of her jaw was set so hard. Her voice was so steady but sardonic. It was ringed with subdued anger. Paul said nothing. He merely looked at the ice floating in the caramel-colored Scotch in his glass. He shook it around once or twice, finished it in a single, defiant gulp, and went to bed without a word.

Chapter 8

"Sleep, il mio tesoro, sleep!"

The racecourse at Campiglio was set up on the exceptionally steep and doubly named Tre Tre Piste on the southwest side of the rocky Brenta Dolomites, which were once known exclusively for some challenging ice climbs. More recently, Campiglio had become a premier Italian resort attracting local skiers from Trento, Bolzano, and Verona, as well as the chic of Europe.

Ethan's practices had been well spent. Slowly, he initially cruised the downhill run, feeling the terrain and letting his skis swim softly over the snow. This was one of the rare World Cup venues where snowmaking was available. The skiers noticed its texture right away. With its great pack-down ability, the artificial snow sometimes afforded great speeds at a high level of comfort. All the racers were expected to take advantage of this significant race. Winding down toward the end of the season, total points were paramount. Friendly conversations among the top-rated skiers ceased as each racer turned inward and selfish, determined to snuff out one another.

Ethan needed a win here to vault into a situation where he might overcome Garmisch on the last race of the season, two weeks ahead in Val d'Isere. On race day, Ethan's concentration level was so high that he forgot to look for members of his fan club, who had promised to line up near the final jump toward the bottom of the course. He thought about it after he had passed the spot during his final inspection of the slope. At the time, his eyes and mind were on the snow, the gates, the ruts, and small bumps. He joined arcs and lines to the snow with his brain, sending the message of the proper line to take down through his body to his feet and skis. Nothing else mattered.

By virtue of the draw the previous evening, Ethan skied fourth. It did not matter to him if he skied first or last. He was determined to win this race, not to do just good enough.

He got out of the chute with the velocity of a crazed bronco rider, taking the risk of speed against the danger of a slight mistake on the precipitous head wall. Passing the first gate, he was in a groove that, if maintained, would propel him forward with a minimum of effort, just as good gliders wanted it. The first jump approached. Ethan relaxed his torso to absorb the force of gravity.

That was the last thing he remembered.

"Atwood is down," the PA announcer shouted to the crowd, intruding on their frenzy. A groan rose up the mountainside, drowning the cow bells and horns. A relative silence followed, the uneasy wait before information, good or bad, about the fallen athlete.

When Ethan crashed, the sky flipped. His head flung back upon the ice with a yellow, electric flash. Then there was dark nothingness. He never felt the pain when the tendon attached to his left kneecap suddenly let go, snapping the rubbery band in two and flinging his patella up toward his thigh, where it pounded against nerves and muscle. It was a place the kneecap was not intended to be. He awoke twenty minutes later, strapped in blankets in the sled carrying him slowly head first down the steep incline. The pain and tears watered his eyes. The green branches of evergreens in his line of sight were like dragon fingers. His world was skyward now. Occasionally, a dark face came into view.

"We're here, Ethan. You're gonna be okay," said the voice of Emil Gerard.

Ethan saw a gray band of swiftly moving clouds. He heard the whirring roar and felt the stinging wind of chopper blades, flinging ice and snow in all directions.

They lifted the whole sled into the helicopter. Ethan saw steel walls painted a dull olive color. A red, green, and white flag was embossed on its side. Girard and the US Ski Team doctor, a graduate student from Oregon, bounded in while the patrollers, hunchbacked under the whirring blades, scrambled like crabs through the snow. The noise muffled shouts. In the chopper, Ethan choked, fighting not to scream, as unseen hands cut away the tight skin of the gleaming red racing suit from his left leg. They needled morphine into him, and the dark blind fell again.

"Good news, bad news, I've got tons of it," said Quinn ten hours later. He and half the ski team had driven down the mountain through a snowstorm to the small hospital in Brescia. On the third floor, in a white-stricken room, Ethan lay in a white metal bed over which a small black crucifix hung. He had regained a portion of his brain, but his tongue was thick as he tried asking what happened.

"You went down," said Quinn. "The tendon snapped, right below the kneecap. You hit your head. You got a concussion. That's the bad news."

"Wush-h-h...goo-h-h?" asked the crippled skier.

"What's good is that the knee's gonna be stitched back tomorrow, by none other than Peter Rogers, that is, if they can get the swelling down."

Ethan recognized the name and frowned quizzically. Rogers was an eminent orthopedic surgeon from Denver nicknamed "Doctor Knee" because of his reconstructive prowess in that area. What was he doing here?

"Luckily, he was on vacation, skiing up in Davos. He saw what happened on TV and called right away. He wants to do the surgery."

Ethan shook his head affirmatively.

"How ya doin', Ethan?" asked successive ski team members as they filed in twos and threes up to the bed. Through glazed eyes, he recognized them—Rutledge, Klecko, Whitney, Schultz, and Ann Messner, a slalom skier. Others were beyond the bed. The room was packed.

"Is he awake? Can he hear us? Yo, Ethan, we're here. Hey, Ethan, at least you're going home!"

Through the shrouds of dulled pain pulsing through his left leg and up his body, Ethan repeatedly turned the word "home" in his brain. His thoughts were unconnected. "Home! What is home? Where is home? I want to go home, I don't want to go home! Season's over. Life is over? No, career is over. No, life is over. Mary Ann."

"S' Mary Ann here?" he asked.

"No," said Klecko. "Mary Ann called. She'll talk to you when you're able. And your Mom, she called. They were going to come over, but the doctors say you can go home in a week or few days after the operation."

All of Klecko's words blurred in an optimistic verbal soup. He was smiling though, and that made Ethan feel better.

"Well, you can see already what a difference twenty-four hours can make," said an unfamiliar voice. He was talking over his shoulder to somebody standing behind him in the hospital room. Outside, the sky was black. Night had crept in. Another night? How many nights?

"Well, there you are," said the voice. The man wore a stethoscope around his stout neck. His hair was graying at the temples, and he had gray, kindly eyes. "I'm Doctor Rogers, Ethan. Glad to see you coming around." He stood rather triumphantly tall with his arms crossed in front of him. "How are you feeling?"

"I think I feel a lot better than I did a while ago? Did you operate? Is it all over?"

"Yes, but you're not going skiing today," said Rogers, softly grasping Ethan's wrist while staring at his watch. "Surgery was a success, but we did a helluva lot of repair work. You blew out your whole knee."

Ethan forced his chin into his neck as he tried staring down at the left limb, the object of everybody's concern. It was wrapped in a long, bandaged box. It looked like a carton that flowers were delivered in.

Quinn, a shadow in the corner of the room, slowly stood and approached the bed. "Hiyah, kid!"

It took Ethan awhile to catch his breath and get his emotions under control when he saw the coach. He tried swallowing, but it was difficult. Finally, he whispered, "Bill, I let you down, just as things were goin'…".

"Bullshit! You just can't have any control over a knee like that. When it pops, it pops. You're one helluva a great skier. You'll be back. I ain't worried."

"I hurt it in Kitzbuehel!" Ethan said, clearing his throat. He was suddenly animated and incredulous. "But it was just a little strain!"

"It obviously happened on the jump," interrupted Rogers. "All you have to do is contract the quads, and any sudden movement like that can tear the patellar ligament. You also ripped the lateral patella retinaculum and the medial patella retinaculum. They're the two supporting cables."

"But," he said loudly and not without a touch of pride, "the surgery was a success. Everything—and I mean everything—looks good."

Ethan took a deep breath, but before he could open his mouth, Rogers rolled on, "I know what's coming next, and the answer is that the knee will have to be immobilized for six weeks. That's six weeks in a long leg cast, and then rehabilitation of about four-and-a-half months."

Quinn looked down and began counting on his fingers: "Six months, you'll be skiing in August, just in time for South America!"

"Jesus Christ!" murmured Ethan and looked away at the wall.

An hour later, when they had all left, Mary Ann's call came through. It was mid-afternoon in Lowgate Springs. She was at his house and insisted he talk to his mother first and then his father. The conversations were brief but upbeat.

"I'll be skiing again in about maybe five months," he told his father.

"The doctor said I can be skiing as soon as midsummer, probably three or four months," he lied to Mary Ann, who smilingly and silently added a couple of months.

"You'll never change your optimism," she said.

"What do you mean?"

"I know you well enough. You always say, when we're driving somewhere and I ask how much longer, you say, 'oh, about a half hour.' An hour-and-a-half later, we get there. You always like to give the best picture. Well, now listen, I know a little bit about knees. I'm on a ski team too, you know. I know it's going to take a good, long time before you're out of the cast and a good several weeks of therapy. I'm not going to let you rush it, just because you want to walk to your wedding. That's what you're talking about, right, hon?"

He laughed for the first time, "Yes, you bet that's what I'm talking about. I can put off skiing for a while, but I'm not going to put off you much longer. I love you. And, oh my God, it'll be so good to see you!"

"And I you!"

In the night, when the nurses, that is, nuns wrapped in cream-colored cassocks who sometimes murmured in melodic Italian, quit fiddling around his bed with their silent ministrations, the now black walls began closing. He stared out the window, desperately trying to find a light...any light, even a glimmer...but there was none.

In Vermont, the night traveler could occasionally see a cabin window's white dot pinning the mountainside, a couple thousand feet above the road. Ethan did not know if a mountain, an olive grove, field, or junkyard was outside his hospital window. All that he knew was that it was deathly quiet and deathly black. His room was at the end of the hall. It was far enough that he could not hear the happenings at the nurses' station or even see a faint light.

A steady, dull pain drummed from his boxed leg. It pulsed with the healing surges of the blood beat. A shot had been administered to dull the ache. His eyelids grew weighted and closed. Sleep came deeply and soundly.

In the middle of the dark, quiet night, some of the slumber lifted. He became aware of heat in the room. He was sweating. There was a movement to the side of the bed that was closest to the window. His sleep-filled eyes could make out nothing. Just shadows. The faintest sound of fabric moving.

From between his legs came a feeling of velvet, or silk. He was aware of an erection, now hard and pulsating. It was like his leg, but minus the pain. Suddenly, the nearby shadow stealthily climbed onto the bed, came on top of him and pulled up the hospital gown to above his waist. Just as quickly and softly, the shadow dropped down...then up...then down...and then up. It slowly repeated the soft, sweet rhythm and carefully avoided touching the leg.

Ethan's eyes popped wide.

"What!" he whispered. "What!"

"Shhhh!" she said, taking form.

Ethan grasped Lina's arms. With one sudden, spasmodic, thrusting, upward movement of the hips, he let loose a winter's worth of frustrations. It was a lightning burst that, for that moment, exorcised every dark demon that caged his soul and body. In a split second, Mary Ann's face appeared, as in a video. But it was not Mary Ann.

Lina flung back her head and shivered violently as her hips drove down upon him. She felt her eyes roll up toward the back of her head as they felt the rush of blood and then tingling through both their spines. He grasped her buttocks and squeezed every last bit of ecstasy from her body and his.

Soaking with sweat, he let his muscles sink deeply into the bed and turned his head to the side in wonder. He then looked back and up, as if to see if she were still there. He felt the heat of her inner thighs upon his.

Lina carefully rose to her knees. Bending over, she kissed his dampened hair, her nipples barely touching his chest, and quickly and silently dropping to the floor, began putting on her clothes. She kissed him fully and longingly on the lips, which he had neither strength nor desire to resist. She moved her lips to his ear and whispered, "Sleep, *il mio tesoro*, sleep!"

In the morning, as the sun filled the room with golden brightness and a winter bird sang wake-up calls in a tree outside, the nuns, two on each side, laughingly lifted Ethan from the rumpled bed while another ripped away the sheets from beneath him. They quickly unfolded clean sheets and wrapped them to the mattress.

As they left the room, one nun teasingly wagged a finger at Ethan. All of the other nuns smiled.

He knew then—or suspected then—that it was not a dream. Oh, it was a dream of course. A beautiful celestial being had been sent to ease his pain, to warm and then cool and soothe his tired flesh. But how did she get in? Did it really happen, or did the nurses think he masturbated? That must be why they laughed.

In mid-afternoon, the phone rang. Lina's voice came through, speaking before he had a chance to question. "You must forgive me. I wanted so badly to see you and try to heal you. You hurt so bad. I felt so sorry. I wish I had been there when you fell. I heard it on the loudspeaker. Oh, oh, I was so terrified!"

She explained, ignoring his interruptions, she snuck up the back stairs of the hospital. She knew the building well because her father was a member of the hospital's board of directors and a major supporter and equally enthusiastic fund-raiser. Because of her father's connections, Lina had access to many places in Italy.

"Only you know I was there. No one else. Do you remember?"

Ethan squirmed in bed, a sudden pain shot through his entire leg. He winced.

"I thought I was dreaming, but why...you know, I told you..."

"Please don't be angry. Tell me, do you feel better?"

"Yes! Of course I feel better, but that's not..."

"Then I did the right thing, a friend who cares for a friend by making him feel better."

Ethan was at a loss to grasp any feeling or reaction that made sense. What happened was wrong, and what happened was so right, so good, so desperately needed, and, in the sense of purging, so wonderful. Confused, he could not say anything. They said good-bye, and he slumped back on the pillow in the same dazed bewilderment of the night before. Suddenly his thoughts were of Mary Ann and the mountain top near home, the first day of their love together. A pang of guilt dismissed the thought. His troubled mind wandered and his thoughts fell on his hands upon Lina's round, smooth buttocks, squeezing. He thought of the soft kiss upon his lips and the velvet touch of her breasts brushing his chest. He became aroused once more.

Chapter 9
Home

The Alitalia plane from Milan to Boston glided over Newfoundland, high above the small bays and larger waterways where brown, dead grass stood out against the frozen mire. The sun cast brilliant silver splinters upon the flat, but rippled, gray water of the salt marshes. Home, pretty soon, home. Mary Ann had promised to meet him at Logan Airport. Normally, he would take the shuttle from Boston to Burlington, but the seating in the smaller plane did not accommodate a busted leg in a flower box. Mary Ann readily agreed to make the three-hour drive.

Just the sight of the North American continent worked to dull the keenness of Ethan's recent European memories. Six hours on the plane afforded some time to judge all the good and bad things that had happened to him these past several months. Soon, home and its familiar contents, its warmth and immediacy, would come again into play.

Sorting it out, Ethan concluded a most successful racing season was undeniable, despite the crash of the last race. He had met a goal to do well and had gone even further, a heady experience that told him he could do even better. His bolstered maturity would accelerate his rehabilitation, and, more importantly, entry into marriage and a subsequent, fulfilling life with the girl he adored. He realized his life would never be the same.

They would settle in their own place, perhaps it could initially be a cabin or hunting camp high up in the woods. He paused in his thoughts with the realization that, with the endorsements he had earned from his good performances, he could buy a house or have one built. But would the endorsements continue to come? How can an athlete with a mending limb sell watches or skis for somebody? He chased the negative thought from his mind.

The plane droned onward towards Boston, sailing high above the coast of Maine now. The Down East Islands, 3,000 of them, were simply dots floating in the offshore bays.

Inevitably, his thoughts returned to Lina. They were not immediately of what she had done to him, but they were about their conversations.

"You live with your grandparents?" she had asked.

Did she think it odd? Did she appraise it as a curious American thing to do? Lina's worldliness was a bother. He tried not to dwell upon who she was or what she was. He was not sure whether the overt sophistication and the material ease of her life, compared to his, was worthy of looking up to or down upon. She did not have any experience with hard work. If she had lived in Vermont, she would be classed with the people known as trust fund babies. They were the ones with trophy houses, wealthy second-home owners. Some had abandoned Boston and New York to live permanently and idly in the serene Vermont mountains. Some had a hobby business, like manufacturing cheese from goat milk. Lina's future goal, which was more of a delusionary boast than real, was that she would someday go into the apparel designing business. She had attended the Milan School of Design for a year, but she had dropped out after an argument with her father. While he had persisted in pushing her to study harder, he was at the same time barreling around Northern Italy, the Cote d'Azur, and Capri with a succession of female flummoxes, some of them married to other men. Many of the women were Lina's age.

Ethan pondered that for a while, attempting in vain to concentrate on an in-flight magazine that seemed to contain nothing except advertising for luxury goodies. He attempted but could not obliterate the details of the night with Lina. He wondered how he would act when he saw Mary Ann for the first time upon returning? What he would say? Mary Ann had powers of insight, which sometimes frightened him. She despised secrets.

"You don't have to tell your girl anything because it didn't happen!" Klecko said urgently during the morning he helped his crippled friend leave the hospital. "Sure, it happened, but not the way that women will see that it happened. You tell her, and your ass is in the fryer, cooked. You'll be in the biggest god-damned jam of your life."

"But Mary Ann and I..." Ethan pleaded. "We don't have...I don't want to start..."

"Listen, women don't see what happened to you in the same way. Do you understand that?" Klecko spoke in an emphatic whisper. It was urgent but subdued as one of the nuns came into the room to redo the bed. The old love bed. The guilty, sin-filled love bed.

"Ethan, you were victimized, but it doesn't count. You got it? You were raped, you know. But that doesn't matter."

"I wasn't raped," said Ethan.

"Yes, you were!"

"I can't say that because...Oh, Christ, I don't know. I know this," Ethan said, gritting his teeth and looking out the hospital window as he steadied himself on his crutches. "I needed it, by Christ did I need it. And she was there when I needed it!"

"That's it, and you were victimized!" said Klecko. "Why the hell are you feeling so guilty about something you had no control over? A beautiful girl comes into my hospital room when I'm flat on my back, immobilized, and jumps on my Clyde. I'm the luckiest man alive, but I don't tell nobody that. If I'm caught, I'm a victim of circumstances. I don't care who's waitin' for me at home. You've gotta stop thinking guilt! Don't tell Mary Ann. Keep your mouth shut. It was just an incident, an unfortunate incident that, as far as you're concerned, never happened!"

As the plane taxied to the terminal and a flight attendant cautioned passengers to keep their seat belts buckled until the plane came to a complete stop, Ethan wrestled with the plausibility of whether it was ever possible for a mature male with average hormones to be sexually assaulted by a beautiful, young woman.

Two flight attendants eagerly helped place him, the rape victim, in a wheelchair. They lifted the foot bed to cradle the big, plaster box that held his fragile leg, now slightly pounding with a dull pain from the change in air pressure. Then an airline employee came and pushed him up the tunnel ahead of the other passengers. Ethan was the first person Mary Ann saw. As she ran to him, kneeling on one knee to smother his face with kisses, all the fear, guilt, and doubt vanished with the joy of seeing her. He was home.

"There's that skier," a flight attendant passing in the hall whispered to a colleague.

"Yes, Atwood. Ethan Atwood. Isn't it a shame? Didn't he win something?"

"He won some big race in Europe and then he fell down and ruined his knee. I guess that's his wife."

"Or girlfriend!"

Mary Ann wheeled him to the luggage area and then left him on the sidewalk outside while she went to the parking garage to get her dad's station wagon. The air felt cold, damp, and filthy from the exhausts of buses, cabs, and cars, each jockeying for an advantage with bursts of horns. Piles of dirty slush from a recent snowfall were splashing everywhere. People shouted, and doors slammed. The walls and ceilings of concrete amplified the echoes.

Mary Ann returned and loaded Ethan into the middle seat of the big Chevy with his leg stretched out. His luggage, several duffel bags mainly, barely fit inside the car. His skis were being shipped separately from Italy.

Going up Route 93 toward New Hampshire, there were newer homes surrounded by trees and lawns that were connected to busy ribbons of roads with a mall and gas station here and there.

Then there was the dark, New Hampshire woods. Tall fir trees hid lakes and rivers with names like Massabesic, Piscatoquog, and Souhegan.

Ethan and Mary Ann made plans. Through his agent, Red Everts, a ski team sponsor had promised him a four-wheel drive truck. He would have to ask for one with an automatic drive so he could get around without having to use a clutch.

"And I'm going to move out of the house," he said. "I just don't feel like being a dependent anymore I guess."

"Moving out? Isn't your timing a little off? Who's going to take care of you? Open doors? Cook meals?"

"Yes, I'll need someone to fu…tuck me into bed"

"Oh, I am, am I?"

Sitting comfortably in the backseat as the comforting sight of lakes and woods swept by, he stared at Mary Ann's profile while she drove. She chattered nonstop, bringing him up-to-date on valley gossip.

"Alec Ventnor quit his job as base operations manager at Maple Glen. Well, that's what he said. Actually, Bruce White was going to fire him. He and Bruce had a huge fight."

Ethan studied the right side of her face, barely listening. Often, the curled wave of her hair, golden brown and shining, bounced gently on her neck as she talked. She wore simple gold-plated earrings, a rare adornment for a Vermont girl. It was a conscious decision to look a little pretty after the months of separation. Dark, long lashes curved in small upward cuticles over her right eye.

"Soft and creamy," he whispered to himself as he studied her complexion.

A high cheekbone said intelligence and strength, and the curve of her chin was symmetric. Some would call it a square jaw. The part of the lips he could see was red, slightly moist and full. He winced a little as he leaned forward and placed a hand firmly on her shoulder. He had never seen Mary Ann more beautiful. She smiled, bent her face, and kissed his fingers.

Early March welcomed a reprise of winter and a couple of heavy snowfalls. Skiers from cities flooded the happy valley while Ethan began the ascent to recovery.

The ski team headquarters in Park City sent him a plethora of guidelines, magazine articles, medical and mental treatises, every printed word on the psychology of injury and how to cope with it, particularly how to combat the inevitable depression, frustration's loyal sidekick. Ethan had steeled himself mentally for the road ahead. In a week, the cumbersome cast would come off, and he would be able to get around much easier. He reacquainted himself with the training room at Spring Mountain Academy, where there was a physical therapy clinic for banged up racers and other jocks, as well as normal village types, including a daily visitation of geezers with arthritic joints.

Therapy began, initially for short hours. Longer periods followed. He did straight leg raises while lying on his side. He then laid on his back and stomach, lifting the leg barely from the floor, just setting it stiffly in motion to strengthen the quads and calf muscles so they would take the stress away from the healing area. They then added weights to his ankle...first one pound...then two. The weight increased weekly. Soon, he began flexing and riding a stationary bike.

Donny Naples, the old boyhood buddy whose bubbling enthusiasm had a way of energizing those around him, joined Ethan nearly every morning at the gym. He had been, superficially at least, good-natured about the loss of Mary Ann as his Number 1 girl. Because he had other girlfriends besides her, he felt it somewhat just that he had to give her up. He was aware enough of the circumstances to see that Mary Ann and Ethan were deeply involved with one another.

Despite one feeble protest from his grandmother, whose maternal caregiving instincts were being usurped by Mary Ann, Ethan rented a cabin deep in the woods on the westward side of the mountain, away from the Maple Glen ski area.

Rose Delahanty harbored a subliminal fear of people living alone in isolated places, particularly on remote farms or deep in the woods. In the years before Medicare and private health insurance, both her parents died remotely. Her father was first, found at the bottom of a hayloft with a pitchfork at his side. Her mother was next, sitting stone cold dead on the floor of her kitchen, the old clock ticking away on the wall. The latter death occurred when Rose and Big Ethan were enjoying a weekend in Boston. Such was death in rural New England before nursing homes.

Ethan's cabin, first constructed as a one-room hunting camp, had a succession of owners who had added rooms over the years to fit the sloping terrain. The result was a charming series of connected step-up rooms with knotty pine walls and lots of shelf and closet space. The present owners, a New York dentist and his wife, sublet it for the winter ski season, but they were willing to let Ethan have it longer into the summer, at least until August when he would finally leave for summer training in Portillo, high in the Andes.

Returning to the States and picking up his life where it had left off so many months ago was no longer within Ethan's realm of possibilities. Though there would be breaths anew within the same old comfort zone of familiar things and familiar people, life would never be the same.

He had left in November for a World Cup season with a modicum of celebrity. He returned as a full-blown icon in the community. Being injured only increased his familiarity. His stature was more prominent. People he had never seen nor known took the opportunity to commiserate. He and Mary Ann dropped into the Frost Heave Saloon, a local bar where visiting skiers every weekend and nights in between got downright stupidly drunk and sated on ear-piercing rock band music. The bar was at the base of the long access road up to Maple Glen Ski Resort, a winding road where local smugglers spirited farm goods and other contraband into Canada during the 1812 trade embargo, away from the eyes of customs inspectors. During Prohibition, the secret traffic of Canadian whisky was smuggled in the other direction. Now, the road mocks its history with restaurants and bars, ski shops and boutiques, gas stations, condominiums, and motels.

On the log-hewn walls of the Frost Heave were hung new posters and old photographs of the local boy turned hero. Ethan would have to get used to being stared at, yelled at, and laughed with. He could not even go to the men's room without someone telling him, "There's the man!"

In this swirl of noise and adulation, Mary Ann remained one of the few fixed certainties of his life. Steady and pretty, her flaws were so minor as to be almost positives. A nose with a small bump at the bridge where it was broken in a volleyball game. Cute! Squinting to improve her vision when she was not wearing her contact lenses. Also cute! A sentimental trait that made her cry at all the particular sadness she encountered, including bad movies.

Ethan reckoned the moment she became his paramour for real was because of that kind of breakdown, when she became so blurry-eyed over their discovery of a baby's grave that wonderfully fateful day in the mountains when Mary Ann ceased to be Donny Naples' girlfriend and became Ethan's.

"Our Mae they called her," Mary Ann had said so sadly of the Hathaway child, the baby lying beneath the stone. In subsequent conversations, Mary Ann said, "I want to name our first baby girl Mae."

"You're kidding!" responded Ethan, although he had no objection.

Mary Ann and Ethan's families were the only ones who failed to sympathize openly about Ethan's wounded knee. They knew that too many "too bads" simply retards healing. At this stage Ethan did not need to dwell upon losses or setbacks. An exception perhaps was his father.

Paul Atwood was in his third round of Alcoholics Anonymous. This time, he had been sober for two years, two months, and twenty-nine days. In that time, he had grown enough to think about the past in terms of what he had failed to do, not with all the drinks he had consumed each day to escape the failures. For the first time, he reflected that a man cannot raise children properly while fighting his own demons. The cold shoulder he had turned to his wife so many times over the years must have affected his son. The boy's relentless reticence was proof. As a child, Ethan hated to show his face to anyone. Even though he had a mostly happy countenance, which was a very slight grin, he kept problems deeply folded within, rarely discussing them with anyone, except perhaps Mary Ann and, of recent times, Lina.

The first weekend Ethan was home from Europe, when his parents visited, Ethan was mildly surprised his father asked to speak to him alone. They walked out back into the yard, behind the old, red barn on the lane that Ethan's grandfather kept plowed all winter. Ethan was now making long strides with the crutches. They looked up at the meadow in the distance where the tops of the high dead grass were stiff and brown above the clumps of snow. Compared with the week before, when an Alberta wind had picked apart dead tree limbs and scattered them to the snowbound floor below, the day was mild.

Paul's face looked pleasantly weather-beaten and healthy. His eyes were bright.

"I don't know how to tell you this," he began. "The reason is because I was never much good at telling you anything. I never even tried, did I?"

"Oh gosh," Ethan broke in. "You were...you had your work... your..."

"My booze, boy! My booze!" He laughed, grinning widely.

Inspired, he turned and looked at Ethan. "Tell me you had a breakthrough year. You did. Of course, you know that. But, there had to be a day, a time, or a particular race when you felt it coming. Am I right?" He looked straight at Ethan again.

"Yes, yes, it's true," Ethan said. "There was a breakthrough. It gave me chills."

His father interrupted. "Well, that's what happened to me. There's a helluva difference in my breakthrough, and forgive me for making the comparison. But, my switch to sobriety didn't really begin until the day I actually admitted I truly loved whisky and beer and wine and anything liquid that had a jolt to it. I had always used the excuse that I drank because of stress. There was stress on the job. The stress to succeed. The stress to pay the mortgage. To raise your kid properly. Stress, stress...Everywhere I looked, I could find it. Any one more reason to take another drink. But, as I was saying, I didn't really quit until that first day I decided, 'You're goddamned right I love whisky. Scotch, rye. Irish whisky. Bushmills or Jameson's. I can still feel that soft burning with the first taste. The great heat in my mouth, the warmth. It was like gold going down my throat. And then the leap when it hit my stomach. The spontaneous jolt. By God, it tasted good!"

Ethan looked at his father with his head tilted slightly. A small smile of understanding crossed his face. He nodded.

"I think you know what I mean. I couldn't accomplish a damn thing as far as being sober was concerned until I faced up to that fact that I actually liked the stuff!" said Paul.

They walked on in silence for a few hundred yards, up the hill toward where the old family spring used to be. It was now overgrown with weeds and spittles of snow that were turning to crystals in the warmer days.

"Just one more thing," Paul said.

"What's that?"

"I just want you to know that I am so goddamned proud of what you have done this year. So proud!"

Ethan said, "While you're at it, do you have any advice to give a young guy on the eve of his marriage."

Paul stopped, surprised, turned, and looked. "Yes," he said. "The way to a woman's heart is for a man to pick his socks up off of the floor."

Ethan laughed aloud.

"Believe me," Paul said, "you'll get more mileage out of that than anything else you do in life!"

Chapter 10
Mary Ann and Lina

Mary Ann was at school. A rainfall, shrouded in gray fog, draped the woods and old logging trails crisscrossing near the cabin. The phone rang.

"Salve, Ethan, hello!"

His stomach leaped, triggering a paroxysm of cold sweat.

"My God! Lina?"

"Si, Leeena!" she said invitingly with a grin in her voice. "You will never guess where I am."

"No!?"

"I'm in Barr...ee, Baree, Vermont. I just arrived yesterday. I told you I would come to Vermont some day. Here I am. My papa, he has relations here. And here I am on a visit. Will you let an old member of your fan club come and see you?"

Ethan's reaction was that of an ambush victim startled in the dark. With time to prepare, his answer would have been...well, he would not have been home. He would be far away, way far. Or, he would have hung up, disguising his voice and saying weakly, "Wrong number." Or, he politely would have told her to get the hell out of his life and get back to Italy where she belonged. Or, he could have told her, "How nice that you're here. Have a pleasant visit, and maybe we'll bump into each other some day."

Taken so by surprise, he found himself impaled on a vague promise to meet her, show her around, and, at Lina's insistence, introduce her to Mary Ann.

"We're getting married soon. We're making wedding plans," he said with affirmation.

"I cannot wait to meet Mary Ann," said Lina, sending another cold pulse shooting up the middle of his back.

An hour later, Mary Ann called from Burlington to tell him she was going shopping and would be late coming home. He tried keeping the unease out of his voice, "Remember my fan club in

Italy. I told you about them. Well, you'll never guess." He cleared his throat, thankful she could not see his face. "One of the members, Lina Biancavella...well, she's visiting some relatives in Barre. Imagine that! She's making some kind of skiing exodus, spending a month or so in Vermont. Then she's moving on out to Colorado and Utah and ski until the snow's gone. I guess she's got the money. Her dad's an auto executive in Italy."

"Well, what a coincidence!" said Mary Ann, surprised by the information and nevertheless slightly pleased at the opportunity to tease her lover. "I hope she's not here to pursue her downhill hero."

"Oh Christ, no," he said. "I'd like you to meet her. I think you have a lot in common." He winced at the last remark, but he reasoned illogically that, ignoring Lina while she was close by would somehow reveal or tip off news of the moment of surprise and lust, Mary Ann would suspect it. Ethan saw himself confessing in a prone position at Mary Ann's feet.

He prepared to see it through, as Klecko would do. What exactly would Klecko do? He would boldly push the two women together and boast of his affection for both, one, of course, real, and the other, of course, a necessary show. He would depend on the naturally strong perceptions of Mary Ann and Lina to be able to size each other up, consider all things safe and harmless, and, once and forever, banish jealousy and fear from the door. Wouldn't it be wonderful if Mary Ann and Lina became close friends? He shuddered again.

They agreed to meet at Maple Glen. It was Mary Ann's idea. She suggested she and Lina ski a day together. While Mary Ann took Lina to the rental shop, Ethan hobbled the stairs of the ski lodge to the bar and ordered a sherry, glancing stealthily at his likeness pasted to a mirror behind the bar. Instead of an image of shame and deception that he expected to see, there was only fame and achievement. He hunched over the bar. He was hiding, lest others seated at tables would recognize the poster and the real person seated there as one and the same. How could anyone confuse the two? Right now, he could have given anything not to have been himself. As the girls headed uphill on the base lodge lift, Ethan sipped the sherry, ordered one more and than another. In a half hour, he was relaxed enough to channel his thoughts elsewhere. When some skiers from down south recognized him, he began animating eagerly, answering their awed questions about World Cup ski-racing. Meanwhile, out there on the slopes of Maple Glen, his fate was in the hands of the Almighty.

The girls were gone two hours and then three. He squirmed on his barstool, trying futilely to concentrate on the NBA game on the television and questioning the time on the Miller Beer clock stuck up behind the bar next to his poster. He made about six trips to the men's room, staring hard at the mirror for telltale signs of betrayal. At several tables, couples drank and ate lunch. He wondered how many men there had been in the same fix at one or more times in their lives.

He finally decided the girls were gone so long because Lina had revealed all to Mary Ann, how she snuck into her lover's hospital room on the darkest night and took from him that which belonged to Mary Ann. He could see Mary Ann suddenly wheel and stick Lina with the sharp steel point of her ski pole and then flog her to death right there on Sidewinder, a horrific scene witnessed by dozens of other skiers. The wide-awake nightmare continued with himself on the witness stand, relating the testimony that would send his beloved to life in prison. He ordered another sherry, wincing when he accidentally put weight upon his damaged leg.

At last, Mary Ann and Lina appeared. From the huge window of the bar, he saw them ski down the last few hundred feet to the lodge area. Both were doing neat, completed tight turns. Oddly, even though he faced a firing squad, he studied their techniques, a habit deeply ingrained from, it seemed, birth. As they stacked their skis at the rack, he noticed their lips moving and smiling. They seemed to be chattering, and they came bursting into the bar laughing together. A smile creased Ethan's face, the biggest smile he had since he could not remember when.

"We had a wonderful time," said Lina. "She is such a good teacher!" she yelled, pointing to Mary Ann. "She's gonna teach me to really ski. I know it."

Mary Ann came up, planted a buss on Ethan's cheek. "We had fun. She's great fun!"

In spite of and because of his handicap, Ethan was finding time to see the world around him in shapes and shades other than the rigid terms of professional racing, where the investment is in self, the ego, and the body. If not nurtured and both pushed and protected, the body performs less than adequately. The athlete is then out of a job. The forced relaxation and respite from the regimen of racing nudged him—albeit slightly—toward other appreciations and the thought of a family of his own. He and Mary Ann practiced domesticity. From his propped up position on the couch by the wood stove, he enjoyed watching Mary Ann alter the interior of his cabin, "our cabin." She bought lamps, adding them throughout.

"The trouble with cabins is that they're so damn dark," she said.

At least one of the owners had imagination enough to locate a picture window in the broad but narrow kitchen that looked to the south and sun out over a meadow where a moose and sometimes wild turkeys ventured before twilight. Ethan brought home a gray cat at the humane society. To their delight, he and Mary Ann discovered it playing with a river otter early one morning. Like snakes, the two animals rolled over each other and down the slight slope to the pond, now covered with ice a couple of feet thick. As his knee healed and he was able to limp about more readily, he began riding his new snowmobile, streaking up and down the mountain along the forest trails, a couple of which led all the way to the top of Spring Mountain. He found a route to give him access to the upper trails of Maple Glen. It was a convenient discovery because, if he ever accepted Bruce White's invitation to join Maple Glen someday as a skiing ambassador, that trail would give him carte blanche access to the mountain, especially the upper glades, the off-piste poaching areas where he and other students from the academy used to sneak and do wild things in the snow in those days long ago. It would also save a good fifteen-minute drive up and over the Gap Road to the Maple Glen base lodge.

Once a week, he and Mary Ann ventured out. They often went to the movies and then to the Frost Heave. Ethan's limit was two

Long Trail ales, while Mary Ann appreciated bottled spring water with a slice of lime. They eschewed the Frost Heave on weekends when the young condo skiers, up from Boston and New York, took over the bar with noisy après-ski drinking and dancing. They all wanted to get to know the guy who won the Kitzbuehel race and showed so much promise for an ailing and perpetually failing US Ski Team.

Weekdays at the Frost Heave were for the locals, ski patrollers, instructors, lifties, cooks, maids, and bartenders who worked the resorts, ski bums barely stretching their dollars for food and lodging. Almost all were single. It was just not possible to support families on six dollars an hour. In the summer, some worked in the woods as foresters or for the resorts running chain saws, cutting brush, mowing lawns, and waiting tables. These were jobs that were always available to the economically unskilled. Many of the crowd were educated dropouts, ones who at one time were speeding in the fast lane and then suddenly found themselves pushing the brakes. They abandoned everything citified in their lives, rushing to the mountains in order to breathe again and to willingly accept the trade-off of low wages in favor of a quality of life that was the envy of their urban friends.

Lina, with her cute Italian accent, fit in beautifully with the ski bum crowd. Ethan and Mary Ann often met her and her cousin Agnes—whose home Lina was staying at in Barre—at the Frost Heave. Lina was not the first from foreign soil to intermingle with the valley people. Ski instructors with Austrian accents were sometimes in great demand, and any number of people from Australia and New Zealand could boast of year-round skiing because of the flip-flopping seasons when they went home in the summer. In good times, when local help was scarce, young people from Europe and South America filled resort jobs.

To Ethan's surprise, he noticed that Mary Ann and Lina genuinely got along. Suffering shyness and the defensiveness that accompanies the ailment, he was in awe of people who automatically befriend others, even strangers. He attempted to analyze the Lina-Mary Ann relationship and noted both were outgoing and self-confident. Both were good listeners and better talkers. He could never though get inside their heads. For all of her casualness, Mary Ann also dissected Lina's apparent motives. To Mary Ann, Lina was another pretty girl who liked Ethan, but she liked good times more. Lina was lots of fun, but she could be easily distracted. As soon as Mary Ann suspected doubts about her, Lina would move on.

Mary Ann introduced Lina to her mother, Emma, who, for Lina's benefit, immediately traced her ancestry in Italy and tried finding connections. Emma had come from near Naples though. Most of Lina's family was northern with traits and lighter-skinned physical features quite far removed from their fellow Italians from the Mediterranean.

The first signs of winter's dissipation were evident now. Ice melted and dripped from the eaves of roofs, creating slush beneath one's feet. People talked about going someplace warm to escape the clutches of the northern New England mud season, a time generally agreed upon as being unfavorable to both soul and body. It was a time when the chilling dampness and fog of early spring replaces the dry briskness of winter cold. Still, the skiers would not give up. On the slopes, light jackets and shorts replaced heavy ski clothes. Sunny afternoons were like a day at the beach, and a strong set of legs was demanded of skiers to in order to plow the heavy kernels of ice called corn snow.

Ethan and Mary Ann invited Lina to attend the Easter Sunrise service atop Spring Mountain, when churchgoers riding ski lifts would stand shivering on the frozen crust as the resurrected eastern sky grew pink. Then, after thanking God for the gift of snow, the ones—that is, the ones who could—would ski. Ethan, of course, would download on the lift like the rest of the non-skiers.

A few days before Easter, Mary Ann coincidentally ran into Lina and Agnes at the University Mall. She heard Lina's happy shout, "Mary Ann!" above the puddling and plopping sound of the water fountain in the center of one of the mall corridor intersections. The mall was crowded with mothers anxiously towing their distracted children, who were caught up in the atmosphere of yellow and purple decorations hanging just about everywhere.

"Here Comes Peter Cottontail" blared tiredly through loudspeakers.

"I'm buying my Easter outfit," said Lina with a smile.

"Easter outfit? But aren't you meeting us for the sunrise service?"

"Si, but I must have new Easter ski clothes," answered Lina, prompting a rolling of the eyes by her cousin Agnes, who shared a short laugh with Mary Ann at Lina's expense.

Agnes had not liked Mary Ann when they first met. She had some fixed working-class attitudes toward Mary Ann's social and economic status. Particularly, she had accepted from others the contemptuous regard toward students of the Spring Valley Ski Academy, believing their reputations to be that of spoiled, middle-class, privileged brats.

The first time that Mary Ann, Lina, and Agnes had skied together at Maple Glen, Agnes had showed up in jeans, which Mary Ann, to Agnes's surprise, pretended not to notice. Agnes was surprised several days later when Mary Ann dropped by her house with a couple pairs of her ski pants and a jacket.

"Please, we're the same size," she said to Agnes, who stood with gaped mouth. "Would you like to borrow them?"

Later, when Agnes tried returning the clothing, Mary Ann said, "No, no. Please, I want you to keep them."

Agnes, like Lina, was quickly won over by Mary Ann's lack of pretense, her honesty, and generosity. Learning later that Mary Ann's mother had been a Barre girl, an Italian at that, explained everything, thought Agnes. Mary Ann had been raised correctly.

They sat in the food court for lunch, laughingly commandeering a tiny table no sooner than its previous occupants left. Lina, who had been bubbling while showing off her new, white jacket with the fur collar, ordered only tea. As they talked, she began fidgeting and grew silent.

"Are you okay?" asked Mary Ann.

"I must excuse myself," Lina answered, looking pale. She pushed back her chair hurriedly and left.

"Is she all right?" Mary Ann asked Agnes.

"She'll be okay. She's been sick all week," said Agnes, who caught a breath, deliberately looking away. She returned Mary Ann's concerned stare. "I think she's got a stomach virus. There's a lot of it going around in Barre. My mother just got over it."

Mary Ann suddenly arose from her chair, pushed it back, dropped her napkin on her plate. "I'll be back," she said. Agnes stared with a frightened look at Mary Ann as she left for the bathroom.

Pushing open the door, Mary Ann heard the troubling sounds of Lina upchucking in the stall, groaning and coughing. She was about to say, "Are you all right,?" but for a reason she could not immediately comprehend, the words did not come.

She could hear Lina pulling at the toilet paper in the stall, still coughing. The toilet flushed. Lina came out, her face gray, looked up and saw Mary Ann. The two women said nothing. Lina's face contorted to one of shame and sadness as she stared with imploring eyes. Eyes which begged forgiveness.

Mary Ann ran back to the table, grabbed her purse and without looking at Agnes, said, "I'm sorry, I have to leave." She hurried out of the mall and did not stop to think until she was seated in the car, then let her chin drop and her body sag.

She returned to the cabin before Ethan got back from his appointment with the physical therapist. The cast was now gone, and he was happy to begin the long hours of stretching, lifting, and cycling that would return him to full strength and back to skiing.

She turned on every light available in the room because she wanted to see his face and what the mirror of his mind would reveal when she confronted him.

When she heard the truck tires splashing through a puddle in the dirt driveway, her pulse quickened. She felt a chill. Her hands were tightly knotted before her as he entered through the back door, carrying a bag of groceries.

"Oh boy, I can't tell you how much better I feel after that workout. A lot of the stiffness is just gone completely. Tomorrow, they're going to up the weights...Hey, why are all the lights on?" He looked at Mary Ann and saw the disturbance in her eyes.

Quickly, she said, "Please put the groceries down." She turned to walk toward the living room.

When he came in, she walked closely to him and looked directly in his eyes. "I know why Lina's here. She's pregnant, Ethan!"

The words, though softly spoken, thundered at his ears. He stared with his mouth dropping open. When he saw the tears as well as the mixture of love and confusion on her face, his shoulders sagged. He dropped to the couch, still saying nothing.

"I want the truth!"

He put his hands to his face, rubbed his eyes, and then the back of his neck. When he could not look at her, she knew.

"She came to me," he whispered hoarsely and cleared his throat.

Mary Ann wheeled and walked to the picture window, looking at the meadow and the cold, brown trees. Some were just starting to bud. The snow on the ground was turning brown and lumpy. It was all there, the outside world. It was basically unchanged. What she heard was real. This was happening. The most devastating news she had heard in her life was true, simply that Ethan and Lina had made love and that Lina was carrying his baby.

"It wasn't the way you think," he said, his voice finally rising as it sought the words to explain what happened in the hospital. He heard Klecko's voice, those foolish words. "Don't tell her." Even though he had mentally rehearsed this moment when Mary Ann might find out, he did not know what to say now that it was upon him.

"It wasn't the way you think!"

"What are you going to tell me next, Ethan? It isn't your baby? It's probably somebody else's? That could be! Sure it could be! But it doesn't erase the fact that you slept with her, does it? You made love!" Her voice was rising, saying what she thought was impossible.

"What was she, Ethan? What was she?

"Nothing, nothing! Mary Ann, please listen!"

"Nothing?" she mocked. "Nothing? You mean like nothing, just another trophy? Just another medal to be picked up along the way?"

"Mary Ann…"

"What a fool, what a fool I've been! You're like the rest, aren't you? You're like that goddamned Klecko!"

"It didn't happen…it didn't happen the way you think, Mary Ann!"

"It wasn't the way I think, Ethan? Tell me what to think. What can I think? Do I know how it happened? Yes, I do know. It's called fucking!"

When the bitter word reached her lips and was spat out, she felt her skin turn to terrible icy flesh and her shoulders tremble. She grabbed her coat and ran out, not hearing his shouts.

He stumbled to get up from the couch, "Mary Ann! No! No! No! Come back! Don't leave! Mary Ann!

Chapter 11
Awakenings

The overhead street lamp did little to light the way as Ethan got out of his truck, carefully stepping over the grimy clumps of ash-dirty ice and snow that the snowplow had pushed onto the curb. The three-story house with white asphalt shingles perched on a hillside, overlooking the downtown area of Barre, where tiny spots of white and red lights weakly glimmered through the fog.

A dog barked from the backyard as Ethan, clumsily walking with one crutch, tripped over a snow shovel that had been left leaning on the wrought iron railing at the top of the concrete stairs. He pushed the doorbell and shuffled impatiently until Agnes opened the door. She was not surprised to see him, but her face showed pity and resignation. She invited him in, but he said:

"Could you ask Lina to come outside? I have to talk to her."

Lina appeared, walking out the door while throwing a jacket over her shoulders. Her eyes were wide with terror. She stood silently on the porch as she shivered in the night air. Her shoulders were stiff, and her arms were folded in front of her.

"Please come with me a minute, Lina," he asked.

In the pale light, she noticed his sunken eyes and the several days' growth of beard. He was not wearing a hat, and his curly hair was matted to his forehead.

"I just want you to sit in the truck with me."

"No, I'm afraid!" said Lina.

"For God's sake, I'm not going to hurt you. We have to talk, Lina!"

He opened the front passenger door. She immediately slunk down in the seat. Ethan, in the driver's seat, exhaled. He put the key in the ignition, but he did not start the engine.

He began by recounting for her the facts leading to the moment. "You came to me in the hospital, remember? You came to me. I was half-drugged, asleep, out of it. I didn't know what was happening?"

Lina said nothing, comprehending everything and understanding fully. The sweet, hot love of the night in the hospital had turned to an all-enveloping bitterness that now had trapped three people and a soon-to-be fourth.

"I want you to tell Mary Ann the truth," Ethan said, looking out over the dark mountain, just a line now in the starless sky.

"How do I do that?" Lina asked in a low, deep voice. She stared toward her feet.

"Simply tell her what happened. Tell her it wasn't my fault!" Ethan said, his voice rising despite the promise to himself that anger would not overcome reason. "Whose fault was it, Lina? Was it my fault? Did I invite you? Did I chase you? Did I knock you down? Did I rape you? Did I even encourage you at all?"

"You did none of that!"

"Did I, in all those weeks, lay a hand on you? Did I come at you?"

"No." She began crying.

"You knew. Goddamn it, you knew how I loved Mary Ann! There was no doubt about it!"

"Yes, I knew. I thought…"

"You thought? Lina, you even said it. 'You're so in love.' Jesus Christ, why? Why did you do what you did to me? You killed me. You killed my life. You killed Mary Ann. You don't even know us. You don't know me!"

"Stop! Please, please, stop!" she cried, suddenly turning her face, wet with tears, to him. She was sobbing.

"Tell her! Tell her!" he shouted.

Lina put her face in her hands. Her shoulders shook convulsively.

Ethan waited for the crying to subside. He did not dare touch nor comfort her.

A moment passed. Sobbing subsided; Lina sat up straighter and blew her nose on a rolled-up handkerchief she had crushed into her fist.

Finally, she said, "I don't know if I can do that…tell her."

Fighting to control his anger, he said, "You have to do it! Why can't you tell her?"

She finally looked at him—at the tormented face that stared at nothing through the windshield.

"Don't you think, Ethan, I haven't thought about it? I have hard time with that because…" She gulped, fearing him now. She feared what her words would provoke. "It's because I respect Mary Ann."

"Respect?" he interrupted.

She went on, "Can't you see…how difficult…When I met you," she said, finally getting some courage to continue, "I thought, of course, here this American skier, handsome American racer. Most handsome of all! I wanted to date you, to get to know you. And I achieved that. I got to know you, and you told me about Mary Ann. I tried not to believe, at first, you had a girl. Oh, I don't know why I did that. I don't know why."

She looked at him through her tears. "I did not know she was so special."

"Special? What the hell do you mean special?" He exploded. "She was my girl, and I was going to marry her. I told you that!"

Lina looked anxiously back at the house. "Shhhh!" she said. "Everybody hears you shouting."

He started the car.

"Where are you taking me? Stop, Ethan! Don't!"

"I'm not going anywhere. We'll go around the block."

They sat silently while he drove to the corner, turned right, and parked at an overlook high above the town. The fog was starting to lift. Even with the lights, Barre looked cold and quiet, except for the distant slamming of a door.

Lina, feeling more at ease, continued talking.

"I know you told me all about Mary Ann, but let me explain. When I made love to you, do you think I cared at the time what I was doing? No, I was a foolish girl who was doing what I wanted to do. I did not care. I wanted to make love to you, to comfort you. You were in pain."

"Christ!" said Ethan.

"Your girlfriend wasn't here…in the hospital…I thought," said Lina. "I was foolish. I thought I would do for you what she would have done."

He began protesting again, but she interrupted. Her voice rose. "Of course I wanted you. Even when I come here, to Vermont, before I knew Mary Ann, I think I maybe have chance to take you away from your American girlfriend. All the time, we in Europe hear American girls are silly. They are vain. They are possessive."

Ethan wanted to shout, "Scheming, lying, little bitch!"

Lina continued, "Then I got to know her, and I got to know you better. I wake up every morning sick. And I pray to God. Please, God, don't let me be pregnant with Ethan's child. I knew by then how foolish I was. Mary Ann is the most wonderful person I have ever met."

She turned to look into his eyes. "I cannot face her. What I have done to her, what I have done to you?"

She began sobbing again. "Oh, Ethan," she cried, "I am so sorry what I did to you!" In anger and self-contempt, she made her fists in her lap. "I could tear my guts out."

Except for the monotone whirr of the heater fan, there was a long silence in the cab of the truck.

"Why don't you?" he whispered coldly.

"Don't you think I don't want to?" she shouted. "I can't. Everyone in that house knows I'm pregnant. And God knows how many more people know. Do you know what my father would do to me if I killed this child?"

She stopped speaking and whispered, "Besides, I can't help it. I want the baby. I am weak. I am nothing but weak. I want to have your baby now. It is all I have left in the world now."

Ethan said nothing. He would not pity her.

Lina, after a long silence, choked back more sobs and whispered, "I will write to Mary Ann. I cannot face her. I will have to tell her that way."

Riding away toward home, down the dark, steep stretch of the interstate highway that overlooked the valley, Ethan reconstructed all that Lina said. Three months ago, she did not exist. Twenty minutes ago, he wanted to strangle her. Even now, moving away from the bitter intensity of the confrontation with Lina, he guiltily wished her dead. Then the thought appeared. It was a realization this strange, young woman, by carrying his seed, caused in him a precipitous leap to adulthood and, most probably, a life of shame, drudgery, and ruination.

Perhaps for the first time he felt the dread of his own being. His selfishness had given birth to this awful problem. Had he not skied...had he not made the ski team...had he not won...had he not been injured. Now, there were two—perhaps three—ruined lives.

Another week of desperation passed—unreturned phone calls, tearful messages left on the Queensbury family's answering machine, and trying unsuccessfully to meet Mary Ann at school and outside her home. Nothing worked.

He believed Lina when she told him she had written to Mary Ann and mailed the letter.

"She must have it by now," Ethan said.

Ethan wrote to Mary Ann himself, again pouring forth his anguish. When he heard nothing in reply, he called Donny Naples. "I have to see you, Donny. Can I meet you someplace in Montpelier?"

Donny, who, along with several others, had heard about the scandal by now, knew what to expect, but he was ill-prepared for the details, listening with open-mouth fascination to the story about the girl jumping upon his friend while he lay helpless in a hospital bed. Most men would regard such an incident as a fantasy certainly worth having at least once in a lifetime. However, as Ethan experienced and Donny realized, considering the circumstances, it was not one worth repeating.

"I should have talked to you sooner, but I don't know if it would have done any good."

Ethan told Donny the whole story of how he met Lina, the innocence of the encounter in the beginning, and how it literally erupted in passion in the hospital.

The thought also raced through Donny's mind that it was Ethan who won Mary Ann's heart, not he. "Serves him right, maybe. Why should I pity this guy?" It was a thought that Donny just as quickly thrust aside. Ethan was his very best friend.

"I'm asking for your help. At the same time, I'm asking you not to explain to Mary Ann the gory details. Could you just tell her that it wasn't my fault? Oh, it was my fault, my naiveté all right in meeting with the girl in the first place. I could have known better, and I did think she was maybe just after my ass or something. But, I swear, under normal circumstances I'd have been able to hold her off. Don't you think, Donny? But, Donny, I was flat on my back, asleep in the hospital. Full of drugs, painkillers! I didn't know what happened until it happened!"

Donny took a deep breath and said, "Wow!" He looked at his friend for several moments, a mix of awe and sympathy passed over him.

"My God, man," Donny said. "I never ever heard of such a thing!" Yet, he did not doubt that it happened, not the least that it happened to his close friend, who could not and would not make up a story like that.

"I'll do it, buddy, I'll do it," said Donny. "I'll talk to Mary Ann."

"She'll listen to you!" Ethan said eagerly.

"I'll try, Ethan. Honestly, I'll try, but there's only one thing wrong."

"What's that?"

"It won't erase the fact that another woman is now carrying your child."

A few days later, the letter came in the mail. Ethan waited until he got outside the post office and into his truck before opening it. He failed to hear Mrs. Patterson, the postmistress, say, "Hello, Ethan, how is your leg coming along?" She watched the young man stumble out of the building, oblivious to her hello. She turned and shook her head.

"Oh no!" Ethan said silently before he opened the envelope. The sunlight was glinting harshly through the windshield, half blinding him. Between his fingers, within the envelope, he could feel the tiny lump of the engagement ring inside. "Dear Ethan," the letter began.

"I understand you and believe you when you tell me what happened and that you were faultless. I am not blaming you. I could never blame you for any of the things you have done since I have known you. I still care too much for you. And I know you love me as much as I love you. The problem is that that perfection we had together has a tarnish that I don't think can be removed. I cannot think. I don't believe I'll ever be able to think or see things clearly again in my life. It is why we can never marry. I don't expect my feelings to change. You have a responsibility now that lies elsewhere. It could never be with me, our family. I hope, my God, I hope and pray for your happiness."

She signed it simply, "Mary Ann."

The letter was achieved after a week of the worst conflict for Mary Ann. It took all her forbearance to keep reason ahead of emotion. Each night, while she cried in bed, she searched for truths and logic, particularly being aware of her own stubbornness. This was the 1990s, various friends had told her. Some of them regarded sexual dalliance as a symptom of the age more than a failure of mutual faith between a man and a woman.

However, "never a secret" is what the two had promised. And here it had been broken only weeks before the impending marriage.

Would she get over it? Would she forget? Would she forgive? She finally believed Donny and everyone else who told her Ethan was innocent. How could Ethan be otherwise? The fact that gnawed at her most was that he failed to tell her in all the weeks after he came home, in all the days that Lina was with them. They were now bitter days of deception.

Her mother, Emma, and her father, Thomas, were supportive but not interfering. Mary Ann, precocious in childhood, had not heard a real parental lecture in years.

"We know she's stubborn," Emma said late one night.

"I know. I don't think we can tell her what to do," said Thomas, who, as a doctor, had witnessed the consequences of unplanned pregnancies many times. If he had to counsel Lina, he would have worn the robe of professional passivity and told her about the options, but he would never, never force a decision upon her or any other woman.

He raised his own daughter in ways that he prayed would avoid Lina's predicament. Now Mary Ann was one of the victims, entrapped in the consequences of casual sex.

Even though both parents adored Ethan, they were aware of his immaturity and vulnerability. Subconsciously, so was Mary Ann. Emma sometimes fretted about what Ethan would do as a wage earner, especially if his ski-racing career would not work out. She had liked Donny Naples also, though, in the beginning of the relationship between her daughter and Donny, she thought him as witty, brash, and funny...but conceited. Donny's father was heir to one of the granite companies in the region. Just one generation before, when Emma was growing up, a natural social and class chasm existed between the wealthy entrepreneurs and the mostly Italian employees who worked for them. When Mary Ann and Donny were going together, Emma, deeply aware of the past, was nonetheless pleased that her daughter had broken that pattern.

Mary Ann finally arrived at her decision following a reflection that, for most of her life, her judgment of things around her had never failed her before. It had given her strength of character. Her steadfastness would lead her on. She would never be so happy again, but she would be right in her decision. There was no other way.

The days that followed Ethan's receiving of the letter found him in a depression that absolutely nothing, it seemed, would overcome. Finally, upon waking one morning, he decided that self-pity was far from virtuous. He had always told himself many times, especially after doing poorly in a race, that he would never feel sorry for himself, and if he did he would get rid of the feeling. But spite soon followed misery, as did anger, caused by the unfairness of it all.

A final decision about what to do with the rest of his life came after a phone call from Agnes.

"I know this is not the right thing for me to do, Ethan," she said, "but we are worried about Lina."

"Why should I care about Lina?" he answered.

"I know, I know, you have a right to be angry. But it's something more than that. She bought a plane ticket to return home to Italy, and was going to leave yesterday, but she never moved. She sits up in her room and says nothing. She can't eat, she can't sleep. When I tried to talk to her, all she could say was, 'It will soon be over'. Ethan, I'm afraid she'll hurt herself."

He listened and thought, and was ready to respond that Lina's future held no interest for him, but a very small part of him objected. He agreed to talk to Lina, to try to resolve something.

The night before Agnes had called, he had had a long conversation with his mother, Marge, who did best to reassure him that pain goes away, and that life goes on. She had experienced it, and her resolute decision not to abandon her husband turned into something positive.

"People change," she told Ethan. "Change for the better, sometimes."

He came close to saying, "Not Lina!," but recalled instead the anguish and pain in Lina's voice and face just a few nights ago in Barre. "What I have done to you," she had said with such bitterness and self-reproach.

"The trouble with Lina and everyone like her is that they can't see beyond that particular moment," his mother continued. "She never for a moment considered the consequences."

"Oh, she knew what she was doing," Ethan interrupted. "She wanted me, she told me that. She didn't give one shit about Mary Ann. Now she does! Now she regrets it! Now it's too late!"

"Well, if she learned something that's a beginning."

"A beginning?" he asked contemptuously.

"Yes, a beginning. You said that she told you an abortion is out of the question..."

"She's afraid of her dad and she said she wants the child."

"Then that's the beginning," said Marge.

She turned to him and emphasized that whatever hatred or by now disaffection he had for Lina, the two of them would have to meet some day and resolve how best to get through the present ordeal, which meant agreeing how best to make an effort to ease a new life into a painful world.

"Whether you like it or not," Marge Atwood told her son, "You have a new responsibility. I swear I won't let you run away from it."

They met on a sunny morning on the front porch of the house in Barre. Lina was dressed in jeans and a white turtlenecked sweater which would have set off her face—eyes and lips that were normally bright, engaging and seductive, but now were bleak and desolate.

She spoke in monotone, grief somewhat exhausted for the moment. Her confession was straight forward, laying out the details of what led to this moment.

"I came to you," she said meaningfully, purging it all. Looking up into Ethan's eyes, "I am so sorry for what I have caused you. I will do anything—anything to make it right."

He reached and drew her to him. A week later, she and Ethan moved to Colorado together.

Chapter 12
Going West

Dillon is a small town in Summit County, Colorado, that was once old and was now new. The entire town had been relocated three times, the last time in the 1950s to make way for a huge water supply reservoir for the Denver Water Board. Interstate 70 runs alongside the town and Lake Dillon. Equidistant from the big and popular ski resorts of Copper Mountain and Breckenridge, with Keystone and Arapahoe just up the mountain road and Vail less than an hour west along the pike, Dillon was positioned as a town with room to grow. It depended on the fortunes of the ski industry surrounding it.

Therefore, Dillon residents had shucked off the old and embraced the new with a blind enthusiasm that was typical of the settling of the west. They would take what came, day by day, and never look back. Ethan, on the long, exhausting trip out there, tried also to tell himself that people who dwelled in the past had no future. His credo from now on would be to always look ahead.

But gathering strength and vision after a fall is more easily attained in thought than in doing. Predictable bursts of behavior, explosions of anger, disappointment, sullenness, and peevish and somber undercurrents frequented the recently joined couple's trip from Vermont to Colorado. Silences boomed in their consciences like thunder. Outbreaks would occur particularly late in the afternoon when they tired from driving 500 miles. Ethan's damaged knee seemed to constantly ache. Sometimes it would itch and sting. Alternatively, it would be pierced by what felt like a sharp hook. He took frequent breaks. Whenever they got out on the open highway after leaving a metropolitan area, he let Lina drive, even though they should not have risked being stopped by a cop because she did not have an American driver's license.

With Lina at the wheel one afternoon, Ethan nodded off in the seat beside her. She tried keeping her thoughts focussed on the road, but when the thought of her plight became dominant, she pushed harder on the accelerator with anger, fright, and disappointment rushing to her brain. The truck sped ever faster—ninety, one hundred. The irrational decision was welcomed, making all the sense in the world. A rush of the speed could carry her away from her troubles and from this vast, monotonously foreign countryside. She would go faster and faster, letting the big car take off like a jet on a runway as it carried her and Ethan to the vastness of the sky. The speedometer read 110, climbing still.

Ethan awoke with a "Jesus Christ, Lina, what are you doing?"

She pushed the gas even harder. He grabbed the wheel, yelling, "Stop! For Christ's sake stop!"

He glanced quickly behind him. Surely, a cop would be in their wake by now. He grabbed the steering wheel again, but he resisted yanking. Tears flooded Lina's eyes, blinding her. She took her foot off the accelerator, and the truck's speed slowly backed down. She sat sobbing as he put his arm around her shoulder and pulled her to him. He kissed her hair.

"It's all right!" he whispered. "It's all right!"

At night in roadside motels, the arguments were interspersed with forced solicitude at first. Contrarily, in bed, he sometimes thrust himself roughly upon her. At other times, their mutual touch was tender and caring, and moved to a passion neither had experienced before.

On a rain-filled, gloomy night in a motel off Interstate 80 between Toledo and Chicago, they fought again. He was in the bathroom, toweling himself after a shower, when the towel accidentally swiped a bottle of Lina's body lotion to the tile floor. It shattered in dangerous pieces that mingled with white globs of goo.

"Why the hell do you have to carry so much shit with you?" he yelled. Lina was not just a clotheshorse. She was both parfum queen and pack rat. She carried small beaded and plastic bags of lip gloss, eye shadow, hair conditioner, and shampoo. Ethan's countrified toilettes would never agree to Chanel, Givenchy, nor even Revlon. He had no use for vanity in the first place. Never an overweening spoiled brat and selfish meddler.

He heard the front door slam. When he yelled "Lina!" and looked into the room, she had gone off into the rainy night.

Before he could slip on a pair of pants and race to the door, he heard the truck's engine start and a squeal of tires. He saw red tail lights bounce over the curb and down the highway.

At two AM, while lying on his back in the dark and pressing his fingers into the sheets, he heard the key click carefully in the latch. She came to bed without a word.

The next afternoon, after driving silently all day, they pulled wearily into the lot of a Ramada Inn on the outskirts of Chicago. It was a rendezvous point that Ethan and his father had arranged during a phone call that Ethan had made to Albany. His mother, Marge, acutely worried about her son, made him promise to call every other night. Paul Atwood told Ethan he had business in Chicago and they could maybe meet for dinner.

Both Lina and Ethan forced smiles when Paul hailed them from across the dining room. He was seated in a dark-colored booth off in a corner. Lina felt uncomfortable in the presence of the two men. She had met Paul only briefly once before and had noted his handsomeness. She searched out the similarities of father and son, the high cheeks, half-smile, and lightness to the eyes. Now, she smoothed and patted the front of her dress, as if to hide any sign of pregnancy. She cleared her throat anxiously as she leaned forward to receive Paul's kiss to her cheek.

When the waitress came, Lina briefly considered ordering white wine, but quickly changed to "just water, with ice." Her decision to not drink during her pregnancy caused a sudden warmth to pervade her body. It was a pleasant feeling and for the first time in days she felt serene. Ethan ordered a beer.

"Tonic with a little lime!" smiled Paul. He then grinned at the pair. He sensed their uneasiness and pictured what kind of trip west they were having.

All the while, Lina was wondering why Paul was there. Ethan wished he weren't.

Paul gently deflected attention from the two by talking casually about himself. He wrapped one huge hand around the glass of tonic, stared at the glass, tipped it and said, "You have no idea how refreshing this is!"

Ethan, eager to mix in some small talk, said, "It doesn't bother you at all anymore, does it?"

"Not at all!" said Paul, knocking a couple of times with his fist on the table. "It's not even day by day anymore. I can go to a party and watch everyone drink. I think, 'These poor bastards. They'll wake up tomorrow with lead in their head. I won't, thank God!'"

Paul began talking more about the wondrous, healing waters of sobriety. Then his face darkened. He surprised even himself as he began relating the moments of anguish that finally tipped him over the edge.

It had not come easily. Most of the time, the ghosts that were exorcised one by one by embarrassed men and women at the AA meetings failed to haunt Paul or touch his conscience. In the beginning he had even gone to the meetings half drunk—until that one night in the paneled room in the basement of Trinity Lutheran Church in Albany.

Paul began relating to Ethan and Lina the tale of a man who had fallen to the bottom and had tasted the bitterness brought on by his suffocating addiction to booze. As Paul spoke, he visualized that night in the church. He could see even the portrait of Christ hanging near a poster of black children in Africa.

"I lost the job. Believe me, that was nothing," said the penitent, a soft-spoken man in early middle age, as he stood before the gathering on wobbly legs. "The worst was when the wife left and took the kids with her. She had warned me plenty of times. I guess I never took her seriously. Even when she told me that last time and started packing a suitcase, all I could think about was getting a drink!

"By God, how insane I was!" the man said with his voice trembling. "They were walking out of my life, and I was glad when the door shut and I could put the bottle out on the kitchen table instead of sneaking down to the cellar where I had hidden it.

"Worse came to worse. I asked my wife to come back, and she said the only way she'd live in that house is after I'm out of it.

"So, I left. I tied the house keys to a brick and threw them right through the front window of her mother's house where she and the kids were staying. Then I went and got an apartment. I couldn't even hang onto it because I had no money. So I got a room. I lost it when I couldn't pay the rent, so I got a real cheap fleabag. Each step was a step backward.

"Once, I was hanging out on the corner, like a bum, waiting for a drinking buddy to come by. I was in real bad need of a drink. I was out of work, dirty and alone. I was standing on the street corner when the bus went by. It was late in the morning. I looked up at the bus and saw my daughter at one of the windows.

The man paused, cleared his throat, and struggled to continue. He suddenly felt that he no longer had the ability to breathe. "She's working her way through college now without any help from me. By God, I don't know how she does it! But anyway, she's looking out the bus window at me, and I'm looking back at her.

"We just stared at each other. She didn't wave. She didn't smile. She just stared at me. She just had such a look of sadness and pity. Her pity was for me. I thought I could tell that she still loved me.

The man fell silent and then muttered as he exhaled and choked on the words, "That's the only reason I'm here tonight."

Paul had not intended to tell this story, and he was still surprised at himself when he finished relating it. There was more to add, but not this time. He was not at all sure what to say next. He sat up brightly when the waitress came with their orders.

Lina leaned across the table toward Paul and touched the sleeve of his jacket.

Whatever the message by Paul Atwood, the remainder of the road trip between Chicago and beyond Denver to Colorado's Front Range occurred under the banner of unwritten truce, with the door to each day's end closing softly. Neither Lina nor Ethan spoke of it, but Paul's tale carried the message that a step back can turn into a step forward.

So it was. Physically tired and emotionally whipped from the mostly anxiety-laden, cross-country journey, Ethan and Lina stopped at the first real estate office they saw in Dillon. Without much consideration, they chose to rent a small, furnished row-style condo abutting the lake to the north. It was within walking distance to the town's center. The boxy little home was one of a half-dozen strung together with red brick and white aluminum siding. It had two small bedrooms and a bath upstairs. There was a living room, kitchen, and dining area downstairs. Skiers, resort personnel, or merchants with shops downtown owned most of the houses.

Many, like the one they chose, were rented to itinerant skiers by the season. Not much to look at either inside or outside, the keystone location of the unattractive development was its singular allure. Toward the southeast, there was an arresting view of the frozen lake. In its not inconspicuousness background, there were the buxom mountains. The small lawns sloped to the lake's edge, now made invisible by the still-heavy blanket of snow upon the ice.

Guided briskly by the real estate agent, a tall, gangly, young man with a crooked smile and large ears, they peeked quickly into each room. The hot water faucet handle in the shower came off in Ethan's hand when he turned it, and the broom closet smelled of cats. Large scratch marks, the blazes of a large dog, were gouged into the front and back doors.

"One of the previous tenants had a dog. Worked at Copper as a lift op. Not the dog, the owner," said the realtor, chuckling. "We've reduced the rent because we've got a little bit of damage."

"I think somebody had a cat here, too," offered Ethan.

"Yes, the most previous tenant had, I think, two cats. Some of our condo owners won't lease to people who have animals. Others don't care."

"We'd like it through July if we can do that," said Ethan. This drew a puzzled glance from Lina, who felt slighted that he had not bothered to consult her on the decision. But, looking down at her stomach, it was something she had to get used to.

"Through July is all right," said the realtor.

That night in bed, Ethan wondered if the rest of his days and nights would be so unfulfilling, so temporary and fleeting, without serious meaning, as these last several days had been. They could have settled into a larger place. They surely had enough money to rent any one of several log style homes in the mountains. Lina would have preferred that, but she bowed to Ethan's haste. It was as if he wished to speed through each day as quickly as one could and then move on to whatever else life offered. Lina began dreading thoughts of the future. She became quieter each day as she concentrated her conversation on small talk. She tried maintaining a calm that belied her normally buoyant and self-assured personality.

No one, absolutely no one in sympathy with the victim, can fully share the pain of loss of a loved one or the associated pain of guilt at having been the cause of such a loss. Of course, news of the broken affair, the wrenching schism between Ethan and Mary Ann, reached Europe. Coaches and fellow skiers called to chat up their fallen colleague. The men offered brief condolences and suggested that fate works matters for the better.

"Hey, you'll be back here racin' in no time, Ethan!" yelled Klecko into the phone. "You'll probably have a helluva year. And listen, pal," his voice lowered, "you could do a lot worse than to end up with a doll like Lina. Look at the bright side."

Men, discussing other men's problems, tended to sidestep the perplexity, especially the emotional overtones, with practical forecasts. It could always be worse.

Klecko had gone over the "Ethan situation" many times with Morgan Rutledge. "I know Ethan's girl, Mary Ann, was a real doll and a beautiful person. But that Lina. Jesus, what a firecracker. I wouldn't have minded blastin' off in that one myself."

"You never did, did you?" asked Rutledge, seriously.

"Shit no, uh-huh! Oh, wait a minute. You don't think I…" Klecko protested so earnestly that Rutledge smiled. "Hell no, man. Absolutely, hell no. Never touched Lina, so help me God."

The two young men discussed what they would have done had they been caught in the same predicament as Ethan, knocking up a virtual stranger.

"I probably would have just made the payments," said Klecko. "Not that Lina needs child support. Her old man is loaded! But, I guess I would've run." His voice was casual and honest. "I'm not made the way Ethan is."

"I know what you mean," said Rutledge. "I don't know what I'd do if I knocked up a girl that I didn't care for. You know though, I used to think sometimes that Ethan was this big, dumb guy who couldn't help himself, you know, especially socially. He seemed so awkward a lot of the time. But, what he's doing—I talked to him, and he said he feels a responsibility, even though it wasn't his doing, his fault. He said he's got a kid to look after now, and he's not gonna walk away from it. You know, I have to admire that. Sometimes, I think Ethan's got more sense than any of us. It's like that's what made him such a good downhiller. He not only has balls. He has that sense of being responsible...for winning and not losing. You know, every time he did bad in a race, his first thought was that he let down the team."

He paused. "Shit, here I am talking about him like it's the past tense or something. I keep forgetting that he's still a part of this team and that he'll be back."

"Yeah, he'll be okay by summer," said Klecko. "He'll be with us in Chile. You know, he'll come back strong and have a good year. It's because he's got nothin' else now but racing."

"Racing and a kid. Don't forget the kid," reminded Rutledge.

"Yeah, I guess you're right. The kid."

"I like the way the sun curves around the lake each day," said Lina as she stood at the rear kitchen window near the sink with her arms folded. "It starts over there," she said, pointing eastward where a strip of road was barely visible at the icebound rim. "And then it goes all around here," she said, sweeping her arm as her fingers glided backward. Ethan took in the soft, white hands, the breast swell of her sweater, wavy hair, molded hips, and still-firm tummy. Times like these mollified the periods of anger and loss that he felt coming cross-country in the truck while unpacking luggage into the motel of choice for the night. He could have easily strangled the breath from her body. Often, he had wished her dead.

"It was not my fault," he said to himself so many times.

He cursed himself and told himself that many men would have left Lina. Millions do in identical situations and do not consider another thought about abandonment. Ethan could no sooner leave his unborn child than he could leave the ski team. Was it in his genes? Responsibility. His mother, Marge, disgusted over her husband's alcoholism, nonetheless pledged to stay with him. Making it work is the cliché.

However, the temperament of Ethan and Lina swung in the dark of night. Shades opened to the lake. Occasional moonlight sought the walls of the mostly bare room. With caressingly soft fingers, lips, and tongue deftly touching, Lina loved like no other. He cradled her then. He cradled mother and child, as she opened up her body and, little by little, her soul.

As a child, Lina became lonely. She was just ten years old when her mother, Joanna, died of pancreatic cancer. Alone with her father in Milan, Lina turned to him with such smothering attachment that it bewildered her when he had to leave the house. But Benito did leave. It was not just days at his office, where his draftsmen bent silently over their tilted tables. It was also at night when a variety of whores and married women kept him sated with all the love he desired and needed.

For his daughter, Benito reserved the fatherly affection of head pats, fixing the beret in her hair, touching her cheek with the backs of his fingers, and generally ushering her along to school or to play.

"He indulged me." she said. "Both me and my brother, but it was me especially. He never spent time with me playing though. I wanted to hold his hand always, always. I wanted him to take me places, to the zoo and even to his office. He would never, almost never. He left me with Nanny instead.

"When I became a teen, I started going out, like he did. Of course, I never went to the same places. All my friends and I, we went to discos. We danced and drank 'til dawn. I almost always paid. He never minded. My father never cared. Even though I had such great fun…ah…I thought it was great fun. It troubled me so that he didn't care. When I was a child, I would wish, daydream, that a nun or a priest would stop him on the street, and scold him.

"'Look after your daughter, who loves you. Stop this running around.' Alas, it never happened."

Chapter 13
The Lake

"Guess what!" said Lina, her eyes bright with good news. "We're invited to a party!"

He stood with his back to her, gazing absently out the window as he sipped a cup of tea. "Where?" he asked indifferently.

"Right here, down the street. The Mick So-and-Sos. Mick Something. They live the last house on Tenderfoot. You remember them."

"McGuires," said Ethan. They had met the day he and Lina moved in. They were still tired and irritable from the last 400 miles of their journey through the plains to the Front Range. He had paid little attention to their introductions. He failed to register the couple's first names and barely remembered McGuire. The wife wore glasses and had brown hair. Her husband was big with black, curly hair. Both smiled a lot. That was all Ethan could remember, except they were pleasantly surprised that a World Cup skier was moving into their block.

He did not want to go to the party and said so. Lina, who spent most of her days alone since they arrived in Colorado, was fairly desperate for some entertainment and diversion. She was tired of skiing alone. She tired of walking from shop to shop downtown. Although delighted by the abundance and variety of factory stores in the nearby town of Silverthorne, she often would come home exhausted. Most of her concentration there was on maternal necessities—cribs, strollers, and baby clothes. It was an occupation of time that left her with a mix of joy and sorrow. Ethan would come home from the gym or from visits with Dr. Rogers in Denver. He would then squat on the sofa, reading ski publications or Tolstoy or Turgenev. He talked little. He was glum much of the time.

His social life, however, was as full as he wanted it to be. When not at the gym, riding the bike, carefully lifting weights, and sitting in the whirlpool, he consorted with the skiing elite of Arapahoe, Breckenridge, Copper, and Keystone, a handful of local extreme skiers, some aerialists, and bump skiers. Breckenridge, with its topnotch freestyle facilities, attracted athletes from around the world who bordered on the wild side. They kept Ethan entertained. In turn, they enjoyed being in the company of a World Cup downhiller with a reputation for guts, just like themselves.

Lina finally pleaded her case successfully as she used a succession of pouts and turning her need into his need. "It will do you good, do us good."

Still, the party was not that difficult to enjoy. They were an older crowd in their thirties and forties. It was couples mostly, skiers and snowboarders all, chattering about famous back bowls, secretive off-piste areas, what skis are hot, and the learning curve of snowboarding. They talked about the changing weather, the anticipation of a new season of mountain biking, fly fishing, hiking, and water skiing.

Because of his now-famous and widely respected bum knee, Ethan was given the seat of honor, the middle of the couch in the tiny, crowded living room. He was flanked on either side by Ann McGuire and Barbara Jones, who, when not asking a thousand questions regarding ski-racing, were strenuously disagreeing with each other over which had the best skiing, the Alps or the Rockies. Ethan, of course, was forced to choose.

"I'm probably the wrong person to ask. Anybody on the ski team would be the wrong person. We don't do it like the tourist. I see the towns. They're lovely. I like the ambience, but I generally don't like skiing in Europe all that much," he found himself saying.

"I guess it's all that packing and unpacking," said Ann helpfully. "Going from hotel to hotel and town to town."

Barbara wanted to know about his injury, something he could talk about easily by rote now because it was an everyday topic. Yet, he tired of it.

"It just went," he said of the patella. "There wasn't that much strain on it. Most doctors will tell you that you can snap those ligaments just standing still if they're weak, which apparently mine were. When they're ready to pop, they pop."

"I'll bet it was awful lying in that hospital," said Barbara, a thin-lipped girl with a deeply cleft chin. "Was your family there? Was Lina there?"

"My family wasn't, but Lina was," he said, staring deep into the wall and then fixing his eyes on Lina, who was across the room. She was standing with her back turned, facing the table containing chips and dip. Beside her was Ralph Lawrence, a squat, burly guy wearing a ten-gallon hat who lived next door. Ralph and Lina were banging hips, playfully pretending that each other was in the way. Ralph sold stocks in town and looked like the kind of man who banged hips with young women at every opportunity. He owned a huge, black Labrador named Buster. According to Ann McGuire, who volunteered some low-down information on the party attendees, Ralph enjoyed wrestling on the lawn with Buster in the summer, wearing nothing but tight-fitting shorts. Muscular and athletic, he had spent time roping calves on the rodeo circuit.

Ann excused herself when she heard her ten-month-old baby crying in an upstairs bedroom. Ethan was eventually left pretty much alone on the couch. Though he had managed of late to master a degree of social ease, engaging in occasional repartee above the small talk, he would eventually find himself alone in a room full of people.

"I just run out of conversation," he would tell himself. Prior to this past year of his life, he often found it difficult in crowded, noisy rooms to concentrate on what other people were saying to him. He would think instead of his own prepared reply. With small talk zinging overhead, he would hear enough to mutter a semi-intelligent reply. Eventually, he would be left alone.

He preferred to observe and now saw Lina wearing a white, woolen turtleneck that set off her wavy, dark hair and coal black, dreamy eyes. Flushed with the good health of childbearing, she was also gaining weight. She stood next to Lawrence, who was into his fourth or fifth rodeo anecdote by now.

"Bulls, I don't mess with. Horses neither, except to ride 'em after they're broken. I just rope calves, little shavers about this high. I'm just a rodeo sissy."

He promised Lina, when the weather got better, he would show her how to spin the lasso. "We can practice roping each other," he said grinning.

After a minute, Ethan got up with a beer in his hand and walked to the other side of the room. He nodded to Ralph and put his arm around Lina. He whispered in her ear, "I've noticed you're getting a little pudgy." He smiled down at her.

"Pudgee? What is pudgee?"

"Chubby, corpulent!" He laughed.

"No!" she gasped. "I am?" She immediately put down the cracker and cheese on the small plate in front of her.

"It's okay. I like it." He bent and nuzzled her neck. "I like you a little succulent, a little ripe." He felt overwhelmingly horny and whispered, "Let's go home." He then kissed her hair.

As they walked the few steps to their own condo, they were startled at the sound of what could have been a small explosion. Instead, it was more of a sharp, whomping sound, like two forces colliding.

"That's the ice. On the lake. It's breaking up," Ethan observed.

"My God, that frightened me!" said Lina, taking his arm and squeezing it tightly. From overhead, a bright, full moon illuminated the flat, white plain of the lake. This day had been colder than most in the preceding week, but generally, with the approach of May, warmer days were taking over.

Even though he could not ski and could not even reach these steep peaks and snow-filled crags 12,000 feet in the sky and run their feathery powder, Ethan found himself enjoying the bustling distractions of his new ski towns. Cars plowed the slush now in Breckenridge, causing pedestrians to skip backwards out of the way. At the base of the ski slopes, brown-colored snow was forming as the early spring mud made its seasonal claim.

He rode the Summit Stage, a free bus that carried skiers and workers from resort to resort. From his seat, he could see aerialists practicing jumps on the freestyle ramps up toward Peak 9 of the Tenmile Range. Impulsively, as the bus turned the corner near the Beaver Run Resort, he yanked the cord to signal the driver and hobbled off.

By now, he was able to work his crutches as second nature. The increasing strength in his arms and shoulders surprised him. He was amazed at how far they could lift him, even in the snow. Still, it took about twenty minutes for him to climb the slight hill. The pedestrians packed the snow along the walkway. Despite the thaw, it made it easier for him to plant the crutches. Well-wishers who recognized him occasionally detained him. A small child stood still as Ethan autographed his white helmet with a black, felt tip pen. The kid's mother beamed as the boy looked up at Ethan as if to see if the cause célèbre was worth all that fuss.

Ethan, who was a spectator himself today, felt the need for some mental freedom. The jumpers who took off from icy ramps and headed straight for heaven, a spring blue canopy of sky, gave it to him vicariously. It was optimal freedom to be able to launch like that, to have the ability to ignore gravity for a few seconds at least, until it won and brought you down to earth. The trick was to get your skis down before your rear end or your head.

A pretty, blonde girl stood poised with her skis sideways to the hill, digging in her edges. She pumped, inhaled deeply, and then quickly twisted her body as she let the skis go. Ethan watched the golden sun glint off her helmet as she cleared the lip of the ramp with her arms outstretched and her feet together. She appeared to be in the air for minutes, a birdlike victor over the pull of the earth. She floated and spun backward. Her skis were still parallel. Then twisting, her arms were folded across her chest. Once...twice...she twisted three times while her small body performed a double flip at the same time.

"Difficult!" Ethan gasped to himself, entranced by the free fall.

However, her perfection in the air did not carry over to the landing. As the skis hit the ramp, she slap-backed. She came down on her heels and then on her head. She walloped it against the stiffened snow so hard that spectators choked. After she stopped sliding, she lay lifeless while coaches and other staff raced towards her.

She was on her side in a half-fetal position. A leg then stirred, and she moaned.

Their fears lessened, trainers and coaches began asking routine concussion questions, "What day is it? Where are you? Do you know your name?"

Eventually, she was helped to her feet, amid scattered applause from the few people watching. She was then half-carried to the sidelines.

The pretty girl's eyes were wide and vacant, blind on the inside to the world they were looking at. Her zombie's stare went right through Ethan as she wobbled on unsteady feet to a small grandstand where her friends carefully sat her down.

Ethan shuddered before quickly turning and walking downhill. He had seen enough. Grace...beauty...freedom...then the fall. "Just a concussion," the athlete would say. Ethan was beginning to think he knew better, despite his efforts not to connect his own fall with the confusing, uncontrollable events that had followed the night in the hospital in Brescia. Those events led to what he thought—in unguarded moments like this one—was the collapse of all that he had ever desired in life. He glanced at his watch. It was 3:00 PM Mountain Time. It would be 5:00 PM in Vermont. They would be sitting down at the dining room table. Mary Ann's father liked an early supper.

There were many more painful reveries, despite Ethan's resolve to live the day. Once, when the vision of Mary Ann became too much, he called her home in Montpelier. With his heart pounding, he was half-relieved when Emma answered. Their conversation was brief with Emma exclaiming, "It broke all our hearts. But Mary Ann won't back down."

There was a long silence. Emma finally said, "Ethan, dear, it's best you not call again. Mary Ann is trying to forget. You both have separate lives. And she's seeing Donny again."

The phone rang. It was an invitation from a Denver television station.

"We're feeding into a network wrap of the ski-racing season," said the woman from the television station who invited him. "It'll be shown nationwide. It looks like some sponsors want to put money into the ski team.

"I think you had something to do with that," she said with a smiling voice.

"Well," Ethan interrupted, "I'm making no promises for next year. Coming off an injury. It'll take some time to get back."

"Oh, you'll be back. I think it really looks exciting for the team, and a lot of people think that," she said. "There's a lot of excitement."

He silently agreed to the interview, recalling that both Klecko and Rutledge finished in the top fifteen in the final two races of the season, helping the U.S. Team to fault into third place in the World Cup standings, up from tenth the year before. And Klecko, buoyed by those successes, decided to stay on for another year. If Ethan could achieve anywhere near his performance of the past year, the team's future looked secure, especially for the next Olympics. He repeatedly pledged to himself that he would be ready.

He arrived in Denver fifteen minutes ahead of the scheduled time for the interview. He parked his truck in a space marked "Visitors" and took a quick look around the neighborhood, noticing its industrialized appearance. There were two-and three-story concrete buildings with flat roofs. Traffic zoomed noisily on the nearby interstate. It was so different from other so-called snow country towns like the Alps and New England. Though a mile high, Denver was as flat as the plains to the east, while, to the west, the massive mountains of the Front Range though close, appeared hundreds of miles away.

As he started toward the door of the building with a huge KDEN-TV emblazoned on its façade, he imagined the kinds of questions that would be asked during the interview. She said it would be seen nationwide. Generalities upon generalities. He rehearsed his answers in advance, suddenly stopping short because Mary Ann's image came clearly into view, as did her house high on the hill in Montpelier. Dusk would be falling. His mind flashed visions of the Vermont countryside, old clapboard homes with wood smoke spiraling from chimneys. He saw rolling snow-covered fields and lanes where newly budding trees kept sentinel. Sugaring season had been underway for a few weeks now. It had to be. God, has it been that long?

As a small boy, he would stick to his grandfather's leg like a fly to flypaper because he was afraid of the roaring, yellow fire under the boiler and the sweet, sticky smell of maple sap in the air. On those cold, dry nights, the flame would shoot straight up and out the chimney, lofting orange sparks from the fire into a sky filled with stars, as numerous as plankton swimming in a black sea sky.

Ethan sat back against the fender of his truck, breathing deeply. His thoughts were stifling. "She'll see my face. She'll know. And I have to be on. I have to be smiling. I can't!"

He told himself that doing a television interview was no more difficult than going into the start shack, except there wasn't a downhill race hairy enough or important enough to scare him as this upcoming exposure would do. Mary Ann can see through every disguise, every affectation.

Across the street was a tavern.

"Stupid!" he said under his breath and walked to the windowless stucco building. He opened the door and entered the smoky, dark room with a pool table so close to the door that a cue stick almost stuck him in the groin. The pool player holding it stood straight. He glanced at the well-built man before him and said, "Scuse me, buddy." The man bent again to the green felt and said, "Three in the corner."

Ethan moved to the bar and ordered a shot of vodka "with a little water." He was thankful for the semidarkness, but he was annoyed with the cigarette smoke that stung his nostrils and eyes. He quaffed the shot in one gulp, grimaced, and ordered another.

It was amazing, he thought as he walked across the street to the station. A little bit of fluid fire in a tiny glass creates just the right kind of confident glow. The nerve ends that trigger smiles were working again.

The interview lasted about fifteen minutes. Probably two of them would be used on the air. Most likely, the fatuous comments would be preserved for the tape.

"We feel very positive about next year...

"We've got a good nucleus."

At the end, as he unpinned the little mike from the front of his shirt and shook hands all round for a job well done, a voice said, "Phone call for you, Ethan."

Ann McGuire was on the line. Her voice was tremulous and frightened.

"There's been an accident! Hurry, hurry!"

No sooner had Ethan run through the clinic door, Ann was up to his side and explaining to him what had happened.

Lina had been shopping. She was carrying a plastic sack of groceries in one hand and a large bag in another with the printing "Just for Baby" on the side. As she walked on the footpath, the sun was showing a pink upper lip as it sank over the mountains. It cast massive, dark shadows upon the lake and the town. She loved the purple twilight when the harsh contrasts of daylight became blends of pastel. People moved indoors. She looked around, counting dots of white and yellow lights of windows. She failed to notice that the snow-packed trail made a hitch to the left. The faintly dark roofline of the condos was just ahead. The snow crunched beneath her boots.

She heard nothing when it happened, only a sudden coldness around her ankles.

"My God."

She knew immediately and screamed as a small blanket of ice began slowly collapsing beneath her, sucking her legs and lower body into the lake.

The bags flew in the air as she flung herself on her back, arching her stomach. At the same time, she flailed with her arms, attempting to keep her weight distributed over the cracked and broken surface. An icy path of cold water began shooting down her neck and spine. Her legs were already heavyweights. They began aching. Her heart raced wildly. Panic-filled eyes fastened upward at an evening star and then to the shore onto the little row of houses. The lights of neighbors' kitchens were only a few hundred yards away, but it was an eternity in time. Would they hear the screams? Again and again, she shouted, "Help!" In Italian, she yelled, "Aiuto!" Lina kept her arms flailing backward with her back and head against the ice. She must not go under!

A dog began barking loudly. A light went on at the back porch of the end condo, but Lina could not hear the voice of Ralph Lawrence, who yelled, "Yo, Buster, what's the matter?"

"Help!" screamed Lina, as she sunk in the water to her armpits. She was holding the ice now with her arms.

Ralph could see her shape about fifty feet from shore.

"Jesus!" he yelled. He had no idea who or what was in the lake. He thought it was probably a neighborhood kid. This time of year, they were always running across the ice with reckless unconcern about the vagaries of the weather and testiness of the spring thaw.

"Hold on," Ralph yelled. "I'm coming."

His rowboat lay beneath a tree. It was half-buried, upside down in the snow only a few feet from the edge of the lake. Wearing just a sweat suit and moccasins, he grasped the gunnels of the small boat, but he could not lift it. Both the boat and anchor rope were frozen to the earth.

He ran back to his kitchen and grabbed a knife. By the time he reappeared, other neighbors were on the run. Lina was screaming, and the dog was barking. Doors were opening, and people were now shouting.

It took four of them to "One, two, three, heave!" to release the boat from its icy grasp. Ralph grabbed the anchor line and cut it close to the prow where it was tied. He ran to the edge of the shore while the other men grabbed the boat and carried it to the water's edge. They slid it onto the ice. The boat would be of little use, however, with the ice and lack of oars. Someone brought out a powerful flashlight and shined it on the struggling woman. Darkness had engulfed the major part of the lake.

"I'm throwing the anchor. Hold on!" Ralph yelled to the form in the lake.

He tied one end of the rope to his waist, left about eight feet of slack at the anchor end, and then began slowly twirling the anchor in circles around his head, faster and faster. He then let loose in Lina's direction.

Lina felt she was losing consciousness. She fought to stay alert, kicking. Her legs and lower body were dredged in cold pain and weighed a ton.

"I've got to live!" she yelled to herself. "Live, live, live!" she said.

The irony of the past weeks of regret and remorse was swept away with the need for survival. She thought of Ethan and the baby.

The anchor went sailing over her head, clanking on the ice beyond her, but the rope lay a few feet out of reach.

Ralph ran up the beach to position the rope closer to Lina.

"Grab it!" he yelled.

She tried, but she could not hold on. Her head dropped to the ice. He started pulling, letting the anchor approach her. Then, when it was a few feet from her body, he gave a furious yank, hoping one of the flukes would catch a piece of her jacket.

With her last bit of strength, Lina grabbed the rope and twisted her arm around it. She then held on with both hands. An anchor fluke caught her wet jacket and pulled it up to her armpits, exposing her bare back to the wind and cold water. It held fast.

Ralph and the other men, some of whom had broken the ice and were now in the water up to their waists, began pulling.

"Slowly, slowly, guys, or it'll tear right away from her!"

By force of will, Lina held on, and she felt her body come loose from the icy well.

They pulled her to shore and wrapped her in blankets. By now, the entire neighborhood was on hand. Medics took over, trundled her small body into the ambulance, and sped to the Summit Health Services clinic in town.

When Ethan arrived, Ann grabbed his arm and squeezed it tightly.

"I'm sorry, Ethan. I better tell you. She's all right. But the baby didn't make it. The baby's gone. The baby! I'm sorry."

Ethan stroked Lina's dark hair, which looked even darker against the whiteness of the pillow. He warmed her cheeks with both hands and put his face next to hers. He covered her upper body with his, holding and warming her.

"I'm sorry," she said, still shivering.

"No, no, no," he said softly, holding her small cold hands in his.

She said nothing, but, in a few seconds, she swallowed hard. The tears flowed steadily. She attempted to smile, but she could not.

"You're free!" she whispered hoarsely.

"Shhh," he said, kissing her cheek. "Don't talk. Thank God you're all right. You're going to be okay. You'll be fine. We'll be fine! We'll be fine!"

Lifetime surprises usually flash abruptly, hurriedly. It is why they are called surprises, instant eruptions of elation or tragedy. It is correct to assume that neither Lina nor Ethan had prepared themselves for what happened in the days and weeks that came after her accident.

Ethan asked himself repeatedly, "Why am I feeling this way?"

They loved, laughed, and held the other tightly that spring and on into summer. While he healed physically, the spiritual side of his mending came by degrees. However, it was seemingly on the increase with each sunrise. Life had taken on a fullness again. Was Mary Ann out of mind? Never. Nevertheless, Lina's effervescence had also advanced each day with the realization that Ethan's angry wall of reserve was coming down. She had set him free by virtue of that terrible accident. Ethan told her he did indeed choose to be free now that the opportunity was upon him. He surprised himself and Lina by choosing her, and he was ever surprised that she had become a meaningful, valid part of his existence.

Lina, also free, knew she could never return to the groupie lifestyle that led to the present. Her maturation into womanhood had begun unknowingly with the subconscious realization that men and women can—and do—become enjoined in one deep love. The irony was that she learned it from Ethan and Mary Ann.

So, with a renewed spirit, Lina and Ethan vowed to give it a try. On his part, Ethan reentered as a man the real world that he had left in Vermont as a boy.

Of immediate concern was how to thank Ralph Lawrence for pulling Lina from the icy lake. One happy evening, they took all of the rescuers to dinner. A couple days later, a large crate arrived at Ralph's house, containing a new Evinrude outboard engine.

Chapter 14
Papa

As the jet began lowering altitude on its approach to Milan's Malpensa Airport, Lina could make out the rugged peaks of the Alps through the clouds, an undulating bed of nails poking from the rough landscape as far away as one could see. Looking sideways at Ethan with her big smile, she saw he had fallen asleep, despite saying during the flight that he couldn't sleep on airplanes. He had been anxious and as tense as a crouching panther before leaving for Chile in August to join the ski team. He returned high, not quite mighty. He was relieved and now finally relaxed. His preseason had gone well. Only once did he have a serious fall to test the repaired knee, and it had held up well. He felt ready.

They had left for Europe a full two weeks ahead of the rest of the ski team. Ethan had to get permission from his coaches. They gave in, thinking it might be well for their rising star of a skier to acclimate himself to his surroundings before plunging into the grind of the European season. Quinn and the others were fully aware of Ethan's rocky love life. It was not uncommon for racers to have hitches in their romances. The coaches took the problem rather lightly, but they pledged to carefully monitor the psyche of this particular racer. The Ethan they had known in the past bruised easily.

Five kilometers outside Milan, Lina slowed the little Fiat, braking it to a stop on the shoulder of the busy *autostrada.*

"Your turn," she said. "See how fast you can make my little Spider go."

He grinned and nodded at the challenge. A few seconds later, he gunned the small, bright red sports car to 100 kilometers an hour...then 120...140...160. It was an unseasonably warm day in November, and, after the cramped space of the airplane, the wind flooding past and into the open convertible was indeed welcomed.

"I forget how fast I'm going," he yelled. "In miles, I mean."

"What does it matter?" shouted Lina, her hair flying horizontally behind her. "They will not stop you. I know every *poliziotto* on *autostrada*!"

Ethan was surprised how well the tiny car hugged the road. "It's like a...Ferrari!" he yelled.

"It is a Ferrari!" she yelled back, laughing. "Almost Ferrari! Fiat owns Ferrari!"

Together, they let their lungs fill and refill with the warm, moist air as they approached the flat country east of Milan, on their way to Lago de Garda.

Ethan, driving in the passing lane, slowed down to ask, "What's our exit? I don't want to miss it."

Before Lina had a chance to answer, a glance in the rearview mirror recorded the flashing of headlights, a huge automobile that seemed magnetized to the rear bumper of the Spider.

"Jesus Christ!" Ethan yelled, suddenly swerving the car to the right and out of the way. The silver Mercedes swept past him in a rush. "What the hell was that?"

"You aren't supposed to slow down in the passing lane in Italy...in Europe!" yelled Lina, holding her sunglasses to her forehead as she turned to shout at him. She was laughing.

"That was a Mercedes!" said Ethan.

"Si, yes!" said Lina. "The Germans, the Austrians, they come roaring down out of the Alps, and they don't push the brake until they get where they are going! They will push you out of the way!"

Ethan laughed and filed the metaphor into his brain under "R" for Racing: "Just like they ski. Just don't get in their way!"

He pressed the accelerator, chasing the Mercedes. It was like an orgasm. He felt the speed and a beating heart creep closer to his throat. Both hands gripped the steering wheel tightly, just the same way they were on the handlebars of his bicycle the day he, Mary Ann, and Donny Naples, as teenagers, plunged down the backside of the Mountain Gap road in Vermont. They tested their skills by daring not to squeeze the brakes of the bicycle. It had been Ethan's idea.

"This is how you get the balls...the guts," he told them beforehand, "to ski downhill." And he hurtled forward, letting the wheels of his eighteen-speed roll at their natural progression. He let the downhill force of gravity do its job. All they had to do was steer...and lean...and steer...and lean. First right...then left... right...left again. They dodged small rocks and leaves that could set the bike a few inches off its course and into the woods below.

Mary Ann was the first to chicken out. She called it "common sense." Then the roar of a lumbering logging truck huffing uphill suddenly terrified Donny, who squeezed the brake little by little.

The road was flanked heavily on both sides by pine trees, birches, and boulders as big as porch chairs. They were in the middle of the Green Mountain National Forest, a wildly beautiful area where the nearest house was two miles away.

The truck driver saw a speeding shape coming around the next bend and hit the air horn. The loud "Blat!" caused birds to take flight. Ethan's bike followed, which did not have anywhere to go except off to the opposite side of the road where there was not any guardrail. He sailed through small limbs of a stand of saplings. They ripped at Ethan's skin and lashed his face, chest, arms, and knees. Luckily, the bike splashed down in the near middle of a beaver pond. Rider and bike, still joined together, bobbed once atop the waterline and then toppled to the right side.

Donny had braked in time to avoid the truck. Mary Ann arrived in seconds. She dropped her bike and dived head first into the water, which was clear but dark with the stain of cedar. Within seconds, in waist-deep water, she had Ethan grasped under the arms. The truck driver, a barrel-shaped man, made huge waves as he leaped in to help her.

With terror in his heart, Donny ran to the pond in time to see the burly trucker, his soggy, wet jeans hanging dangerously low on his hammy buttocks, gently place Ethan on the ground on his back. The boy was conscious and grimacing, but he was managing to work in a grin between the shocks of pain pounding against his ribs and shoulder.

"Some ride, huh!" he gasped.

"Kid, I hope you're all right!" yelled the trucker. "You musta been doin' eighty comin' down there!"

"Think so?" Ethan asked hopefully and then winced as he eased his back into a comforting bed of mud.

He throttled the Fiat to the floor, feeling with pleasure the tug of its roaring engine at his feet. The front bumper crept closer and closer to the Mercedes. He drafted the bigger car for a quarter-mile and then suddenly whipped to the left. He let the suction of the air whiplash the Spider forward, alongside the Mercedes.

The driver glanced sideways, caught Ethan's eye, and pretended to be bored. He let the little, red convertible spin away in front of him. The German knew that—anytime he wished—he could take the Italian with ease.

At a rest stop, Lina took over the wheel. From time to time after leaving the devilish, high-speed throughway, Ethan, now seated in the passenger seat, caught glimpses of the distant big, blue lake, past vineyards with scrawny strings of vines and wooden posts planted in dusty, weak-looking soil and bright terra cotta, roofs of stuccoed houses. From the road, he could see a skinny peninsula of land to the north. It was protected at its end by a castle-like structure that poked into the blue water of the lake.

"That's like a fairy castle!" noticed Ethan.

"It's Sirmione. The Scaligero castle is what you see. We will go there this week. Very medieval."

Going through Brescia, Ethan turned to crane his neck toward the hospital where he lay that night. He grimaced and looked at Lina to find her expression. She smiled, but she did not look at him. She stared straight ahead at the road that was soon flanked by green foothills on the left and the lush coolness of the lake on the right.

"No wonder you liked Dillon so much," said Ethan. "It must have reminded you of home."

She nodded.

They reached a torturous winding road outside Salo. The small car hugged the curves at high speeds as if it was glued to the asphalt. Lina was a good driver who had been taught by her father.

"Respect the car! That's what he always told me. It is a work of art!" she shouted in imitation of Benito, kissing her fingers with her lips and tossing the kiss skyward.

"He helped design this car," she said.

"You mean under Pinin Whatshisname?" shouted Ethan, bracing himself for another curve.

"Pininfarina, the great Pininfarina!" she yelled back.

Once past Gardone, Lina braked and eased the Spider into a driveway flanked by coarse brush so thick it was impossible to see through it. The curvy drive had been laid in salmon-colored brick. Ethan thought it curved needlessly because the terrain really did not demand it.

"You Italians like curves," he said as the car wheeled from side to side, rocking its inhabitants.

Again she nodded as she brought the car to a stop outside the villa. Immediately, they felt the wind's warm kiss from the lake. Late-season insects buzzed in the air, surrounding trees of lemon and eucalyptus. Lina honked the horn, but no one came.

"He is not home. I am so disappointed," she said.

Meanwhile, Ethan strolled the manicured lawn that was shaved similar to a golf green. Benches of stone and mortar were placed throughout. A sprinkler made a "patta patta patta" sound in a corner of the garden, nourishing beds of brilliant red and yellow roses. There were arches that seemed to float from the façade of the pink, stucco house. "Mansion" would be a more appropriate description. To the left, a long, flat-roofed garage squatted beneath some towering palms. Ivy grew on white-painted lattices up the side of the garage.

"Look through the window," Lina advised.

Cupping his hand above his eyes to ward off the glare, Ethan peered upon a dozen, shiny vehicles that were lined in a precise row. He saw a Maserati, Lamborghini Countash, Uno, Lancia, a red Ferrari, a white Ferrari, a chocolate brown snub-nosed X1-9, a dark blue Alfa Romeo Milano, and, oddly enough, a white Corvette.

Later, on the inside of the house, past the curving, teak, cantilevered staircase that hung unsupported from the wall, he could see room after room descending in a split-level pattern toward the part of the house that obviously faced the lake.

Eventually, he came to the last room before the lake, the dining room. Massive chestnut beams towered above a twenty-foot long table of darkened mahogany. Silver candelabra braced the table ends. Fresh flowers stood in a pot in its center. In the room's far corner, a stone fireplace, as tall as a man with a marble mantle supported by gargoyles, was flanked by silver-plated fire tools and an old broom made of twigs, the kind Ethan had seen all throughout Italy. It occurred to Ethan that people were always sweeping in Italy.

Lina opened the double glass and wood door outwards to the tiled veranda, a large portico with an iron railing draped in roses that looked to the water.

They smelled the sweet but acrid odor of leaves burning in the distance. From high to the north, the massive purple peaks of the Dolomites rose. To the east, the blue lake, deep and placid, sat with little sailboats rocking at anchor hundreds of feet below.

She took him to her room, a surprisingly modest, white-stuccoed but charming room with a view of the lake. The brass bed was huge and engulfed them both as they made sweet love on satin sheets. He ran two fingers over her olive skin. He began at the throat and ran them over the curve of one breast and her flat stomach, where he fingered her belly button. He made larger and larger circles against her skin with his hand. She made weeping sounds, as if she was out of breath, as he plunged into her. Both then succumbed to a deep, mid-afternoon sleep. It was only 6:00 AM in Colorado. Sublimely exhausted with jet lag, Lina, before closing her eyes, watched him sleep. For the very first time since they met, she was content; they were secure and happy together.

They slept through the evening and into the dark of the night. Awakened by a sound, Ethan leaned on one elbow. He studied a few twinkling lights far across the bay, which let a streak of moonlight stab its width. His watch, by the light of the moon, said 2:13 AM. Below, in some other room, he heard a woman's voice softly laughing. He could tell by its pitch that she was young. Lina lay sound asleep beside him, unmoving. He listened hard to hear another sound. But silence returned, as did sleep.

Benito Biancavello was finishing a piece of fruit in the shiny, modern kitchen. He grinned while a silver-haired, old woman, bent with osteoporosis, scolded him in a cackling, dry, irritated voice for getting mud on her floor. He had been out on the lawn, still wet with early morning dew, poking at the rose bushes. He was sorry for them because they were beginning to fade from the shortening days of sunlight.

When Ethan and Lina walked in, Ethan was certain the old crone in the kitchen could not have been the woman's voice he heard from the night before. He did not say anything except "Hello, Sir" when introduced to the squat, muscular man holding the half-eaten pear.

Benito switched the pear to his left hand, wiped his right hand on his pants, and extended it quizzically to Ethan. He did not smile and seemed to regard the introduction as nothing more than the ceremonial recognition of one more of Lina's temporary conquests.

"How are you, Papa?" said Lina

"You look lovely, child," said Benito, regarding his daughter. He finally took her hand and ushered her to the veranda. Lina signaled for Ethan to follow. Outside, he sat in a wrought iron chair, uncomfortably listening to the father and daughter chattering in Italian. Occasionally, Lina would nod and smile to Ethan, but Benito took no heed. She got up to fetch breakfast from the old woman in the kitchen. When Benito lit a stogie, the breeze caught the pungent smoke and sent it Ethan's way. With an automatic wave, Ethan wiped the air, causing Benito to smile.

"You do not like smoke?"

"Afraid not, honestly," said Ethan, half-smiling.

"I forgot. You are an athlete," said Benito, looking at the blue lake while letting the smoke curl up from his hand and around his arm.

Lina and Ethan spent the afternoon and the days that followed exploring the lake side. They lunched in small village cafés. On one warm day, while Lina drove, they sped around the lake in Benito's speedboat.

"It's too bad it is too late for water ski," she said as her eyes sparkled in the Mediterranean sun.

"Do you know how?" she asked.

"Yes, I know how," said Ethan laughing. He suddenly tickled her midriff, which made her laugh so hard she took her hands off the steering wheel. The boat made slow crazy turns in the lake while they kissed.

Chapter 15
The Renaissance

Lina took Ethan on day trips to the medieval cities of northern Italy. In Venice, during an unromantically cold, wet drizzle, they hired a guide who promised to trace the footsteps of Casanova.

Huddling for warmth in the Calle Mala Piero, an alley hardly five feet wide, they watched the sharp wind toss whitecaps upon the Grand Canal. They then entered a small dead-end courtyard, where the guide, a pretty, wide-eyed brunette, told them—in an upstairs English accent—about Angela, one of the many women who befriended the great lover.

"She, however, was a platonic friend," said the guide, an assertion that—considering Casanova's risk-filled lifestyle—raised Ethan's eyebrows.

Looking around at the water-locked landscape, it occurred to him why Casanova was the champion lady-killer of his time. Venice is not a city made for fast getaways.

Later, the gray, swollen sky cleared. Sitting at a sidewalk café in the Piazza San Marco, facing the afternoon sun and the tall brick Campanile a block away, Ethan refrained from complaining about the twenty-dollar bill for two six-ounce bottles of San Pelegrino mineral water and a small piece of apple pie he devoured in two gulps. He reflected it was hardly overcharge for the privilege of a front-row seat. From there, he and Lina could watch tourists, with cameras poised, throwing peanuts into the air. Flocks of pigeons flickered five feet above the pavement, a dizzying mix of feathers cast like a fishing net. Before them was a stage of brilliantly colored façades. Balconies and loggias were guarded by unearthly marble gods and saints, lions with wings, frescoes and mosaics styled by Moors, Byzantines and Romans, and inside the Basilica of St. Mark and the Palace of the Doges, gems and marble, copper statues turned black with age, bas relief portraits of Noah and the Flood, the Resurrection of Christ.

How many millions had met at this beautiful crossroads by the sea? How many besides popes, kings, and conquerors, like Napoleon or the Borgias? Ethan watched a boy about ten years old with an inexpensive camera. He was shouting in Italian, attempting in vain to get his younger brothers and sisters to stand still for their photo. They would form a staggering line to pose when one would lead a sudden breakaway, screaming with glee to chase another pigeon, which escaped from his or her grasp at the very last second.

Someday, probably like the millions more before them throughout the centuries, one or more of the children would count that day as among the freshest of their lives, a day spent chasing pigeons in St. Mark's Square.

In Milan, Lina and Ethan fed even more pigeons on the Piazza del Duomo in the shadow of the looming, buttressed cathedral. They strolled through the Galleria Vittorio Emanuele, the century-old precursor of the shopping mall with a huge iron lacework dome hanging above it.

In Florence, Ethan stopped and ate pasta in seemingly every other *ristorante*.

"Got to load up on the carbs!" he said before racing nonstop up the stone steps of the bell tower, where he waited for a panting Lina to crawl up to him. From up there, with a strong wind nipping, they looked down on all of Florence.

"You're gonna hate me for saying this," his eyes sweeping the several piazzas with their exquisite marble and bronze statuary, "but this town reminds me of Vermont."

Lina cast a furrowed brow.

"No, I mean, Florence impresses me as a somewhat hick town, a farming town. Except on every street corner, there's another work of art." He pointed. "There, a statue. There a fountain. The statues, the fountains, Christ, they're like cows in Vermont. They're all over the place."

Lina laughed. "In your country, you regard art as something special for rich people. They hang it in museums or in some rich man's private gallery. In America, you hide art. In Italy, it is everywhere. Michelangelo and Botticelli, they lived here. They were here! It is easy for Italians to pick up this artistic idea. Everything we touch, we try to create in the eye of the Creator. Even my father's cars! They take years to design. They must contain beauty and utility, form and lines."

That night in bed, she continued her linear appraisals on Ethan's physique and psyche. "For me, your body is art. You are my David," she purred, touching a shock above his ear.

"Cut it out!" He stared at her wide-eyed. They were lying in the raft-sized satiny bed, his forearm and elbow were propping his head.

"When I first saw you ski, you came downhill so fast in that skin tight suit, and you skidded to a stop. You sprayed snow all over us. Then you took off your helmet, and I saw that curly hair. I don't think I ever saw hair so beautiful in a man! And a body so beautiful. And I thought, 'That's my David. That's the David of my dreams!'"

He stared, as if waiting for her to continue. "And what?" he asked. "What about my slingshot?"

She laughed and punched him playfully on the chest.

"And that's the origin of the Ethan Atwood Fan Club?" he asked.

"You got it, kid!" she said, stabbing his thigh with her fingernail. She was trying to dent the muscle. "Your legs are like marble. You have no fat!"

Chapter 16
"Theesa Leetle Boards…"

Ethan entered a Ski Europa race to warm up for the serious competition that was to begin in a week at Val d'Isere. He finished tenth. A few days later, he joined and won another Super G race at Chamonix. He beat several other World Cup skiers, but not Franz Kluckner or Otto Gerbisch, the two in particular who were ranked above him and did not enter the race. Klecko finished fourth, and Rutledge finished eleventh. It was not a bad beginning to this season of promise.

Lina stayed behind at Lago di Garda to spend some time with her father. She would catch up when the team got to Wengen in Switzerland.

The race at Val d'Isere had to be canceled because of a lack of snow. The gloomy, brown mud that occupied the finish area pervaded the skiers' souls, distractions that Coach Quinn tried to offset by treating his team to a sextet of horror films on video. That afternoon, Klecko sneaked out to a toy store and bought a pair of plastic vampire teeth, which he flashed at the waitress serving them supper in the hotel restaurant. They laughed and drank white wine. Ethan fell asleep with a headache. The next day, the skiers could not wait to get out of France.

At Val Gardena in Selva, the Italian Dolomites, Ethan rented a private room in the Alpenroyal Hotel with a large window facing the mountains. He had asked specifically for a room with a decent view and cozy interior. There was a king-sized bed, plenty of closet space for Lina's vast supply of clothing. The walls held several pastel watercolors of Alpine villages with high-peaked gables and balconies draped in brilliantly colored flowers.

The evening's clock ticked slowly while he read ski magazines, including an article about himself. He winced when he read his own vapid quotes, "The team will go as far as the present talent takes it. I'll certainly give a hundred and ten percent." He vowed to obtain a fresh collection of generalities. Again, he read his watch, listening for footsteps.

Lina finally showed up late at night. Her face, which had been radiant of late, appeared drawn and fatigued. Her shoulders were slumped.

"Are you hungry?" he asked. "Let's go down and get something to eat."

"I'm too tired," she said, "Besides, you must ski tomorrow. You should sleep now."

"Is anything troubling you?" Ethan asked, bending to peer directly into her eyes, which she cast downward.

"I'm just tired," she said, slumping into his arms. Her head was on his chest. They did not make love.

He finished twenty-seventh in the next day's race, a mediocre start to the season. However, it was not an alarming one for a racer attempting a World Cup comeback after knee damage. He barely heard Emil Girard and Bill Quinn uttering, "Good job. Nice going, Ethan!" When the race day was over and he tiredly climbed the two flights of stairs to the hotel room, he threw his jacket at the chair, where it slid to the floor and slumped in the chair next to the big window. He did not make any attempts to pick up the jacket.

Lina, who was in the shower, had slept all day and had failed to get to the race.

"Where were you?" he yelled over his shoulder. "I was hoping to free ski a little with you after the race?"

She emerged from the bathroom, wrapping her wet, dark hair in the white, thick towel.

"I am sorry. I was so tired," she said, walking to the chair and bending behind him to stroke his chest. She kissed his ear while he gently pulled her arm. He turned her around where she slumped to his lap.

"There are just some great runs through the forest over there. We haven't skied together in months." Her robe fell open to her waist. He kissed her breasts. She turned and knelt. Her knees were on each side of his feet. As she bent toward him, he kissed her neck and shoulders, cupping her buttocks in the palms of his hands.

At dinner, Lina grew quiet again. She nodded subconsciously as he related the trouble he had with both the first and last gates of the racecourse. The dining room was quiet. An elderly couple sat in the corner. The old man had his hand upon the woman's hand and was staring intently at her. Outside, a feeble bell sound collided with a distant hum of a vacuum cleaner being pushed in the hall of the second floor. The waiter approached. He bent and lit a single candle in a star-shaped crystal holder.

Again, Ethan asked if she were feeling poorly. A thought flashed suddenly that she may be pregnant again, a conditioned fear that quickly subsided surprisingly. She took the pill regularly now, but, even if she would become pregnant, it would be different now.

"I had an argument with my father is all," she said finally as they left the hotel dining room and strolled over to the little mountain railway station, where skiers caught the train from the center of town each morning. Ethan wiped fresh powder from the red wooden slats of a wrought iron bench, and they sat down. A bell in a nearby tower pronounced seven o'clock. Above, directly over the Eiger, the sliver of a new moon did not cast any light.

"It is nothing," she said.

"The hell it's not nothing. Come and tell old Father Atwood. C'mon, confess. Say 'Bless me father…'." He put his arm around her.

She smiled. "I can't. It is a father and daughter thing."

She shrugged, finally inventing a story about getting up the nerve to criticize her father for his continuing wayward habits of the flesh. With his preoccupation with self, his work, and his women, he was repeatedly cold to her and her friends, including Ethan. He was also short of rudeness to Ethan, which was evident to her.

"He was not nice to you!"

"Ah, I didn't notice."

"You did, you did! Stop pretending that things don't bother you!" said Lina, her voice rising. "You put up a shield, a wall. When something bothers you, it is not right! He hurt you. My father hurt you. I could tell."

Ethan tried projecting his nonchalance, but she would have none of it. The recent argument between Lina and her father was genuine. It was heated and volatile, especially on her part. Ethan was part of the argument, the major part, but she hid the truth from him.

She had yelled to her father, "I'm not a child anymore. Neither is Ethan!"

"You are a child. You're both children!" Benito had said with a calm assurance that made his daughter hate his superiority. He was sitting on a steel garden chair, leaning back and puffing a stogie. The apparent ease underscored the contempt held for his daughter's latest dalliance.

"This time a ski-racer. What's it to be next, a high-wire circus performer?"

Lina's knuckles went white as she grasped the iron railing against which she had been leaning in frustration and anger.

"He has no occupation, no training for the real world, this Ethan?" Benito asked.

"He's a skier, Papa, a professional racer. That is his job. That is how he makes his living," she said bitterly with deliberate coldness in her voice. "He makes a good living, he is one of the best. The car he drives," she said, "courtesy of the sponsor. They give him that car because he is a good professional. That's how he earns his living. He does well. He is a champion."

"You wait!" she screamed. "What if he wins the Olympics? The whole world will know who he is, better than you." She spat the words bitterly.

"So, he is no better than a movie star!" said her father with an insulting grin on his face. "What is he? What are they? They are nothing, froth. Froth is what they are! They have nothing in here," he said pounding his chest, "or in here." He touched his head.

She was shouting over his words now. "His clothes! Courtesy of the sponsor. Prize money, courtesy of the sponsor."

Later, on the train from Milan, she cursed her loss of control, her inability to reason with the old bastard, and her dumb words. "He is an artist, like you think you are, you who draw lines on paper."

"Art? You call what he does art? He skis!" He deliberately broke into English, mockingly, "He puts onna theesa leetle boards, and he wobbles downa hill lika this!" he said, holding his hands as in prayer, moving them side to side in slalom fashion. "Where did he go to university, this Ethan? I want to know!"

"He doesn't need to!" she yelled, running from the veranda. Lina stormed from the room, slamming the door behind her. She raced upstairs and began throwing her clothes into the suitcase on her bed. She left the house without saying good-bye.

She drove to Milan and boarded the first of three trains that would take her to the Dolomites. On each segment of the trip, she replayed her conversation, framing arguments that would make sense to anyone except her stubborn father, who would never ever see his daughter as a woman. He would only see her as a transparent, little girl who skipped from one inconsequential relationship to another.

Benito contented himself with the thought that he had tried as a father to interest his daughter in learning. He sent her to art school in Bergamo and then paid for her to take design classes in Milan. The fact that she dropped out both times, in spite of an initial zeal that showed some talent in fashion design, showed that none of that was his fault. She knows how to buy clothes and wear them. Not design them, not sell them. Wearing them is all she is good for. It was all she knew.

In Kitzbuehel, the mail from home finally caught up with the ski team. Joe Parkinson, who was handing media relations for the team, handed Ethan a pile of letters and magazines that were bound by a heavy rubber band. There was a letter from his mother. There was one from the ski team describing a ridiculously expensive insurance program for the skier to purchase if he or she ever left the team. Another letter invited him to appear in a celebrity race at Aspen in the spring. There were several skiing magazines and the most recent edition of *Ski Racing*. There was one, stubby envelope that was cream-colored and made of expensive heavy-stock paper. It had been addressed to Ethan

Atwood and forwarded from the U.S. Ski Team headquarters in Park City.

It took only seconds for Ethan to guess the envelope's contents, yet he opened it with a tingling mix of fear and dread.

Doctor and Mrs. Thomas Queensbury
request the honor of your presence
at the marriage of their daughter
Mary Ann Elizabeth to Donald James Naples
Saturday, the twelfth of November at twelve o'clock
St. Margaret's Church Montpelier, Vermont
and afterward at the reception
Green Mountain Country Club.
R.S.V.P.

Chapter 17
Donny the Rock

Emma Queensbury twisted the dish towel in her fingers. With a similar knotted concern on her face, she said to Mary Ann, "I don't know why you're inviting him, dear. He can't come anyway."

She paused to lift a stack of lunchtime plates from the dishwasher and place them in the cupboard above the butcher-block table. "Or is that why you're doing it? The fact that he can't be here?" She let the questions escape with as much softness as possible, with kindness, concern, and motherly love in her voice.

Outside, rain was falling heavily upon the single, old homes that guarded the long, steep road from the town proper uphill to the city park, a place where Mary Ann had learned to ride a two-wheeler, ski, and play tennis as well as gather leaves and walnuts in the fall.

Mary Ann sighed, sensing the direction the conversation was taking. It was one of many tiresome lectures her mother would launch lately on the Ethan theme. What would her mother know about love or the problems of love? She married the only man she ever dated, one who was loyal, never cheated, worked hard, and never failed to call when he would be late for dinner. Mary Ann pulled on her jacket and began zipping it up the front. Her thumb and forefinger tightly pinched the zipper.

"Mother, he has to know. He has a right to know I'm getting married, and he has a right to hear it from me and not from anyone else."

When Emma began gently protesting, Mary Ann spoke louder. She grabbed a container of yogurt from her mother's hand. She yanked open the refrigerator door and stuffed it inside. She closed the door with enough controlled force to relay her anger and frustration.

"Do you think I want to forget that Ethan ever existed? I know that's what you're trying to make me do. And mother..." her voice softened, "I appreciate what you're doing, but how can I convince you that it's wrong to pretend there was no Ethan in my life?"

Emma opened her mouth to speak, but Mary Ann charged on. "He was there. He existed. I loved him," she said, slowly and carefully measuring each small sentence. "I'm trying now not to love him. It isn't fair to Donny. But do you think it's going to help Donny and me by suppressing everything and pretending Ethan was never there?"

Emma twisted the towel and reached out. "I'm only trying to help."

"Help! Yes, help! I know, mother. I know your intentions. You say help and..." She fought to hold down the volatility that was building up, "I see interference!"

"I'm not interfere..."

"Mother, goddamn it, you are! Every time you..." The words were hammer thuds. "Shit, I can't even think anymore!"

As her mother involuntarily recoiled, Mary Ann stiffened and continued, "Every time you bring it up, your goddamned helpfulness, mother, your so-called understanding, I take another step back. I've been trying to put it all aside. I have to! I'm getting married. But the reality of it is that he happened. Ethan was real! He was alive! He happened! He was in my life!"

She clutched at words the way a drowning victim futilely grabs a floating leaf. She attempted calmness.

"He exists," Mary Ann continued, clearing her throat, "and he's still my friend. I'm not going to throw that friendship away." Stopping, unable to speak another word, she turned and left the kitchen.

Emma winced as she heard the back door slam and then the car door. She watched out the window. A stream of water from the mudroom roof drummed loudly on the metal lid of a trash can against the house. She gazed sadly through the rain as Mary Ann, only a shadowy form in the car, dropped her forehead to the steering wheel. She remained fixed that way for a couple of minutes, twice as long as Emma watched. Mary Ann then raised her head, turned on the motor, and slowly backed the car out of the driveway.

Mary Ann had been working full-time since her graduation from college that spring in the marketing department at Bruce White's Maple Glen Resort. Bruce had hired her personally. He had known her since she was a child and student at Spring Mountain Academy. He noticed her intelligence and direct, but not pushy, manner. He saw her ability to articulate as well as that wide, easy smile with matching good humor.

"She's customer-friendly," said Bruce, who liked to sprinkle his speech with marketing bits. Mary Ann first came to Bruce's attention years ago through the parents of a little girl who had become stranded on a black diamond trail way above her ability. The child could not ski down and was terrified.

Skiing with other Spring Mountain students, Mary Ann dropped out of the racing lesson to approach the child, who was sitting in the snow halfway down the notoriously steep, mogul-filled Thunder Roll trail.

"What are you doing here?" Mary Ann asked.

"I can't get down," the girl, who was about nine years old, said. "I took the wrong turn and ended up here. I don't know how else to get down."

"Look, I'll help you," she said, getting the girl to her feet. She made her wedge her skis, and then Mary Ann, skiing backwards, stood downhill of the frightened child. Slowly and carefully, she guided the youngster to the bottom of the hill.

The letter the girl's grateful parents wrote to Bruce White told about "a girl named Mary Ann who was wearing a Spring Mountain jacket who took the time to help our daughter down the mountain. We just want you to know how grateful we are to her and hope she will be acknowledged for her kindness."

Bruce trotted over to the academy the next week and asked the director to place copies of the letter on the school's bulletin boards, which academy officials were only too happy to do, especially for the opportunity to thwart an ongoing criticism by many townsfolk about some of the snotty attitudes of the rich kids up on the hill. Mary Ann was a refreshing antithesis to that reputation. She was a giver and a doer, certainly not a taker.

After hiring her, Bruce did not hesitate to put her out front for the resort, making her visible to the people in the community, the business leaders, and especially the temperamental environmentalists with whom he was doing polite, but potentially bloody, battle.

Most of Bruce's encounters with the Keep-It-Green Society faltered because of his stubborn incapability to present an argument in any view except his own. There was no meeting on a common ground for Bruce. There was no seeing things in a different view. His father had been an Army colonel who had taught philosophy most of his life at the Army's Military Academy at West Point. Bruce grew up learning dictums that would stay with him the rest of his life. He was proper and intelligent with a basic mind-set of completing tasks in a geometrical fashion. That is, he took the shortest distance between two points. "Straight thinking, straight talk, and straight action." He mistrusted people who wavered. He disliked even more those souls with a temperament and way of thinking that were as resolute as his own, but who held an opposite view.

Just the sight of major antagonist Emily Davenport sent icy fingers up his spine. A retired elementary school teacher, Emily had been an unrestrained tree hugger who tried teaching students in her classes that unregulated businesses like ski resorts would destroy the earth. Bruce regarded her as the "wicked witch of the East, the most dangerous woman in America."

"Did you ever get a good look at her? She looks just like what she is—long, old nose, pointy chin to match her pointy head, tiny little spectacles over her tiny-ass squinty eyes."

So, on the other hand, Mary Ann was a quiet brook to Bruce's rushing storms. She was widely known and well-liked, even by Emily Davenport and the Keep-It-Green Society, who monitored Bruce White's and Maple Glen's every move to expand the ski resort's reaches into the surrounding woods and countryside.

Mary Ann hiked the fragile mountaintops and understood the delicacy of plant life in those altitudes. She swam and fished the rivers and lakes. She biked the mountain trails, and she was familiar with the need to keep up oxygen levels in the river. She recognized erosion problems and the need to preserve animal habitat.

"She's at least as knowledgeable as the so-called experts in the so-called environmental movement," Bruce said at the board meeting when he promoted her as "my point man...woman" in the state capitol at Montpelier. She would work with the industry lobbyists in both protecting and advancing Maple Glen's interests.

She took up the position eagerly. She wanted to stay in skiing, but she definitely knew her competitive skiing days were at an end. The University of Vermont ski team dominated the eastern college circuit and often won national titles. Though Mary Ann had done well as a member of the slalom team, her star would not rise any further. She was smart enough and mature enough to realize it, and she had prepared well for the future by taking several courses in environmental studies and ski industry management.

Currently, Maple Glen was engaged in a financial and permit-laden effort to build a 3,000-foot lift up the northeastern face of Spring Mountain to open up some exciting new black diamond terrain. Years before, skiers like Ethan, through their off-piste explorations, convinced Bruce that the steep woods, with its severe head walls and drop-offs, had exciting potential.

"How do we present this?" Bruce said to Mary Ann one afternoon as they bounced uphill in a pickup to join surveyors already at work on the mountain. "The first reaction will be that we're destroying the habitat of the shrunken skink or something else. Do you know what these people, the environmentalists, do to me? They give me nightmares. I have a world-class ulcer. The other night I dreamed I was arrested for sneaking up on a tree and wringing the neck of a baby owl. They took me in handcuffs to the courthouse."

Mary Ann laughed, and asked, "Did you ever think about buying an ice cream store or doing something safe?"

"All right, now how would you handle this?" Bruce asked.

"Meet them halfway," said Mary Ann. "Meet them more than halfway. Look, did you know I was a member of the Keep-It-Green Society?"

Bruce had stopped the truck at the end of the work trail. From here, they would hoof it uphill. Bruce looked surprised.

"Well, I am. I'm an environmentalist, too. I love the environment. We all do in different degrees. Everybody who breathes is an environmentalist. And I love to ski in a safe, clean environment, too. I love these mountains enough that I wouldn't think of causing them or what's in them irreparable harm through my skiing. That's how you have to present it, and you do it by working with the environmental people, not against them. What will work for both of us? What works best for the community and the future?"

"That I understand," said Bruce. "I also know the pitfalls and the contradictions. The bear habitat, for instance. We're limited in how, where, and when we can put that lift in up there. We can take up no more than fifty feet wide to cut the lift line. We can cut down only so many beech trees in order to protect the bear corridor. Thirty-seven trees, thirty-seven beech trees exactly. That I can understand, and that I can accept. But you know what drives me crazy?"

"What?" said Mary Ann.

"We're not allowed to work putting that lift up in December. We have to stop work for a month. The state says so. Do you know why?"

For the moment puzzled, Mary Ann said, "No."

"Because it's bear-hunting season. We're not allowed to build the lift during bear hunting season so the bear hunters can go up there and kill the god-damned bears we're sworn to protect. Now, answer that one for me!"

"It's Vermont!" Mary Ann said, laughing. You've got two power groups making the rules, the environmentalists and the hunters."

Driving home that afternoon, she dwelt on the conversation and told herself it was not enough to just shrug off a problem with a "that's the way it is" explanation. She thought that, what is true is that we were all part of the mix—bears, people, and trees. None of those groups can survive without the strength of the others. We were on top because we have the brains, and the only way we can stay on top is to use them. If all the trees go, the bears go. Eventually, so will we. Only humans can protect all the species.

That the community responded well to Mary Ann was not altogether due to her popularity nor brilliance in front of a crowd. Because of the broken love affair with Ethan, she was an icon of sympathy, the injured victim, and the betrayed one whose betrothed ran off with a dark-eyed Italian bombshell.

Her loss was also Ethan's. However, what she gained in sympathy, Ethan lost, at least among the majority of neighbors, skiers, and friends who knew nothing of the behind-the-scenes details of his entrapment. In the valley, prejudices were not always in the forefront, but to say that Ethan's reputation suffered is an understatement. The tiny, tightly knit villages that comprised the valley were mostly an understanding, forgiving, liberal community where class and economic distinctions were rarely measured. Abner Dean, the wealthiest man in the valley, whose family made a fortune dealing in lumber, dressed about as nondescriptly as did old Ed Phoebe, the scruffy house painter. Side by side, at least from a distance, one could never tell who the millionaire was.

Neighbor met neighbor at the post office, the general store, and the churches. The man who made six dollars an hour at the Dean clapboard mill was just as welcome at the church's chicken supper in the fall as the ones who lived in expensive homes on the mountain and who owned private planes that were used to commute to their offices in Boston, New York, and Montreal.

When Ethan went away with Lina, friends who had known both him and Mary Ann since childhood were dumbfounded. The marriage had been predictable.

For the sake of Ethan's grandparents and parents, who still had a presence in the valley, feelings were at least publicly ameliorated.

"I heard it wasn't Ethan's fault."

"That Italian girl came after him. He didn't go after her."

"Ethan never could turn anybody down."

"But for Mary Ann's sake, you'd think he would have...I feel sorry for both of them, Mary Ann and Ethan"

"Yes, but especially Mary Ann."

There were questions rolled over day after day by Big Ethan and Rose Delahanty and Ethan's parents.

"I don't know what happened," said Rose to her best friend, Jean Stallings, at the Valley Market one day. "I know he got the girl pregnant. But what led up to it, I just don't know. I just think there must be so many distractions over there in Europe."

Mary Ann, by plunging her energies deeply into her work, managed to keep the aftershock of her disastrous love affair at bay. It was always there, however. It was like trying to push a beach ball under water. The minute she let go, the more severely the fearful truth of what happened to her and Ethan would rocket to the surface.

She gave Donny Naples the freedom to keep her distracted, though telling herself she could not begin to abuse his friendship. She knew he wanted her and her feelings for another man would never be the same as the ones she had for Ethan, but she nevertheless needed someone badly.

Donny had done what Ethan had asked him to do that worrisome day. "You've got to convince Mary Ann it wasn't my fault."

Donny told Mary Ann the truth, but he excluded the details that Ethan had asked him to do. Donny was relieved he would not be forced to explain how a tiny, Italian girl could rape a grown, strong man, bad knee or good knee. Mary Ann never learned what took place that night in the hospital in Brescia. All Lina's letter of confession told her was that the seduction was all on her part and that "Ethan was a victim of my selfish actions."

The facts, even if disclosed in full, would not have mattered to Mary Ann. Her life had taken its new turn during the seconds after she heard Ethan had impregnated another woman.

It was Donny who nursed Mary Ann from her depression. Her parents, listening and consoling, also helped. However, it was from the perspective of a parent assisting a child. Donny, on the other hand, reminded Mary Ann the world was not all that bad. There were other real people, genuine people, existing in it, and all of them were in need of something. He reminded her she was young, healthy, smart, and vibrant with the best of her years ahead of her.

He took her to the movies, took her bowling, bought her drinks, and made her laugh. He did not kiss her once in the months they dated.

On the first day of June, the first really warm day after the doldrums of mud season, they drove out to the islands of Lake Champlain and took the ferry to New York state for a day in the Adirondacks. The sky was a cobalt blue, and insects were just beginning to buzz in the fields and woods. On the ferry ride back, Mary Ann's mood changed with the weather. As clouds boiled in from the west, the wind kicked the waves of the lake ferociously. Mary Ann insisted on stopping outside a chapel on the island.

"To pray?" joked Donny.

"No, to sightsee." she said with feigned rancor.

Once inside, she did pray and lit some candles. When they left, she grew even more somber, refusing to talk on the trip home.

Donny gripped the steering wheel, peering at the wet highway through the windshield wipes.

"Look, Mary Ann, I've been your friend for a long time. You know, you can do just about anything to me that you want. I really wouldn't mind because you're not the kind of person who would deliberately hurt anyone or cause them any pain or anything." He paused. "But lately..."

She looked at him.

He kept his eyes straight ahead on the road, regretting what he was saying. "You get moody, and I hate to see you moody. I'm here for you because I want to be, because I think you need somebody and I want to help. But I have feelings too. And lately sometimes, you get so, so damn glum." He turned to her and put his hand on her knee. He patted it, and, just as quickly, he withdrew it. "What the hell, I'm sorry. I just want you to know I'm fond of you."

That was all the courage he had for the moment. Mary Ann stared at Donny for several seconds. Her face softened to a sweet, sad smile.

"You're a good guy," she said as her feelings lifted. "C'mon, let's stop and eat. I'm hungry, and I'm buying."

The following month, Donny's father, who was in his mid-sixties, suffered a heart attack. He recovered as a much wiser man who admitted the next one would kill him if he did not slow down in his attempts to keep his business, the Bader & Naples Granite Works, from losing money.

Donny was eager and willing to step up and take over the business that had been in his family exclusively since his grandfather had bought out the major portion of shares owed by his long-deceased partner, Thomas Bader, in the 1920s.

"I've been at this since after World War II," said Donny's father. "Now, it's your turn."

As a teen, Donny had worked summers in the granite sheds by cutting and polishing stone, putting muscles on his short but rugged frame. He knew enough about the hands-on part of the business to earn the respect of the tough, rough-handed workers at his side. He had worked in the 500-foot deep quarries and once watched a sixty-ton slab of stone slip from the grasp of a derrick and fall upon a worker, whose body was a mash of red-soiled clothing with barely an outline of a human form when they got the stone off him.

He had grown up in an industry that, for decades, turned profits generally because people died and deserved tombstones. However, it was a business that had slipped badly over the past several years as it lost to imaginative competitors who broadened their markets beyond the cemeteries and skyscrapers.

"We've got to make smaller, polished wares," said Donny at his first board meeting. "Forget about tombstones and building blocks. Architects want lighter, stronger materials for their buildings. We need to get small if we're to survive. Even though we've got enough stone here to last 4,500 years, we've gotta produce smaller ornamental stuff—business signs, garden furniture, and desk sets—all made of granite."

Some of the older board members joked about his goals, calling them "granite tinker toys."

However, none could doubt the young, new executive had vision. His first deal as head of the firm was made through Paul Atwood Sr. He called him in Albany and obtained contacts within the corporations that were leasing space in the industrial parks that

Atwood had designed. Donny went to work selling granite signs to be implanted on lawns.

He then hired a marketing firm to make videos and brochures tracing the history of stone as building blocks, from the building of the pyramids to the making of Manhattan skyscrapers in the twentieth century. He hired a design studio to conceive products to be used in the home, like picture frames, statuettes, bookends, and smaller items that might be mass-produced. He created a much greater profit return on a single slab of granite than would come from a couple of markers for the dead. A major effort went into fitting large blocks of natural-looking granite to be planted on hillsides and made into cascading pools of water. In the first year of that venture, he had sold the idea and the product to a new resort in the Caribbean.

Donny's energies conversely created an immediate loss for his company because of increased costs of advertising, design, and development. However, over the months ahead, things began turning around, at least enough to get him recognized in the local business community as an up-and-coming innovator.

"You're as steady as a rock," said Mary Ann, leaning her head on Donny's shoulder in the front seat of his new Nissan 300ZX one summer night.

"Thanks a lot," he mocked. "A rock? A rock? You're comparing me to a piece of granite!" he yelled teasingly.

"No, I don't mean you're hard. You're really soft and understanding. I can't tell you how much you've meant to me these past months. What I mean is that you're durable. Always there."

Donny squeezed her hand affectionately. His steadfastness to Mary Ann was slow, methodical, and as precisely calculated as one of his business deals. He wanted her badly, but he would win her in terms of being needed, not through the false passion of love on the rebound. He knew she could never love him completely, but, by God, he would make sure she needed him and he would always be there for her.

When he proposed to her three months later, she accepted without hesitation. Their honeymoon night at a beachfront villa on Virgin Gorda was the first time they made love.

Chapter 18
Nightlife

Since joining the World Cup circuit three years before, Ethan had never had great difficulty maintaining the comfortable anonymity of his shy youth. He watched when greater known skiers were mobbed by fans. He studied how the skiers held themselves—if they smiled and how long it took to write an autograph. He otherwise enjoyed the rewards of mediocrity.

That had changed since Kitzbuehel the year before and, prior to that, the publicity he received due to his wounded thumb.

Now, with fame achieved, sometimes he—and Lina as well— were set upon by Italians, French, Germans, and vacationing Americans. Even sportswriters from the States began showing up. Favorable reports were printed about the chances of the US Ski Team to climb in the world standings once Ethan Atwood regained his top form.

"He's about eighty percent," said Bill Quinn in an interview with *Ski Racing.* "We're being patient, and so is Ethan. He's not the kind of racer who will stay put just being an also-ran."

Klecko unconsciously dropped his underwear to the floor. Ethan bent and picked it up with the tips of a thumb and forefinger. His face bore a sign of mock disgust.

"This goes in the laundry bag or back in your suitcase, not on the floor," he said matter of factly.

"Well, look who's gone domestic on us?" smirked Klecko, swiftly snatching the underwear from Ethan's outstretched hand. "Here's the guy who wore socks that smelled like a gorilla's armpit."

"I appreciate finer things in life now," said Ethan. "I've been with women."

"Well, your sure have!" answered Klecko, exhaling with a sudden awe. He was impressed with the worldly growth of the one-time bumpkin from Vermont. "And, by the way, where's the latest? You never did fully explain why you're bunkin' with me again."

"Well, it's only for a while," answered Ethan, sitting down on the side of the bed. "Lina's gone back to school, design school in Milan. She'll team up with me again on weekends, race weekends anyway."

"Is this?" asked Klecko, not quite sure how to ask if Lina's absence was due to another romantic upheaval. He waggled his hand above the floor, as if to indicate uncertainty as to whether the situation could be this way or that way.

"No, well, she says she thinks she's distracting me." Ethan smiled and snorted. "Thinks my skiing's not so sharp because she's with me. At least that's what she says."

"Well, I must admit she sure as hell would distract me!" said Klecko. "But not on race day."

Since the day Ethan reported Lina's hot-blooded, sexual introduction to him in the hospital that night, Klecko had difficulty looking at Lina without a misty, weak-kneed feeling of lust, a distraction not encouraged by Lina and one that would go no further so far as Klecko was concerned.

The social rules predicated, for the sake of team unity, you do not hit on a teammate's woman. Klecko liked Lina, but he admired his friend Ethan much more. As teammate-roommate, he felt that part of his responsibility was to provide the soundest advice his many years on the World Cup circuit could offer, right or wrong notwithstanding. The non-racing life of the ski teams generally adhered to narrow simplistic confines of meals, sleep, and relentlessly difficult travel in a bouncing van. Whatever love life occurred in the meanwhile was to be treasured.

A teammate with a wife or regular girlfriend waiting at night and chauffeuring him between cities was a covetous anomaly. Lina's sudden disappearance may have been a source of curiosity, but questions were not necessarily raised in Ethan's presence.

"Do you think she's what's affecting his skiing?" asked Mack Schultz, who had been beating Ethan's times in trial runs lately, despite never finishing above the middle of the competition himself in a single race.

"No, no! No way!" responded Klecko, who disliked theories of mental lapses affecting the abilities of athletes. "If you've got what it takes physically and you know what you're doin' mentally, you should be able to win a race on the day of your mother's funeral. The only thing wrong with Ethan's racing is a bum knee that takes time to heal. That's all. Ethan will be back."

The next weekend, the American skiers tore up Crans-Montana's Piste Nationale downhill course. They did not win, but they put Ethan on the podium in third place behind rivals Gerbisch and Kluckner. The three of them spritzed each other with champagne. As Ethan turned the bottle toward the press photographers in front of them, he felt the kind of elation that can only come with winning.

"I'm back," he thought.

With Klecko and Rutledge finishing seventh and eighth respectively, the team appeared solidified, on its way to a good season.

"See, you don't need me. I guess I'll have to stay away from you forever if you are to race well," said Lina teasingly as she pressed closely to Ethan in the smoky, dark hallway outside the bar of the La Grange. A discordant rock band's chaotic sound was blasting through the wall of the barroom, where dancers were literally elbowing each other from the floor. The dance floor was too confined for that many whirling bodies. When Ethan was suddenly hipped out of the way by a short-haired blonde, he pretended to lose balance completely. He grabbed Lina, with whom he was dancing, and fell through the doorway. He regained equilibrium in the hall.

The hall, with its dull, beige wallpaper, was narrow and dark. A single bulb in a dirty white globe overhead provided light. She pushed him up against the wall and began kissing and teasing. Both were feeling lazily high, their bodies swaying in the odor of spilled beer and cigarette smoke.

"You see what happens to you the minute I let you out of my sight," Lina said, touching Ethan's lower lip with a forefinger. "You win a race. You don't need me. We are finished. I am so sad. I will have to find another lover. I think he will be a fat, rich German this time."

Ethan could not help laughing. "You do, and I'll find me a nice, fat German as well, a busty Wagnerian blonde with pigtails. One of those women who wears an iron brassiere. That's what I need. I need some big, muscled woman to wrestle with. I'm gonna give up skinny, little, Dago girls."

"I am not Dago!"

"You are!"

"I am not Dago. I am Florentine." She turned her head to profile her noble, little nose. "And I have to pee. You wait for me here while I pee!"

She tripped down the narrow, dark corridor. She lost her balance once and fell to the wall, where she let her shoulder bang her upright again. She then bounced off the opposite wall and disappeared into the bathroom, whose door was on a heavy spring, slamming her small but stocky body nearly into the toilet.

Almost immediately, two more bodies came sailing out from the dance floor. They were laughing so hard they could hardly stand. One was the same blonde who had bumped him. The other was a tall, thin Italian boy in a woolen turtleneck sweater. His sleek, black hair was pulled back, Valentino style, from his forehead. Together, they looked at Ethan and laughed.

"You are Ethan Atwood," said the blonde, thrusting her bejeweled arms from the sleeves of her floor-length fur coat and wrapping them around Ethan's shoulders. She planted a wet kiss on his lips before he could move.

No longer incredulous at the impulsiveness of European women, Ethan grabbed the blonde's wrists, squeezed them firmly but gently, and held them away from him.

"Yes, I am!" he smiled. "And what is your name?"

"My name is Lolita!"

"Probably not," Ethan said. He turned to the young man. "And what is your name?"

"Paulo," the boy said. He looked sadly at the blonde and then at Ethan.

"Well, for God's sake, what a small world. That's my dad's name, Paulo. Well, Paulo, will you take Lolita here and take her outside for some fresh air?" he asked, depositing the girl onto Paulo's chest. He pushed them both toward the outside door.

"And Lolita, you stay with good, old Paulo for the rest of the night because he's a nice, young man. You stay with who brung you. Okay?"

Lolita yelled back over her shoulder, "You are nice, too, my Ethan!"

Together, she and Paulo headed out into the frosty air. Ethan caught a glimpse of heavy flakes drifting down beneath the street lamp just as Lina emerged from the restroom.

"C'mon, Florentine! Let's go home."

He awoke the next morning with a head full of oyster shells. Their sharp edges stabbed his inner eyes and sinuses, which were also swollen and clogged. He needed cold, fresh air.

Carefully, he sat up on the side of the bed and repositioned the heavy quilt over Lina until just the very top of her head and the dark, bright black of her hair was visible. She slept deeply.

Outside, the entire sweep of the Rhone Valley was awash in sunshine. A briskness to the air that was so sharp that it was like breathing pepper. He took careful, lung-filling gulps, deeply inhaling as he walked past the tidy boutiques and little hotels up toward the train station, whose peaked, Tyrolean roof still held big globs of freshly fallen snow. Dressed in only a sweat suit, he jogged to keep warm, pulling the knit cap down over his ears. The snowy street curved past little old stuccoed homes with carved wooden balconies, fashioned by people who, over the centuries, passed time by making clocks and watches and making their surroundings snug and pretty against the grandeur of the mountainous backdrop.

He recalled the blonde and the boy with slick hair and wondered where they were now, what they were doing, and what the blonde looked and felt like without her furs and jewels. Like his skiing, his perspective of life was advancing now at a faster pace, swift and anxious. Around him in these castles washed in snow and sun were mostly happy people. They were content if even for only a brief holiday. They were primed for fun, breathing air that made them dizzy. They loved life and being loved. Ethan could be one of them, capable of attracting good-looking women, probably as many as he wanted or needed.

All his life, he had never dated more than one girl at a time and was steadfastly loyal to each. Not that he would cheat now on Lina. Just the idea that a rendezvous with a strange woman was possible gave him fuel, the kind of oiling his ego badly needed.

He laughed silently at the recalling of the junior prom dance, long ago in the Starlight Casino Café on Mallets Bay. Donny Naples had to coax Ethan into the blind date. He pleaded, cajoled, and all but forced him to call Angela Simone, a busty girl from Montpelier, whom Donny ended up calling himself and making the arrangements. Donny had asked Mary Ann to go to the dance with him, and he was nearly paralyzed with fear because he adored Mary Ann and held her high on an adolescent pedestal. He needed company, and Ethan, who was awkward enough that he would never show up Donny, fit the bill.

The dance went fairly well and was without serious incident. Ethan had even kissed Angela on the cheek when he walked her to her door after taking her home. He took her to the movies twice after that. The second time, he dredged up the nerve to place his arm around her shoulder. He waited until a particularly comic part when she began laughing and then sneakily poked an inquisitive finger into the hole of her sleeveless blouse. His stomach heaved when his fingers felt the filled-out part of her upper breast.

She stopped laughing and leaned to Ethan. She whispered with her jaw tight and teeth clenched, "Move your hand, or I'm going to bite off your goddamned finger!"

Jolted upright and flushed with guilt, he took her home and never called again. He recognized the vast gap between her worldly society and his, the big hick from rural Lowgate Springs who had light years of growing up to do.

As he ran uphill, breathing harder, he wondered what Angela would be doing now, Nursing quadruplets? He then thought about Mary Ann and how she looked at the prom on Donny's arm. She wore a strapless, pale orange evening gown. With her braces and glasses gone, which were replaced by contact lenses, she had begun to fill out as a woman instead of a stringy, teenage girl. Her bosom was also high. He thought her legs were brown and firm. Breathing steadily now with the uphill climb, his memory recollected a sociological dilemma posed by a professor at the academy who had been lecturing about the relativity of goals.

"Would you prefer her to be with you and love him, or would you prefer her to be with him and love you? Think about it. It's your dilemma for today. Most of you will face it sometime in your life, probably the next few years. It is not uncommon."

How quickly the unanswered puzzle had swept him up and tossed him aside in a heap of remorse and self-pity. It left a scar as hard and ugly as the one that crossed his left knee, creating the dull little ache as he ran.

"Mary Ann is with him and loves...I am with Lina and love..."

It was a test. That was all it was, one that hardens and matures as it speeds one along toward manhood. Thank God he had Lina. Despite the irony, she, the protagonist, now belonged to him.

"I won't let her go," he told himself."

Part II
Chapter 1
A Year Later

The Eiger, in southern Switzerland, just south of Interlaken in the Jungfrau region, is one of the earth's most difficult mountains to climb, particularly up its north, mostly vertical, face. Sheathed almost always in ice, the climber digs toehold steps uphill, often in inches, against temperatures that seldom rise above zero degrees Fahrenheit. Abetted by a nearly constant wind, the real effect of the cold can be minus thirty degrees.

Climbers often spend three days going up the 13,025-foot mountain, clinging like lizards to the ice, crampons on both feet and an ice axe in each hand. They move to stay warm. The first time men went up the north face of the Eiger was in 1938. It took four days, and Adolph Hitler awarded the climbers who performed the feat gold medals of the Berlin Olympiad. In bad snowstorms, some climbers get pinned for a couple of days in exactly the same spot, unable to move up or down as they contemplated the wall of ice on one side and eternal infinity on the other.

"What is he doing now?" asked Lina, toweling her hair and walking toward the big window facing the mountain.

"He's standing still," said Ethan. His left eye was shut, and his right eye was squinting through the long, telescopic lens aimed like a rifle at the tiny ant like figure that seemed tacked to the icebound granite a half-mile up Eiger.

He and Lina had come south after the doctors had canceled Ethan out of the race at Wengen. His left knee was bloated and swollen. Ethan, sullen and angry, protested.

"You need time to let the swelling come down," the doctor had said.

"I have to race!"

"You have to rest!" interrupted Quinn testily, who demanded that Ethan cancel out of the race and take some time off.

Ethan and Lina had gotten to the town of Kleine Scheidegg by way of the Jungrau Railway to Junfraujoch, the highest rail station in all of Europe. From the hotel, they could see the Eiger and the little dot groping its way up.

"Christ," Ethan said, "I feel as though I'm up there with him." He had stopped looking at the dot and turned to face Lina, who was pulling on a pair of jeans while balancing on one foot.

"I'm like him."

"Like who?"

"The mountain climber, that guy up there. He's been in that spot for twenty minutes, not able to move."

Outside the hotel, the wind was whipping the Swiss flag atop a nearby bell tower. On the mountain, the gusts would be stronger.

"He keeps stopping and then going up a little. It's so funny. Here, I make my living speeding downhill, and he does his thing going up, step by step, slowly, like molasses."

"You are faster," she said, reaching up to massage his shoulders.

"Huh, yeah, I'm fast all right. Glacier speed. That's what I have."

"You have bad knee."

"I have bad knee," he echoed. "Bad knee, yeah."

Ethan was now into his second season as a recuperating racer on the so-called comeback trail, a pitiless road that figuratively climbed uphill. He and Lina had been together a year-and-a-half now. Loving comfortably, they had a relationship that saw one leaning on the other without any long-range hopes and goals. Ethan's concentration was on healing, the thousands of hours in training rooms as he rode bikes that went nowhere, rowed machines fixed to the floor, climbed steps to no greater height than eight inches. All forced upon him a self-indulgence so intense that the outside world became superficial. The ski team became mired once again in mediocrity. At the end of the previous season, he had minor surgery again and spent the summer healing and resting. He had been told that a tiny splinter of bone, barely larger than a grain of sand, had broken off and was rubbing into the fleshy tendon, causing a throbbing pain. When it was scoped out, the doctors warned him that arthritis, the old man's disease, was likely to pay a visit to the wounded area.

He and Lina divided time between Europe and Vermont. After three weeks of training in Portillo, Chile, Ethan went into the next season prepared to do better. But he had so far failed to win another World Cup race. The long season was another climb up the Eiger. Crawling and waiting. Standing still on a precipice so tiny. One slip would send him downward. In February, a dozen races into the season, still in constant pain and finishing no better than forty-third, he told Coach Quinn he was going home to Vermont.

"I'll sit out a year to rest and recuperate some more. I'll be back. You know I will."

Chapter 2
Coming Home

"Well, guess who's coming to work for us?" Bruce White said no sooner than he punched open the wooden door to his outer office. He carried a pile of mail and dropped it on his secretary's desk. Before she could ask, Bruce said, "Ethan Atwood. I got a letter from him this morning and opened it right away. It's from Switzerland. In a way, it's sad. He's giving up racing, at least for this year, because of that bad knee of his."

"I heard. He hasn't won a race," said Sarah Thomas, beginning to sort the pile of envelopes and bills on the desk before her.

"He's going to represent the mountain, be our skiing ambassador. I told him years ago that he always had a job here after skiing. He'll be a tremendous representative for us. Local Vermont boy, World Cup racing. Good-looking." Bruce already had visions of what the posters would look like. Ethan Atwood would be taking air off Thunder Road or maybe Exterminator. It had to be with something recognizable in the background. It needed a church steeple. No, that was too corny, but it was Vermont. He decided the poster would give him something to think about at lunch. He hurried into his inner office to put in a call to his marketing department.

In the next room, Mary Ann, listening to her boss's announcement, stood with her mouth open. She then composed herself and stared out the window. She was glad no one was in the room to see her face, which reddened with shock when Bruce first yelled out.

Mary Ann had, of course, kept an eye on Ethan's career. More than once, she wondered what he was doing certain hours of the day. He was among her "God blesses" each night when she went to bed, albeit at the tail end of a short list that included, first, her husband, Donny; her little newborn daughter, Ellie; and her parents. And, after a pause, she would say "Ethan."

The Naples had built a huge new post-and-beam home by a stand of maple and birch trees at the north end of the valley on the western side of Spring Mountain. After weeks of hesitation, Mary Ann had decided the western view was lovelier because they could watch the sun set. Being so high up, on both clear and hazy days, particularly in summer, the rewards were literally heaven-sent. It was pink or orange or as red as a sumac in autumn. Donny had cleared some trees to create a meadow sloping from the front porch. They could sit on the porch, which wrapped around two sides of the house, to take in a view of the farmlands with barns and the narrow river, green or white depending on the season, coursing through pastures. The size and comfort of the new home reflected that Donny was becoming one of the more prosperous citizens in the valley as he shuttled back and forth between his home and the business in Barre, which was doing progressively well under his new stewardship.

Little Ellie, just learning to walk, had short legs and a broad forehead like her father, but she had her mother's piercing brown eyes and curly hair. When not working, Donny could not let Ellie out of his sight, including letting her perch on his lap while he rode the mower back and forth across the broad, hilly lawn. Mary Ann would watch worriedly from the porch.

"You be careful, Donny. Don't let her fall." She stopped short of demanding an end to the dangerous practice.

She had made a conscious effort not to counter Donny in almost every situation where she could have—and should have—a courtesy she thought owed to him. Simply put, her love for him was not as strong as his love for her. Each knew that and understood it. Hers was a compromise.

Still, they were a relatively happy, mutually caring, little family, which worked and played well together. Mary Ann and Donny skied many weekday mornings before going to work, depositing Ellie in the resort's day-care program. On winter weekends, Mary Ann stayed home tending the house and Ellie while Donny worked as a ski patroller. Never a competitive skier, he still enjoyed the mountains, and, he said, the camaraderie of the other patrollers.

"You like patrolling because you like being the cop," Mary Ann teased.

"You said it," said Donny. "I love the power that red jacket gives me. The other day, I busted two snowboarders for jumping a lift line."

"Why do you dislike snowboarders?" she asked.

"Because they're snot-nosed, punky kids who ruin the snow and make life miserable for the skiers."

"But," said Mary Ann, "that's what the kids want to do today. It's like skateboarding on the snow. They'd rather ride than ski. When they grow up, that's what they'll be doing and what their kids will be doing. Snowboarding, not skiing. Bruce said we have to make room for them because they're here to stay. Plain economics. Let them in, or the ski resorts will perish."

"I know you're right," said Donny. "Bruce's right. I wish I could clean up their language though. It makes my blood crawl, hearing a pretty, little thirteen-year-old girl yelling fuck this and fuck that!"

Mary Ann laughed. "I remember when Bruce enlisted Rose Delahanty. Years ago. He encouraged her to take up snowboarding. She and that friend of hers. I can't think of her name. Bruce thought Rose, because she's an elderly woman, a grandmother at that, would put a good face on snowboarding. I know the main reason Rose accepted was because Bruce gave her a Gold Pass for the season."

Mary Ann started laughing harder. "Rose's first day out on the snowboard. It's a steep learning curve. She's is a great skier and has that lithe, athletic body. She was still having problems controlling where she was going. Up on Ramrod, which is kinda steep!

"She started downhill, and her snowboard clipped the back end of some guy's skis. And Rose couldn't stop. She kept going.

"The guy races downhill after her. When he caught up with Rose, he's yelling and screaming. She...Rose..." By now, Mary Ann was laughing uncontrollably and could hardly speak. "She looked like a little boy with the goggles, helmet, and those baggy snowboarding clothes. And the guy, he's middle-aged. He calls her a little prick!

"Oh God, I wish I had been there. Rose took off her helmet, and that crazy, gray hair came out. She later said the guy's jaw dropped, and he just started sputtering. He couldn't talk!"

The Alitalia jet, with its white lights flashing on its wing tips, slid through the fog and touched the runway at Kennedy Airport.

"It will be only for a short while," Lina said sadly as she placed her hand on Ethan's knee as the plane taxied to the terminal.

"You promise you'll come up this weekend."

"Si, of course, I promise."

Her plan was to spend that first week in New York City. She had a friend, Emilio Poli, who worked at the Evermayer, Inc., corporate office in Manhattan. Poli, whom she had met in Milan, had already raved to his executives about her work and her future.

"Designing is in her blood. Her father, Benito Biancavello, designs sports cars in Italy. He has his own studio."

Lina was enthusiastically anxious about starting a career, especially in New York, a city whose cosmopolitan tone she very much wished to test. Her deeper reason for hesitating to join Ethan in Vermont was also difficult to hide, one that Ethan was also aware of and respected. Yet, it was one he wanted to put behind him. Lina was still "the other woman."

On all of her recent visits, Ethan had to plead with her to leave the cabin and go to a restaurant, the Frost Heave Saloon, or the movies.

He coaxed her again this time, making her promise.

"Remember, you can take the train if you want. It stops in Waterbury. I'll be there to pick you up. Or you can rent a car. Oh God, do you have your driver's license? You'll have to make sure you can drive in the states. Can you do that? Will you do that?"

"Yes!" said Lina, somewhat irritated by his demands. Her mind was half-floating between what he was saying and thoughts of the upcoming excitement of her first encounter with the city. Her fears of Vermont lay now in the background, and she resented that Ethan kept bringing them to the forefront.

Before he put her in the cab to take her to the Evermayer office, they hugged each other tightly, kissed, and parted.

"Next weekend!" he said.

"Call no later than Thursday!"

"Si, yes! Ciao! I love you!"

"I love you, too!"

He rented a Jeep and headed for the New York Thruway. Snow would be on the ground back home.

Home. It would be good to be home. Luckily, the cabin he had rented years before was still available. His thoughts as he drove, though, were with his real home, the old, yellow Delahanty Greek Revival farmstead that stood at the edge of Lowgate Springs Village. It had been unchanged, except for an occasional coat of paint, for 150 years. It was a clapboard, L-shaped house with the barn attached to the woodshed many years ago

Vermont beckoned with familiarity as soon as he crossed the state line toward Rutland. The many billboards that dominated the horizon in New York state disappeared from the landscape as he turned onto Route 22A through the flat, valley farmland east of Lake Champlain. In the 1960s, Vermont had legislated billboards from the roadways, which created a huge leap in tourism. No state east of the Mississippi has such uninterrupted scenery as Vermont. Turning onto the Gap Road for the steep climb up the western flank of the mountain, a soft rain that had pelted down in the valley changed over to wet snowflakes the higher the Jeep climbed. The Jeep snaked back and forth on the dangerous switchback road. No sooner did the car arrive at the summit where the Long Trail crosses than the road began its sudden plunge downhill on the other side. He was home.

He decided to stop at Grigsby's General Store on the way and call his grandparents to see if he could bring them any last-minute groceries. Allen Grigsby, the teenage son of the owner, was the first to greet him.

"Well, look who's here. Hiyah, Ethan!"

Several others in the store, old familiar faces since childhood, stepped up to greet him and console him on his bad luck of not being able to compete on the World Cup circuit.

He took a long look around the store, thankful that absolutely nothing had changed since he last left. Grigsby's wasn't a store so much as a barn-sized farming outlet, spectacular for its abundance and the weight of hardware and feed that it put on the wide, planked floor. In the grocery and canned goods section, a monstrous wood stove put forth a fiery heat from an orange glow within. Ethan recalled the oddly comforting feeling of burning on one side and being blue with cold on the other whenever he came inside the store on bitterly cold days.

He called home. After the excited greetings and learning Rose had a roast turkey in the oven, he asked if they needed anything. After a pause, Rose said into the phone, "Your Grandpop said to get some ten pennies."

Ethan laughed and said, "Okay."

It had been a long-standing joke between him and the old man, one that had originated when Ethan was about five and Big Ethan said he had to stop for "a coupla things. Need some ten pennies."

"Ten pennies?" asked Ethan. "What do you need ten pennies for?"

"Ten penny nails, son. Nails are measured in pennies. Goofy, huh! There's ten pennies, eight pennies, six, four, all different sizes. Remember last summer when I built your slide and swing in the yard? Ten penny nails, that's what I used."

The next time Ethan entered the store, he put a pile of copper coins on the worn counter and asked Old Man Grigsby if he would turn them into nails for him. The clientele roared when they figured it out. For a time, he was "Nails Atwood."

After dinner and after speaking by phone with his parents in Albany, Ethan begged to leave for his cabin. "Jet lag's starting to hit me. Been up since midnight your time."

He got home and called Lina at the Southgate Tower Hotel where she said she would be staying. No one answered. He went to sleep.

Ethan's contract with Maple Glen called for his presence a fixed number of days. Many were special events, such as locally sponsored races and holidays. At other times, he would be called to ski privately with celebrities or other special guests. He was asked to set up racing clinics once he had become acclimated to the job. As always apprehensive about his short supply of social ease, he thought about asking Bruce White what demeanor he expected, but he hesitated, for fear that Bruce would lose confidence in him.

Had things been different, Mary Ann would have been the one person he would permit to offer advice on how he should behave. He thought about it the next day and decided to risk a telephone encounter. What the hell, he was an old friend.

"Hello Mary Ann," he said, gulping once while waiting for a reply.

"Ethan! Oh God, it's so good to hear from you. How have you been? Where are you? When are you coming to work? I think it's wonderful. Everybody, especially Bruce, is so excited to have you…" The sentences spilled from Mary Ann in a seemingly continual gush, making him feel instantly relieved and grateful. She had never lost the knack of making him feel at ease, even now.

His second day on the job at Maple Glen, Ethan had caught a glimpse of Mary Ann at the other end of the cafeteria, eating her lunch with several office colleagues. He declined to go up to her, satisfying himself with a few, but priceless seconds, of noticing what changes married life had done for her. Her face was just slightly fuller than before Ethan left the last time for Europe, but it was still the same high cheekbones and bright eyes beneath hair that was still the chestnut brown he had remembered. Her hair was cut in a shorter style. Her bangs were gone, and he was not sure he liked that.

On the phone, they chatted ten minutes, catching up on harmless matters.

"Wait 'til you see Little Ellie. As the mother, I'm not ashamed to say she's adorable."

"I can't wait," Ethan interjected and immediately pondered what kind of gift he could buy the little girl.

"Mary Ann?" he said hesitatingly.

"Yeah?"

He was able to relay to her in a few humbling sentences that he was not sure how he should behave in his new job. "Should I be glad-hand? Big toothy smile? Laid back? Quiet? Talkative?"

Finally, she told Ethan, "Bruce doesn't expect you to be some kind of rah-rah host, glad-handing everybody you meet. Just be yourself." She emphasized, "Be Ethan. Nobody else."

When he was assured he was getting the message, she asked in a lower, slower, more deliberate tone, "How is Lina? Is she here?"

"She's in New York, applying for a job actually. She completed design school and has a chance to go to work for Evermayer."

"The ski clothing company?"

"Yes, if she gets it, the job that is, she'll be coming up here on weekends."

"Oh, that'll be good." Mary Ann ran short of harmless platitudes, not offering any "Give her my regards" or "I'll be anxious to see her."

Ethan was still glad the way she broke the ice for him and for Lina. She could always make it easy. He would be anxious to tell Lina he had spoken to Mary Ann and that she was the same, old Mary Ann. "She asked how you were doing, and when you were coming up."

On Friday night, Lina arrived after driving a rental car from New York City. Still, when Lina arrived, she insisted on not leaving the cabin, not even to ski or even get pizza, as Ethan suggested. She did not even want to visit the Frost Heave Saloon or visit his grandparents. She spent the weekend on edge, still not knowing if the work samples she had presented to the high-fashion, expensive skiwear company were good enough. Ethan could tell that working in New York City would now be her priority. Still, they held each other, like two lost puppies in a kennel that were waiting to be adopted.

When she left Sunday afternoon to return to the city, Ethan asked, "Next weekend?"

"Of course, next weekend. I'll call tonight to let you know I got to the hotel all right."

"Good, I worry about you all alone in that big city."

"I will take care. Remember, I'm European cosmopolitan girl, a Milanese!"

"I thought you were a Florentine."

"That too! Ciao!"

Chapter 3
The Family

Up on Thundercloud, a late winter sleet stung Ethan's cheeks, prompting regret at not wearing his heavy ski mask, which covered all except his eyes, nose, and mouth. He had forgotten, after Europe, how fiercely New England weather could attack the unprepared. However, the snow being relatively soft, a corduroy laid down by the groomer of the night before. The terrain afforded a cautious but safe test of his dully aching knee.

Taking slow, GS turns, by the time he paused at the entrance to Rodeo, a usually bumped-up mogul run, conditions underfoot had changed. The sleet was changing to frozen rain. He stooped and grabbed a handful of snow. He gripped it tightly to see how moist it was, testing the flakes for ice. Concluding the snow was still soft, he decided to risk the bumps. He skied as slowly as he could, letting the quads and calves stretch the tendons, which was doing most of the work absorbing the ups and downs.

"Christ, what if I get hurt skiing here, on this job?" he thought. "Then what will I do?" He reminded himself he was falling into what Klecko would call a negative trough.

"Once you get in there, you have a helluva time getting out. Keep it positive. Keep it upbeat. If you can't be upbeat, keep it neutral." Klecko would say.

God, how he missed Klecko!

He spent the better part of the afternoon at the cabin on the phone with his agent, Red Everts, who had been busily assuring sponsors that Ethan Atwood was only temporarily delayed on his mission toward a World Cup championship. He had contracts with Subaru, Rossignol, Marker, and a cluster of ski wear. With their patches and decals appointed on available spaces of his civilian property, he was a moving billboard and a valuable chip in the commerce of the industry.

"They're staying with you, pal. The only thing is they want you for celebrity stuff. Races out West, like Vail, Aspen, and Whistler. Can you do some half-ass races? Of course, that may be down the line a bit when you're more in the healing process."

"I'll do anything they want. I have pain, sure, but I can still get down a hill fast on skis. I've been testing real easy on bumps and stuff. I just can't do the serious downhill anymore, right now anyway. I can't compete on the same level. I just can't afford to take the risks."

"You're in PT, I suppose?" asked Everts.

"Three times a week at SMA. Stretching, mostly. Weights will come later."

While Lina's new life showed hints of flourishing, Ethan struggled to maintain some professional equilibrium. She called one night to say Evermayer hired her. They liked her stuff, and she was giddy with excitement.

"I will do design for collars for the new season. They want wider neck with longer collar so, when is turned up, the wind stays out and the heat from your body keeps your face warm. Does that make sense?"

"I guess so. I don't know about racing. I don't wear collars."

"I don't talk racing collars, silly. You racers wear nothing, nothing, just that skin that wraps you like a snake. Oh, you look so good in snakeskin. I can't wait to slither up to you in your nice skin."

He was relieved. "I'm really, really glad to hear that. I was afraid, with your new job, you'd be making ex…having to work or something."

"No, I don't work this weekend. I want to see you, but can you come down here?

"To New York?"

"Si. You must see my office…well…not office…my…how do you say, coo-bik-ull. But it is so nice. I am so happy, Ethan. And I want to show you off. There is nice ski bar here on Eighth Avenue. All skiers hang out there. To see you, wow, they go crazy!"

"Uhhh!"

"Pleeze, I come up there all the time. Please come down here!"

"All right," he said.

They spent the weekend dashing the streets of the West Side, arm in arm, laughing and dodging traffic. From her office/studio near Eighth Avenue and 40th Street, they stopped at the Downhill Bar & Grille. They then went by taxi up Broadway to 63rd Street, where they had dinner before going to Lincoln Center and the Metropolitan Opera House. Lina had bought tickets for *La Bohème*.

In the restaurant, even though it was late afternoon and the sun had not yet set, the place was filling up. Tables were spaced closely, making it necessary to wiggle sideways to get to one that was now being cleared by a busboy. Lina sat with her elbows on the table. Her chin was cupped in her clasped fingers. She looked at Ethan, seated across from her, admiring his new green, wool sports jacket, which he wore over a white, cotton, turtleneck shirt. It was dressy for him, but it was casual for New York, passable for the opera. There were multilingual conversations occurring at every table, offering a dulled cacophony with lots of laughter. They ordered beer, which arrived in frosty mugs.

"It's like being back in Europe again." Ethan said.

"You feel at home here?"

"Not home, comfortable. Except it's a little tight in here," he said as a man bumped his chair from behind. "I think I figured out New Yorkers. Actually it's something my father mentioned years ago."

"We get a lot of New York people and Connecticut and Boston people skiing in Vermont. The New Yorkers, I swear by God, they stand out by being so pushy and demanding. And my dad, he explained one time, that New Yorkers are so accustomed to subways and elevators, fighting to get a seat and jostling for space, that it's a hard habit to break. They come skiing in Vermont and spend all day charging lift lines. They have terrible reputations."

"And that too is because Vermonters are slower," said Lina.

"I don't think we're slow," said Ethan. "We're more laid back."

"No, I watch you," she said. "You move like a turtle until you get skis on. And the clerks in your stores; they take forever to make change." Then she laughed and paused.

"You never talk much about your father anymore. Why is that? And he is such a handsome, nice man!"

"Well, I never talked much about him because I guess I don't really know him. Of course, I lived with him as a child, but he's not an easy man to know. He's been sober now for a long time. But I guess I don't like to think too much about him because I never know if he'll fall of the wagon."

"Fall off wagon? What wagon!"

Ethan smiled. "It's an expression from years ago. I don't know where or when, but they had temperance parades or holiday parades at least with a temperance wagon in them. Drunks from the crowd would suddenly jump on and announce they were willing to be saved. Then they would embrace sobriety. Most of them, a week or so later, would sneak another drink and then another and another. Before you know it, they had fallen off the wagon."

"You are afraid of this," she said, "about your father?"

"Yeah, I guess. I guess its part of my makeup. Why I'm always cautious in many things, except racing, of course. I don't..." He stared out the large, plate glass window. Pedestrians scampered by, holding the collars of their coats to ward off the cold wind and squinting against the fog of whirlpool dust.

"My father is capable of going into hiding in a crowded room. Mom said he's always in his head. That was an expression she used. And I guess that's so. I know he's a good architect, always planning and always thinking. I think that's how he came to observe the New Yorkers. He said they lack space in their lives."

"Your father is designer like me," said Lina.

"Yes," he answered, emptying the mug and looking for the waiter to order another. "His spaces are a little bigger than yours."

"Do you like your father?"

"Yes, I do. In fact, I wish I knew him better. Mom sent me to live with Grandmom and Grandpop when I was about seven."

"Didn't your father decide to send you up there, too?"

"No, I don't think so. I think it was her decision alone. Nobody told me at the time, but you pick up things as you grow up. I know my mother didn't like my dad drinking so much, and I think she wanted to get me away from that. Well, for sure, that's what she was after. We can't kid anybody about that."

"He doesn't drink anymore, you said."

"Yes, he has stopped for several years now. I think the first time was right around the time I first went to Portillo, right when I got on the ski team."

They left the restaurant and headed toward Lincoln Center.

"You will like this opera," Lina said as they walked across the broad, windy sweep of concourse to the brilliantly lit glass façade of the opera house. "You know why? It is set in winter and has snow," said Lina.

Ethan laughed, "Still trying to ease my education into the cultural arts, aren't you?"

"You do not have to ease into Puccini." she said. "Puccini eases into you! His music is very sweet and lyrical. You will like it because it is also sad and dreamy. And happy too!"

"It is sad and happy, both?"

"Si, sad and happy," she said as they entered the huge lobby with its curving, sweeping balcony that was milling with people. Many were in evening dress, making Ethan search for someone dressed more casually.

Lina chattered on, "There is always happiness when there is sadness in the opera.

"And in life!" she added with emphasis. "You can't be sad without first being happy." She turned her head to look up at him with a broad smile and squeezed his arm. "Don't you know that?"

"I think I know that better than a lot of people!" he said.

Back in Vermont, as he was driving into the Grand Union parking lot to shop for groceries, Ethan caught a glimpse of Mary Ann getting out of her Saab several rows away. He braked and waited, staring at her as she pulled the tiny child, bundled in snow clothes, from the backseat and hurried inside.

He parked next to her car, got out, and peeked cautiously through its rear window, looking for clues or something. He was not quite sure. The interior of the car was clean. This was not unexpected because Mary Ann had always been neat, clean, and tidy, except when she exercised in the summer heat. He could see her standing at the mountaintop with sweat clinging to her hair and shirt. He remembered how he had buried his face in her hair that first time, kissing her throat as she held back her head.

He yanked a cart from its long row outside the market and pushed it inside, wondering which aisle he would casually run into her and Ellie. He would feign surprise. Other than brief small talk in the Maple Glen administration building, he had not the opportunity to chat socially.

As he looked over the bananas, she yelled from across the store, "Ethan!"

They hugged.

"This is Ellie."

Little children who can neither talk nor understand their surroundings are remarkably wonderful inventions. Ethan was able to divert his awkwardness by turning his entire attention to the small, fat bundle of clothing plopped in the metal seat of the shopping cart. He smiled broadly and said, "Hi, Ellie. I'm Ethan!"

The child, who was chomping on a pacifier, gazed at the dark-haired form before her and worked to affirm his presence by turning to her mother for a sign of acknowledgment and approval.

The worst was over. A flurry of small talk aborted the blank wall.

"Donny's anxious to see you. Please come for dinner. Sunday. How about Sunday?"

"Well, uh..."

"I forgot. Does Lina come up on weekends? Please, both of you. Come!"

Lina would not go. He knew this before dialing her number. He pleaded over the phone.

"I cannot. Please, Ethan, don't ask me. Maybe later. I am honest. I could make excuse that I have to work or something, but I just can't see her right now. Please understand."

"Well, what am I to do?"

"Go, you go see Mary Ann and Donny. I stay in New York."

"Well, Christ, are you going to hide in New York City the rest of your life now?" he asked irritably.

"I do not hide, Ethan! Please, try to understand me! I will see you the following week."

"Where?"

"Vermont. I will come up. I promise. I will come to your place. Maybe if we meet Mary Ann all of a sudden some place, that might be easy. I cannot go to her home. Please, please understand that."

Sunday came. He made the visit solo, and he made excuses. "She's been very busy."

While Mary Ann was alternately attending to the baby and the roast in the oven, Donny showed Ethan around his small estate. It was 200 acres of largely woodland. Most lay uphill with a single dirt road about a half-mile long that wound through the trees before connecting to the Mountain Gap Road, the main highway that crossed over the mountain.

The home was wide, tall, and spacious. Its post and beam construction afforded openness. Its cathedral ceilings and large loft overlooked a stone fireplace that stacked up two floors. A small, iron wood stove stood on the fireplace hearth. As big as the house was, it spread its glowing heat throughout, even into the second floor. Donny had also installed baseboard hot water heat, but they only needed it on particularly cold days.

"You must be planning a big family," Ethan said to Mary Ann as she escorted him through the four bedrooms upstairs. Donny dropped out of the tour to feed the two big Labs who bounded about the yard.

She grinned. "Don't ask. Ellie's a handful. I take it one day at a time."

"Look," Mary Ann said, pulling a baby's garment from a drawer. It was a pair of pajamas, soft, white cotton with lace edges. "Lina sent it."

"I had no idea," Ethan said, honestly surprised. He altered the conversation. "Ellie looks like you."

"I think it's too early to tell. To be absolutely honest, all babies look like babies to me. She was small though. Six pounds, twelve ounces. She may look more like Donny when she grows up."

"Donny's not small. He's built like a horse."

"He's short," said Mary Ann.

"A small horse. A pony."

"A mule!" she said, suddenly laughing very hard. She tried not to be too loud about it. She need not tell Ethan that Donny was a stubborn, purposefully driven individual who set goals and met them. Ethan could see it all around him in the house and grounds. Though much of Donny's wealth was inherited from his father, his playthings were work-related, from his high-priced Macintosh computer system to the three different garden tractors and a basement workshop with new table saw, lathe, planer, router, and such.

Donny showed Ethan a garden wall made from flat fieldstone that he put together himself. It snaked through the backyard, creating two levels of lawn. On its lower plateau in the summertime were his and Mary Ann's vegetable and flower gardens. He built a small greenhouse at the end of the yard where they raised tomatoes and other plants from seedlings to give them an early start in the brief Vermont summers.

The new six-car garage contained a four-wheel drive sport utility truck, a Chevy pickup with a snowplow rig attached, the Saab that Mary Ann drove, and a new Polaris snowmobile.

"A man after my own heart," Ethan said, crouching over the snowmobile to admire its metal innards more closely. "I just ordered the same model.

At dinner, they talked of skiing and the future of Maple Glen.

"Bruce wants to put a new cluster of condos in over by the South Mountain Road, if the zoning board lets him," said Mary Ann.

"They'll let him," said Donny.

"And how do you know?" asked Mary Ann. "There are a lot of people in the valley who think the place has gotten too big already."

"Yeah, and they're the ones that don't work there," said Donny. "Their livelihoods don't depend on it, or they think they don't depend on it. If anything, Bruce's too shortsighted. I'd open up that whole North Ridge area."

"Why don't you suggest it to him?" she asked, slightly sarcastic.

Donny, slabbing a thick slice of butter on his piece of homemade bread, looked at her and said forcefully, "Please don't give me any ideas, sweetheart. That's all I need right now, running another business. I have enough to do with my own, although I think I could show Bruce a thing or two. No thanks, I'll stick to ski patrolling two days a week."

Throughout the conversation, Ethan remained mostly silent, absorbing the dining table give-and-take, reflecting how different conversations are in Vermont compared with New York City and Milan.

"So, how do you like the new job?" Donny said to Ethan.

"Not too intimidating, I guess. The season will be winding down in another six weeks. Bruce said there won't be much doing the rest of the year, but he has big plans for promoting me next season, even though I hope I'll be back with the ski team. Who knows, I may be here another year, maybe for good."

"How's the old knee?"

"Old is right." Ethan shook his head from side to side and frowned. "Dull ache, all the time. I can ski with pain, but I can't get the goddamned speed up. We're talking decimal seconds. In a long downhill, they add up. I'm two to four seconds behind everybody else."

"The real good ones anyway, I guess," said Donny.

"Anyway, I go back to see Rogers in Colorado in the spring. I'm afraid he may have to cut again."

"Oh, dear," said Mary Ann with a worried look.

"If that happens," said Donny, "If he has to cut, that'll lay you up even longer."

"I could miss the beginning of next season. Christ, the Olympics! I dreamed about that all my life!"

Mary Ann stood and walked to the stove to fetch the coffee. Her back was turned away from the table. "You'll be there!" she said, struggling to keep her voice from quavering.

Chapter 4
Hathaway Child

Lina's creative world was so absorbing that it left little time for casual thoughts. To her, New York City was a whirlwind of work and hurried lunches. You threw yourself each day into its vortex, side by side with other inventive, exciting people. At day's end, you were spun out, either into the nightlife or exhausted into your bed at home. People in New York City constantly invented glamour and money, and ski clothing was at the apex of fashion.

"Thank God, they destroyed the hot pinks," she said to Ethan on the phone. She lay on her back on a queen-sized bed, massaging the back of her neck with one hand. "Now it is dark earth tones in the clothes. There is strong American Indian influence. Indian colors. You must take me to the West again. I must see the ones. They live in caves. P…P…P something."

"Pueblos," Ethan said. "They lived in caves centuries ago. I think now they live in condos and sell pottery in big discount warehouses along the highway."

"But I know nothing of them, and that's the rage. Our ski clothes. Next year, they will all be clay colors, like tiles with triangles and diamonds. They taught me so little of Pueblos and Aztecs in design school. They say next year will be breakthrough for Western motif. You must get rid of those awful ski jackets you wear with all bright colors. Trust me, you will be sooo handsome in dark colors!"

"Who cares, so long as somebody else is paying for it?" he replied. "I'll wear anything and everything they tell me to wear."

"Anything?"

"Almost anything!"

"Get rid of that awful hat!"

"It's warm!"

"Other hats are warm and stylish. Yours make you look like Dopey, the dwarf."

Ethan laughed. True, the large fleece hat he had bought years ago from the country store named Grampy's while skiing at Stratton did indeed flop around his head except when he skied. Then he would pull it snug, turning up the brim in front to make the rest of the silly hat lie closer to his scalp. It was warm. It was a very warm, fleece hat.

When she visited that weekend, they skied in brilliant spring sunshine under a deep blue, cloudless sky. Temperatures climbed to about fifty degrees, leaving drifts of corn snow that crunched so very softly beneath their skis. They went down Widow Maker, a steep, straight shot that was wide and smooth. They made turns in rhythmic patterns. The sometimes cruel and challenging ice patches had vanished. The skiing was easy and lazy.

"Why don't you come to Colorado with me?" Ethan asked as he put his arm around her on the lift ride up the mountain.

"I can't. I have to work."

"For a weekend?"

"No, we are so busy! I am sorry, next time." She then kissed him on the cheek.

On the drive down the mountain road, past a rushing stream galloping like a spring racehorse toward a finish line, they saw a line of cars and trucks parked on the shoulder near a field. "The kayakers are out, catching the rapids in the gorge," said Ethan.

They caught glimpses, through the budding trees, of the bright-colored, cigar-shaped craft playing in the rushing river. They swept back and forth and side to side, like water bugs. One kayaker was plunged beneath the surface, and the craft then twirled him upright.

Weeks later, when he finally got on the mountain bike, strength and high spirits returned in spurts. Pedaling uphill caused the most strain, but he felt overall stronger than when he left the circuit in February. The August sun was directly overhead. Very little of the road lay in shadows. He was glad to reach the top of the summit, where the view of Lake Champlain came to him as did the gray, strong mountains to the west. Taking a deep breath, he decided not to pause and let the bike plunge downhill on its own. He did let his hands carefully touch the brakes. No more would he test his courage as he, Mary Ann, and Donny did in their youth as crazy, kamikaze kids.

He let the wind rush through and around his body, drying his torso. By the time he pulled into the parking lot of the Frost Heave, the perspiration was gone, except for a narrow band on the brow where his helmet rested.

"A big, boiled ham sandwich with mustard on one of those hard rolls and the biggest, frostiest mug of beer you can come up with," he said to bartender, Connie Rich. Only a half-dozen other people, a couple of truckers and four tourists who poured over maps and brochures on their table, were in the saloon at this lazy, noontime hour.

Connie leaned her elbows on the bar and watched Ethan take big bites out of his sandwich.

"Been bikin,' huh!"

"Yeah, up and over from Lowgate Springs."

"How's the knee?"

"You had to ask, didn't you?"

"I'm sorry, Ethan dear. Just making conversation…and being polite!" she scolded.

"No, I apologize. I have to expect people to ask about my goddamned knee because my whole life revolves around it. People are just being courteous, but I get so damned sick and tired."

"You get sick and tired because there's no change, is that it?"

"That's it, I'm afraid."

"What did Doctor Rogers do?"

"How did you know I saw Rogers?"

"Christ, I read the newspapers. Ethan Atwood will have his bum knee examined by famed surgeon…"

"Well, he didn't operate, which is what I was fearing he would have to do."

"What did he do?"

"Scoped it out again. Scrubbed away the scar tissue, and told me to get back into therapy. Mildly exercise, and try it out again next month."

"You mean South America?"

"No, Mount Hood, in Oregon. I'll go out in September and ski the glacier."

"How's your girl? What's her name, Lina?"

"I haven't seen her in a month. All right, I guess. She's supposed to come up this weekend before going back to Italy to see her father."

When he pedaled back to the cabin in the afternoon sun, intent on taking a shower and then a nap, he was surprised to see a bicycle he did not recognize leaning up against the porch steps.

He walked through the front door, letting the screen door slam behind him. He then heard her voice. "Hey, I'm out here. Out back."

Mary Ann sat slouching back in one of the Adirondack chairs in the shade beneath the big eastern pine.

"Sorry for dropping in, but a neighbor can only wait so long for an invite," said Mary Ann, smiling.

"I'm sorry. I should have invited you and Donny over long ago. I fully intended to, but it's always one thing after another."

"I know, I know. Don't apologize. You're probably busy. I guess Lina comes up on weekends."

Ethan looked down at his bike shoes and stared at the way the toes pointed up, like those of an Eastern caliph.

"How is she?" Mary Ann probed.

"You know, that's the trouble, Mary Ann," he said, taking a seat in the chair beside her.

"I don't mind talking, Ethan."

"She...when she comes up here, I can never get her to go over and see you and Donny." He looked at Mary Ann. "She says she's embarrassed."

"I'd be embarrassed, too," said Mary Ann. She quickly added, "But I'm not going to bite her head off. Look," she said, "this is a small town. We're all small town people here. We live here. We were born here, you, Donny, and me. And we don't have secrets...or, to put it another way, we don't have problems we can't share with others. What happened, happened. What's important is that we get on with it. Get on with our lives."

"Yeah, but..."

"But…but what? If Lina is to come here, to stay here, to be with you, or whatever, I don't like the idea of her mousing around, feeling guilty. How the hell do you think I feel?"

"She's not mousing, Mary Ann," he said irritably. "She's not anything. She's not…Shit, I'm not even sure myself what she's doing. It isn't going well, she and I. I haven't seen her in a month. She's all wrapped up in her job. I honestly feel as though we're going in opposite directions. She's going up, and I'm going down."

"What do you mean, down?"

"You know what I mean," He pulled at some blades of grass and tossed them. He then looked at her. "For the first time in my life, I'm scared. Scared of my skiing. Scared of my future."

"You mean, if you can't race, what will you do?"

"I put it all into racing. Every goddamned inch of my life, every fiber of my body!"

"You've got two problems then."

"Two?"

"Racing and Lina." When he looked at her, Mary Ann asked, "Do you love her?"

He looked far off to a hawk or raven. It was difficult to tell because they had similar wingspans. They had small, fingered feathers that hung at the end of broad wings, scarcely moving in the thermals. "I had one…" He hesitated and then held up a forefinger. "One love. Just one!"

He turned to look at her. "Do you know who I am now?" he asked. "The Hathaway child, the baby on the mountain. The one that's buried."

She looked at him so tenderly. Her fingers clenched the arms of her chair, as if to spring up. It would have been easy, but she sat back stiffly and stared toward the woods.

They sat quietly. After a minute, she stood up. "I have to go."

"Mary Ann!" he yelled, but she hastened off across the lawn, around the side of the cabin, and vanished on her bike.

Lina did come up that weekend. They argued furiously in his cabin, negating cool, clear, sunny summer weather with the storm they made between them. The reason was the same.

Lina stared out the picture window toward the woods, repeating she was ashamed of what she had done to Ethan and Mary Ann and would never get over it.

"You cannot understand that, can you, Ethan?" she said, suddenly wheeling in his direction.

He was sitting on the long divan in front of the fireplace. A blue ice pack encased his left knee.

"It didn't shame you that night in the hospital," he said bitterly.

"Why do you have to bring that up? Why? Why? I told you I didn't know Mary Ann then. I didn't even know you then. Do you understand that was a foolish moment that changed my life, yours, Mary Ann's? Of course, I never forget. Don't you see, I've changed since that moment. Mary Ann Queensbury is the goodest, best person I know. It was like I stab her in the back. I have hard time facing her."

"Lina. Please, listen to me." he said, getting up from the couch and wincing. He took her gently by the shoulders and held them at his arms' length.

"It's not like you're forced to face your accuser. Mary Ann has gotten over it and wants you to get over it. Oh, I know we can't forget it, but we can push on.

"Look at me!" he said. "Look at me! I fell. I busted up my leg so bad I couldn't walk. I need this leg to make a living. What am I doing? Quitting? Hell no! I'll never quit. My life must go on. Yours too, go on, forward."

"It is going on, my life!" she yelled. "I have life in New York. Ah, I come up here, and you tell me to forget. I don't forget."

"Mary Ann has," he sputtered, biting his tongue because he knew it wasn't quite true. "She has…"

But Lina interrupted. "She has? She has? Bullshit, Ethan! I see her. She says go on and forget. But I see it in her eyes."

"Let me put it this way," Ethan said, massaging his neck while regrouping his thoughts. He knew enough not to rile Lina's tempestuous Italian temper. He could see her walking out the door. In his thoughts, he begged God, "Jesus, don't let her leave."

He continued, "What you did before had guilt and shame all over it. That night and what happened after. But what you've done since has remorse all over it. Shame and remorse. To me, that means something. To Mary Ann it means something."

"Why is it always Mary Ann?" Lina shouted. "Always Mary Ann, always Mary Ann. It always comes to that."

"I don't...Jesus Christ!" moaned Ethan, unsure now where the argument was headed.

"I'm sorry." He moved to her. She was staring out the window again.

"I don't mean it that way, Lina. Please, please, let's you and I have something together."

"What is have something, Ethan? We have each other, yes, in bed. We have each other, yes, in guilt. There is no brightness anymore!"

When she spoke about the brightness, Ethan trembled.

"What the hell do you want me to do, Lina, marry you?"

She turned and stared.

"Well," he said, turning to peer out the window. "I guess that's the one thing I'm not doing right. I think it has to do with punishment. My punishment, your punishment. I guess not offering you my whole life, my entire life, is my way of getting even. I'm sorry. I guess I've got some growing to do, too."

The remainder of the weekend was passed in a cloud. They did not fight anymore. Lina had made it clear there was more depth to the problem than the remorse over a single mistake.

"There is no brightness anymore," she had said.

Chapter 5
The Race

In mid-September, mellow daytime temperatures cast by usually bright sunlight fit sharply but nicely with the cool nights of frost upon the leaves and thin glimmers of ice upon the ponds and lakes. Soon, tourists with cameras, maps and guidebooks would commandeer the dirt back roads, slowly chasing the ever-changing scenes of vermillion and orange.

The quiet of Ethan's nights was deafened still by the silence from New York, leaving a cold, queasy void in the pit of his stomach. It was a malaise he had felt only a couple of times before —when the coaches ignored him and he couldn't guess if he'd made the ski team or not and when Mary Ann closed the door for good. Though he and Lina had never committed to a life eternal situation, the void was there. His mustering of spirit came all too infrequently in spiked and artificial spurts. They were forced bursts of enthusiasm, vastly outnumbered now by the letdowns.

He called and left messages at her hotel and Evermayer. He could tell a coworker, Joyce Benfield, was making excuses.

"She's out to lunch.

"In conference."

"Down at the garment shop."

"Shopping. I'll tell her you called."

On his way home from physical therapy, when he stopped at the post office, he put his hand in the little box and pulled out a stack of bills, invitations, and shopper throwaways. There was also an envelope on which he recognized the taut, upright penmanship, an almost Gothic, typically European script.

I'm returning to Italy for a few months; they gave me time off because I can sketch over there as well as here. I need time to think. My path in life seems to be taking another course. Forgive me, I could not live in Vermont with you, but I think you know that. I need time to think. Please don't be harsh with me.

Lovingly,

Lina

He called and was told that Lina had gone.

He called her home at Lago di Garda. The elderly, ill-natured housekeeper, bothered by the phone call interrupting her scrubbing of the kitchen floor, shouted back. Through the garble of the language difference, she made clear that "Lina no here. In Roma she is."

"Just barely home and she's off to Rome? Why? With whom?"

On the way to Oregon, Ethan stopped at Denver for a strength checkup with Doctor Knee, getting a "knee-looks-fine" prognosis.

"I wouldn't push it too hard, however. You're going to have to be careful the first few weeks, maybe months. I honestly see no reason why you can't rejoin the team. Don't expect top results right away is all. Ethan, this is going to take time."

At Mount Hood, Ethan joined some ski team members, mostly B-and C-teamers, hankering to join the big show. He forced his thoughts and energies into skiing, consciously striving to push down the anger that welled inside. Bad knee…bad love life…bad luck.

For a time, the younger ski team members were able to lift him from the doldrums. They paid for the beer. He went to the bar to get it because they were underage. One night, telling of life in the World Cup, he got sauced in his hotel room. The next day, it took several hours for the crisp air to scrub his lungs.

For the first time, he had thrown up from drinking too much.

"Hey, Ethan, wanna race?" came the taunt from young Drew Wallace, a promising downhiller from Heavenly, California.

"No, I'm here to R and R. Got to take it easy."

Wallace was an ambitious, talented skier, and hustling was part of his scheme. He reckoned that winning junior and Nor-Am races was not a sufficient test of his true ability. Beating a World Cup racer was.

Every day it was the same.

"Anytime you're ready, Ethan."

"Oh, for Christ's sake, Drew, I can take your ass anytime I feel like it. But not today."

Still the taunts came.

"I don't mean with the clock, Ethan, I'd like to go head-to-head with you. First one down the mountain wins."

It was a cloudy, cool day atop the Summit Express Chair. Around them, the mountain dropped into 360 degrees of skiable acres. Most of it was soft, forgiving powder. In the distance were the volcanic cones of Broken Top and the Three Sisters, a mountain-perfect scene whose backdrop afforded easy loping, frolicking in the snow, or a chance to let it all out to unburden and to triumph as well as to casually hammer this annoying kid down into his deserving place in life.

"You son of a bitch, all right, let's go!" Ethan answered. "I'll take you on."

"You guys are nuts, don't do that!" yelled Peter Simeon, who was younger than both skiers but old enough to see through fools.

"I'll count down," yelled Drew. "Five…four…three…two…one…Go!"

They hurtled, neck and neck, skating to pick up speed on the mildly pitched hill. They turned left in the same position to avoid a patch of hemlocks and to pick up the Wanderer, which had been groomed and was swift from the day before. However, a new, six-inch blessing of powder had softened it. Though not steep, it was a challenging sidewinder, offering natural gates to test a skier's slaloms.

Ethan, being a glider, was at a disadvantage. The younger skier could put brute force into work as he carved perfect turns in the constantly shifting curves.

Ethan felt himself falling behind. The wise thing to do would be to pull up, shout "You win!" shake hands and call it a day. He would save face, and the younger skier could brag he beat the great Ethan Atwood in a 2,000-foot race.

However, Ethan's energies and instincts were overpowered by a will that was stronger than both. He knew, by skiing smart, he would beat the kid by several seconds.

"Take the line. Take the line," Ethan repeated, promising to let the mountain decide which route to take.

Drew was several lengths ahead now, but a long, sweeping turn arose where the wind had swept the new powder away, leaving a hard pack that was more like a genuine racecourse. They had left the glacier area, and they were below the tree line where shadows worked the snow.

"Aha! C'mon ice," Ethan said. "Let me have ya!"

"Yeah, ice!" he yelled as he chose the quicker line.

Drew, suddenly wary of what his skis were feeling beneath him, dug in his edges as best he could. Ethan was coming up on his left, threatening to pull ahead. Drew let the downhill edge grip tighter, pushing with all his might on the inner part of his left boot.

Suddenly, it gave way. His skis went sideways, crashing his hip to the ice and bouncing him directly into Ethan's path.

Both went down, reeling off course and into the trees.

Drew was unconscious for ten minutes. He awoke with a headache and resulting concussion. It was a convenience for him, albeit weak. Not having a clear memory allowed him to rely on gibberish to deny the foolish act.

Ethan's immediate self-perception was of virtual doom, an abyss in which he alternately felt himself tumbling or confronted with obstacles piling one upon the other. The knee, which had been the center of his physical awareness, had failed again. His ribs were cracked from the impact with Drew, and his right shoulder was found to have a chipped humerus. A tiny piece was floating in the upper arm, which made it painful to raise his hand above his shoulder. These were microcosms of a much bigger problem that Ethan was then incapable of putting a label upon. Much more therapy seemed the easiest way out in order to get back to his proper place in the ski-racing world. The once new and inviting season lay dormant, if not totally dead before him. It had been eliminated forever or postponed until who knows when. The larger question, survival of a psyche, was spinning in a dark void.

Chapter 6
Moonlight

"Have you seen Ethan lately?" asked Donny, dipping into a bowl of green beans. Outside the first snowflakes of October were racing the few brown leaves still falling to the ground.

"I haven't seen him in weeks, at least to talk to," Mary Ann said, aware of a minor sidestepping of the truth. She had, of course, seen Ethan at Maple Glen and shopping in the village. Since they met last on the day in his backyard, she had avoided him. She uncomfortably watched him one September day as he parked his car and entered the drugstore. She quickly ducked into the Grand Union with Ellie under her arm, hoping not to run into him.

"I've been hearing some sad things," said Donny, not looking up as he grabbed the gravy boat.

"Like what?" said Mary Ann.

"Like hanging out at the Frost Heave all afternoon. He's down, I guess, since what happened out at the ski camp. You know, he just didn't have a fall."

"What do you mean?"

"I heard he was racing some kid on the Development Team, some kid who taunted him into racing. Frankly, Ethan had no business putting that kind of pressure on his knee."

Mary Ann looked up. She had heard the details, but she let Donny tell the story as if she was hearing it for the first time.

"It was the kid's fault, but it was also Ethan's fault for giving into him. Honest to Christ, he does some of the dumbest things out there…skiing."

"He could never back out of a challenge. And, even when he wasn't challenged, except by himself. I remember he skied while once wearing a blindfold. When we were kids at the academy. He made me follow him down Juggernaut, yelling turn left and turn right. Then there was that time on bikes. You remember that."

Mary Ann cleared her throat and shook her head affirmatively. She tried to smile, but she could not.

Donny laughed. "Up there on the Gap Road. 'Let's go down without using our brakes,' he said. What a nut, and we were nuts for letting him get away with it!"

"Well, whatever happened out there in Oregon, it's probably destroying him right now," said Mary Ann. "Do you think he'll ever get back on the World Cup?"

"Not the way he's going, he won't." Donny added, "I'd better give him a call. See if we can't do something. I think I'll invite him to Mike Scott's roast."

"You mean the retirement party for Mike?"

"Yeah, it'll do him some good to get out, and see people instead of moping around. Especially drinking in a bar all afternoon."

Ethan was warmed by Donny's invitation to the dinner and by the invitation implied in his concern.

"I have to learn not to let all this crap bother me," Ethan said. "But truthfully, Donny, I have been down…then up…then down again. I've been forcing myself to get outside and test the pain. The more I concentrate on something pleasurable and good for me, the easier the days go by. I'm really glad you called. I need a few laughs."

Donny was the master of ceremonies at the farewell dinner for a longtime ski patroller who was hanging up his red jacket. His old legs were no longer able to bear the weight of the skiing wounded.

The night of the banquet, even though Ethan had agreed to meet them, he failed to show up. Mary Ann had been on his mind. He wanted to see her, but he had changed his mind at the last minute while sitting in his cabin.

"It wouldn't do any good," he told himself that morning. It had been an unusually long night. He awoke every time his body wanted to turn to a different position. But, throughout it all, he had slept for ten hours.

In sweatpants and wearing only a T-shirt, he sat stiffly on the front edge of an Adirondacks chair on the porch, careful not to lean back. Getting out of a chair, any chair, required a test of will in order to steel the muscles around his pained and weakened ribs. Moving from a reclining position in an Adirondacks chair was as difficult as moving an elephant's ass out of a large bucket.

He sipped hot coffee and took deep breaths, hoping the crisp air would wash out the dustbins in his head.

At the roast for Mike Scott, Mary Ann searched the door whenever anyone walked into the lodge, glancing at her watch each time. The banquet was held in the Green Mountain Room of the new Maple Glen House, a combination hotel and conference center recently built at the base of the resort. It was a large, white, frame building. Though it could boast modern facilities, such as a fitness center, state-of-the-art kitchen and dining facilities, and apartment condos with hot tubs, it was constructed with Old Vermont in mind. Its green shutters set off its white clapboard siding in a way that was not intrusive to the surrounding countryside, thanks in part to the Keep-It-Green Society, which orchestrated several plan revisions before the architects "got it right."

About fifty people at the dining tables were already on their way to a merry evening. The drinks before the dinner had done their work, and Donny Naples did the rest.

"The man we're honoring tonight needs no introduction…" he said, pausing a moment before adding, "and certainly deserves none!"

The howls of laughter set the tone for the evening. At his right sat a white-haired man with a rugged, red, wrinkled face. He smiled bravely under the torrent of Donny's well-meaning jibes.

"Mike Scott has had the distinction of bringing down—and I mean literally bringing down—some of the most famous skiers in all of skierdom. Twice, he pulled the toboggan that bore the almost lifeless body of a one-time governor of Vermont, who never could ski anyway. He also carried away two movie stars, a famous outfielder with the New York Yankees, and half of a hockey team from Montreal. That's quite a career."

Mary Ann once again glanced at her watch and sighed. It would be a long evening. She and Donny had taken two cars because she did not feel like joining in at the bar when the banquet was over. Donny said he would be home late. He enjoyed these moments when his wit was on stage and he could be the center of attention. He had just been elected president of the Maple Glen Valley Chamber of Commerce, and he was certainly one of the most widely known young executives in the valley. He was also one of the most popular, having demonstrated with his volunteer ski patrol work that he was still one of the boys.

Big Ethan Delahanty sat at a table about halfway from the podium, looking at Mike Scott and remembering when he also said farewell to the Maple Glen Ski Patrol nearly ten years before. He also wondered if Mike gave it up because of the ache in his legs or the one in his head from all the increased paperwork required by the insurance companies and the lawyers. When Eddy Schultz was made a defendant in a liability case, when he was sued because the drunk he treated for a sprained ankle continued skiing until he broke it and Schultz and the resort were held liable, that was when Big Ethan decided he had had enough.

"All the shots are being called by the lawyers and insurance men," he complained to Rose.

It had been an effort to quit, and he felt sad for Mike. However, he laughed heartily when Donny said, "And, after tonight, Mike, you can retire to the old farts' table and sit with Delahanty and the rest of the gang."

When Clayton Undermacher, the mountain manager, momentarily took over the dais and spoke in a monotone voice through his "loyalty" speech, Big Ethan decided to get some air and light a cigar. The rules also changed on smoking. Even though Big Ethan agreed it was probably for the best, especially regarding cigarette smoke, he wondered how anything so sweet smelling as his Royal Havanas, which he bought from a Montreal cigar dealer who made regular trips to Cuba, could possibly offend even the daintiest of noses.

He went outside, and Mary Ann followed him into the starry, moonlit night. Ethan was genuinely happy to see the young woman to whom his grandson was once engaged.

"Mary Ann, dear, it's been so long. How are you? When are you goin' to drop by and see the missus. Rose misses you. She'd love to see you."

He bussed here on the cheek, and the girl blushed with a little pride at the fuss. She loved the old man for more than one reason, particularly his once-curly hair now turned to silver that had been passed down the line.

"Here, you better stand downwind from this chimney of mine," he warned, beckoning her to join him on his other side.

"I don't mind it. Cigar smoke, at least some. Yours is okay."

Big Ethan finally broke the short silence. "I'm worried about Ethan," he said, not looking away from the full moon, which cast long shadows over the now brushy lawn. The great steel base of the Green Mountain chair lift, standing skeletal in the distance, looked like a deserted amusement park ride.

"I tried to get him to come here tonight," Ethan said, "but he wouldn't."

Mary Ann kept silent, fighting a lump in her throat.

"He's getting moody, like his dad," said Ethan. "At least like his dad used to be. I...oh...I shouldn't be so harsh. Paul's a good man, moody or not, and so is Ethan. I just wish there was some way to break that spell."

"What spell?" asked Mary Ann, suddenly feeling foolish. She had only been half-listening. The other part of her was wondering where he was.

"Well, the other day, he and I went hunting up in back of the house. I thought shooting a few birds might do him some good, and he's always been so eager to go along with me," Big Ethan said. "Well, he went anyway, and I suggested we cut through the woods that used to be around that old farm, the Hathaway Farm."

"So, we went," Ethan continued with Mary Ann now staring silently into his face. Her attention was secured on his every word. "And we got up there where there's this old meadow. It's pretty overgrown now, but he stopped and bent over this little tombstone. It was like that's where he was headed."

"And he began...he's on his hands and knees now!" Ethan said worriedly, a frown and puzzle across his brow. "He begins digging at the weeds, scattering them in all directions and making the grave tidy. I tried not to think much of it and thought, 'Well, here's this sensitive kid.' Ethan was always like that, sensitive to animals or other things. I think you know what I mean."

"But, I finally looked at the stone. And it read Mae Hathaway or something like that. The dates were in the 1890s, but Ethan said, "She died when she was two-and-a-half.""

"And I said, 'You musta been here before. You act like you been here before.' And he said…and I swear, Mary Ann…he said, 'It's my child!'"

"That's what he said, and I laughed. I don't know why I laughed. I guess because I didn't know how to react to what the hell he was saying. I thought maybe he was jokin' or something, but he then looked up. He was trying to laugh it off, but he got all moist on me. He actually misted up around the eyes."

Big Ethan looked down at Mary Ann, whose face was shining in the moonlight now. She put here hand to her mouth. Ethan continued, "What do you think that's all about now, Mary Ann?"

"I…I think I know," she answered softly, trying to keep her voice from trembling. "I think I know," she repeated. This time, it was louder. She cleared her throat and added, "I have to go back in."

She stopped and turned to face Big Ethan. "Don't worry about Ethan. He's going to be all right. I know he will." Her voice was determined.

Big Ethan said nothing more, just sighed and pulled deeply on the Havana while he watched the blue smoke drift uphill on the moonlight, up toward the tops of the mountains.

Mary Ann hurried back to her table and leaned to Florence Johnson, with whom she was sitting. "Please tell Donny I have a headache. I'll see him when he gets home. I'm leaving now."

Outside, she raced to her car and, before securing the seat belt, roared from the lot with her tires screaming.

The car sped down to River Road, where she turned left through Lowgate Springs Village. She then turned left again for the steep, uphill climb on the Gap Road. She plunged down the western side just as the moon slid behind a cloud. A half-mile later, when she reached the dirt lane leading back to Ethan's cabin, she drove past a grove of tall pines and a slanting meadow. She murmured, "Please be home." She was relieved to see a light shining through the trees. She stopped the car in the drive, behind Ethan's truck, slammed the door shut, and raced to the front porch. She did not knock. When she pushed open the door, Ethan stood with his mouth agape. He was holding two logs, about to push them into the wood stove.

"Ethan!" Mary Ann whispered as she stood in the doorway. She was breathless, and her arms were straight down at her side. Tears poured down her face. He carelessly dropped the logs to the side of the stove as she stepped toward him. Her eyes were on his until her face was inches from his. No word was spoken as their arms wound tightly around each other. It matched a passion felt years before, the first day they loved on the mountain, when she astounded him with the words that she loved him, whispered so softly but urgently.

"Ethan, Ethan, Ethan, hold me!"

He held her so tightly. He had to let go and finally kissed her forehead. Both were crying.

"My ribs!" he said, grimacing.

"I'm sorry. I'm so sorry," said Mary Ann. "I'm so sorry for everything. Please forgive me." Her face was drenched. It was screwed up like a baby's. Her eyes were reddened. She rubbed them and kissed him again.

"Please forgive me!" he said. "Mary Ann, oh Mary Ann," he said as he kissed her throat and her hair. He felt her back and body with his hands.

When they finally parted, he sat her down upon the sofa facing the stove. The cool, autumn night air had invaded indoors. He placed an afghan over her shoulders while he went to the refrigerator for some wine.

They drank and talked for the next three hours. They let the words fall, releasing pent-up tensions. Ethan finally was able to tell her, with surprisingly little shame, exactly what happened between him and Lina that night in Brescia.

He told of the move to Colorado, of Lina nearly drowning in the lake, and how the rodeo performer, Ralph Lawrence, rescued her.

"And I never liked him, didn't trust him, before that. I misjudged many people. I guess I've grown up some."

"We all have," said Mary Ann, relating how the steadfast loyalty of Donny got her through the worst time in her life. She told how the birth of her daughter gave her a purpose, a reason to live.

"Why did you come?" he asked, kissing the softness of her hair.

"Tonight, you mean?"

"Yes."

"I was at the dinner for Mike Scott, looking and waiting for you. I talked to your grandfather on the porch. He told me you and he went hunting and that you stopped at Little Mae's...the Hathaway grave."

She began crying again, and Ethan cried with her, but happily now.

"That day, that first day," he said. "Do you remember? I thought you were a little nuts, the way it all struck you, finding an old grave of a little baby. Then I saw how much you cared. My God, Mary Ann, my heart just melted that day. I wanted to grab you right there to tell you I loved you. I couldn't though. I didn't have the guts. I thought you were still Donny's girl. I respected that!"

"I know," she said.

"Then you did it for us. Remember?"

She smiled as they both sat silently, mutually reflecting for only seconds about that day. The heat of that day on the mountain had overwhelmed the moment. He kissed her throat, and neither could hold back that powerful tide. On the way back down the mountain, Mary Ann made Ethan walk ahead when they reached the stream.

"You were my first love," she said.

"And last, Mary Ann. I want to be the last.

She started to stand up from the couch. "I've got to go!"

"No!" he urged, pulling her back down and laying her gently with her head snug against the arm of the sofa. With his hand, he began rubbing her thigh.

"No, we can't." She pushed him away. "Please!"

She stood and pressed her clothes with her hands to tidy them up. "I have to go to the bathroom." There, she washed her face, put on lipstick, and then forcefully wiped it off again with paper tissues.

They stood at the open door, unaffected by the night chill as the moon crept away from captor clouds, rolling a mat of white light across the lawn and cabin. The light fell across the doorway into Mary Ann's eyes.

"When will I see you?" Ethan asked.

Mary Ann looked away. "We can't. You know we can't." She kissed him again and cried, "Oh, I don't know why I came? I'm here. I had to see you, I had to hold you just once more!"

"Mary Ann, no!"

"Yes, I have to go!" She tried to pull away, but he held her.

"We can't, Ethan. We can't. You know we can't!"

"Mary Ann, I have to see you. I'll die without you! Mary Ann, please!"

"It's Ellie!" she blurted. "I can't because of her. I won't ruin her life!"

They embraced once more, saying nothing. A sudden, snapping sound came from the woods. They then heard a thudding of heavy footsteps toward the lawn.

Mary Ann froze with her mouth open.

Ethan laughed. "It's all right. It's a moose! See, there, right where the woods meets the lawn. He pointed, just as the huge ungainly animal changed direction, heading through the meadow toward the bog at the other end.

He finally relaxed his hold on Mary Ann. She slipped from his grasp and held his hands.

"I'll call you!" he said.

"Don't!" she said, backing across the porch to the steps. "You can't!"

"I have to!"

"No, no!" She then whispered, "Yes! No, Ethan, I'll call you! I'll call!" She turned and fled to her car.

She broke the speed limit on the winding dirt roads between her house and Ethan's cabin, It was deserted except for a few darkened homes she passed on either side. When she raced through the front door, the apology to Jeannette, the teenaged babysitter, for being late was out of her mouth before she had her coat off. The girl said it was okay. Ellie had slept most of the evening and was not a bother. Mary Ann was relieved that Donny had not come home yet. She was thankful the party must still be going strong. She crept into bed and barely closed her eyes when she heard his car pull into the driveway.

Chapter 7
The Audition

The worst time was Christmas Day, the holiday spent alone except for the company of his parents and grandparents at the farmhouse in Lowgate Springs. He got an Irish wool sweater from his parents and a new pair of lamb's wool slippers from his grandparents.

Opening the gifts, he harbored fears about a life spinning backward. He was eight years old again, dependent for companionship with his elders and his daily moods riding a roller coaster.

That Christmas morning, he looked once again at the tiny package he had hidden in his bureau drawer. It contained a gold bracelet, and the card read, "Mary Ann. Love, Ethan." He could see her opening it, hopefully on the day they were finally to be together again for the remainder of their lives. Somehow, he saw that day coming. How it would happen, he did not know. However, that thought alone kept his sanity intact.

"You're another Herb Score," said Big Ethan at the dinner table while carving the roast turkey. They had been talking about Ethan's chances of returning to professional skiing, though no one held out full hope because it was now approaching two years since his one World Cup victory.

"Who's Herb Score?"

The old man was pleased to relate the unfortunate true tale of "probably one of the greatest left-handed pitchers, at least the most promising. Played with the Cleveland Indians, tore up the Major Leagues for a couple of years, led in strikeouts. Then a line drive hit him in the eye one day."

"Dad, that's a fine thing to be telling him," said Marge Atwood, sitting next to Ethan.

"Off the bat of Gil McDougald," Big Ethan continued. "Gave people one more reason to hate the Yankees. I'm sorry."

"It's okay," Ethan said, laughing and trying to set the conversation at ease. "I know what he means. I'm not the only professional athlete to see his career busted up by an injury."

"There are hundreds of them," said Ethan. "Guys who never made it because of arm trouble, pitchers anyway. Knee trouble for the football players and skiers. I'm taking it one day at a time. Slow, real slow. On the other hand, it's nice to savor the downtime. Just let things go."

Ethan's dad looked at the half-empty wine glass in front of Ethan. He said a small prayer.

Early in January, when he was back on skis again, even with the injuries, his knee surgically repaired for the fourth time, the shoulder still aching, and facing arthroscopic probing to remove the bone chip, Ethan was still skiing as well as any of the advanced skiing guests thrust his way by Bruce White.

A long-distance call from Klecko and Rutledge buoyed him. They were at Val d'Isere, and both had scored in the top ten. The team was not doing badly without Ethan; however, with him during his prime in the days after Kitzbuehel, they would have been in superb position to challenge the best of the Europeans.

"We need you, Ethan!" yelled Morgan through the phone, standing in the lobby of the Fleur de Lis Hotel.

"No, we don't!" Klecko yelled over him. "I wanna be the star. How the hell can I be the star when Atwood is around?"

"Don't listen to him!" said Morgan, laughing.

"Don't worry. I stopped listening to him the day after he gave me a language lesson. Remember?" said Ethan.

They all laughed. Klecko was the loudest. "Hey, I miss you for that, Ethan babe. I'm not havin' any fun. These dumb assholes don't let me pick on them the way you used to."

"What a shame!" Ethan replied.

"Hey!" Klecko yelled. "March 8th in Aspen. Be there!"

"I've got it circled on my calendar," said Ethan, referring to the World Championships, the last set of major races on an international level. "Nothing will stop me from being there."

On a day he skied with some TV sports executives from New York City, he suspected they were not there simply to enjoy the company of a World Cup skier in Vermont. Instead, they were there to assess his skills of elocution. Always looking for the right color commentator to relate the rush of competition to the viewers, especially with the Winter Olympics coming up, Ethan Atwood could be the choice, depending on how well he handled a microphone.

Curious and anxious the day before their arrival, he called his agent, Red Everts, to see if he could flush out what the TV people had in mind.

"I really don't know," said Everts. "Would you be game for that, being a color commentator? You have to talk on cue, you know." Everts' concerns were really assessments. He knew Ethan's personality. He was more quiet than talkative. He was passive most of the time, except during competition. Everts knew Ethan was literate and well-spoken when he chose to be, but Everts wondered if he could make it work through the TV medium. On the other hand, his chiseled good looks would sit well with viewers.

"I wanna be there," said Ethan, "be involved somehow. And I can't think of a better way. Especially when there's money involved."

Everts paused as he looked out his window at the flat, Camden waterfront across the Delaware River from his high-rise office in Philadelphia. He then replied, "Gimme an hour or two. I'll call New York and see what I can find out."

A while later, Everts concluded in his return call to Ethan that, "I think that's what they're after. I called a sports guy I know at NBC, and he got back to me on the Q-T. He said he nosed around, and it seems that's what they're doing. They have a couple of skiers in mind. You're at the top of the list." He laughed. "They like your looks."

"Shit!" said Ethan. "Looks shouldn't count."

"They're probably not going to tell you right out what they're doing there today, unless they ask you to come down and audition. They're more than likely there to size you up, see if you brush your teeth and can keep up a stream of bullshit."

"You're scaring' the shit out of me right now, Red, and you know it," Ethan replied honestly. "I have to meet them in an hour."

"Comb your hair," said Red.

"Kiss my ass!" replied Ethan, who nevertheless went to the bathroom medicine cabinet. He self-consciously grinned for the mirror, opened the cabinet, and took four 200-milligram tablets of ibuprofen from a large, plastic bottle.

He returned to the kitchen sink. In the cabinet above, he kept the vodka bottle and poured a generous three or four fingers into a glass. He felt his painkilling combination of Motrin and alcohol was more sensible than some codeine-based elixir that might do the job better but also pooped all over your brain. He would take a little pain and mask it with a little booze.

"Insurance," he said and then added some water. He popped the 800 milligrams of painkiller into his mouth and washed it down with a grimace.

"The World Cup," the executive named Fred Glazer said to him on the lift. "Must be a heckuva lot different from skiing with a couple of New Yorkers in Vermont." "Well, skiing's skiing," said Ethan. "I enjoy it no matter where."

Glazer and his companion, Philip Emerson, who said he worked in media relations for the network, began their conversations by hopping from one generality to another. As the day progressed, their questions grew more specific.

"What kind of a chance do you think the U.S. Ski Team has at the Olympics?" asked Glazer, suddenly leaning almost into Ethan's face as they sat in the warming hut by a blazing fire near the top of the mountain. They had skied four runs down a big cruiser named Little Elbow, so-called for its sharp bend at the bottom of a head wall. The skiing was icy and difficult. "And I mean, without you on the team and without you racing, what kind of a chance does this team have?"

Hesitating for a few seconds, carefully choosing his thoughts and how to put them into words, Ethan looked directly at the questioner and then sat back in his chair before answering.

"I can't answer that, and I'll tell you why," realizing too late these guys were here for some kinds of energetic snippets that would keep viewers glued to the screen, not comments like "I can't answer that."

He continued anyway, "When I won my first race, nobody knew it was coming. That was Kitzbuehel."

The men nodded, pushing closer to the table. Besides the scrawny kid behind the counter serving up soup and sandwiches, only a half-dozen other skiers were in the tiny cabin-like room. Most of them were senior ski bums, retired, old locals who met and skied every day at Maple Glen. They were old men with gray hair and bright red cheeks, laughing a lot at old versions of familiar stories.

"Nobody, I mean nobody expected me to win that day. I wasn't even sure myself. I just wanted to race my damnedest, excuse me, my best. It's the way it happens. Somebody on this year's team could be ready for that kind of breakthrough. You have to look at their results up to now. They're young, therefore they're unpredictable. Can they outrace the Austrians? Probably not. The Swiss? Probably not. Germans? Not the way they've been going lately."

"Can the United States pull off a couple of surprises? Bet your ass they can!" said Ethan. "The Olympics. I was never there, but I know how big the race is. Guys get pumped. Some get over-pumped. They're so tight they ski out or go down." He sat back and laughed. "Like me!"

The other two smiled, but they said nothing, looking at him to continue.

"Others, their coaches tell them, 'Look, just have fun. This is an honor to be here! Go out and enjoy yourselves.' Well, some of those skiers are relaxed enough to win. You never know what's going to happen!"

"Interesting," said Glazer and then looked around the room as though he was searching for a change of subject.

The rest of the afternoon, Ethan spent mostly quietly and silently cursing.

"I blew it! I blew it! I blew it!"

He thought it was a most unpleasant day, aggravated even more in the extreme by the uneven skiing conditions. A thaw, typical of January in northern New England, invaded the mountain a few days before, letting fog and rain rape the slopes of its best snow. When the temperatures dropped at night, what was left in the morning was an unwelcome icy hard pack that the skiers called bulletproof.

"Have a good trip back," Ethan said, poking his face in the window of the rental Ford Explorer. "I hope I see you guys again!"

They thanked him, as one said, "for a great day of skiing. Call us again if you get some real snow up here."

"Well, they're expecting a big storm in a couple of days. The way the temperature's dropping, it'll be powder. I'll certainly let you know."

He rode the lifts up toward the high pines where he had stashed his snowmobile, trying to avoid re-creating the morning's events. He put himself at ease with the promise that a few swift runs downhill would work wonders for his burgeoning self-contempt.

Total quiet lurked in the trees. They were fully green and dark from the recent rains. Examining the woods in all directions, hating the new sneak thief within him, he yanked the vodka bottle from his saddlebag and swallowed long and hard until the heat hit bottom. He then fired his brain with warmth as he pushed off downhill, carving beauteous, confident turns on the hard pack.

Out in the open, he hailed a couple of Spring Mountain students riding the lift above. Doing so tipped his balance. An edge slipped, and he went down with enough force to pop his bindings, crack his head on the ice, and knock the wind right out of him. Embarrassed, he bounded upward as soon as he could gulp some air. He steadied himself on his ski poles as some of the locals in the lift above pounced to the occasion with automatic glee.

"Yo, Ethan, do it again! Yard Sale!"

"See, I told ya!" said one student, "Even the best of 'em go down on this shit."

"It ain't shit, man. It's slippery concrete!" said another.

He sprawled in bed late the next morning while he contemplated a dash for the bathroom, wondering and worrying if he would need a Motrin cocktail to deaden the pain of his head and body. He had drunk heavily the night before to neutralize the new bumps and bruises he had suffered in his fall. Stumbling from bed, he scrambled to the toilet, bent over, and puked. He felt his gut contract into an uncontrollable knot as it forced up air and saliva, the contents of an empty stomach. They called them dry heaves, a wrenching, involuntary payback from the dissipation of the night before.

Hollow-eyed as he faced the mirror and fingered the large welt on his head, he scolded himself for not wearing a helmet. His old Dopey hat did not work against solid ice, the ultimate hard pack. He went to the kitchen, pulled out the bottle of vodka-laced orange juice, and drank an eight-ounce glass. He shuddered as it hit his stomach with a hot burst that immediately flushed out the haze and the pain. He waited a minute before holding his hands out straight, palms down, letting them relax. When he did not see any tremors, he pulled on the heavy bathrobe Lina had given him, stirred up the logs in the stove, and cooked a big breakfast of bacon and eggs. Then he napped until noontime, waking to the dry tune of twigs scratching the side of the cabin. Clumsily stretching with great pain to reach the remote control on the side table, he flicked on the Weather Channel and watched the scrolling message. This time, it was white letters against an orange background, not the usual blue. It warned of a "Winter Storm Advisory. Heavy snowfall whipped by high winds will form blizzard conditions, especially in the higher elevations. Temperatures will drop to way below zero."

"At last, some decent snow," he said, dropping his head back onto the pillow. He drifted in and out of slumber. Thoughts of warmth broke over him—brown eyes and soft hair.

"What the hell, I'll risk it," he said, getting up and rekindling the fire. He held his outstretched hands over the stove to let the heat soothe. He knew Donny was most likely at his office in Barre.

He held the phone in his left hand and looked at it curiously before dialing.

"What if Donny answers? Well, it's not like we don't know each other? I'll ask him how things are? Ask him to go skiing when he gets the chance.'

He went to the vodka bottle in the cupboard and drank it straight from the neck. He then dialed, letting the phone ring two…three…four…then five times.

She answered, "Hello!"

He pushed the reset button. At the other end of the line, Mary Ann said "Hello" twice more before hearing the flat tone, signaling nobody there.

"Jesus," he said, walking to the big window overlooking the lawn. Big, gray clouds were moving in from the west. He tried to focus on how good the powder would be in a day or two.

He dialed another number, a long-distance number.

"Lina is not here anymore," said the pleasant, female voice. "She doesn't work here anymore. She went back to Italy and then joined a firm in Paris. Yes, designing. No, I don't know her forwarding address. You could reach it long-distance, I'm sure."

Chapter 8
"My pain, my shame"

Mary Ann held little Ellie in her arms so the child could see the black-capped chickadees feasting in small flying circuses around the feeder hanging from the big maple not ten feet from the window. The steeply pitched roof of the small feeder held a pillow like glop of snow, a fairy tale castle.

"Birdie!" said Ellie, pointing at the small balls of fluff.

The day was dawning beautifully, although it would take another hour before the full sunlight skirted the mountaintop to the east. Grotesquely shaped soft, white mounds covered each pine branch. Some were gargoyles. Others were creeping fat cats. Others were simple snowmen. So much snow had fallen from the storm of the night before that it had drifted above the top of the barn door.

Donny had just finished plowing out the lane and came onto the back porch. He stomped his boots. Entering the mudroom, he stuck the heels of his boots in the bootjack. He slipped them from his feet and then placed his feet in slippers before entering the kitchen.

"More coffee?" Mary Ann asked.

"Yeah, one more cup. It's not that cold anymore, and the wind's died down. But it's brisk." He rubbed his hands over the stove.

"How's the Gap Road, I wonder?" she asked, not having heard the plow truck's slow roar as it labored up the mountain for a while. In heavy storms, it would make several sweeps in a night, scooping ocean waves of dirty snow to the sides of the road in ever-increasing piles and laying down little circles of sand and salt from its pinwheels.

"It's pretty good from what I can see," said Donny. "It better be, or Bruce White will have a shit fit. The locals'll wanna be all over that powder this morning. They sure as hell better be able to get up the mountain roads to get there!"

After Mary Ann dropped Ellie at the nursery in Lowgate Springs and drove through the village uphill to Maple Glen, a state police car roared past her about halfway up the mountain road with its lights flashing. She was concerned and wondered why. She hoped it was not anything serious. Some kids had broken into the money-changing machine in the downstairs locker room of the main lodge the week before, and she wondered if it had happened again. Or could it be some other break-in that occurred? Either way, the cops would not rush up the hill like that just to investigate the vandalizing of a coin machine.

Soon, another police car rushed by, passing her on the left with its red lights flashing. From above, she heard the whap-whap roar of a helicopter. As Mary Ann parked her car in the administration building parking lot, Bruce White's secretary, Sara Thomas, approached her. She had run from the building without wearing any coat. Her arms were wrapped tightly over her midriff to keep warm. Her face was twisted. It appeared to be puzzled with grief as she grasped Mary Ann by the arms.

"They found a body on the Summit lift, frozen to death." She held Mary Ann by the shoulders. "It's Ethan!"

By noon, the news that the lifeless form of Ethan Atwood had been discovered frozen on a chair lift at Maple Glen had rocketed through the valley. By mid-afternoon, the wire services had notified the ski-racing world of the bizarre death of the former World Cup downhiller.

The news went through the valley and the state like a rocket burst, hurting, saddening, and mesmerizing in its wake. It created an equal mystery in the skiing communities of Europe and the American West.

"Did you hear? About Ethan Atwood? He's dead, they found him frozen on a chair lift!"

Vermont was a place virtually dominated by tranquility. Even though violent death was not a stranger, the occasional highway accident, skiing accident, or hunting accident were mere misfortunes compared with this single unexplained tragedy that would stir disbelief in townsfolk for months to come.

It took several days before the resort returned to any sense of normalcy. Phones rang. Reporters gathered outside a makeshift pressroom in the cafeteria part of the lodge. Television cameras and wires poked their intrusions into every available space. People asked questions that were never fully answered. Bruce White bore most of the hammering. He was confused, angry, and remorseful, a reflection of the feelings en masse throughout the valley.

The news of Ethan's death took on a bizarre prominence because of the manner in which death came. People buzzed about it. Though skiers had become stranded on ski lifts every day, for minutes or even hours, they eventually were rescued. Nobody could remember anyone being caught overnight on a lift. Like all tragedies that were so odd and so frightening, people who had never heard of Ethan nor had never followed racing were drawn in by the macabre imaginings of the death. It could happen to them. How awful. It was like being trapped in a mine, thrown overboard in mid-ocean, or being buried alive with the suffocating weight of dirt being piled on top of the casket. You knew, if you did not escape soon or if you were not rescued, you would die.

Film clips on television that evening repeated Ethan's thrilling come-from-behind race on Hahnenkhamm. Barely out of the starting gate, he took the wrong line, and his knee scraped the snow. He struggled to regain his balance and barely clipped the next gate. The announcer was shouting, "He's out of it! He'll never make up the time!" It was then the split-second that uprooted tradition, an American won Kitzbuehel. A curly-headed kid from Vermont beat both the fabled Hans Gerbisch of Germany and Franz Kluckner of Austria. For a brief glittering moment, it set the European skiing world, at least, on its ass.

Big Ethan caught his breath as he watched the film on television, even though it was just a slice of the video he had watched dozens of times in the past. It was stored next to the trophies on the shelf of the living room. He heard Rose's footsteps coming from the kitchen and swiftly clicked off the television, wiping an eye with the knuckle of a forefinger.

"It was about Ethan, wasn't it?" said Rose, untying an apron.

Big Ethan nodded.

Ethan and Rose asked the same questions that others asked, but they asked them to each other in the privacy of their old home, not at the General Store in Lowgate Springs, also called "Gossip Central." The same questions were asked all throughout the skiing world.

"Why did Ethan Atwood die in such a gruesome way?"

Nobody has died overnight on a ski lift. Or have they? Men connected in the executive offices of ski resorts searched their records and asked questions.

"No, never happened before."

"Not supposed to happen."

A suicide? Accidental death? Homicide? No, it was out of the question. Then, at the Frost Heave Saloon, old chums lining the bar speculated as best they could when fortified with a few drinks and the power of hindsight.

"I wouldn't have been surprised if he wrapped himself around a tree on his Harley or in that pickup truck," said Theron Walls.

"Or mountain bike," echoed another.

"Yeah, that too. Speed came as naturally to Ethan as breathing. But this, Jesus Christ, I just can't believe it."

"Ethan was drinking a lot lately," said Walls, casting a glance at the bartender, Connie Rich. She looked away.

Ethan had some good reasons to be in a down mood. His racing career, which had been so bright with the promise of not just winning but perhaps dominating, was on hold due to a succession of unsettling injuries. And his heart ached heavily. His love life was in an unrecoverable shambles.

So, what was the cause of death? Not giving a damn? Gross negligence? Recklessness?

"Perhaps," thought his neighbors and colleagues.

They could not wrestle with the thought of what was known absolutely about Ethan's last hour. With difficulty, they had to accept that it was something that seemed dumb and remote. Freezing to death on a chair lift is slow and painful. It happens only to the helpless.

"Unless the victim is drugged or drunk beyond caring," said Walls.

Roger Walls arose at 4:00 AM and looked out the window to where the barn was lit by the strong floodlight hanging from the rear of the house. His parents were sleeping in the front room. He could hear his father's snores. Beside the barn, in the glow of the light, was his 1984 Ford pickup with the long bed and large cab. It was the one his father had angrily insisted cost too much money and was a waste. However, today, Roger was to make a killing, earning more money than he had ever seen in his eighteen years. He had prepared carefully by buying a new plow with infallible hydraulic fittings. It would last for years. From the window, he admired the shiny yellow of the big blade, underscored in red. No scratches or dents. Ass-kicking new!

Charles Cummings, the funeral director, told him the cow pasture next to the funeral home had to be free of snow by 8:00 AM, long before the viewers were to arrive. Lowgate Springs would never see a funeral like this one.

The line of mourners stretched a quarter-mile. It went all the way to the general store at the opposite end of town. They stood patiently in line. Some stamped their feet to keep warm. They were bundled up to the ears against the cold that could not be pierced by the bright sunlight.

In the four days since the big blizzard, more snow fell every night, piling high against the white-painted porch of the funeral home. The highway crews had been working around the clock. The roar of their heavy diesels and clanking of chains would drown the conversations in the line of mourners.

A roofless tunnel had been dug through the eight-foot pile of snow in order for the crowd to reach the porch and then file inside. Sinewy branches of mordant lilac wrapped through a trellis at the end of the porch. So many people were filing into the funeral home, it became impossible to keep the front door closed between each entry. Charles Cummings, tall and angular who held his bony hands before him most of the time as if he was in constant prayer for the dead, had turned the thermostat in the large viewing parlor to ninety degrees, an almost feeble attempt to offset the cold that crept around the ankles of the mourners inside. Closest friends and relatives attended a private viewing by invitation the night before. Lina, who flew immediately from Paris, finally embraced Mary Ann in a side room where overflow sprays of bright flowers had been stacked. They held each other for a long time, but they exchanged few words other than soft, expected pleasantries until Lina said, "I must speak with you. In private."

Mary Ann asked the undertaker where they might talk. Sensing the urgency in her nevertheless controlled voice, he said, "Use my office." He opened the door and ushered the two women inside with a sweeping gesture of his arms.

The office appeared to be pretentiously leather-bound, at least the furniture was. Situated against the handsome, dark mahogany of the wainscoting and pastoral wallpaper, it seemed unlike Vermont. Lina stood by the window. She faced Mary Ann, who sat down in one of the leather chairs.

"I want you to know," Lina began, "that my sorrow is strong for you. Stronger than it is for myself. I *did* love Ethan. I not ashamed to say that. Maybe not like you loved him, but in my own way." Flashing just faintly in the background of her confession were words like selfish and immature. She quickly added, "Once I saw how perfect you and Ethan were together…and innocent.

"Forgive me, this is difficult for me to say this."

Mary Ann, unsure of her own feelings, whispered hoarsely, "It's all right."

"In those few weeks, when I was here and when I first arrived in Vermont, I suddenly see you two, innocent lives living together. Warm, you were warm. Ethan was warm. And I destroyed that. I took that which was good and innocent and trashed it, just for the sake of a stupid night. How stupid! How stupid!"

She stared outside the window where the snow went on and on over the fields in massive, silent, glacier form. "I hate the snow," she thought.

"I just want to say I regret what I caused. I thought I could win him from you."

"You did," Mary Ann said abruptly.

"No, no, I never did!" Lina pleaded. "I never knew how strong love could be until I saw it in the two of you. I wish I had abortion right when it started. How foolish I was."

"Would that have mattered, Lina? Unless, of course, you assumed I would never have found out."

"You would find out. I know that now!" Lina suddenly stifled her involuntary urge to shout. "I know Ethan well enough, knew him enough to know he never could hide his love for you. Never.

"I don't know what it's worth," said Lina, dabbing at her eyes with a tissue. "My pain, my shame follows me."

"You don't have to…" But Lina interrupted.

"I'm not asking for forgiveness." She faced Mary Ann directly and looked straight into her eyes. "If I were you, I would never forgive me for what I did. I do not ask for that."

Mary Ann said nothing, but her eyes softened, accepting the apology, knowingly so now, on this day. She absorbed a self-guilt sharpened over this past year. It probed deeper inside her, the guilt that said repeatedly she could have solved everything by accepting, just once in her goddamned life, the flaw of her misguided perfection. She could have so easily understood and forgiven others. Her fault was in not even once giving herself the same standards she so willingly gave to others. She had even locked that most proper virtue, being a walking paragon of steely merit, onto Ethan. And that was wrong.

For now, Mary Ann would reserve some forgiveness. She went closer to Lina, who was openly crying by now, put her arm around her, and said, "C'mon, we have to go now."

Lina flew back to Europe the same night.

There was no internment, which was typical of a winter death in northern New England. Bodies are kept in vaults to await the spring and the thawing of the frozen ground. Paul and Marge Atwood decided to have the body cremated and the ashes scattered at the mountaintop when the weather got warmer.

Chapter 9
The Last Chair

The medical examiner's inquest was held two weeks after Ethan was found and all the lab tests and autopsy results had been returned. The courtroom in Montpelier, though well-lit, was a somber, dignified oak-paneled place that was packed to overflowing. Friends, acquaintances, several coworkers, and skiers at Maple Glen and from Stowe, Sugarbush, Mad River Glen and Killington all jammed the pews. They wore their work or play clothes, mostly wildly colorful ski jackets.

Ed Phoebe, sad-faced, removed his graying yellow vest and stuffed it beneath the pewlike bench. Ethan had been the most famous person that Ed had known, and he had always been a joking, fun-filled friend. Most of the time, Ethan's job called for skiing with well-heeled patrons of the slopes, television and magazine executives from New York City, movie stars, and other entertainers. However, Ethan still found time to mess around on the slopes with the locals, including Ed, urging him to tuck "just once in your life and challenge the mountain." He called the old man "the greatest downhill house painter I ever saw!"

For the loved ones closest to Ethan, they knew the inquest proceedings would be more difficult to get through than the viewing. Rose Delahanty refused to go. Big Ethan, on the other hand, concluded, "I have to find out what happened up there!"

Just an hour before the proceedings started, Mary Ann decided, as an afterthought, to attend, although Donny had tried to talk her out of it. They sat toward the rear.

"I may not be able to stand this," she told Donny. "I want to sit here."

Strangely, most of the people who filed into the small, paneled courtroom failed to greet each other, as if each was expected to be there and that the proceeding were merely a continuum of the initial wake. The mourning had become ritual.

Only the lawyers wore suit jackets and ties in the court. Wearing a checked sport coat over a white turtleneck, Bruce White, his bald head reflecting the artificial light, sat near the front. He held a briefcase in his lap. Two lawyers and an insurance agent accompanied him.

Bruce was somber, concentrating on the pre-hearing drill that the lawyers put him through. He was prepared to explain how Atwood was employed by the company as a celebrity host, a young man whom everyone loved. His vision of Ethan still was that of the strong racer on the poster. He was speeding downhill and busting through a gate with his broad shoulder punching the plastic pole. His downhill leg was extended, knifing the ski into the snow. Bruce was nervously aware of the grim business side of this affair. The liability. An apparent breakdown in safety rules had not only caused a tragedy, it found a victim whose fame had propelled the incident to a worldwide level that Bruce White did not welcome.

The tragedy had already collected other victims. First and immediate was Emma Casey, only twenty years old. She was the bottom lift operator when the lift was shut down for the final run exactly at 3:45 PM on Tuesday, January 6, about five hours prior to what had been reckoned as the time of death.

When Emma had been told the next morning that a skier had died overnight on her lift, she collapsed and had to be revived by her roommate. When learning the skier was Ethan Atwood, despair plunged deeper. How, she asked herself repeatedly in the days that followed, could it have happened?

With permission of the court, Emma took the witness stand with George Alston, the lift operations supervisor, who was her boss, at her side. Though a legal proceeding, a medical examiner's inquest, whose goal is to determine the cause of death, is a less rigid procedure than a full-blown court trial. Dr. Thomas Rowles, the medical examiner, handled much of the proceedings.

Alston held the lift log of the day of the mishap. He related the record showing that Emma had placed an orange cone on Chair No. 27 at about 3:45 PM and the top lift operator, Jason Duvall, had counted eleven chairs after Chair No. 27 had passed by him before notifying dispatch that the lift was stopped and shut down for the day.

"Why eleven chairs?" asked Dr. Rowles.

"It's standard procedure, sir, to count eleven chairs after the last chair had passed the bull wheel at the top," said Alston. "It's a safety precaution to ensure that no one had gotten on the lift after the last chair had been marked."

"But, in this case, it appeared that someone did, isn't that correct?"

Before Alston could answer, Maple Glen attorney Morris Schick interrupted. "Objection, sir! I advise the witness that it wouldn't be proper for him to assume that which he does not know."

Dr. Rowles leaned to one side, cupping his mouth while he conferred with Sam Adamson, the state's attorney seated next to him.

Rowles asked Emma to backtrack, detailing her actions prior to calling the last chair.

Taking a deep breath and with eyes wide, she told about placing a double cross of bamboo across each of the two lanes leading to the lift ramp to prevent skiers from entering the area at lift-closing time. Skiers and snowboarders were always racing to the lift at the last seconds like drunks to the bar for last call. Many of them would playfully swear at Emma when deprived of their one last run. Sometimes she would return the laugh, depending on how tired she was from the stressful rigors of the day. Standing in the cold, she braked each 300 pound chair with her forearm as it swiveled toward the waiting skiers. She sometimes had to quickly punch the emergency stop button when a skier fell on the ramp. There were moments when the job was worth a lot more than the $5.50 an hour that Emma earned.

"Then what did you do after you fenced off the area?" asked Dr. Rowles.

"I started taking in the cones and put one on the chair," Emma answered nervously. The purple vest she wore, marked with the Maple Glen insignia, swelled with each hurried breath.

"By taking in the cones, what do you mean?"

"The orange traffic cones on each side of the ramp. We have to have four cones on each side," she said, feeling as if the explanation was a trifle silly. It seemed so difficult to make clear.

"The cones are there for safety then," said Rowles.

"Yes, sir."

Dr. Rowles began asking another question, but he was interrupted with an "Excuse me, sir" by Sam Adamson.

"Isn't it possible, Miss Casey," Adamson queried, "for someone to slip under the rope and hustle onto the chair while your back is turned?"

"Yes!" Emma shouted, her voice rising in fear. "But I saw no one. No one did that. I swear I would have noticed!"

"At any time, during say...five minutes after you put the cone on the chair...was your back turned to the lift?" asked Adamson as pleasantly and as carefully as the decorum of the occasion demanded.

At this Emma sobbed, "Probably, I guess so, but I would have seen!"

"When you put the orange cone in the chair, that signals to the top operator that particular chair indeed is the last chair of the day, doesn't it?"

Yes," said Emma, "but you also have to call him on the sound phone and...and tell him the number of the chair so he can watch for it...when it comes up." Her voice was trembling.

"And what is the sound phone?"

"It's a direct line to the top of the lift, I guess. You just push a button, and it rings. Then you have to hold down a green button when you talk. You have to tell the guy at the top..."

"Guy at the top?" interrupted Adamson.

"The operator. The top operator. You have to tell him the number of the chair where you put the cone."

Five more minutes of verbal scratching over the details by Adamson and Rowles ended Emma's testimony. With a sigh of only momentary relief, she got out of the chair, hoping, perhaps futilely, that the testimony to come would somehow exonerate her terrible guilt.

Jason Duvall's answers did little to help. He was eighteen, a high school dropout who was determined to maintain that academic record. He was focused in life with becoming a snowboarding virtuoso on the Maple Glen mountain or any other mountain. Becoming a liftie was only a means to gaining a season pass.

"When you saw the last chair pass by at the top and you counted eleven more empty chairs, what did you do?" asked Adamson, who had picked up the bulk of the questioning from Dr. Rowles by now.

"I called dispatch, but not right away. I was raking the ramp, putting more snow on it to fill in the holes and get it ready for the next day. A few chairs went by before I went back inside and called."

"How many chairs?"

"I don't know, maybe a half-dozen."

"But there was nobody on the lift that you could see. Is that correct?"

"That's correct, sir," Duvall said puffily, pleased he remembered Morris Schick's coaching to insert the phrase "that's correct, sir" from time to time instead of "yeah."

The medical examiner and the state's attorney huddled some more, quietly whispering to see if there was anything they forgot to ask.

Morris Schick took the opportunity. "I'd like to ask the witness, if I may, if there was any more communication between him and Miss Casey prior to your calling dispatch. In other words, doesn't it really take the two of you to stop the lift, at least the two of you communicating?"

"Yeah…uh, that's correct, sir, I called Emma on the sound phone. You can't shut down the lift when there's a chair hanging on the bull wheel."

"Why is that?"

"Well, they don't like the weight on the bull wheel overnight. Somethin' like that, I think," shrugged Duvall, evoking a few smiles in the audience. "Emma has to tell me when there are no chairs riding on the wheel down below, and I can't shut 'er down up top until the chairs are clear of the wheel up here…up there."

"But then, when you did finally stop the lift, were there any chairs riding the wheel at all, top or bottom?"

"No, no chairs. We were all clear."

"But how many chairs did you have to let go by before none were riding the wheel?"

"Oh, just a couple."

Adamson, not at all agreeable to taking over of a crucial point of the proceedings by the well-paid corporate attorney, interrupted, "So, if the last chair was Number 27, then you counted eleven more?"

"Yes sir," said Duvall.

"And how many more chairs went by after that until the lift was finally stopped?"

"I thought it was only about a half-dozen."

Adamson leaned forward. His shirt collar dug at his red, mottled neck. He examined on the yellow pad the figures he and his staff had repeatedly worked on in the past several days. It was simple arithmetic. The figures added up to precise numbers that stared back at you, yet still not offering an explanation.

"So, actually, you may have been looking at Chair Number 48, give or take a few, when you pushed the stop button."

"I thought so, yes," said Duvall, squirming in his seat. He began to sweat because he knew Ethan Atwood's body was found on Chair Number 7. For the next several minutes, the lawyers, the medical examiner, and Maple Glen officials studied their yellow pads. Conclusions were not satisfactory, and they knew it.

The lift was 5,400 feet long and contained a total of 108 chairs. Each was spaced fifty feet apart. If Chair Number 48 was parked at the top for the night, as Duvall had calculated, that meant Chair Number 103 would have been at the bottom. However, the frozen, stiff body of Ethan Atwood was pulled from Chair Number 7, meaning an additional twelve chairs had passed beyond Duvall's estimate.

"How long does it take for twelve chairs to pass a given point?" asked Adamson.

Alston, sitting behind Duvall, piped up, "It takes a little more than a minute at normal speed." He explained the average lift speed was 540 feet per minute and that it took about ten minutes for a skier to reach the top after boarding the chair.

Adamson asked a few more questions about weather conditions. Duvall confirmed that visibility at the end of the ski day, because of the then-driving snowstorm, was not good.

"It was maybe "a 100, 150 feet.""

The following questions were still unanswered: How did Ethan Atwood get on the lift without anyone seeing him? Where was the chair he was on when it was shut down? Why didn't he shout?

There was no getting into the dead man's mind. Lacking that, the investigation centered on his known activities before the lift closing for the day. The several patrollers who pried his bent, stiff body from the chair told of finding his snowmobile parked in the woods about 200 feet from the bottom of the lift. That was not a mystery. Ethan frequently drove his "sled," as those who own the powerful machines call them, up and over the top of Spring Mountain nearly every day. The log cabin where he lived was only a half-mile down the western side away from the resort. By riding his sled to work, Ethan not only saved a trip requiring nearly four miles by car or truck, it also allowed him to ski where he wanted, including his favorite "poaching" areas. These were places declared off-piste, out of bounds, but it was where the adventurous, both skiers and snowboarders, sought out radical cliffs and chutes to match whatever kamikaze yen they were after.

Roy Ferguson, the head patroller who directed the removal of Ethan's whitened corpse, could not release from his mind the nagging lectures he had thrust at the former World Cup skier, many times over the years or at least since Ethan was a wild teenager. They were mostly one-way conversations. He could see Ethan's slightly grinning, apologetic face. He had been giving the boy hell ever since he was a child and a student at the Spring Mountain Ski Academy years before.

"Ethan, look, I know you're gonna ski out of bounds. My patrollers do it. I used to do it before I got so goddamned old, but, for Christ's sake, stay the hell out of these bowls and trees, and offa these cliffs where the public can see ya. All it does is encourage the dumb buggers to get up there and join you. Believe me, I got enough to do without peelin' somebody's ass out of a tree well up there!"

Ethan, laughing, would reply, "Gotcha, Roy baby! I understand."

However, the off-piste visits to rocky outcrops, the "lump in the throat" jumps, and the blinding rush through the pines would never stop so long as Ethan and his fellow poachers could strap skis to their feet. The dangerously steep, high mountain ranges were shrines, meant to be worshiped and visited often. And Ethan reveled in the role of high priest.

"We'll, I guess you stopped now, old buddy," whispered Roy to the wind on that quiet morning. He stared at Ethan, at the familiar lump of a man who lay bent, his frozen haunches overlapping the rescue sled. It was impossible for the patrollers and state police, who had arrived by helicopter, to straighten Ethan's body. They tied it to the sled with yellow cord and covered it with blankets. They had pried off his goggles, revealing a contrasting strange line of curly black hair against the ghastly white. Ethan's eyes were closed in peace, sculpted shut by the frozen hand of winter.

"Do you think he jumped on that chair?" asked a state cop before ordering the body be taken down to the waiting helicopter.

"How the hell else would he get there?" snapped Ferguson. "Seriously, he was always pulling shit like that. I loved the guy, but he was sometimes a pain in the ass."

Ferguson blinked. The tears froze instantly, sealing his lids like Ethan's. He turned away, yanked off a glove, and warmed his eyes with his hand until they opened.

At the inquest, Ferguson described the day's end routine where patrollers swept the mountain for the last skiers and riders who had not departed to the lodge and parking lots below. A patroller traveled each trail, looking right and left while searching the darkening woods and eyeballing the lifts in the swirling snowstorm.

Paul Myers took the witness stand and told of sweeping under the Summit lift on the Thunder Roll black diamond trail at closing time on the day in question. It was not just steep. The trail was pocked with icy moguls that had been sculpted by skis and snowboards. The falling snow only made it harder to see the ice. At best, Myers, a good, strong skier, groped his way down, but he diligently searched for stray skiers to his left, his right, and above him on the lift. There reached a point in the trail when a rocky outcrop leaped down from the mountain. The trail then cut to the left, departing from the lift line, until it reached the adjoining Silversides trail. Below this juncture for a distance of about 200 feet, it was not possible to observe the cables and steel towers, nor the chairs.

Adamson also asked if the lift was visible from the base lodge, the parking lots, and roads leading to the mountain.

"No, that lift is high up, way above the lower ridge line. There's like a hump in between. It's not visible at all from down below."

Adamson picked up the questioning. "So, in this area and in a heavy snowstorm, you really can't see if anyone is up there on the lift or not. Isn't that correct, even from your vantage point coming down Thunder Roll?"

"Yeah, I guess you could say that," answered Myers, whose face reddened with annoyance at having to answer the question. "But, even though I couldn't see up there and couldn't really sweep that area, if everybody does their job, things like this don't happen."

"You son of a bitch!" George Alston whispered through clenched teeth, loud enough for everyone to hear in a five-foot radius of where he was sitting. "You didn't have to say that, asshole!"

Registering Alston's frustration, Bruce White wrinkled his brow. He saw this coming, the waves of reaction.

Tragedies work their way through small communities like worms through soil. They tunnel and undermine everything they touch. An accident that ends a life first sends a shock in the form of disbelief and frustration. Grief follows. Then there is a search for a cause. Guilt takes over until it reaches a dead end and one or more scapegoats can be found. Bruce White felt guilt because he owned it all. He was the overseer. Beneath him, the feeling spread down directly to mountain operations director, Clayton Undermacher, to Alston, the lift operations supervisor, and then ultimately to Emma Casey, who must have been—probably was—

looking in another direction when Ethan jumped on a moving chair.

There would be no shortage of scapegoats by the time this was through, thought White.

But then one more was added. Ultimately, Ethan himself was to share the blame. The testimony of witness Connie Rich came closest to penetrating the dark unknown of Ethan's role in his own demise.

Chapter 10
Ethan's Role

"Would you tell us your occupation, Miz Rich?" asked Adamson, leaning forward and revealing a charming, penetrating smile directed solely to the pretty, dark-haired, young woman seated before him.

"I'm a bartender at the Frost Heave Saloon," she answered, evoking some slight smiles. This was not the first time the good old Frost Heave would bear mention in public inquiry. The most popular après-ski bar in the valley, it was the occasional target of liquor control agents seeking underage drinkers, who were mostly from New York, southern New England, the Middle Atlantic States, and Canada who faked their way past the bouncer at the door with the wiliest of forged credentials. Then there were traffic accidents, cars driven by tipsy drivers, spinning out of control on the sharp bends of the Mountain Pass highway on which the bar was located. Hardly a week went by in winter without mention of the Frost Heave in the weekly *Valley Sentinel*. Even the DUI arrests, "Driving Under the Influence," could be traced to the Frost Heave depending upon the location of the bust.

The saloon was a barn-red clapboard building with little outside adornment except for a four-by-six foot sign on its porch roof. Inside, the ski world motif dominated the walls with posters, photos, and trophies hung amidst various pairs of old wooden skis and poles with leather baskets. A half-dozen large, red and blue posters of Ethan touching his heels in mid-flight lined one wall alone.

Connie Rich, like many young people in the valley, was a dedicated ski bum. She had worked there three winters. She told Adamson she knew Ethan "probably better than most people." She then blushed at the implication of what could have been meant by her answer. The truth was that she indeed did know Ethan well enough to hold his hand that day across the bar, look into his eyes, and listen with tenderness to what he said and, more revealing, did not say.

Adamson questioned Connie for at least a half hour, politely asking about Ethan's state of mind, about how much he had to drink, how long he was at the bar, the time that he left, whether he was alone when he left, and whether he was driving his car.

"He seemed sad one minute and carefree another," said Connie.

"Can you explain that further?"

"Yes, Ethan was generally cordial and even carefree. When you talked directly to him about anything except a problem he might have, he spoke as if there were no cares at all in the world."

"Well then, how do you know he was sad?"

"When I waited on other customers. If my attention was directed elsewhere. Out of the corner of my eye, I could see him looking down. Looking at himself in the mirror. Rubbing his eyes. I could just tell, I guess, when someone is out of sorts."

"That's sort of a bartender's gift, isn't it?"

Connie chuckled slightly. Many in the audience laughed louder.

"But no, I know he was down. I know his girl, Lina, had just left him. That was days or weeks before. She left him and never came back."

"She left weeks before. In other words, she didn't just leave him recently, is that correct?"

"Yes, but this guy, Ethan, he couldn't shake it loose, the fact she was gone and probably wasn't coming back. He was just as down and out as…well…like she picked up and left the night before. He couldn't seem to get over it."

Connie knew of Ethan's long-ago romance with Mary Ann Queensbury, but, like many of the valley residents, she was not aware how deeply affected both Mary Ann and Ethan were over the loss of each other. That was ancient history as far as any public surmise was concerned. The affair with Lina was not, however.

"He was despondent?"

Mary Ann, still sitting in the rear of the room, squirmed and looked at the ceiling. She then shut her eyes briefly, feeling her heart race.

"Yeah, I'm afraid he was.

Adamson then stood squarely before Connie, as if blocking her way. "And how much did he have to drink that afternoon?"

"Five or six vodkas," she answered reluctantly with her eyes downcast.

"Was that five or six single vodkas, or five or six double vodkas?" asked the lawyer, knowing already the autopsy report showed Ethan's blood-alcohol level measured 0.17 percent, more than double the amount considered unsafe for operating a motor vehicle.

"Doubles," admitted Connie, fearing another citation from the liquor control board for serving visibly intoxicated customers. "It did not matter," she thought. "A good human being was dead." Not only that, it was her friend that was dead. That's what mattered.

"When Mr. Atwood confided in you about his remorse, was he emotional at the time?" asked Adamson.

"You mean, did he cry or anything?"

"Yes, was he visibly upset? Could you describe him as desperate?"

"No, Ethan didn't like to reveal what he felt. I've known him a long time. He kept things bottled up inside. You had to talk to him to get it out. Ethan smiled most of the time. He was generally happy most of the time, and I think…I think…he was able to smile even when his thoughts were bad. Except this time."

As she spoke, a mirrored, hazy image of just she and Ethan at the bar appeared before her. Ethan stared at the moth-eaten old moose head that hung above the cash register. The knuckles of his right hand were knotted in a fist below his nose, covering his mouth. As Connie made small talk, he pretended to smile, but he could not. When she tried looking directly at him, he lowered his eyes to the bar, focusing on the shot glass in front of him.

"Jesus, man, you still hurt, don't you?" Connie said, unconsciously wiping the bar with a cloth. "Hey, look at me. Yoo hoo! Anybody home in there? Hey, Ethan, she's gone. Kaput, vanished. Get on with it!"

"I can't get it out of my mind," said Ethan, squirming on the stool as if his back and legs hurt. He was dressed in ski pants with a bright gold and red jacket unzipped over a white, turtleneck shirt. His floppy, old hat seem plastered to the back of his head.

He wanted to say more. He knew Connie fairly well. Well enough, at least, to know she cared and that whatever went between them would stay that way, not to be shared with others. But, he thought of what he would have to say. "I'm in love with a woman who is married to someone else, one to whom I was betrothed, one to whom I belong, one I should have, possess, care for, love. All of that was taken away from me by a stroke of fate. Beyond my control."

He also thought of the involvement that came later with Lina, his sudden love for her and what it meant. Was it a rebound? A safe haven in the storm of life? He did not have any answers and realized it. He kept silent.

Connie waited for him to say more.

"I wish I could help you to forget. I guess I wish I was woman enough."

She bent forward in an exaggerated pose, trying to look Ethan directly in the eyes. She wanted him to know she meant what she said, that her door was always open and all he had to do was walk in.

Ethan's eyes studied the grain in the old, oak bar. He traced one with his forefinger. After a bit, he said, "Thanks, Connie."

"You know, Ethan, I can't force you to do anything. I have to say this as a friend and as a goddamned bartender. You were like this the other night. I hate nagging. I don't want you to stop coming in here. I worry about you. But you're putting away an awful lot of booze. You even had a bad fall skiing yesterday, didn't ya?"

When Ethan looked up, suddenly startled, she said, "I heard about it. The great Ethan Atwood caught an edge." She laughed. Her warm eyes tried making him smile at least once. "Oh, did I hear. They said you had a yard sale up there. Skis one way, poles the other!"

Ethan emitted a halfhearted chuckle, but he suddenly froze again when she said, "I know why you fell." She picked up the shot glass with just her thumb and forefinger, holding it up for his inspection.

"This, pal, is no good."

Ethan's parents sat at the back of the courtroom, fixing tightly on every word and searching for clues about their son's last hours alive. Connie wished she were somewhere, anywhere but here, and that she did not have to answer any more questions, except maybe the obvious facts. But she did not want to say anything more about remorse and sadness, feelings that should not have to be noted on official reports. But she did not hesitate to tell the court that Ethan finally left the Frost Heave about 3:25 in the afternoon. It had already begun to snow. He told her he was going skiing, and she warned against it.

"You know what happened the other day."

"You know, Connie." Ethan stood up and inhaled a deep breath. "I hear what you're saying. But what do you want me to do? Go home, and stare into the fireplace. Skiing's the only way I know to wring it all out. It's what I've used all my life. It's how I solve problems. I don't know anything else, not a god-damned thing. It's what I do. It's what I'll always do. I'll probably die doin' it!"

"When he left the bar, Miss Rich, did he leave in his car, truck, or some other vehicle?"

"He had his sled in the parking lot."

"By sled, you mean snowmobile."

She nodded and said faintly, "Yes."

"Are you sure he left on the snowmobile? Could you see out the window?"

"I didn't have to. Ethan put his ski boots on in the bar. He had them with him. You can't drive a car with ski boots. Well, you can. Some people do it. But Ethan often went up to the mountain from here on his sled. He went everywhere on the sled. Besides, I could hear it."

She was dismissed and left the stand with a feeling of relief mixed with tension. She would ask her boss for the night off.

Customers would be asking her a ton of questions and volunteering as many ill-founded solutions as to why Ethan died. Connie had enough for one day. Most of the six jurors followed her with their eyes. Some of the men maybe were just looking the way men look at pretty women. Most of all, they were still absorbing the events she had described. They were making up their minds about what happened to Ethan and why.

Chapter 11
Toward Death

When the time came to determine the central motive for the inquest, which was to decide the actual cause of death and whether it was accidental, a suicide, or homicide, Adamson called Dr. Rowles as an expert witness. The cause of death was a simple case of scientific facts, he said. His reading glasses were perched precariously on the end of his nose. "Cardiac arrest, brought on by severe hypothermia, which, in itself, was hastened by the amount of alcohol the deceased had absorbed.

"The alcohol led to an increased loss of body heat through vasodilation."

"Which is?" asked Adamson.

"Dilation of the blood vessels."

"Was Mr. Atwood dressed properly to ward off the terrible cold of that night, doctor?"

"He was if he had remained active. But he was trapped on a chair lift. I don't think he realized, or cared, what was happening to him. That part I can only guess at. But the circumstances tell us he could easily have fallen asleep once the chair stopped moving, become drowsy with the alcohol. He was dressed warm enough for that. But temperatures dropped to minus twenty-three degrees that night. There was a lot of wind and a lot of snow. No human being could have survived for long under those conditions."

Could you describe what happens to a person in that kind of extreme cold?"

Dr. Rowles squirmed in the leather-bound chair, as if he was experiencing what he was about to relate. "The body begins shivering at first. It's the body's way of increasing the production of muscle heat. It usually occurs while the body core is still relatively warm, 98.6 degrees or even ninety-six degrees. But, by this time, it becomes difficult for the person to do coordinated tasks. You would have to assume that Mr. Atwood, under normal conditions, would attempt to climb down somehow from the chair, even if it meant shimmying up to the cable overhead and making his way to a tower. He was pretty close to prime physical condition, and, of course, he was an athlete."

"You say he could have gotten out of that situation?"

"If he had been aware, yes. But, under the influence of alcohol, his motor functions would have deteriorated rapidly in that kind of cold. In a manner of minutes, under cases of even moderate hypothermia, that's when the body core temperature drops to ninety-five or ninety-three degrees. The victim is dazed and barely conscious. He can't do simple tasks with his hands, like zip up a parka. That would be due to the restricted peripheral blood flow. There is violent shivering, slurred speech, and, sometimes, irrational behavior.

The people in the court sat silent as Rowles spoke. Some were on the edges of their chairs, listening to every word as if they were absorbing themselves the terrible product of that cold, cold night.

"In this case, one of Mr. Atwood's gloves was missing." Rowles continued. "The glove for the right hand."

"And what's the significance?"

"I was saying that a hypothermia victim will often begin to undress,

"You mean, start to take off his clothes?" asked Adamson incredulously.

"Yes. Totally unaware that he is cold. He, the victim, no longer cares."

Throughout the testimony, Donny glanced sideways at Mary Ann, who was seated to his left.

"You okay?"

She had loudly sighed when the ski patrol told her of pulling Ethan's frozen body from the chair. However, when Dr. Rowles attempted to explain the missing glove and "the victim no longer cares," Mary Ann got up and hastened from the room, covering her eyes with her hands. Donny raced after her, catching her on the landing to the stairs.

"C'mon," he said, holding her in his arms while she sobbed on his shoulder, "Let's go home."

Adamson turned his back to the witness, checking the clock on the rear wall. "What happened to the glove?"

"We don't really know. I understand the ski patrol, state police, and the sheriff conducted a thorough search of the area beneath the chair lift, but found nothing."

"Is it possible he removed the glove and simply dropped it?"

"Yes."

"Was he still wearing the other glove, the left glove?"

"Yes, it was a distinctive racing glove, made by Invicta, with leather palms. It was colored white with a long cuff and red and blue stars. The snow was very, very deep that night. I'm sorry to say that the missing glove may never be found until spring."

Rowles paused to pinch his nose and wipe his reading glasses.

"Dr. Rowles," said Adamson, "Mr. Atwood's condition was diagnosed as experiencing severe hypothermia, is that correct? Could you describe what happens under that condition?"

"Yes, this is usually what occurs when the body temperature falls below eighty-six degrees. The shivering comes and goes in waves. Very, very violent shivering for a minute or so. And then a pause, followed by more violent shivering. The body is trying to shunt its heat, which means the blood tends to flow, in a manner of speaking, inward." He placed the palms of both hands on his chest. "To protect the vital organs, the heart and lungs."

"You mean the blood actually races toward the vital organs?"

"Yes, the best I can explain is that it's like rallying for a last-stand effort, to protect those most vital organs. But, after a while, the shivering stops because the heat output in the muscles is not enough to offset the decreasing core temperature. What happens is that the body shuts down its shivering in 6order to conserve glucose.

"By this time, the victim literally falls or curls up in a fetal position. Mr. Atwood was discovered sitting almost upright, however, probably because he could not remove his skis and, more probably, because he had passed out long before. Anyway, the muscles become rigid, the person's skin becomes very pale, the pupils of the eyes dilate, and the pulse rate drops dramatically."

He hesitated here, drew in a breath, and said, "There's a term called metabolic icebox. That's when the temperature drops below eighty-six degrees. A person looks dead but is still alive."

"Beg pardon!" said Adamson.

"Still alive! I can't say this is what distinctly happened to the victim. I'm merely describing it as one of the steps that takes place toward…toward death."

"Go on, sir."

"This is followed by very erratic and shallow breathing. The victim is, at best, semiconscious. Cardia arrhythmia occurs. That's an irregular heart beat. Then the heart simply stops beating, and death occurs."

"When was the last time anyone actually froze to death in this area of Vermont?"

"It happens. I can't recall a specific instance in recent years. Not that I handled. It used to happen every now and then years ago. Old people living alone. I know also of a case in Burlington not long ago. A college student was found frozen to death in the snow after an all-night fraternity party."

"And was that alcohol-related?"

"Again, I didn't handle it, but, yes, the victim had consumed too much alcohol."

"Dr. Rowles, were there any other marks or discoloration on Mr. Atwood's body other than those created by the hypothermia?"

"Yes, there were a few bumps and bruises, including one to the head. But I understand the victim had occasioned a rather serious fall, at least for him, while skiing the day before. I conclude those extraneous marks were the result of that fall."

Dr. Rowles looked up from his report at the clock on the wall, a simple, professional reflex, as if he was noting the time of death.

"What you have described about the hypothermia is mostly hypothetical, wouldn't you say, doctor?"

"Yes."

"Are you prepared to swear these circumstances pretty much match the conditions of the deceased prior to him actually dying?"

"Yes, I am."

As the six jurors stood stiffly to depart to the deliberating room, several of the spectators breathed deeply, relieving a bit of the tension they felt inside. Some cried softly. Marge Atwood sobbed with her head held down.

When the jurors were assembled in the back room, Adamson came in and sat at the table with them. He was much more relaxed and informal than in the court. He took off his jacket, carefully hung it on the back of his chair, and loosened his tie. He had a fleshy face with beagle brown eyes. Approaching forty-five years old, he had a gut getting out of control. The overworked waistband of his pants turned slightly down toward the floor.

He explained, as he had at the outset, a medical examiner's inquest was a legal vehicle to affix the cause of a person's death. It was not a trial to determine anybody's guilt or innocence. Most medical examiner's juries tend to agree with the findings of the medical examiners and the lawyers representing the state. Ethan Atwood's death could not have been much simpler. He froze to death on a chair lift, forty feet above the ground. He had been too drunk to help himself. It did not take the wisdom of Solomon to figure it out.

When everyone had relaxed a bit, Adamson asked if they had any questions about the testimony.

"I keep asking myself," said Leona Kurtz, "was it a suicide? It really looks to me like…If he didn't kill himself deliberately, he really didn't care what happened to him."

Three or four other jurors spoke up with the same conclusions and began speaking at the same time.

The lawyer put up his hand, a halt signal. "What you say has validity. It appeared he was despondent. We had direct eyewitness testimony to that affect from the bartender. Also, the fact he apparently jumped onto the chair—you might say actually snuck on at the last minute when it was being shut down and when the operator had her back turned—that all leads in that direction. But, and this is a big but, there's a huge gap in the evidence. He never told anyone he was going to kill himself. The state police interviewed everyone he knew. Not once in the weeks preceding his death did he indicate he was suicidal.

"People who knew him knew him as a determined athlete who had suffered a setback. It happens all the time. Yet, he had intentions of rejoining the ski team and competing. Outwardly, he was happy most of the time. He also left no note of any kind. Suicides often leave clues. He really left none of the kind except there was evidence he was despondent, perhaps even clinically depressed despite the outward appearance. But there's no professional evidence of that. We can't get inside his head. To rule suicide invites a lot of complications."

"Yeah, but where does that leave us?" asked Kurtz. "What do we do? Can we just leave it at cardiac arrest?"

Adamson stood and moved to a window, looking out at the traffic creeping along the street. Occasionally, a car tire would pop a piece of ice, sending it spinning to the sidewalk. It was nearing rush hour. The statehouse and other public buildings were closing for the day. Adamson, from experience, knew this particular proceeding was over, but he felt, aware of the celebrity of the victim, he should stretch things out a bit. Out of respect, perhaps.

"Well, not knowing Ethan's true state of mind gives us an out," said Adam-son, returning to the table and leaning on it with both hands, "and it's a legitimate one. The hypothermia we know about. The booze we know about."

He stood erect and looked to the ceiling. "The awful cold weather we know about."

"So it could be accidental," said juror Mike Weathers. "Is that what you're saying?"

"You're giving Ethan Atwood the benefit of the doubt," said Adamson, "but you have every valid reason to rule this an accidental death."

So, six hands were raised around the table agreeing that death was caused by cardiac arrest, the result of accidental circumstances.

Marjorie and Paul Atwood held hands, clenched tightly, at their seats near the front of the courtroom. She sobbed again when she heard the words, yet there was a blur of relief that Ethan's death was not a suicide.

Funny, but nearly every chapter of her son's life ended with some questioning of motive. There were his bursts of restlessness, not just a fidgeting but a dangerous need for speed and action. At the opposite end of his emotional scale were the silences, the problems kept opaque in the dark closet of his mind. When Rexie, his pet terrier, disappeared for a week after chasing a deer, with the fear in everyone that he might have been devoured by a fisher or wildcat and would never be found again, Ethan hardened, stubbornly refusing to show remorse. He cried only in bed at night with the covers pulled over his eyes. He kept some things inside.

The Atwoods and all the other spectators left the courtroom. Except one. Still seated in the middle of the room, his shaggy, gray, unkempt hair an anomaly in the polish of the judicial setting, Ed Phoebe stared at the floor and then toward the desks up front, as if he was unable to make up his mind about something. The lawyers and officials of Maple Glen were gathering papers and notepads and were stuffing them in briefcases. At the same time, reporters were questioning them.

Still, Ed Phoebe sat. He had not even fetched the dirty, old, puffed-up vest from beneath the bench below. He finally caught the eye of Bruce White, who stared at the old man curiously. Something in Ed's pained face made Bruce curious. He knew Ed and Ethan had been good, though casual, friends. Ethan loved teasing the old man about his skiing, but, at the same time, he admired the crispness of Ed Phoebe's style and always had a favorable word.

"You okay, Ed?" asked Bruce.

Ed Phoebe shook his head slowly from side to side.

"Are you ill?" Bruce asked, walking toward the old man.

"No, I ain't sick!" But his eyes betrayed him, and his hands trembled.

Bruce bent over the bench. His hands were clasped on the back upright of the one in front and the other on the upright of the bench where Ed was sitting. "What's wrong?"

"It weren't no accident!" whispered Ed, his voice hoarse and breaking.

"What do you mean? 'It weren't no accident!'"

Chapter 12
Encounter in the Woods

The picture on the camera's screen was of a chubby bear cub squatting on its rear and examining a pretty, pink lady's slipper, the delicate woods-loving plant that was glowing in the sunshine.

Mary Ann, her finger on the button, hesitated before pushing to the next slide, waiting for the few "ahhs" to subside.

"Cute!" said a deep voice from the rear of the Odd Fellows Hall. "Tryin' ta soften us up, huh, Mary Ann!"

"Nobody can soften you up, Howard!" replied Mary Ann as laughter rose in the room, easing the slight community tension. This was Maple Glen Resort, Inc. versus the Keep-It-Green Society.

The chuckles were the correct reaction that Mary Ann sought to evoke from the outset of her dog and pony show. She knew by first name just about everyone in the audience. These were community people, neighbors to the giant ski company that had a goal of tearing a slice through the South Ridge mountain woodland in order to build a new ski lift and a half-dozen new trails.

"We know the bears are up there," Mary Ann said, flashing to the next slide, a photo of a beech tree, standing tall and majestic in the sunlight with sharp scratches up its gray elephant-like hide.

"Honestly, that is not a local bear," she said, flashing back to the bear slide. "It's a stock photo, but that's what we're talking about anyway. The bears are there. We know it, and we want them to remain there. I hope to be able to show you over the next half hour what we plan to do, how we plan to do it, and how we will do it with the least amount of intrusion into the bear habitat."

A PR show to be sure! Mary Ann went through all the statistics made available to her by Bruce White and his staff, especially how, if Maple Glen was to remain competitive in the industry and provide jobs to the local community, the resort needed to expand.

Probably half the community supported the resort. Almost all of the valley residents had some—sometimes many—family members who worked the seasonal jobs, albeit low-paying ones that barely paid the rent and bought the groceries.

The rest of the year, they painted houses, cut firewood, mowed lawns, ran catering services and clerked at grocery stores and gift shops. Some held two or three jobs yearlong. An oft-seen bumper sticker read, "Moonlight in Vermont or Starve!" It was all part of the Great Vermont Trade-Off, low-paying jobs versus high quality of life, a good, crime-free place to raise kids, outdoor life at your doorstep, and, with Vermont being one of only three states to ban billboards from the countryside, stunningly gorgeous to look at.

After the slide show, several in the audience came up to Mary Ann and complimented her on the presentation.

Many, familiar with her past, knowing of her involvement with Ethan, searched for pain in her eyes, some lines or wrinkles perhaps, or a gray hair. She knew they wanted to help, but they politely refrained from probing. Only her closest friends could dare ask before they could console. It was not easy to comfort a married woman over the death of an old boyfriend or, as a few had suspected, a lover up until the time his body was found.

Mary Ann eagerly took up Bruce White's newest venture, giving it a secret cause. Ethan Atwood was one of the skiers who persuaded Bruce the South Ridge terrain, because of its steepness and the fact it was mostly in shadows throughout the day, offered not only good natural snow but exciting skiing. All he had to do was run a new lift up there and trim out some of the hardwoods and he would have some of the best tree skiing in the East.

Mary Ann arrived at work early and went home late. Often, by the time she got home, darkness had settled on her side of the mountain. She could hear the spring peepers down in the pond below the meadow. They arrived like clockwork every year about April 15.

"At least I know when the tax bill is due," Donny would say. "I just have to listen for the peepers and run like hell to the post office."

Donny was not approving of Mary Ann's new work habits, but he refrained from complaining, knowing it was part of the healing. They talked little about Ethan's death. He would never bring it up unless Mary Ann broached the subject first and then he would entertain that conversation only with reluctance.

However, in the small valley and in the little towns that had risen 100 years before around the mills and farms, gossip flew like buckshot. There were rumors about Ethan's death not being what it seemed. Suicide was one conjecture. Murder was another.

Murder? How and why?

"Don't know," said Emily Davenport on the phone to a fellow harpy. "But it has somethin' to do with Ed Phoebe!"

Most of the people familiar with the investigation into Ethan's death, at least those who attended the medical examiner's inquest and had listened carefully to the testimony, quickly dismissed the rumors of murder as unthinkable. But then Bruce White began receiving phone calls from Lieutenant Jordan Rice, the state police investigator.

Though he spoke to Rice in the privacy of his office, Bruce took a deliberate precaution of shutting the door, arousing more curiosity from Sara Thomas, the secretary, and Mary Ann, whose office was adjacent to the open reception center where Sara worked.

Mary Ann had also heard the rumors, but she denied them for other reasons. The main one being she had exhausted herself with grief over the death of the only man she had ever loved. That was most difficult. By day, she adopted a stiff pretense at bravery. She did not want her husband, nor little Ellie, to see her red-eyed. At night, Mary Ann cried herself silently to sleep.

Still, a terrible chill jolted her spine when the strange phone call came at home that day.

It was just five o'clock when she walked through the door of the mud room, pulled off her big snow boots with the bootjack, unlocked the kitchen door, and burst inside to grab the phone in time. She had hoped it was the babysitter, who was needed that upcoming Saturday night.

"Hello!" she answered.

"Hello, Mrs. Naples?"

"Yes, this is Mrs. Naples," she answered, not recognizing the strange, male voice.

"This is Lieutenant Rice of the Vermont State Police. How are you today?

"I'm fine. How are you!" she asked incredulously to the stranger.

"Is your husband home? May I talk to him?"

"He isn't here. He isn't home from work yet."

"I should have known. I'm sorry."

"Is there any message?"

"Yes, just this. Our appointment for tomorrow? Could you ask him to make it 9:30 instead of 11:00?"

"Yes," Mary Ann finally answered in a hesitant voice. Rice hung up before she could ask what the appointment was about.

She wondered why would the state police want to talk with Donny? What could he be involved with?

Her brain skirted the details of the phone call. 9:30 tomorrow. Is that urgency? What's it about? She knew Lieutenant Rice had been calling Bruce White and suspected it had something to do with Ethan's death, but it now seemed her husband was involved.

"But that's nonsense," she said to herself. Probably something to do with the ski patrol. Donny probably put the arm on the state cops for some kind of contribution to the ski patrol's special equipment fund or some other kind of service. Donny, as head of the Valley Chamber of Commerce, forever had little pots of business boiling. He was a planner, a progressive voice in the valley, and a successful owner of a once-failed granite business who breathed new life into it and the community. Donny was respected and admired for his quick wit and sometimes outspoken behavior. Overall, he was the go-to guy, the one who got it done.

A few days after Lieutenant Rice had called Mary Ann in order to talk to Donny, the rumors around the valley compounded. This time, the story was that both Donny and Ed Phoebe had talked to the state police together. And Rosemary Ann Perkins, a clerk at the general store, had seen Donny's truck pull into the backwoods lane where Ed had his cabin one day.

Mary Ann could bear the mystery no longer. She invited Bruce to lunch at the Moss Brook Inn. This time of year, it was a quiet, little inn halfway down the main access road to the Maple Glen Resort.

"I have to know," said Mary Ann with typical frankness no sooner had she sat down and Bruce had his jacket off.

"All right," Bruce said. "I didn't want to tell you. This kind of crap can be upsetting, and, right now, that's all I think it is, just crap. I'm still convinced Ethan's death was just as it came out at the hearing. An accident. But…"

"But what!" Mary Ann pleaded, leaning over the table. Her arms were folded in front of her, and her hands grasped her wrists tightly.

Bruce ordered a martini for himself and a seltzer water for Mary Ann. "Make it a double gin!" he said as an afterthought to the waitress. The dining room of the rustic, old restaurant was nearly empty. This late in the season, when the beginnings of mud season crept upwards through the melting snow, not many outsiders came to Lowgate Springs to ski. The locals though still took time off from work to get in their early morning runs.

Bruce sipped his drink, wiped his lips with a napkin, and told Mary Ann what he knew, swearing her to secrecy, a promise he need only extract once from her.

"It was about a month before Ethan died. It involved Ed Phoebe. In fact, he's the one who brought it to my attention."

Mary Ann nodded, but she dared not interrupt.

"Ed. Well, you know he's not the youngest guy on the mountain," said Bruce. "He was up skiing Juggernaut, his favorite trail, this particular day when two guys came out of the woods. One was on skis; the other was on a snowboard. Apparently, they were flyin'. One of them clipped the back of Ed's skis, and down he went."

"Ed apparently yelled at him, but the guy on the board just kept going. But his buddy didn't. He stopped and turned to Phoebe. 'Hey, watch who you're callin' an asshole, you old fart! And keep the fuck outta the way! You're supposed to stick to the side of the trail if you're gonna ski that goddamned slow.'"

Remarks that are made in a smart-ass fashion usually relate well with a would-be adversary. This one scored well and gave birth to more. The confrontation became more heated with Ed threatening to 'bust your ass!' He lifted his ski pole threateningly. The boarder grabbed Ed and shoved him to the snow. This time, in a rage, Ed swung the pole at the younger man, who not only seized the pole but used it to come down hard on Phoebe's head. The basket snapped off the pole when it struck his fleece hat. The younger man yelled, 'You fuckin' old asshole!'"

Bruce paused, coughing slightly and taking another sip of his martini. He had softened his descriptive adjectives by telling Mary Ann the man uttered some "pretty rough obscenities."

"Well," Bruce continued, "to get to the point, Ethan, who was skiing in the Upper Woods, but who was pretty far away, saw the whole thing happen. He took off after the two guys."

"They went down Obscurity," said Bruce, referring to a little-used woodland adventure trail that skirted the southern boundary of the resort. It was a difficult black diamond rarely skied when the snow cover was thin. Rocks and bare spots were showing.

Ethan, in a furious burst, skated after the two men. He sped up to Ed Phoebe and stopped only long enough to see if the old man was injured. 'I ain't hurt,' Ed yelled to Ethan, who again took up the chase. Phoebe followed.

Bruce paused. "What happened next is vague at best." He took another sip, finally gulping the gin and vermouth in one move. He winced at the sharpness of the liquor in his throat.

Mary Ann waited.

"I don't know all the rest because everything I know is secondhand. Donny, however, knows this part of the story. He and I were sworn to silence by the state cops. I'm telling you, Mary Ann, only because I know you and want to set your mind at some kind of ease. Otherwise, I'd rather not tell you."

"I understand," she said softly, "and I'm grateful." She touched his sleeve.

"If Donny wants to tell you what happened, that's his business, but I guess, if I tell you, it may be enough," Bruce said. "What I mean by that is that you should be satisfied as to what Donny's involvement is."

"Anyway," he continued, "Donny happened upon Ed probably only seconds after Ethan took after the two guys."

"Ed told Donny what happened, and then Donny took off.

"From what I understand, Donny caught up to Ethan and the two guys down near the snowmaking shed. That Obscurity Trail stops there, and there's no way back to the lift unless you pole through the woods. You know where I mean?"

"Yes, I do," Mary Ann agreed. "That's why I don't ski that trail. Nobody does!"

"Well, the compressors in the snowmaking shed make a lot of noise. The area's pretty isolated, and the shed is a solid, concrete building. No windows. The guys working inside don't hear what goes on outside."

"What happened is that Ethan caught the two guys and proceeded to beat the living hell out of both of them. First the guy who hit Ed with the pole and then the other snowboarder who clipped Ed in the first place. Donny said, by the time he got there, Ethan was out of control. He was a savage and he was beating one guy unmercifully."

Mary Ann interrupted. Her face was reddened. "Bruce, don't tell me. I don't believe this. Don't tell me that, because Ethan had a fight with two guys, that they killed him. That's just bullshit! It doesn't happen!"

"I know, I know, I know!" Bruce repeated, attempting to soften her anger. "I felt the same thing. I still do, Mary Ann. I don't think Ethan was murdered, but, now that you know this much, I have to tell you the rest."

Bruce once again paused, looking at Mary Ann directly. "This is the problem. These two guys live in Brooklyn. New York. Both have criminal records."

"But how did they get away. What happened?" Mary Ann asked.

"Well, Donny apparently pulled Ethan off the one guy he was beating, took stock of the situation, and told the two to get lost. I'm sure Donny will tell you about it, but I'd rather you not ask him now. Both of us swore we'd keep this quiet until the state police completed their investigation, until they come up with something or drop it altogether."

"Ordinarily," Bruce went on, "Donny, as a patroller, would be bound to file a report of what happened. But he realized that what Ethan did—Donny said he was like a madman—it wouldn't look good for us to bring charges against these two guys and then have to face charges of our own because Ethan did justice right there on the spot."

"So, he let them go!" Mary Ann concluded.

"He let them go, yes. Donny told them to get lost, which they did, with relief. They had had enough of Ethan. They didn't want anymore, but they yelled at both Ethan and Donny and said they were going to kill them. Words, really, that's what was going on. Words in the heat of the moment. But Donny followed them to the parking lot to make sure they didn't hang around and try to do something. He got the license number when they drove away. They were with two girlfriends, or wives, who met them in the parking lot. I'm not sure who they were. The car had New York plates."

What had occurred that day in the space of twenty minutes was uncontrolled rage from Ethan, which was followed by a searing hatred and promise of revenge by a thug named Yummie Antolucci, the man who had suffered the worst of Ethan's attack and his buddy, Tony Albright. Antolucci sat in the backseat of the Ford Ranger with a T-shirt wrapped around a handful of snow held to his left eye by his girlfriend, Peg.

"Da son of a bitch done know who I yam!" said Yummie through clenched teeth. A patch of dried blood coated his chin.

"You said that six fuckin' times already, Yummie!" yelled Albright over his shoulder. "Peg, tell 'im to shut up!"

He flinched when he involuntarily gripped the steering wheel hard with his right hand, which was swollen from striking the side of the concrete snowmaker's building just an hour before, a wild punch thrown unsuccessfully at Ethan's head. The side of Albright's face was, like his companion in the rear seat, bruised and swollen.

"Who was the guy?" asked Peg. "He musta been a madman! Look at you, oh my poor baby!" she cooed, wiping a trickle of fresh, red dripping from Yummie's painfully swollen nose.

"He whad dat skier guy, dat ski team jerk. Atwood! Atwood!" said Tony. "His pitchers all over da place!"

"You mean that cute guy!" asked Peg.

"Shudda fug up, Peh-h-h!" yelled Yummie. Because of a fat, red lip and gap between his front teeth, which Ethan has separated with one blow, the words came out slurred and comically clipped, the grown-up voice of a snaggletooth. "Shudda fug up!"

"Ya know, Yummie," interrupted Tony, braking for a patch of ice that appeared suddenly beyond a bend in the darkening road. "Youse could sue him for damages. Youse could sue the whole fuckin' ski team, the whole state of Vermont!"

"I ain't soo-in 'im. Nobody dud sit lie dat da me!" countered Yummie. "I' kill 'im. I' kill 'im," he murmured. The air in the truck reeked by now of marijuana smoke. Peg held the joint once more to Yummie's swollen lips, but they were closed. He appeared to have passed out.

Chapter 13
Mexico

The end of April brought mud, a brown, slimy diversion to the cold, white crack of winter. Moods already pummeled by the aftershocks of grief descended even deeper, making it easy for Donny to convince Mary Ann the two of them should get away.

They flew to Cozumel. On the hot, sandy beach of the Caribbean island off Mexico's Yucatan coast, the cold pain in Mary Ann's heart became less pronounced, as did the tension in her voice and face. They drank cocktails at pool-side and scuba dived on the great Palancar Reef. In the evening, they walked to San Miguel, a pretty, little town of small, white stucco homes, whose neighborhoods were being steadily eclipsed by the high-rise tourist hotels.

Even in spring, the Mexican sun can be searing. Neither Mary Ann nor Donny could lie for long on the beach beneath its glare. Soon either or both would be back in the clear, tepid water. Donny had put his glasses in the breast pocket of the T-shirt he was wearing, one with a logo of a scuba air tank with the message "All gassed off and ready to go!" in bright-red flowing colors.

When he saw her coming out of the water, he initially supposed her to be a lithe, Mexican woman with long, muscled legs. Slogging through the sand caused her hips to sway.

"Dreamlike," thought Donny.

"I didn't recognize you there for a moment," he said, eyeing where the tight, little bikini tucked into her lower belly.

"Where are your glasses?" she asked.

"Here now," he said, propping them on his nose and peering at the cleavage of her breasts as she sat down beside him. He ran a finger along the strap on her back, brushing away the thin layer of sand that stuck to her tan skin. They had been there only four days, but Mary Ann glowed golden with brown hair tied in a pony tail. Her bright eyes reflected the sun and azure of the water.

Day by day, what seemed cold and harsh in the north, the distracting bad memories, began vanishing.

Just before they left on the Caribbean vacation, Bruce White received the latest phone call from Lieutenant Rice, bringing him up-to-date on the investigation of Yummie Antolucci and Tony Albright.

"Guess where they were when Ethan died. In jail," Rice said. "They had been in jail for a week. Parole violations. Caught with drugs. I told New York PD and the DEA…that's who nabbed them…about what happened up here. They were concerned enough to run a pretty thorough check on those two birds' activities since the day they had the encounter with Ethan on the mountain. Even though they were in jail the night Atwood died, we wanted to see if there had been any kind of a hit set up by the two of them to get even."

Rice half-snickered. He, for one, had begun feeling better about the investigation into the two young thugs in Brooklyn.

"Anyway, just about the opposite happened. They squawked all right. Told just about everybody what they were going to do to Ethan Atwood. And that's the trouble, they both have big mouths.

"They're wannabes!" said Marvin Bright, a DEA investigator in Brooklyn. He told Rice the pair had long harbored ambitions to be in La Costra Nostra, but they had such a bumbling criminal background that not even that organization dared risk the two as confederates.

"Antolucci had an older brother, Mario, who worked for Alitalia Airlines at Kennedy Airport in the warehouse there. He had been set up by some mob guys to look the other way when they were shipping some heroin into Kennedy, smuggled in olive oil tins all the way from Milan. They paid him $30,000."

"But this guy, Mario, got pinched along with about a dozen others, mostly Gambino guys. He was nowhere close to being a made mob guy, and he chickened and began talking to us. He was easy to flip. Now he's in the Witness Protection Program and is getting ready to testify against the other guys."

"I checked all around," said Bright to Rice, "looking into the theory that the Atwood fellow, that skier, was done in by the mob because he beat the hell out of that pair. After Atwood died, there was a story going around in Brooklyn that the mob did him in. Obviously started by those two punks. No way, lieutenant. This young Antolucci kid, he went around bragging all the time about his mob connections. Bullshit! You think the Gambinos want anything to do with a punk like him, especially one with a brother who was already a rat? Loudmouth, out of control half the time. In fact, the Gambinos told him to button it. They said, if he ever went anywhere near Atwood, he'd be sorry. That was even before Ethan was found dead."

"You know what I mean?" asked Bright. "The mob doesn't want to attract that kind of attention. I don't think they killed Ethan Atwood, but, just in case, we'll keep our ears and eyes on those two."

Therefore, the door was closed, at least for now, on the possibility that Ethan had been killed as an act of retribution for an altercation on the ski slopes. Those involved in the short-lived probe—Bruce White, Donny Naples, Lieutenant Rice, and even old Ed Phoebe—breathed easier.

Phoebe still considered Ethan's death with doubt. He refused to believe Ethan died accidentally or through the influence of alcohol. When Bruce White asked him why he waited until the end of the inquest to come forth with the account of Ethan's defense of him, Ed replied, "I dunno. I guess I thought it would all come out at the hearing. When it didn't, I just couldn't sit there any longer until I told."

Mary Ann's overall mood had been up and down. Her anguish traveled deeper than everyone else's to begin with. She had difficulty separating present from past, fact and reality from fantasy. She sometimes dreamed of Ethan climbing the podium at the Olympics with a gold medal around his handsome neck glimmering in the sun. She fantasized about him holding her in his arms as they sat on the swing of the old Hathaway farmhouse, which, in her reverie, they had purchased, renovated, and cared for. They trimmed the weeds from around the grave of "Our Mae" and watched the sun set over Lake Champlain. They playfully did figure eights on skis in the snow down the mountainside, laughing and panting for breath. They then stopped and kissed, deeply and for a long time, beneath the pines. She remembered every detail of the first time they loved, when she blurted tearfully she did not want him to go to Portillo to join the ski team. Her eyes were blind with images of Ethan frantically kissing her throat and pulling her to the soft carpet of needles beneath the trees.

Her recent day-to-day mood had been uncharacteristically dour, manifested especially toward her husband. He had told her about Ethan's confrontation with the two freaks from Brooklyn who had bullied Ed Phoebe, and he told her of his role in the affair.

She seemed to understand that what happened probably had nothing to do with Ethan's death. She should have been grateful to Donny for revealing the details.

At times, she apologized to him for the grumps. She felt she had not the luxury though to confide in her husband about what a terrible loss she had suffered. He knew, of course. But, she thought talking about it was not the best form between wife and husband. Her mind was working in a trance.

Gradually, the Mexican sun, sand, and warm water performed their healing, improving her mood, appetite, outlook, and her relationship with Donny, who wisely predicted that some underwater scuba excursions would heal the rest. Of course, nothing in Mexico matched the enveloping calm created by the majestic underwater reef known as Palancar. Beneath the surface of the green sea, coral steeples rose like tall, underwater skyscrapers from a thousand feet below.

The first day, she had no sooner surfaced into the warm sun before she began gushing about what she saw. "The reefs, they're like tall buildings! It's Manhattan beneath the sea!" She compared the undersea experience to flying, gliding high above the void below in a watery, green sky.

On another particularly bright morning, at ninety feet, she and Donny drifted slowly together, letting the young dive master lead the way through the maze of columns and pillars. Mary Ann mugged at a large grouper, their faces nearly touching, as Donny recorded their portraits with his camera.

They floated along the head wall, where the sea dropped a mile down into a blue oblivion. In the distance, a couple of reef sharks circled indolently. As Mary Ann and Donny began to surface, the underwater visibility grew less distinct. Usually, a diver could see clearly nearly 150 feet in the gin-clear water, but now it was reduced to about seventy-five to one hundred feet. Donny looked up and suspected a storm had come up over the island. Suddenly, Mary Ann, in a burst of speed, swam in his direction, thrusting her face in front of his. Her mask was full of water. Wide-eyed, she attempted to clear it by tipping the mask at its bottom and snorting through her nose, the prescribed method of dumping water from a flooded mask. But the sea quickly gushed back. The seal of the mask had clearly broken.

Instinctively, she grabbed Donny's vest. He grabbed hers and shook his head affirmatively, letting her know he understood the problem. He signaled "up" with his thumb, and she nodded yes.

Slowly, they ascended. Mary Ann, unable to read her gauges, totally depended on Donny's rate of ascent. On her own, unable to see, and disoriented, she might have ascended too quickly, risking the bends, or even descended dangerously into the depths.

When they reached the surface, still clinging to one another, they found a heavy squall pelting down with a force so hard it stung their faces. The dive boat was nowhere to be found. Visibility was poor in any direction. Suddenly, out of the gloom and the rain, they heard the quick roar of the engines. The boat backed up stern first, and they clambered aboard.

On the way back to shore, the Caribbean squall turned suddenly off as though directed by a hand on a spigot. The sun burst upon the channel and the island, its heat welcome for a change.

Donny sat on the stern board, stealing repeated glances at the young dive master, who, in turn, could not keep his eyes off Mary Ann as she showered off the saltwater in the middle of the dive boat. The water coursed down in shiny braids over her brown skin.

At dinner, feeling warm and lazy from the buffet of red snapper, pork cutlets, chicken, fresh fruit and vegetables, and hot, spicy beans sprinkled with hot picante laced down with white wine, they watched the red sun set over the channel separating the island from the mainland. The lights from gas-fed torches came on. Guitars and castanets were played in the background by black-clad mariachis wearing sombreros as big as beach umbrellas. Beneath a thatched roof covering the outdoor bar, the bartender was leaning on one elbow, talking to two young American girls, who, when not sipping through straws, were giggling hysterically. The music and food, after a day of sun, heat, and water, made the tourists dreamy and sleepy. Mary Ann reached across the table, one of many set up on a huge patio under the palm trees facing the beach. Taking Donny's hands, she said, "Thanks for this morning."

"You mean, the reef? I had nothing to do with it. That's God's work."

"No, silly, I mean taking me up when my mask broke."

"What are husbands for?" he said, half-smiling but totally serious. He patted her hand and whispered, "I love you, Mary Ann!"

"...you too..."

When they retired for the evening about ten o'clock to their seventh-floor apartment overlooking the sea and the festive strings of lights of two big ocean liners in the harbor, Donny asked her to join him on the balcony. Twelve miles to the west was a thin strip of dotted lights from the mainland village of Playa del Carmen. The stars above the now-dark sea appeared larger and closer than Mary Ann had seen in a long time, reminding her of clear spring nights in Vermont. It would still be cold and raw in northern New England.

"Wonderful breeze out here," he said.

She felt the slight caress of air against her cheeks. He turned her toward him. Gently but firmly, he pushed her back against the wrought iron railing and gently slid the thin straps of her dress from her shoulders.

In the semidarkness, she was still embarrassed. From below, toward the bar in the shadow of lanterns, came the Spanish rhythms of the band and occasional caterwaul of tourists dancing beneath the palms.

"Anyone can see us."

"I don't care, I want you here and now," he said as he let her dress drop, sank to his knees, and nuzzled her crotch with his face. He then pulled her down on the air mattress that had been left to dry on the balcony, forcing a lust upon her that she had never felt from him before.

"I want to fuck you here and now!" he said. "I don't care if the whole world sees!"

Chapter 14
PR

"Pray that the summers, though short, are bountiful."

"My grandmother used to say that when I was a kid," said Bruce as he looked from his office window up the mountain toward an ugly strip of dirt and rock that his work crews had gouged from the green. The rain pelting his office window was doing havoc mountainside, despite the several tons of hay in bales they had placed there to check the erosion.

Bruce and Mary Ann both stood with their arms folded, looking uphill toward the stream named Silver Brook, now running brown with mud, in continuation of a season that was so full of rain it mocked Bruce's best of intentions and also his promises.

Besides the interruptions caused by the wet weather, he was committed by the environmental laws to develop the South Ridge into skiable terrain only according to conditions agreeable to nature. That meant those environmentalists hovered over projects like predators. That he felt he could handle. However, construction was delayed, and permits were tediously slow in coming. The architects, constantly revising plans for a new restaurant lodge near the summit, were getting wealthy with work order changes.

"My lawyers are sending children of distant relatives to college on my money," Bruce complained. Everyone was working overtime, including Mary Ann, whose valiant efforts to appease the environmental opponents of the project seemed to consist of a step forward and a step back throughout this tediously wet summer and the slow, tortuous permit process.

"Donny wants me to quit," she said, still staring at the rain.

"I'm not surprised," said Bruce. "I wish things were otherwise, but I understand."

"I'm not quitting," she said firmly. "I want to help you get this through."

Finally, she added through gritted teeth and looking directly at Bruce, "I need this anyway. I have to do this."

"I think I understand," he said.

"If I don't do this, I will go crazy at home. People don't understand that. Donny doesn't understand anyway. I guess I'm not domesticated yet."

"You're domesticated!" laughed Bruce.

Finally, a sunny day returned, flooding the sky and countryside with its welcome, blinding glare. It sucked up little pools left by the rain and turned the mud back into soil that could be worked and walked upon again. Farmers returned to their fields, and the Maple Glen work crews went uphill again.

Mary Ann and Donny, refreshed after a second coffee, kissed each other and laughed.

"Truce!" she said softly, holding up her right hand in pledge.

"Truce!" Donny repeated, hugging her. Both had been in lousy, belligerent moods for days. Some of it had been caused by the foul weather.

"I won't grump today if you won't grump," she said.

"It's a deal," he said, going out the door.

"And don't you grump either, you little devil," said Mary Ann, bending to wipe the oatmeal from Ellie's fat, little chin. The child laughed and spit cereal over the tray of her high chair.

No sooner had Mary Ann gotten to work and hung up her jacket, the phone rang. The menacing, high-pitched voice of Emily Davenport was at the other end.

"I want you know what they're doing up there!" said Emily, deliberately whining in a voice programmed to irritate the listener.

Mary Ann listened, exhaling before she spoke. "Emily, thank you so much, I'll look into it and get back to you. I promise!"

It took willpower to refrain from banging down the receiver. She gently lowering it instead and then she grabbed her jacket. She yelled "I'll be back!" to Sara Thomas and flew out the door.

The pickup rattled and rocked as it raced uphill, scattering stones and twigs and who knows how much wildlife before coming to a stop at the end of the work road.

"Hey, Mary Ann, you forgot your hard hat!" yelled Eric Pancoast, dropping the soggy bale of straw that had washed up against a tree.

"Screw the hard hat!" yelled Mary Ann. "Where is Lenny?"

When she encountered the foreman, an uncharacteristic stream of oaths coursed from her mouth, leaving him speechless and openmouthed.

They had been friends since grade school. The only Mary Ann he knew had been always smiling, caring, and thoughtful. It was not this willful bitch who was letting him have it on the mountainside in front of his entire work crew.

"What in the name of heaven do you guys think you're doing up here!"

"What do you mean?" asked Lenny, shocked.

"Look at this goddamned smoke!" she yelled. "You can see it all over the valley!"

The problem came from Bruce's commitment, at Mary Ann's suggestion, who reacted to an appeal from the Keep-It-Green Society, that only handsaws be used to fell trees smaller than four inches in diameter. The reason was given that chain saws were polluters, fouling the air in the bear habitat. Worse, they created the noise of progress. In Vermont, that was a sometimes unforgivable sin.

One by one, as Mary Ann shouted, the chainsaws became still, their oily smoke ascending in small, vaporish plumes into the trees.

Reddened, Lenny replied angrily, "How the hell am I going to get this job back on schedule if we don't get these goddamned trees outta here, Mary Ann?"

"Do your best, goddamn it! You remember that commitment. Don't go violating it. I don't care how much it rains and how far behind we get."

Furiously, she slammed the truck door closed behind her. She grinded the gears to get into reverse and bounded downhill, leaving a work crew with plenty to talk about the rest of the afternoon. About women! About bitches!

"Yeah, but she ain't usually like that!" was the neutral conclusion.

When she got home that night, as the sun was going down, she kissed Ellie good night and put her into bed. She barely talked to Donny as she got his supper. When she had a chance, she plopped down on the sofa and dialed the telephone to Lenny Dawson's house.

"He's not home, Mary Ann!" said Lenny's wife, Julie. "He's at the fire station meeting."

"Oh damn," Mary Ann said. "I wanted to talk to him, to apologize. Did he tell you how I freaked out on the mountain today?"

"Well..." said Julie. "He did mention something!"

"I'll bet he did! Well, please tell him I'm sorry. If I don't apologize, I won't sleep tonight, and God knows how badly I need a good night's sleep."

"Oh, for God's sake, Mary Ann, he's probably forgotten all about it already. Don't worry about it! But I'll tell him."

"Thanks, Julie, and tell him I'll talk to him in the morning. And I'll wear my hard hat!"

The two women laughed and hung up. Mary Ann felt properly humbled and less stressed. She soon fell off to sleep on the sofa.

Now, in autumn, the daytime temperatures were tepid and comfortable. The nights were perfectly nippy, an ideal climatological coupling for the annual Vermont showcase, the changing of the leaves. The valley, its residents and shopkeepers, buzzed again as tourists swept over the inns and dirt roads. They drove languidly up one lane and down another, going past the farms and through the villages to see the fiery landscape. Thickets of sumac and nanny-berries blazed the way, shining crimson in the valleys and uplands and mocking the lesser brilliance of the red oaks and sugar maples. Travelers from the lower cities who spent their workdays flying down the interstate and waiting and honking in the snarled city traffic luxuriated over the steady thirty mile an hour pace of rural New England. Shopkeepers lured the tourists into stopping by setting the usual traps, rows of brilliant orange pumpkins, arranged by the roadsides. Sometimes carved, they glowed with candles inside at night. Straw cornucopias were filled with ears of dried, golden corn.

The trail clearing was progressing once again at Maple Glen. Mary Ann, sensing a potential public relations coup, invited *The Valley Sentinel* to photograph Lenny Dawson's work crews using bow saws to cut the smaller trees. The photo made the wires and was published by newspapers in Boston, Hartford, and New York City. Above the caption, it explained "a policy to limit chainsaws introduced by the Maple Glen Ski Resort in Vermont to reduce pollution and curb other environmental harm to the woods and wildlife."

Mary Ann found roses on her desk the next day, with a note. "Here we were blundering along, cursing the fates, while you went ahead and turned our gaffe into a public relations masterwork, worth a small fortune in advertising."

Taking her to lunch at the Eagle's Nest Café that day, Bruce startled both Mary Ann and himself by extolling the many gifts of womanhood. However, after ordering a Long Trail Ale for himself and iced tea for Mary Ann, he began with a mea culpa.

"I have to confess something," he said, getting Mary Ann to sit up straight and smile with anticipation. Hearing Bruce White admit to a possible shortcoming was a treat not to be missed.

They were seated in a corner booth, but the room, decorated with corn stalks and jack-o-lanterns, was noisy. A busload of Texans dropped in on the restaurant for lunch. They were hungry and loud, exhilarated by the cool pungency of the day. Though noon, the air remained as it had been in the morning after the sun had burned away the fog—so crystalline and clear.

"I hired you because I was well-acquainted with your gifts," said Bruce. "I knew you were smart, and I later found out you were savvy. But you know why I really hired you?"

Mary Ann, by now puzzled and not just a little edgy, looked serious. "No. Not exactly!" she drawled.

"I hired you because I thought you thought like a man!"

"You what!" said Mary Ann.

Bruce chuckled. "Now, don't get me wrong."

"I'm trying awfully hard not to!" replied Mary Ann, smiling a bit while tilting her head perplexedly.

"Yes, that's right. She thinks like a man! That's what I told myself. Well, I'm now ready to admit," he puffed with satisfaction at what he was to say, "that I made a mistake."

Mary Ann, by now confused, pleaded in a deep voice. "Continue."

"I have to admit now," said Bruce, looking down a little shamefaced at his hands folded across the tabletop. The sun glinted through the window and bounced off his baldish, freckled scalp. "That the reason you're succeeding so well is that you think like a woman."

Mary Ann's mouth was agape. "Which is what I happen to be!"

"No, no, what I mean is that I'm glad you think like a woman. I'm glad to finally admit that your approach to things—I guess it's that feminine approach—is exactly what an executive office needs in certain kinds of turmoil. I like the fresh approach of feminine thought."

She slumped backward against the hard board of the booth. "I can't believe my ears. And what is feminine thought?" she asked, teasing now.

"I'll tell you what it is. It's approaching the problem from your enemy's point of view."

"Go on!" said Mary Ann encouragingly, sipping her iced tea through a straw. Her eyes bulged wide as she stared at her boss.

"You saw a way out of this habitat mess by seeing things the way the Keep-it-Greeners see things."

"Well, thank you, but I think I applied some logic. Not just seeing it their way. They have a point of view."

"That's just it, they do have a point of view, and I refused to see it."

Mary Ann began to say something, but he quickly interrupted. "I always see a problem or see things from my point of view, and I try convincing the other guy that my point of view is correct. That's how I've done things all my life."

"Are you trying to say, in a man's world, that's the way it's done?"

"It is, it is most of the time. And it almost always works, but not against these people."

"The greenies?" she said.

"Whatever they want to call themselves. Anyway, I'm getting to my point."

He leaned forward. "Who do you think my best choice should be to run Maple Glen when I retire some day?"

"You're asking me that!?"

"Yeah, I'm asking you. Who do you think?"

"Well, I don't know. Clay I guess. He's been there a long time and given years of service. He works hard. He's loyal."

"Stop right there," Bruce said, his hairy forearms resting on the table in front of him. "I know he's all those things. He's a good man, but let me say something."

He continued, after sipping from his Long Trail. "Do you remember last Christmas when it rained so hard, wiped out half our snow?"

"Yes."

"And do you remember Clay coming into my office, throwing down all those snow vouchers on my desk?"

"I think I remember," Mary Ann recalled, envisioning a stack of yellow papers with old lift tickets attached. They were office copies of snow guarantee vouchers given to skiers. If skiers and boarders were not satisfied with snow conditions within the first hour of skiing, they requested a voucher to ski again another day, redeemable within a year's time. The idea was bold, revolutionary enough that old industry hands like Clay Undermacher scoffed at the folly of it.

"Yeah," Bruce said, "Clay threw down all those vouchers and said, 'I told you it wouldn't work. There's a hundred of these goddamned things. That's a hundred lift tickets. You do the math and figure out how much we lost!'"

"Yes, I remember," said Mary Ann, perplexed at what Bruce was leading to.

"And I remember," Bruce said, wagging a finger playfully at Mary Ann, "you explaining that many of those people, if not most, who got the vouchers would be returning to ski with us at a later date. They would not just be skiing one day, but they would book two or more days with us and bring, in some cases, their whole families.

"You pointed out that it was a good retention program," said Bruce.

"Well, that's what it is, retention!" Mary Ann said, wondering what the point was.

"Well, that's just it. You took the long view, and Clay took the short view. He saw the idea as an immediate irrevocable loss. You saw it as a future gain."

"Yeah, but you did too. It was your idea, remember?"

"Exactly, it was my idea, but do I need people close to me to keep telling me I've got bad ideas?"

Mary Ann stared. Her mouth was finally open as it dawned on her what Bruce was getting at.

"I'll get to the point," he said, clasping her folded hands in one big paw. "I just want to say thanks and ask you if you will accept the job of assistant to the president."

Chapter 15
Why?

"I was dumbfounded!" exclaimed Mary Ann to Donny, who was stacking dishes in the dishwasher, a chore he jokingly volunteered for when she told of her good fortune. It was his way of rewarding her hard work.

"Well, I guess I just have to accept the fact I'm married to the smartest girl in the valley," said Donny.

"Well, the luckiest, maybe." said Mary Ann, still overwhelmed by the impending promotion. "I thought for sure Clay Undermacher would get it."

"Is he pissed?" asked Donny.

"I don't know, not around me. At least when he congratulated me. And I felt uncomfortable. He just smiled."

"That was probably clenched teeth," Donny offered, hoisting Ellie out of her high chair and taking the washcloth from Mary Ann's hand, "Clay eats raw meat, you know. His wife tosses it on the floor and tells him to go get it!.

"Here, let me do that," he said, picking Cheerios from the floor where Ellie had deposited them.

Mary Ann returned the favor with a small kiss on Donny's cheek.

"He's trying," she thought to herself. "Give it a little more time."

Her silent pledge was an appraisal of Donny's behavior since a near-violent fight of several weeks before. It came the morning after he had all but raped her on the front porch, minutes after she had put Ellie to bed. He had grabbed Mary Ann from behind, pushed her down on the divan, yanked down her shorts and panties, and painfully penetrated her from behind, sweating and panting profusely like a bull in heat.

His sex acts had been like that lately, rough, brutal, spontaneous, and proprietary.

Mary Ann's promotion, the jubilation over it, and the awe had temporarily wiped some of her anger. The morning following

Donny's apelike sexual assault, as she silently picked up the dirty breakfast dishes, she suddenly let them drop to the floor. Bringing up her hands to her face, she was racked with involuntary sobs, which invoked a response. "What's wrong!?"

"What's wrong!?" Mary Ann yelled back through tears.

She raged for five minutes, letting every scorn she had harbored for the past several months hurl at Donny. "You're animal, and you ask me what's wrong.'"

Donny tried interrupting. "I know I lust over you! I guess I can't help it. You're too beaut…"

"That's an excuse, Donny! Don't let yourself off the hook. Whatever you call it," she scoured her mind for the most brutal words, "it's abusive. Disrespectful. Why do you have to be so controlling?" She gasped for breath. "You don't respect me, do you? Did you ever?"

Donny decided to let her rage on, sitting at the kitchen table with his face buried in his hands. He did not move. Instead, he listened to the hailstorm of angry words cascading over him.

When she left the room, he sat still, a pall of fear gliding over him. As if in a trance, he got up and picked up the dishes—two of the larger plates had broken—and put the whole ones in the sink, where he rinsed them before stacking them in the dishwasher. He poured the liquid detergent into the cup in the dishwasher door. He was momentarily cautious. "Is this the right amount?" he asked himself. Then he tidied the kitchen, picked up Ellie and carried her to her bedroom, placing her gently in the crib. The child had sat wide-eyed throughout her mother's exhibition, chewing her fingers.

Donny could not recall any particular conscious effort to make amends to Mary Ann. There was not any overt apology, but life improved for both of them over the next few days, probably because there was no profound apology, no words to fail by. Little by little, Donny took the time to look about him. If he noticed a shirt or other piece of clothing flung carelessly over a chair, he would pick it up and place it in the hamper.

He got the next day's coffee ready each night before going to bed, helped stack the dishes, and picked up the baby's messes.

They did not have sex for a week. One night before she slept, she felt his hand touch her shoulder briefly as they lie in bed.

"You're the most precious thing that ever happened to me," he whispered.

Slowly, gradually, and, most of all testily, conditions in their marriage improved. Day by day, he apologized, not by word, but little deeds. The marital truce had its positive effects.

They decided they needed a date and made arrangements to drop Ellie off with Mary Ann's mother as soon as some chores were completed.

His hand on the snowmobile throttle, Donny let it have just enough gas to boost the machine up the wooden ramp and into the bed of the pickup truck, wiped his hands on his pants, and said to Mary Ann, "I won't be long."

As an afterthought, he hurried to the lawn's edge and kissed her on the cheek.

"Don't forget Ellie!" Mary Ann yelled to him, involuntarily shivering. The sky had become overcast. A slight wind stirred the chimes hanging from the porch ceiling. The leaves had already fallen from the big maples nearby. Over the past week, Donny had gathered most of them and dumped them into the compost bed in the garden. A few brown truants skipped across the still-green lawn. The gray autumn day was turning cold.

"I won't, I won't, I didn't." Donny said, turning to the porch and lifting the child.

"Don't forget, tell Mom I'll pick up Ellie on Monday!" yelled Mary Ann, relieved at the thought of a free weekend without the cares and woes of motherhood. She and Donny had planned a hiking trip to the Adirondacks. They would leave as soon as he got back from delivering Ellie to Montpelier. On the way, he would drop his snowmobile off at Dexter's Garden Supply in the village for its annual maintenance service.

Donny shut the tailgate and drove down the lane with Ellie bound to the baby-seat. As the truck bounced in a pothole on the dirt lane, a piece of rag or something similar, dropped from the hinge of the tailgate where it had been caught.

Mary Ann waved good-bye and walked over to pick it up. As she stooped, she could see it was not a rag at all. Whatever it was, it was matted and caked with many weeks residue of dirt.

She turned it repeatedly in her hands, totally confused. A feeling of fright gurgled up inside her. The flat voice of Doctor Rowles, the medical examiner, echoed in her brain; It was a distinctive racing glove...made by Invicta...with leather palms... colored white with a long cuff and red and blue stars...The snow was very, very deep that night. I'm sorry to say the glove may never be found until spring.

Mary Ann held the glove as though it was a dead unidentifiable animal that had been struck by a car. It was alien, though familiar. She looked closer. On the inside of the cuff, written in faded but decipherable, indelible ink was the lettering, "ATWOOD."

Again, the medical examiner's voice boomed in her head. "The snow was very, very deep that night."

Thunderstruck, Mary Ann raced into the house and closed the kitchen door behind her. She stood panting, unable to catch her breath. She held the glove in her hand, now clutching it tightly, as if never to let it go, as a thousand questions hurtled through her mind at once.

"How? Why? From where?"

The glove, to be so caked with dirt and so wrinkled, must have been lodged in the snowmobile somehow and for a long time. Donny regularly hosed out the back of the pickup, especially when he hauled dirt or something similar, as he did the week before when he brought home a load of peat mulch for the plants.

How did the glove get to be in the snowmobile? Under it? Caught in the mechanism? They said they could not find it.

Mary Ann began pacing the kitchen floor, back and forth. The glove was tightly clenched to her chest. She looked at it again and again, examining the lettering, as if it might change. She read the trademark, "Invicta."

There was no mistake, but how could it have gotten there?

She searched her memory. The afternoon before the big storm, she was home with Ellie, putting away the remainder of the

Christmas decorations in boxes. She remembered Ellie crying when she placed a small angel figurine in its box and how she reopened the box and let Ellie clutch the angel until she put it in her mouth. Mary Ann then said, "No, No, let's put it up on the mantle, and Mommy will let you look at it now and then."

She recalled that Donny worked that day at his office in Barre. "He did, didn't he?" He came home the usual time, after dark. The snow had been falling heavily.

The next day. What happened? She found out Ethan was dead when Sara Thomas came up to her. Donny got up early, plowed the road, and then had gone to work. The men were up on the mountain. There must have been twenty police officers up there and a dozen patrollers. Donny was not one of them. If he had been up there on his sled, that might have been the answer to why the glove had become lodged there. But he wasn't.

Could he have driven over the glove, and had it became caught under the sled on another occasion? No. She remembered he never took his own snowmobile to the mountain. He drove around the woods close to home, through the meadows. He and Ethan sometimes took trips together. They raced over creek beds, down the lanes, and through the pastures. It made her nervous the way they raced.

She stopped short. Her mind was not working, and numbness took over. How could Donny have been there? Was he there? Why? What happened?

"No, no, no!" she cried softly, standing in the kitchen while clasping the glove with both hands. "It's impossible. It could not have happened. Donny would never, never harm him. Not Ethan. No, never. Not Ethan!"

She wandered blindly upstairs and stopped to look into Donny's den, as if it would offer a clue. She walked to Ellie's room. In the crib, she looked down on the child's favorite doll, an old, cloth doll Ellie's grandmother had given her. It was a scarecrow dressed in coveralls. Mary Ann held the doll in one hand and the glove in her other and pressed them to her chest. Her knuckles were white with tension. Why? What could have happened?

She went to their bedroom, fell across the bed, still clutching the doll and the glove, and wept. She promised herself to block out her mind until Donny came home. He would explain.

She must have cried herself to sleep. When she awoke, the room was much darker. Outside, the wind began howling, and rain was sweeping across the lawn. Lightning struck in the distance and then thunder. She looked at her watch, but it was too dark to see. She got up and turned on the table lamp, but it failed to light. The power was out.

Downstairs, her mind raced as she looked for some kitchen matches. With trembling fingers, she lit the oil lamp and placed it on the kitchen table. At the same time an incredible bang came behind her.

"God, the wind blew the mudroom door shut, right out of my hands," Donny said as he hurried through the kitchen door while clutching a large grocery bag. "I got the Thanksgiving turkey. Twelve pounds, on sale. Thought I'd get it now. I hope there's room in the freezer. Oh shit, I forgot the lights were out. I knew they were because the whole valley's in darkness. What a god-damned storm!"

He kissed her cheek. She said nothing, staring into the darkness. Words were unable to come.

"What's that you got?" he asked, looking at the glove in her fist.

"Huh, what's up?" he said, a quizzical but bemused look appearing on his face from the faint light of the oil lamp.

"Mary Ann," he said. "What the hell's wrong? What is this?" He reached for the glove, sensing it to be an explanation of her silence.

She withdrew quickly. She took a couple steps backward and suddenly bumped into the refrigerator. Outside, the rain was pelting the tin roof of the mudroom like a hail of bullets.

"Don't touch it!" she said, "It's Ethan's glove, the one they couldn't find, the one they mentioned at the inquest. It fell out of your snowmobile this afternoon when you put it on the truck."

"What the hell are you talking about?" he said, his voice a mixture of fear and confusion. "Let me see that!"

"No!" she said, clutching it tighter.

"Mary Ann, Mary Ann," he said in a quieter voice. "It's Ethan's glove? Well, c'mon now, how do you know?"

"Here it is!" she shouted, pushing the glove toward his face. She let him look, but she nevertheless held it tightly. "See, it says Atwood on the cuff. It's a racing glove, the one that was missing the night he died. The night he died, Donny! The night he died!"

He stepped back and bumped into a kitchen chair, suddenly pale and feeling weak. He tried speaking, to bring some sense to the room.

Finally, he coughed and said, "How in God's name do I know where it's been? You say it fell out of my snowmobile? That's nonsense, Mary Ann. There has to be an explanation." He thought with difficulty for a solution of his own. "I must have driven over it."

"You said you never rode your sled up there!" Mary Ann retorted.

"Well I did!" he shouted. "Matter of fact, I was up there after his death. That must have been when the sled picked it up. Let me see it. Please, Mary Ann, why are you being so?"

"No!" She backed away.

Donny sat with his eyes fixed on the glove and then Mary Ann's troubled face. He contemplated, struggling for repose, to find the right words. "Mary Ann, look at me!"

She shook her head from side to side. The tears fell rapidly.

"Look at me!" he said softly. "How long have I known Ethan? All my life, just about. We were like brothers. I looked up to him. I idolized him. I would never hurt him. Don't you see, we were too close!"

Swallowing hard, Mary Ann whispered. "I want to believe you."

Donny remained seated, looking at her. From time to time, Mary Ann would bury her face in the glove, which was clenched tightly in both hands. Donny could not take his eyes from the glove. He wanted it in his hands. He had to get it into his hands.

"Just give me the glove, dear. I'll put it on the table. We'll talk. Let me make you a cup of tea!"

"No!" she pulled back. "No more bullshit, Donny, I want the truth. The absolute truth."

"What are you going to do?" he pleaded.

"I don't know. I don't know, but you have to tell me the truth. All of it."

"I told you the truth! I must have driven over the goddamned glove with my snowmobile." Anger flushed his face now. He immediately felt ashamed and tried to regroup. "Oh, Mary Ann, I'm sorry. Please believe me."

She began to back away toward the door.

"What are you doing?"

"I don't know."

"What do you mean, you don't know! What are you doing, Mary Ann?"

He saw the distrust in her eyes.

"I don't know," she repeated as in a trance. "Go to…Go to… I'll take it to Bruce. He'll tell me what to do."

"No, goddamn it!" Donny erupted, springing from the chair while grasping at her body.

She backed away.

"Give it to me! Give me the goddamned glove!"

"The truth! The truth!" she sobbed. "Tell me what happened. Tell me, and I'll give it to you. I'll give it to you. Just tell me what happened."

He sunk back into the chair. His face was a contortion of loss. "If I tell you, you'll give it to me?" he pleaded.

"Yes, yes, I promise!" she sobbed. The tears flowed freely. "Why, Donny, why?" she asked in a softer voice. "Why did you kill him?"

"I didn't!" he said, exhaling and slumping onto the chair at the table. He put his head in his hands. "I didn't mean to. I didn't want to. I wanted to hurt him. I wanted to make him stop."

"Stop, stop what?"

"Stop loving you, that's what!" Donny said, looking up at her with his eyes full of pleading. "I knew, Mary Ann. I knew what was going on. I followed you that night."

"What night?" she asked, suddenly terrified.

"When you left the banquet at the lodge. Mike Scott's dinner. I saw. I saw how you kept looking at your watch. I could see from the table up front, even as I was talking. I saw how you were waiting for Ethan.

"I knew you loved him. I always knew that. I could accept that. But, that night, right after you left, as soon as I could, I left, too. I drove to Ethan's. I knew you'd go there. I saw you. I saw you, Mary Ann, in his cabin. Two lovers. That's what you were, weren't you?"

"No!" she shouted. "It isn't true!"

She stuttered, slobbering with grief now. Her eyes were flooded, and her thoughts were scrambled.

"I said good-bye to him that night! I said good-bye! I told him we could never be together again. I loved him. Yes, I loved him! I loved Ethan so badly I couldn't stand it. I love him now. I always will, but I broke it off. I broke it off for our sake, for your sake, and for Ellie's sake! Don't you see that! Don't you see that!"

"Why did you have to hurt him? Why?" she pleaded.

Chapter 16
Gap Road

Donny's head dropped again, and he sighed. Then he told her what happened the afternoon of January 6.

For weeks, he had planned to confront Ethan. He carefully calculated what he had to say and how he would put an end to the affair his old friend was having with his wife.

He knew Ethan called her. Many, many times. He tried catching the conversations, but there weren't any. Donny listened on the phone in his den. He cradled the phone carefully in the receiver only when he heard it was not Ethan's voice. Several times in those weeks since the ski patrol dinner, the phone rang. Donny heard Mary Ann say "Hello!" only to have the caller hang up. He knew who it was. It had to be a signal. The knowledge his wife loved another man enveloped his being like a stifling disease, dictating his every move and making him conscious that of all the possessions in his life—his job, his home, and his stature in the community—the one thing he valued most, Mary Ann's love, was not his and never would be. An outside force controlled his mind and body now. Embodied in now satanic form was his former best friend. He felt betrayed.

Donny was not a fool. He knew competing with Ethan for Mary Ann's love was an uphill matter. Ethan had the good looks, the athletic ease, and the compelling shyness that appealed to Mary Ann's desire to heal and comfort. Donny used every tactic and facility at his command to first win Mary Ann and then to keep her.

He was sympathetic during her grief. When she literally cried on his shoulder, it took all his willpower, there in the beginning, to keep from smothering her with his affection. He held her in his eyes as the most prized possession of many. He was determined to provide for her in the best way he knew how—a new home, a child, good cars, clothes, and an excellent, secure future that any woman in the valley would be happy with. He needed a contrast with Ethan. Accumulated wealth would certainly help and did.

Moreover, he felt he could compete with Ethan on an ever-widening field through his successes as a businessman and civic and social leader in the community. Donny had put everything he had into his life with Mary Ann. He was not about to let it slip away, not into the hands of a drunken ski bum.

The plotting to confront Ethan privately came easier once he learned his old friend's patterns and his habits during the day were now predictable, thanks mainly to his need to drink. Donny began stalking Ethan, an easy thing to do when you are your own boss. His so-called inspections out at the quarries and lunches with so-and-so were nothing except ploys to divert his secretary and business associates.

The day of the storm, he was not surprised to see Ethan's snowmobile parked once again at the rear of the Frost Heave. With the approaching blizzard, he knew today was the day. All he had to do was wait.

When Ethan left the Frost Heave, his spirits had already lifted a little. Warmed by the drink, the falling snow warmed him even more. It was dry, big-flaked, and fluffy. The feathers touched the ground silently, building depth quickly. *The skiing would be good up on the ridge, so good! Even better tomorrow.*

Ethan made a wide U-turn in the parking lot and let the snowmobile roar off the back lot. He gave it gas to take a short, quick jump from the lot to the meadow beyond. He followed one of the many double tracks laid down over the past several days by dozens of sleds, his included. The deepest grooves were on the regular paths marked with green and red flags, part of the vast snowmobile system that threaded throughout all of the North Country in the wintertime.

At the end of the meadow, as it began coursing uphill toward a stand of white birches, he made a sharp left into the woods along his regularly used path coinciding with the old logging trail. His cabin sat just a few hundred yards to the south. He could drive these trails blindfolded, even in the threatening storm.

Visibility grew even more difficult as he neared the crest of the ridge, the single headlight poking in vain through the flakes pouring down. Still, he knew the trail and gave the powerful machine the gas it needed for the increasingly vertical trail. Occasionally, the tearing treads would send a fallen tree limb flying.

At the very top, it happened. Ethan was suddenly thrown backward as the sled passed between two trees. His hat flew off into the snow. He never saw the taut rope that had been stretched across the trail, never saw its menace as it hit him chest high and sent him reeling over the rear of the snowmobile, which continued for two or three feet more before its dead man's throttle shut off. Ethan landed on his back, but he flipped over to his stomach. Bending his legs, he clutched his chest.

Donny, hiding behind a large maple, ran to Ethan as he lay on his stomach, groping for breath. The force of landing had knocked the wind from him. Donny thrust down with all his might the large limb of a dead tree. It crashed on Ethan's head. He swung it again, hitting him on the shoulder. Ethan fell to his back and rolled to his stomach in pain, trying to get up. As he turned, the branch once more struck. He fell to the snow, not moving.

Donny stood above him. The tree limb was poised high over his head. His arms were outstretched, ready to fling it down one more vicious time upon Ethan's body, but he stopped. Panting, he felt the sweat running down his upper chest and arms, immediately chilling him. His breath came in gulps.

Ethan lay still.

Donny waited about five minutes, assessing the woods around him. He waited for his breathing to subside, waiting for the calm to return and he could think clearly again. There was not a solitary sound, except the wind lifting the boughs of pines higher up on the mountain.

He bent over Ethan, staring at his face. He bent over his mouth to detect breathing and then fumbled through the ski jacket about his neck to feel the carotid artery. There was no pulse. At this time, Donny flung his head to the sky and muttered between clenched teeth, "Why? Why?"

Regaining his senses, he grabbed Ethan beneath the shoulders and hoisted him up and over the rear saddle of Ethan's snowmobile. He stuffed Ethan's hat into a jacket pocket. Ethan's skis, the old Dynastars, and his ski poles were still perched nearly upright in the big, white PVC tube that he had attached to the rear frame. Again, Donny waited in the deepening shadows cast in the trees, checking his watch.

Eyes clenched tightly, Donny focused on the most threatening dilemma of his life.

"It's a complication," he said silently. "Only a problem. You've solved them all your life. Don't panic! Think! Think! Think! Breathe deeply! Calm! Calm! Calm!"

He took off his glove, wiped his sweaty brow and tugged the sleeve of his ski jacket to see his watch. It said 3:58 PM. Seven more minutes and all the lifts would be closed. He knew the Summit chair had been shut down to skiers at 3:45 p.m. It would take the lift operator another twenty minutes or so to bring in the cones and safety poles, get clearance to shut down the lift from the dispatch operator, and then ski down to the lodge. The liftie would not be doing any shoveling or raking tonight because the snow would be piling deeper and deeper. Thank God for the snow. It would cover all his tracks. There would be blankets of it over everything.

He waited five more minutes. The patrol would be finished sweeping the upper trails by then. They would be down the mountain and would neither see nor hear the snowmobile. The upcoming storm was to be his accomplice. No one would be venturing on the mountain until daybreak.

Finally, as the dusk was setting in and putting the mountain deeper into darkness, Donny pushed the start button on Ethan's sled. He grimaced at the powerful cough, which quickly fell to a purr. He carefully threw his leg over the saddle, lifting it high to clear the bent body and then slowly began the short climb to the summit. At the top, he paused, momentarily fearful the headlight would be seen from below.

"Nonsense!" he assured himself.

The blizzard had already assumed its monstrous shape, driving all living creatures, who hunkered down in dens and cabins, out of sight. The very top of the mountain was free of large trees. In summer, the hiking trails crisscrossed the boulders and moss. Now, in the isolation of the storm, they lay buried.

Down the east side of the slope, under the canopy of spruce, Donny could make out the Silversides Trail that would lead him to the base of the Summit chair. He aimed the big sled carefully down hill, feeling the weight of the body pressing into his lower back. He fought to suppress the tears, blinking them away. He had to stop, remove his glove again, and wipe his eyes with the back of his hand. In the cold, he noticed his hand trembling. He sat still for a moment, thinking about turning back and dumping Ethan's body into the woods. No good, they would search. They would find it. There would be evidence.

The thought, sudden but appropriate, of being arrested and tried for a forgivable act was too much. He had not fought so hard and worked so hard to achieve all he had to see it taken away because of one error, a forgivable error. There were to be no compromises. This was better. A suicide! Just an accident! Poor boob got on the lift when he was drunk and fell asleep. He didn't have a chance! This had to be better. "Accidents are always better." This was an accident.

"I never meant to kill. I never meant..." He shuddered again.

He finally mustered the courage to continue to the lift shack, turned off the sled's engine, and waited, listening for any sound that might signal a problem. The wind, however, was picking up, rushing now over the mountaintop and sending snow swirling in an all directions, a whiteout.

Grasping Ethan's body and hoisting it over his shoulders was the hardest part, but Donny was strong and accomplished it with one heave. He waited to regain his breath before taking a step in the deepening snow. Luckily, the area around the ski shack was flat, affording him substantially good footing. Still, he struggled to the chair and let Ethan's body swing down onto it in a sitting position. He pushed the body to the side where it could rest more easily against the arm of the wooden-slatted chair. Then he retrieved Ethan's skis, those old favorite Dynastars and clamped them to Ethan's boots with great difficulty. Donny had to place the ski over his right knee and use it as an anvil almost as he leaned on the dead knee with all of his might to shove the boot home safely into the binding.

"Don't forget the poles!" Donny reminded himself, desperate in his concentration to do everything correctly. "No screw ups! No screw ups!"

On the way back to the chair, he slipped on a patch of ice beneath the powder and fell heavily on his side. He began trembling and crying again. Breathing deeply to calm himself, he got up and carried the ski poles to the bent body, grasping at Ethan's hands to fold over the poles.

Remembering the poles triggered another caution. "His hat! His hat! Where is it?"

He searched his pocket. "Thank God, still there."

When he fit the soft, fluffy hat over Ethan's head, he made sure to put the label, Grampy's, over the dead man's brow.

Again, the tears flowed as he carefully patted the fleecy cap. The memories of two little boys in school, best friends.

"Get a grip!" he yelled, startled at the sound of his voice echoing through the storm.

He stared at the dead man, sitting stiffly and only half-upright, leaning against the armrest. He stared as a sculptor might examine a piece of granite or marble, looking for flaws.

"The glove! The glove!" Donny said aloud. "What happened to his glove? Oh, Jesus Christ, no!"

He fought for control, telling himself he would find it. "Just look for it!"

He carefully searched the ground beneath the chair and then retraced his route to the snowmobile. He poked all around it, through it, and even under the sled. He lifted the flashlight from the leather pouch at the rear of the sled and, with his own ungloved hand, thumbed the switch. Its light seemed terribly feeble in the half-light of dusk and blizzard. He trudged with near exhaustion about fifty feet back up the hill. He retraced his path, looking directly in front of him with the flashlight and letting his eyes sweep both sides of his sled's path. Nothing! He felt an oily sweat trace his spine, chilling him to the bone.

"You can't back off now! You'll find it! You'll find it!"

Again, he returned to the body, shining the flashlight over the stiffening body and searching under the arms of Ethan's jacket and under his seat. He lifted both legs. There was no glove. He shined the light directly into Ethan's face and stepped back in horror. Behind the frosted-over goggles, it looked as though Ethan's eyes were open, appearing to stare directly into Donny's eyes. Donny's fingers trembled as they removed the goggles. Ethan's eyes appeared white.

"No, no, an illusion. A reaction, that's all. A dumb, bodily reflex."

Still, with his hands trembling, he removed his right glove and pushed the lids of the eyes closed with his forefinger. This time, they stayed closed. He carefully lowered the goggles over Ethan's face and pulled the collar up over the nose. He pulled the woolen hat down over the hair, which had frozen into knife blades in places. There was no blood, so far as he could see. He probably just knocked Ethan unconscious. That sudden thought made Donny reel backward.

"If he's alive?" he said. "Alive!"

He stopped to think of the odds of Ethan escaping from the lift if he awoke. He felt for a pulse again. With the wind raging all around them, he could not tell.

"I have no choice," he told himself.

He lowered the safety bar and stood back five feet from the chair, watching the snow slowly build up on Ethan's clothes. It diminished the bright colors of the jacket and covered the small patches that identified the skier. One said "USST." Another said "Nordica." "Rossignol." "Jeep Cherokee."

"No more sponsors after today," Donny thought and laughed aloud at the irony. The sound echoed off the steel overhang of the huge bull wheel.

He shuffled to the lift shack and pushed open the sliding steel door. As a patroller who was trained to overcome any emergency situation on the mountain, he knew what to do. Walking to the control panel, he felt with his fingers the flat cover of the box where he knew the key would be hidden. Trembling, he inserted the brass key in the "Controls On" lock, turned the switch to Drive mode, and listened for the giant horizontal bull wheel to begin to crank. The loud hum of the electrical engine droned overhead.

Slowly, the wheel turned. He watched as Chair Number 7 began its upward climb. Ethan's body diminished in size. It was out of sight, smothered in the blinding storm, almost before it reached the first tower. He would have to estimate as best he could how far the chair would have to travel before disappearing from sight beyond the rocky outcrop a few hundred feet above the lift shack. It was important the chair be out of sight from below.

"One...two...three...four...five." Donny counted the chairs as each approached and quietly moved on. They were dumb witnesses to the brutal truth in Chair Number 7. When he was sure the body was hidden from view, he pushed the yellow stop button and then turned the key. He shut down the power, standing still for several moments while listening to the banshee wind.

He then parked Ethan's snowmobile about 200 feet from the lift in a stand of pines and began the slow walk uphill to the woods and his own snowmobile. He shined the light at his feet to probe for the missing glove, stopping to catch his breath from time to time while looking down into the valley. In ordinary weather, he would have seen the far-off lights of Lowgate Springs Village. In the howling wind and snow, he saw nothing.

Despite the canopy of trees above, the snow had already begun to obliterate the traces of struggle where Ethan was felled from his sled. Donny untied the rope from between the two trees, coiled it on his arm, and stuffed it into the saddlebag of his snowmobile. He then began a fruitless search once more for the glove. Not finding it, he trusted fate to take care of the problem.

At the medical examiner's inquest, he had held his breath when Doctor Rowles mentioned the glove was missing, but he exhaled silently when the medical examiner related that victims of hypothermia often began removing their clothing in a state of stupefying confusion, a legitimate symptom of hypothermia. Donny had read about the reaction in first aid manuals, but he never really believed it to be true.

He recalled, at the exact time that Doctor Rowles was contemplating aloud the whereabouts of the glove, Mary Ann had almost convulsed. He had no choice but to escort her from the courtroom, holding her elbow with one hand while grasping her waist tightly with the other. He let her lean on him.

The silence in the kitchen was a smothering blanket, but, outside, the forces of the storm swept a rocking chair across the porch. It was one of those fall storms that signaled an end to the summer season and the beginning of the next. At higher elevations, snow would probably fall tonight.

Neither Mary Ann nor Donny spoke. Mary Ann stood with her back to the kitchen sink about five feet from the table where Donny sat. Head in hand, he stared into the flame of the kerosene lamp.

"I did it for us, Mary Ann. I had to. But I didn't mean to kill him. I wanted to hurt him. That's all I wanted to do."

He looked at her, imploring with his eyes. The hurt in his face beseeched her, asking forgiveness or understanding.

"I just wanted to hurt him, to make him stop loving you. I was insane with hate, with jealousy."

Mary Ann slightly cleared her throat. Still facing Donny, she slowly moved to the coatrack next to the door. She removed her parka from the hook. Her stirring caused him to look up.

"What are you doing?"

She refused to answer, putting on the parka.

"What are you doing, Mary Ann?" he yelled. "Where do you think you're going?"

"I don't know!" she said. "We have to…have to let them know!"

"No!" he shouted. "You said you'd give me the glove! Now, give it to me! Please, please!"

His pleading softened her faint and confused resolve for a moment. She hesitated.

"I did it for us! For us!" Donny shouted. "He was a drunk, Mary Ann. A loser! A drunken loser. I did him a favor!"

Mary Ann gasped. "A favor! A favor! What are you saying?"

He reached for her arm, the hand holding the glove. She pulled back. As she did, his knee hit the table leg as he rose from the table. The oil lamp rocked twice back and forth. It then tipped and rolled across the table, crashing to the floor and spewing a stream of orange flame across the wide pine boards. It instantly lit the bottom of the heavy curtain that hung from one side of the French door.

Donny, distracted by the flames, leaped to stop their rush up the wall. He grabbed the tablecloth and yanked it, trying to smother the flames. It gave Mary Ann an instant to rush from the door and into the rain. She ran across the lawn and jumped into the first vehicle available, the pickup truck that was facing the road. The key was in it.

Behind her, she could hear him shout "Mary Ann!" as he ran from the house, jumping from the porch onto the lawn and slipping once in the mud to reach her.

She started the engine, slipped to low gear, and spun the wheels in the mud. It tore sideways through the now-dormant flower garden at the side of the yard.

Down the road, the wind was whipping the cold rain sideways, tearing at trees and shrubs. She turned the wipers on full speed, but she could barely see as she floored the accelerator, the truck swaying from side to side, striving for traction on the muddy road. In the rearview mirror she could see headlights. He was in the Jeep, tearing down the road behind her, horn blaring for her to stop.

She was crying hysterically now. She had to get away! Get away! To where? Ethan's glove lay on the seat beside her. Despite the need to keep her eyes on the road and to keep the swaying truck from pitching into a ditch, she looked to see if the glove was still there.

She did not know what to do or where to go. But she had to get away.

At the end of the half-mile lane, she turned right onto the Mountain Gap Road, but the rain was falling so hard she could not see the turn clearly. The truck roared over the mailbox, knocking it aside. One of the rear wheels sunk into the ditch. The force of the fall knocked the steering wheel from her hands. Desperately, she grasped at the wheel, thrust the gears into four-wheel drive, and stepped on the gas. The truck wobbled. Its wheels spun. Suddenly, just as Donny came up from behind her in the Jeep, the truck shuddered and leaped from the ditch and down the road.

The road ran flat for about a half-mile. Mary Ann stayed in the middle, flooring the accelerator. She reached a speed of eighty miles an hour, straddling the yellow line of the asphalt because Donny, horn blaring, attempted to pass her…first right…then left.

Twice, his right fender nudged the left rear fender of the truck. He was deliberately trying to push the truck from the road. At that speed, it would have killed her.

Her mind raced. Where to go? What to do? Her immediate thought was to make it to the top of the mountain and then down a mile or so to Bruce White's house. He lived in a ranch overlooking the top of the Paradise Chair lift at Maple Glen. If she got there, he would certainly help her.

Donny's Jeep raced behind the pickup truck. Being lighter and faster, the Jeep was able to bump the pickup hard from behind, sending the pickup off on tangents. It was all Mary Ann could do to keep the truck on the road, which was now climbing steeply uphill. Soon she would reach the treacherous hairpin turns that followed to the summit of the lonely mountain. A spin off the road in any one of those corners could bring certain death in the rock-bound crevasses below.

By now, Mary Ann was convinced Donny was going to kill her. He would never let her turn him in to the police. He would die before going to jail. He had everything to live for, even, he supposed, Mary Ann. He had a twisted determination to set things right.

"Ethan's dead!" he shouted in his mind. His horn blared behind the pickup, whose tires were burning on the wet asphalt as it tried to keep traction.

Nearing the summit of the Gap Road, where a sharp cliff rose up from the road on the right and a steep drop-off fell to the left into a beaver pond, the asphalt became slippery. Snow was falling. The steeper they climbed, the more the temperature dropped. The big wheels of the pickup no longer gripped the road and began slipping. Luckily, the same was true for the Jeep. It spun crazily in one curve before Donny could get it under control. It was still too early in the season for the vehicles to have snow tires or studs.

Mary Ann's truck sped ahead, gaining ground on the Jeep. She was ahead of him by a couple hundred feet as she neared the summit, where a sharp curve took her to the right and then immediately to the left. As she turned to the right, the gleam of Donny's headlights was suddenly in the mirrors. In anger, he thrust down to a lower gear, gunned the engine, and made up the ground.

The truck dived around the curve, and then Mary Ann yanked the steering wheel to the left for the next sharp turn, once again gaining ground. She dropped down to second gear to increase the hold on the road. From below, she could see headlights approaching. They were coming up the long, mountainous road from the other direction.

"Thank God!" she muttered, bearing down hard, alternately, on the gas and then the brakes. She pumped the brakes to keep them from locking.

Donny now was right behind her again. She braked instinctively hard when another curve approached. The jolt from behind nearly knocked her from the driver's seat. She had had no time to hook the seat belts. Ethan's glove, which had laid beside her, was flung to the floor.

She sped on. Another jolt from the jeep drove her ahead. The headlights from below were getting closer. She could hear the roar of its engines now. As another hairpin approached to the left, before Mary Ann could set the wheel, Donny hit the gas. He drove the bumper of the Jeep hard into the rear of the truck, jolting it ahead like a cannon shot.

Mary Ann was unable to keep the vehicle on the road. The truck shot off the road completely.

As it did, Donny turned hard to the left, not wishing to join Mary Ann's truck in the woods. He did not see the approaching headlights until the very last second. It was the big town plow truck. Its orange lights sent out streaks of warning through the woods. Its driver gave a blast of the air horn. Donny and the Jeep were heading straight for it. He suddenly yanked the steering wheel to the right and hit the brakes. The wheels locked. Tires slid across the black glare ice. They lost traction but not momentum. The Jeep sailed swiftly off the road, taking flight into the steep, blackened ravine below. Its rear end struck the ground first and then pitched forward in a slow, long somersault. The top of the Jeep suddenly faced the ground, upside down. When it landed, it was on its nose. It bounced it up again in another somersault. Over and over and over, the Jeep went. It went down the dark side of the mountain, splintering steel and tree limbs. It finally struck a ten-foot boulder, splitting the gas tank. The Jeep came to a rest. Silence and darkness fell upon it. Then a burst of flames suddenly erupted in a bright orange ball, sending aloft a black plummet of smoke.

Until the burst of flame, the driver of the plow truck could not see clearly what had happened. Both racing vehicles were now beyond his left shoulder. He brought the big truck to a halt in the middle of the icy road.

He got to Mary Ann's truck first and had a hard time reaching even the bottom of the door because the back end was resting on a rock. The truck had slid along the flat top of the boulder, and its front end had collided with a large beech tree, sending its trunk halfway through the cab. Mary Ann, inside, was caught up against the column of the steering wheel. The wheel had broken off completely and had gone through the windshield. Mary Ann's right arm, covered with blood, was thrust through the windshield. Being rendered unconscious was a stroke of fate. Beneath the truck, 300 feet below in the ravine, the dark smoke was still rising from Donny's Jeep as the first rescue trucks arrived. Three miles to the west on the other side of the valley, the turbulent sky was lit in brilliant orange. Somewhere at the base of the flame, the Naples' home and outbuildings, once so seemingly solid and secure, were being reduced to a fire-fed ruin.

Chapter 17
Truth

It was simply a case of sweet, illicit love. It was simply a case of a husband protecting what is rightfully his, seeking vengeance with a blow to the head delivered with too much understandable savagery. By-products of seduction and betrayal as well as hot, white anger blinded Donny Naples.

She felt herself shoving him.

"No, no!" she whispered to her nightmares while knotting the white sheet in her fist, trying to push him away. She beat little fists against his chest. They moved slow motion. They were futile blows, delivered with arms held back by an uncontrollable force. Behind her, she felt Ethan's cold breath on her neck. He sat stiffly, frozen solid, wrapped in white bandages.

"Shh! Shh! Easy!" whispered Bruce White, clasping his strong hands over hers. She was covered with sweat.

"Mary Ann, it's okay!" he hushed. "It's okay."

She twisted her face in feverish grief, awakening enough to see the big, baldish man at the side of her bed.

Drunkenly, she said, "I was trying to get to you!"

"I know. It's all right now! It's over! Rest!"

She had not been conscious when the rescue crews delicately pulled her from the wrecked cab of the pickup truck, which rested precariously on a rock and tree very close to the side of the road. So dangerously poised was the broken truck that a large crane was used to dangle a rescue basket down to Mary Ann's level. That was after chainsaws had toppled several trees to allow the boom of the truck to maneuver. The wreckage was only about ten feet away from the road, but it took two hours to extricate Mary Ann.

Some of the men and women comprising the rescue crew had many experiences bringing rock and ice climbers to safety and finding lost hikers. This was the first time they had to pull a still-living body from twists of cut metal and heavy trunk and branches of a thick, solid tree.

With one man poised on the basket and the other standing on the top rung of a ladder, Mary Ann's limp body was eased onto the basket and rushed to the hospital in the ambulance with its siren screaming. Another siren, the Lowgate Springs pumper truck, echoed. This was followed by firefighters and equipment from four surrounding towns. Mountain fires were the worst, difficult to get to and impossible to subdue when a water supply from a stream or pond was not close by. The night's work was made more impossible by the need to respond to two fires, one coming from a jagged pit in a deep ravine and the other miles away.

The men and women who comprised the Lowgate Springs emergency forces gave themselves plenty to talk about in the weeks —years really—to come. Never were they so taxed as in that one night, except when the 1988 January ice storm toppled transmission towers and trees and cars spun off the icy roads, all in a short space of time.

Of the two wrecked vehicles, little attention was paid to the Jeep, which, an hour after the accident, appeared as a blackened, still-smoking pile of metal debris. They made no hasty attempt to reach Donny's body, which had been totally consumed by fire. Later, when the metal cooled and the smoke ceased, they extricated what little was left of him.

A week after Mary Ann's near-death experience, only the physical pain remained overpowering. Across her eyes, a band of yellowed bruises frightened Little Ellie as her grandfather lifted her to the edge of the bed. But she touched the brown hair and whimpered, "Mommy sick!"

"Yes, Mommy's sick, you dear, little one. But she feels much better now, seeing her baby. I missed you so!"

A concussion had knocked her senses elsewhere for two days after the accident, perhaps a blessing. The pain she felt now in her legs was frightening. Her chest hurt when she breathed, a knuckle of extreme pain pressing against the sternum. But she already noticed, as the doctors predicted, that each day would add to the healing.

The physicians could do little to assuage the emotional suffering. She would take care of that herself. She had already felt some relief in purging when the afternoon session with the state police investigators had ended. With Morris Schick at her side and Bruce White in the corner of the hospital room, sitting deep down in a stuffed chair, she told what happened, matter-of-factly for a moment or two and then weepingly at other times.

She had told Bruce first about what led up to the catastrophe. She would have had an opportunity to lie about it, to cover up all the heated portent leading to Donny's death and her injuries. Donny dead. Ethan dead. Mary Ann was alive, but that was the tipping of the balance, being alive and having to face the future with a small child in a small town with many friends and loved ones. Only the truth would do.

"Tell the Casey girl," Mary Ann instructed. "I know she had to feel badly about Ethan's death. I know she felt partly responsible." She thought—everyone thought—Ethan had gotten on the lift when Emma Casey's back was turned. "Tell her. Tell her the truth about what happened."

Bruce nodded.

The investigators checked and verified all of the particulars that Mary Ann had related—about the glove, about where she found it, and where it had been hidden all these months. At Dexter's Garden Supply, where Donny had taken his snowmobile to be serviced, the police determined that the gears beneath the sled could have caused the gouges and tears in the glove.

Probably, when Donny heaved Ethan's dead weight from the snow and placed the body on his snowmobile, the glove came off and laid on the ground until Donny's own sled picked it up with its treads. The police believed the glove had been caught above the skid plate, where it remained, frozen fast over the winter, and stayed there in a dusty lock all summer.

There could be little doubt about the motive for the killing. Donny's ambition and success had been attained with determination, brains, and hard work. His rise as a successful, well-respected businessman and civic leader had been swift and steady. He possessed money, an equally successful and attractive wife, and a daughter. But they were mere fixtures in his private life. His wife loving another was too much for this particular man to bear.

When all the facts were made known by Mary Ann, they were matched against the already existing evidence, which everyone by now knew was flawed, but honestly so. There was a medical examiner who knew more about hypothermia and the vagaries of New England weather than he did about homicide. Honestly and simply, could the legal system have judged it another way? And what about the victim? He was defeated in the only profession, ski-racing, that he was any good at. He was defeated in love. He was done in by drink, remorse, self-pity, and full-blown clinical depression. Maybe Ethan did not give a damn if he lived or died that day.

His death was now officially listed as a homicide, the eighth of the year so far in Vermont. When more than ten people are murdered in the state, officials and public-spirited citizens begin worrying about a crime wave. Most big cities have as many homicides on two weekends as Vermont has in a year. Yet, the Vermont killings always seemed to rank high on the grotesque. Besides the death of Ethan Atwood on a ski lift, there was the case of a middle-aged man with a record of insanity who drove his car deliberately into the path of a man walking beside the road. The perpetrator hated hippies, he said, and did not like the looks of his victim, a man with a ponytail and goatee. Another case involved murder-suicide. A man who had moved from Pennsylvania after a messy divorce from his wife set his isolated farmhouse afire before shooting his three-year-old child in the head. Then he took his own life with the gun while the house burned down around them.

Near the little town of Dorset, a teenager walked across the road from his home and beat his neighbor, a young homemaker, to death with a baseball bat. He did not know his victim and had no motive for killing her. At his trial, the teen became enraged and wrestled with his own attorneys and court officials after telling the judge who had sentenced him to life to "Go fuck yourself!"

Another recalcitrant teen, a druggie, drove his car into a state trooper trying to hail him down to stop. The trooper died.

"You know, it's so typical of you to be this way," said Bruce, smiling after the investigators had left.

"What way?"

"Honest!" he said. "Just plain honest. You couldn't hide anything if you wanted."

"I don't know any other way," she said, turning her head to the side on the pillow.

"It takes guts to admit everything you have admitted," Bruce said. "Not many women, not many men or women could find the guts to do that."

Mary Ann said nothing, but, in the following hours and days of convalescence, she imagined each old friend in the valley listening to her story. She imagined their questions and their disagreements with it. She knew enough about her neighbors, who had known her since she was a little girl to realize their conclusions would not be harsh, at least not for long. It was not simply an affair of a married woman with a longtime lover and the following revenge. The affair was love, to be sure. Pure and simple unresolved love, they would say.

It would be far more difficult for them to understand the illicit affair was not illicit. Despite one night—one night only—the lovers clung to each other, nothing more followed. No sexual impropriety, only phone calls. Mary Ann's resolve not to allow Ethan to come any closer to her was based on many things. Her moral reserve? Probably. Her middle-class upbringing? Fear of God?. Knowing right from wrong? But there was more. As she lay in bed nursing her physical hurts, the guilt manifested itself. It was not because she loved Ethan, but it was because she chose not to love him.

"What have I done? What a fool! I threw him away because... what did I want? Security. Purity. Comfort. A child. My own selfishness caused this to happen."

She had often fantasized about a life with Ethan after his career. He would be among the best ski-racers in history. They would be wealthy.

She reckoned it was probably about Ethan's weaknesses. The other girl, Lina. Mary Ann could not altogether put all of the blame on an Italian tart. Ethan shared in it.

She rationalized. Her decision finally to marry Donny was based on what? Security, yes. Wealth, yes. Love, a little.

She thought the two men who had loved her suffered a fate far worse than any Mary Ann would realize in the ensuing months and years. Both died, one at the hand of the other. Donny died by his own hand, trying to grasp that which he also loved most in life.

"What do you think you'll do, Mary Ann?" asked Bruce, now holding her hand at the edge of the bed.

"Well, I have to get away for a while. I think I want to go West, somewhere in the mountains, I guess. I can't think of anywhere else to live except where there are mountains.

"Ethan told me, whenever he stayed in the West for any length of time, he felt he had to settle in a town because, as much as he loved the mountains, they were so big out there that he felt they engulfed him. The Rockies made him feel isolated. He said it was like being adrift in the middle of the ocean in a rowboat. Funny, but that's what I want right now. That's what I need. I want to feel some isolation. I want to plan the rest of my life, mine and Ellie's. Thank God I've got her."

"I think I can help. I know plenty of ski mountains who would love to have someone like you working for them, that is, if that's what you want."

"Yes, after a while especially. I need a change…" She stopped mid-sentence when the ghostly flashback occurred, an image of Ethan's smile and the terrifying plunge from the icy road.

Bruce held the shift knob loosely but carefully. He felt the gears grind in the Jeep, which skipped and tugged itself up the mountain path cluttered with loose stones that banged and chopped at its underside.

He and Mary Ann got out and looked over the edge of the new trail, named Ethan's Run, and approved of how it vanished beneath them in steepness.

"This could rival Chapel Rock," Bruce said, glancing over his shoulder to Poacher's Paradise, where Ethan and his gang went to do daring and scary tricks in the snow.

About a hundred yards from where they stood atop of the summit, a stream tumbled brown after a heavy rain, much like a spring freshet, when the strong surge races past fields, woods, and meadows. It would run furiously past nearby houses in the little villages in its path to the river, flooding and scouring the fields and riverbanks. After the fury and the sound would come the calm and sunlight. Always it seemed.

"I changed my mind. I'm not going away." She looked at Bruce, who smiled slightly.

"I figured," he said happily. "Now you know why I didn't fill your job. I was hoping you'd turn around and stay."

"I can't leave. This is the only home I know. If I went, the problems I went through would go with me. I realize that. Here I know they'll diminish."

She and Ellie moved back to her parents' home in Montpelier, where Mary Ann was encouraged to stay. It would help to have an ample intermingling with the people who knew and loved her since she had been a little girl.

One day, weeks after she had come out of the hospital, Emily Davenport, who rarely had kind words for anyone, stood in Mary Ann's path outside the hardware store.

"Are you all right?" she asked. Her expression was still stern, but it was fixed on Mary Ann's eyes.

"Yes, I am, Emily. I'm okay."

"Good!" said Emily. "You're tough, and we need you around here!"

A week after deciding for the final time she would stay, she and Ellie stopped at the school playground. Mary Ann sat on a picnic bench as Ellie joined other toddlers on the swings and slides, running, shouting, and falling. That morning, as she drove the back roads to Lowgate Springs, past the dairy farms and houses, Mary Ann noticed the river fog doing its slow ballet over the water, seeping through unseen atmospheric cracks to hover over fields of corn and then wisp again, touching the gray granite implanted in the wooded hillside. She loved the sharp, distinct weather patterns of the hills and valleys, sometimes giving only a fleeting moment's notice of a storm that followed the sunshine. Mary Ann loved even those gray, dull days because she knew they could be suddenly offset by clearing blue skies The seasons were just as sharply divided by strong frosts that painted warm days of autumn with colors so brilliant they hurt the eyes, reflecting golden rays of shadow chasers. Winter brought virginal snow and bursts of mountain air so sharp it made your lungs burn. She loved especially the web-like fog that, with a ghostly gentleness, laid down the night.

Watching Ellie play with the other children on the swings and slide, Mary Ann reflected on the youngest generation, which, in another twenty years, would be giving adult voices and credence to the everyday life around them. It was hard to imagine little ones like Ellie running the show, making life work, as did the ancestors before them. Mary Ann often reflected on the complexities of lineage. Two parents, four grandparents, eight great-grandparents, sixteen great-great. Who were they? Where did they go? How, when, and why? Who are we? And do we really know one another? What matters?

Mary Ann cautiously watched, ready to spring up, when Ellie stood on a platform of the wooden playground fort, four feet from the ground, trying to reach a vertical piece of pipe that children would grasp hold of and slide to the bed of wood chips below. The child was still too small. Many times, Mary Ann had posted herself within arm's reach to help Ellie extend the last two or three inches needed to grasp the pole. This time she watched and waited, seeing fear, yet determination, in the little girl's eyes. Suddenly, Mary Ann felt the need to get up and race to Ellie, but the stabbing pain still felt in her ribs and chest made her sit down and watch.

A second later, Ellie had leaped. Her little fingers were outstretched. She grabbed and choked the bar. Then her tiny legs wrapped around it, and she hung with triumph and pleasure gleaming from her face. She slid down the pole and ran to her mother with a shriek of laughter and pure joy.

§ § §

Made in the USA
Lexington, KY
08 November 2012